...d in 1745.

Rockingham Pottery and Porcelain
1745–1842

THE FABER MONOGRAPHS ON POTTERY AND PORCELAIN

Present Editors: R. J. Charleston *and* Margaret Medley
Former Editors: W. B. Honey, Arthur Lane
and Sir Harry Garner

Bow Porcelain *by* Elizabeth Adams *and* David Redstone
Worcester Porcelain and Lund's Bristol *by* Franklin A. Barrett
Rockingham Pottery and Porcelain *by* Alwyn Cox *and* Angela Cox
Apothecary Jars *by* Rudolf E.A. Drey
English Delftware *by* F.H. Garner *and* Michael Archer
Oriental Blue and White *by* Sir Harry Garner
Chinese Celadon Wares *by* G. St. G.M. Gompertz
Mason Porcelain and Ironstone *by* Reginald Haggar *and* Elizabeth Adams
Later Chinese Porcelain *by* Soame Jenyns
Japanese Pottery *by* Soame Jenyns
Japanese Porcelain *by* Soame Jenyns
English Porcelain Figures of the Eighteenth Century *by* Arthur Lane
French Faïence *by* Arthur Lane
Greek Pottery *by* Arthur Lane
Yüan Porcelain and Stoneware *by* Margaret Medley
T'ang Pottery and Porcelain *by* Margaret Medley
English Brown Stoneware *by* Adrian Oswald, R.J.C. Hildyard
and R.G. Hughes
Creamware *by* Donald Towner
English Blue and White Porcelain of the Eighteenth Century
by Bernard Watney
Longton Hall Porcelain *by* Bernard Watney
English Transfer-Printed Pottery and Porcelain *by* Cyril Williams-Wood

ROCKINGHAM POTTERY AND PORCELAIN 1745–1842

by

ALWYN COX AND ANGELA COX

faber and faber
LONDON · BOSTON

First published in 1983
by Faber and Faber Limited
3 Queen Square London WC1
Filmset and printed in Great Britain by
BAS Printers Limited
Over Wallop, Hampshire

Also by Alwyn Cox and Angela Cox
The Rockingham Works

British Library Cataloguing in Publication Data

Cox, Alwyn
Rockingham pottery and porcelain 1745–1842.
1. Rockingham Works—History
I. Title II. Cox, Angela
338.7′66′63942823 HD9612.9.R/

ISBN 0-571-13049-6

Library of Congress Cataloging in Publication Data

Cox, Alwyn.
Rockingham pottery and porcelain, 1745–1842.

(Faber monographs on pottery and porcelain)
Bibliography: p.
Includes index.
1. Rockingham pottery. 2. Rockingham porcelain.
I. Cox, Angela. II. Title. III. Series.
NK4340.R6C69 1983 738′.09428′23 82-25158
ISBN 0-571-13049-6

This book is dedicated to the memory
of the Swinton potters

Joseph Flint

Edward his X Mark Butler   Eliz: Her Mark Butler

Willm Malpass   Wm Fenney

Willoughby Wood   John Green

John Brameld   Wm Brameld

Thomas Brameld

G. F. Brameld   J. W. Brameld.

Foreword

The majority of English porcelain factories started as such, and continued as such until their closure. Rockingham is almost unique in having started as a potworks and then branched out to manufacture porcelain. The ability to effect this form of parthenogenesis—Athene created from the forehead of Zeus—is probably due to the other circumstance virtually peculiar to Rockingham. The factory flourished under the aegis of patrons—the Marquis of Rockingham and later the Earls Fitzwilliam—who not only enjoyed the prestige of patronage, but deserved it. Where other managers struggled to make ends meet, and often went under, the Bramelds were able to persuade their benefactors at Wentworth Woodhouse to put up successive large loans which staved off for years the ultimate and seemingly inevitable bankruptcy.

The literature on Rockingham has hitherto tended to concentrate on its porcelain, although Eaglestone and Lockett in 1964 showed proper appreciation of the factory's earlier activities. Since then, fresh documentary finds and a new stirring of interest in the ceramic activity of Yorkshire outside Leeds have put the whole subject in a new perspective, and revivified the pioneer work of such writers as Oxley Grabham and Arthur Hurst. Above all, excavations on the Swinton site, conducted with great success by the authors of the present book, have made it possible to identify with certainty much of the pottery made in the factory's earliest years, as well as throwing considerable light also on its porcelain production. All these factors combined have made it possible to reconstruct a history of the Swinton pottery which it would be difficult to rival for completeness in treating of any other English ceramic concern.

The homely character of the early pottery (to be matched in a number of large and small potteries both in Yorkshire and outside) stands in marked contrast to the ambitious and 'rich' porcelain which succeeded it, underlining the influence of a noble and wealthy patron who not only repeatedly put up money, but stimulated production by the demands of his household and the commissions of friends and guests whom he submitted to the temptation of seeing Rockingham porcelain in his own house. The flavour of country-house high living, as well as the more sober atmosphere of the factory and the counting house, or the earnest aspirations of nineteenth century artists and craftsmen, may be discerned by the attentive reader of what is essentially a ceramic chronicle.

The firm structure of this book, its many new findings, and the mastery of their subject displayed by its authors, entitle it to a permanent place in the bibliography of English ceramic writing.

R.J. CHARLESTON

Contents

Colour Plates

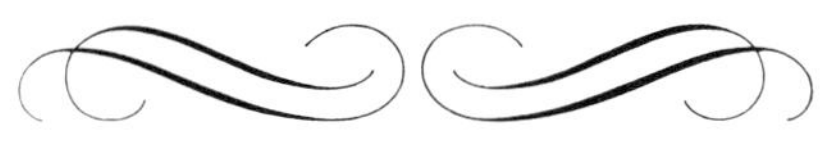

Map

Acknowledgements

We wish to record our thanks to the many people whose help has been invaluable in the preparation of this book. Museum staff were always helpful and courteous in supplying information and providing access to items in their care. Particular thanks are due to Miss M. Pearce and Mr D. Sier of the City Museum, Sheffield; Mr M. Clegg and Mr P. Hall of the Yorkshire Museum, York; Mr M. Densley and the staff of the Rotherham Museum; Mr R. Hughes of the Derby Museum; Mr P. Walton of Temple Newsam House, Leeds; Mrs P. Halpenny of the Hanley Museum, Stoke-on-Trent; Mrs R. Hartley of the Harrogate Museum; Miss E. Leary of the Birmingham Museum; Mr J. V. G. Mallet and Mr D. M. Archer of the Victoria and Albert Museum; Miss G. Blake Roberts of the Wedgwood Museum, Barlaston; and Mr R. A. Crighton of the Fitzwilliam Museum, Cambridge.

We also acknowledge the willing assistance given by the staff of the following libraries and archives departments: Sheffield City Library, Department of Local History and Archives, for their help with the Wentworth Woodhouse Muniments; Rotherham Library, Department of Local History; Doncaster Archives Department; the Borthwick Institute of Historical Research, University of York; and the Estate Office, Wentworth Woodhouse. The Swinton Parish Documents were examined whilst they were kept in Swinton Parish Church; our thanks are due to the Revd. Harris for his unfailing help and courtesy.

For their help in supplying photographs we wish to thank Mr H. Blakey; Mr A. Gabszewicz of Christie's; Mr G. A. Godden; Mr and Mrs B. Newmane; Mrs J. Harland, Assistant to the Surveyor of the Queen's Works of Art; Mr S. Peck of Henry Spencer and Sons, Retford; Mr J. P. Palmer of Sotheby's; and Mr. R. Tennant of Tennant's of Richmond, North Yorkshire.

Of the many other people who assisted us in important ways, we owe a particular debt of gratitude to Mr and Mrs W. Arnold of Swinton for their extreme kindness in allowing us to carry out excavations on land in their possession. Similarly, to the Estate agents Mr A. R. Pelly and the late Mr W. Carr we express our appreciation for permission to excavate on land forming part of the Fitzwilliam (Wentworth) Estate. Especial thanks are due to Mrs E. Cox who, throughout the course of this fieldwork, attended to our every need and patiently suffered the disturbance we caused. Without their help and cooperation, much that is now known about the early wares of the Swinton Pottery would remain undiscovered.

We wish to express our gratitude to antique dealers who brought items of interest to our attention, in particular to Mr B. Bowden, and also to Mrs B. Reed, Mrs S. Davis, Mrs A. Wolsey, Major G. N. Dawnay and Mr D. Wilby.

Equally, we are indebted to the many individuals who assisted us by providing information; their help is gratefully acknowledged in the footnotes. We also wish to thank those people who most kindly invited us into their homes and allowed us access to their collections and who wish to remain anonymous. We trust they have the satisfaction of knowing that they have considerably enriched the contents of this book; and where no credits are given in the captions to illustrations of wares, the pieces are in private possession. We are grateful to the owner of one of the Rockingham Pattern Books we were permitted to examine, for permission to reproduce information from it and for generously providing the illustration shown in Plate 95. Mr R. Boreham, Mr R. Brown, Mr and Mrs D. Cavill, Mr and Mrs R. Hampson, Mr F. Fowler and Mr T. A. Lockett also kindly brought important documentary information to our notice.

We gratefully acknowledge the use of X-ray analytical facilities in the Department of Physics, University of York, for the examination of Rockingham porcelain and brown-glazed earthenwares. For their help in the preparation of illustrations, we express our gratitude to Mr G. Smith and Mr D. Whiteley of the University of York.

Our thanks are due to Dr D. G. Rice, and to the publishers Barrie and Jenkins, for permission to reproduce details of the following Rockingham figures which we have personally not seen, but which are recorded in his book *The Illustrated Guide to Rockingham Pottery and Porcelain*, London, 1971: model numbers 10, 14, 31, 69 and 99.

Finally, we should like to thank Messrs Faber and Faber for making possible the publication of this work, and in particular to Mr G. de la Mare for his patient advice and help. Thanks are also due to Mr R. J. Charleston, formerly Keeper of Ceramics at the Victoria and Albert Museum, for his support during the preparation of the manuscript and for his interest in our researches over the years.

Preface

The Pottery founded in 1745 in Swinton, South Yorkshire, on land belonging to the 1st Marquis of Rockingham, from whose family the manufactory was later to take its name, has attracted writers and commentators on ceramics from the mid-nineteenth century onwards. In spite of so much interest in this concern, there are, however, still many current misconceptions about its history and wares.

In recent years a good deal of new information has come to light. Work done by the present writers on the Swinton Parish Documents, papers relating to the administration of local affairs, and equally important, a re-examination of the Wentworth Woodhouse Muniments, which incorporate the household documents of Wentworth House, the seat of the marquises of Rockingham and their heirs the earls Fitzwilliam, have provided a wealth of new information about the historical background of the Pottery, its artists and wares.

The Swinton Parish Documents have fortunately survived relatively intact, and include militia lists, Poor Law returns, constables' records, bastardy orders, tax returns and sundry other similar papers. They provide much information about the workpeople at the Pottery, their everyday lives, and the prevailing social and economic conditions of the period. The Wentworth documents, in contrast, record in minute detail the purchases of the household, including earthenware and porcelain from the Swinton Pottery, with descriptions and prices. From these it has been possible to compile a comprehensive account of the Pottery's products at different periods, and to give an accurate dating for the various proprietorships.

These documentary sources have recently been supplemented in a most significant way by archaeological evidence from excavations carried out on the Pottery site by the authors. Previous investigations of this kind failed to locate any notable deposits of wares manufactured before 1800, since in general the proprietors sold their waste for road repairs rather than tipping it in the vicinity of the Pottery. However, the chance discovery on private land adjacent to the site of sherds dating to all periods, has helped to establish a full and accurate picture of the wares described in the invoices. Since with one notable exception recognizable factory marks were not in use at Swinton during the eighteenth century, this has enabled early products from this Pottery to be identified and illustrated, and their quality assessed for the first time. It also became apparent that during the early years of the Brameld proprietorship, from 1806 onwards, marks were not consistently used on earthenwares until about 1820, and the archaeological evidence has made it possible to recognize a range of wares hitherto not associated with the Pottery, thus extending the existing knowledge available from marked specimens. This was also true for the period of porcelain production, excavated sherds providing important new details, notably about Rockingham figures.

Additionally, the application of scientific techniques has been informative. In particular X-ray fluorescence analysis has produced some rather surprising facts about the use of the impressed ROCKINGHAM mark on brown-glazed earthenwares—not all of which were manufactured at Swinton. It has also provided answers to certain questions relating to the composition of Rockingham porcelain.

Furthermore, it has been possible to give a revised assessment of Rockingham porcelains, both in the light of contemporary opinion in the nineteenth century, as shown in documentary sources, and also by comparison with the wares of competitors in Staffordshire and elsewhere.

Thus it became apparent that a significantly new account of the Rockingham Works and its wares might be given. The present monograph shows in detail for the first time the development of a country pothouse, which began in a very small way in the mid-eighteenth century making slip-decorated earthenwares, and traces its growth with the introduction of white salt-glazed stonewares and creamwares, and then through all the successive stages to the large and flourishing porcelain manufactory it was to become in the third and fourth decades of the following century. It provides a particularly interesting study, since the Pottery grew up away from the Staffordshire tradition and yet was clearly influenced by it. Probably it is true to say that a similar account could not be given for any other English porcelain works.

1
The Early Years

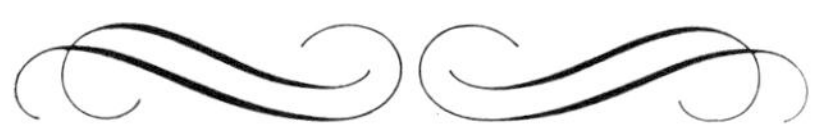

The site of the Swinton Pottery is still one of the most rural and pleasant in England, in spite of its situation in the heart of industrial South Yorkshire. A print of the mid-1820s (Plate 1) shows the Works at the height of its prosperity, as it appeared in the early years of porcelain production, with numerous kilns, a flint mill, workshops, decorating rooms, warehouses and showrooms. One large brick-built hovel (Plate 2) remains today, surrounded by tall trees on a hill top near the junction of roads from Wath-upon-Dearne, Wentworth, Rawmarsh and Swinton,[1] and set amidst rolling fields and woodland. The main buildings, including the flint mill (Plate 3), were sturdily built of stone, but have been demolished over the years, with the exception of one gatehouse (Plate 4), and parts of another structure, which survive as dwelling houses. The nearby Pottery farm was only recently pulled down.

The pottery industry in South Yorkshire became established during the second half of the eighteenth century, as it had done in Staffordshire a century or so earlier, and for the same reasons—the ready availability of the essential raw materials, coal and clay, both of which are found in abundance in the Swinton area. There were pits in Wath Wood adjacent to the Pottery and on Swinton Common itself, coal having been obtained there from at least 1606, when the first references to colliers appear in the Wath-upon-Dearne parish registers,[2] and probably long before this, since coal had been mined in Yorkshire from medieval times. A yellow clay suitable for coarsewares occurred locally and a fine white-burning clay was being dug on Swinton Common in the 1770s.

The second vitally important factor was the early growth of the system of navigable waterways in South Yorkshire. In 1726 an Act of Parliament was passed to improve the navigation of the river Don,[3] and as a result of these developments Swinton had a wharf on the new 'Long Cut' constructed about

1. At this period Swinton was one of five townships which composed the parish of Wath-upon-Dearne (see Revd J. Hunter, *South Yorkshire*, 1831, Vol.2, p.72).
2. An entry for 12 September 1606 reads 'Buried Jo: Beamonte kyld in Addy (*sic*) Cole pitt.' The hamlet of Abdy adjoins Swinton close by the Pottery site.
3. J. Priestley, *Historical Account of the Navigable Rivers, Canals and Railways throughout Great Britain*, London and Wakefield, 1831, p.233. As a result of this Act (12 George I, Cap. 38) boats of up to 20 tons could reach Swinton.

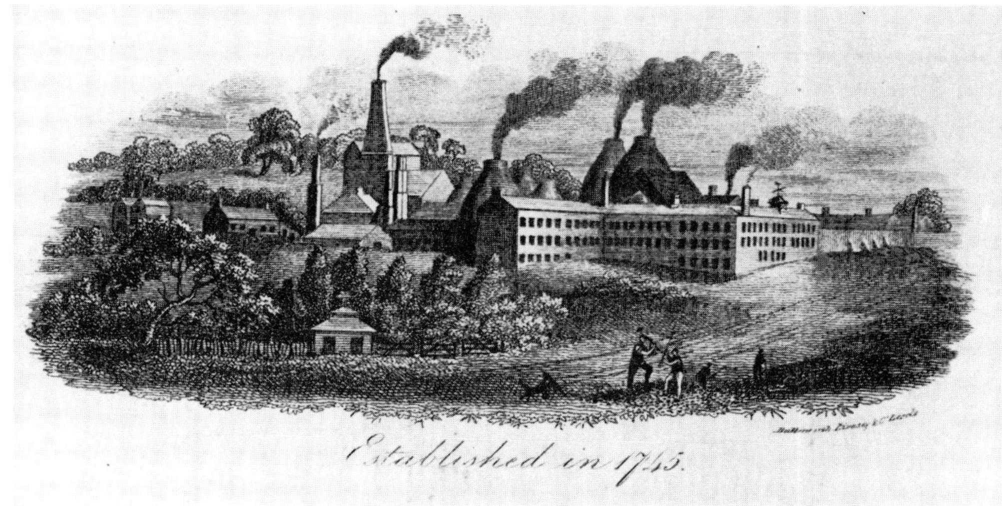

1. THE ROCKINGHAM WORKS. An engraving from a factory bill head dated 1827. *Trustees of the Fitzwilliam (Wentworth) Estates and Sheffield City Libraries.* *See Plate 68 and page 17*

2. THE REMAINING KILN on the site of the Rockingham Works. *See page 17*

3. RUINS OF THE ROCKINGHAM POTTERY FLINT MILL, *c*.1910. The building was demolished shortly after this date. *Rotherham Library.* *See page 17*

4. GATE HOUSES AT THE ROCKINGHAM WORKS, *c*.1910. The building on the left still stands. *Rotherham Library.* *See page 17*

1730, which enabled basic materials for local industries to be brought into the area and finished products to be taken out via Goole to the port of Hull, or along the expanding canal systems to other parts of Yorkshire. The gradual industrialization of the region meant that there was a steadily increasing population available to buy manufactured goods, and as early as 1765 it had become necessary to build a new warehouse on Swinton Wharf to accommodate the general increase in trade.[4]

The impact of canals on the pottery industry was to be significant. Carriage of goods by land was expensive, slow and cumbersome and, given the appalling state of most roads, entirely unsuitable for fragile wares, and whilst pack animals or draught horses could convey a limited amount by road, a horse could haul many tons on a canal. Being purpose-built, the canals took convenient routes and linked the most appropriate centres. Later in the eighteenth century these advantages were to make Swinton and South Yorkshire an important region for pottery production. The earliest proprietors of the Swinton Pottery, however, working in a very small way, using the local coal and clays to provide coarse earthenwares for the immediate neighbourhood only, did not fully reap the benefits of this situation.

Swinton itself in the mid-eighteenth century was little more than a village situated on the river Don and within easy riding distance of the larger centres of Rotherham, Sheffield and Doncaster, with most of its inhabitants still connected in one way or another with agriculture. The most influential figure in the neighbourhood was undoubtedly the great landowner, the Marquis of Rockingham, who from his impressive country seat, Wentworth Woodhouse, some five miles distant from Swinton, controlled in a benevolent way the fortunes of his many tenants, among whom were the first proprietors of the Swinton Pottery.

Joseph Flint 1745–55; Edward and Elizabeth Butler 1755–65

In 1745 one Joseph Flint commenced potting activities on Swinton Common,[5] and had his Pottery not been built on land belonging to Thomas Watson-Wentworth, 1st Marquis of Rockingham,[6] it is probable that we should know nothing of him. Even the ceramic historian Llewellynn Jewitt was unaware of Flint's existence, and he and all subsequent writers gave the credit for the founding of the Pottery to Flint's successor Edward Butler.[7]

4. C. Hadfield, *The Canals of Yorkshire and North East England*, Newton Abbot, 1972, Vol. 1, p. 78.
5. The Common land in Swinton was not enclosed until 1816. The Wentworth Estate's right to the title of this land was to be questioned by the Leeds members of the Greens, Bingley & Co. partnership in 1806 (see page 56).
6. Thomas Watson-Wentworth (1693–1750) was created 1st Marquis of Rockingham in 1746, thus adding to his other titles.
7. L. Jewitt, *Ceramic Art in Great Britain*, London, 1878, Vol. 1, pp. 495–6.

However, the Wentworth Estate records survive, and in the 1745 annual rental, under Wath-upon-Dearne, is recorded:

Flint Joseph for a Brickyard £1.10.0

After 1749, when the details for Swinton are listed independently of Wath, it becomes clear that Flint was working in Swinton, and in addition to his rent he paid dues to the marquis 'for digging clay'[8] on Swinton Common. Flint's Pothouse was evidently a small concern, as were most such country potteries where the potter worked with little additional assistance, digging his own pits and marketing his wares locally. His buildings were too insignificant to be included on Dickinson's map of the district for 1750,[9] but the concern clearly prospered and in 1752 or 1753 Flint established 'A new Tile Yard upon Swinton Common'.[10]

The above evidence might suggest that Flint made bricks and tiles only, but in 1753 there is a note of his buying coal valued at £2.2.6 for the 'Pot house & Tyle yard',[11] and the Estate rental for 1755–6 includes the following entry recording Flint's departure:

Flint Joseph, **For the Pot House**. now Edward Butler ______	£1.10.0
Ditto. **For the Tile Yard**. now John Bette ______	£1.10.0

A further reference on 27 November 1756 makes it quite clear that it was Flint who built the Pothouse:[12]

By Allowance to Joseph Flint for Buildings erected on Swinton Common for a Pothouse and Tile and Brick Yards as by Valuations made thereof by John Bower, Thomas Taylor, and Benjamin Charlesworth ______	£212.2.6
Note. The Ground on which these Buildings stood was heretofore lett to Joseph Flint at the rent of £3 p Ann^m^ they being built by him: So that upon his having the above Allowance made the Pot House and Tile and Brick Yard, which are now lett to Edward Butler and John Bett are Advanced £18 p Annum, which will recoup the Principal laid out in leſs than 12 Years ______	
By half a years Rent allowed to John Bett for Repairs of the Brick Kilns &c. ______	5.0.0
By Ditto to Edwd Butler for Repairs of the Pothouse	5.10.0

8. Wentworth Woodhouse Muniments, A–698.
9. Ibid., MP 95. J. Dickinson, 'A New and Correct Map of ye South Part of the West Riding of the County of York', 1750.
10. Ibid., A–1272.
11. Ibid., Household Vouchers 1750–3.
12. Ibid., A–229, under 'Buildings and Repairs for the Tenants'.

Since repairs were necessary when Edward Butler took over the Pothouse in 1755–6, it had presumably been in use for some time. Jewitt,[13] following local tradition, gave 1745 as the date of the Pottery's founding, and significantly a factory bill head of the early nineteenth century (Plate 1) gives this same date.

Little is known of Flint's business activities, but an inventory of his personal possessions made after his death in 1765 survives, and gives an interesting indication of his relative affluence.[14] He owned a quantity of furniture and effects, although the only pots mentioned were 'some Delf & Stone Ware'.

Flint's successor Edward Butler took over the Pothouse in 1755–6 and continued there until his death in 1763.[15] Unfortunately, no biographical details of Butler have come to light and little is known of his activities at the Pottery. Neither he nor his wife was literate, as is shown by the fact that payment for pots supplied to the 2nd Marquis of Rockingham[16] at Wentworth is simply acknowledged with a cross. In his will,[17] made in 1762, Edward Butler described himself as a 'pottmaker' and it is clear that his wife Elizabeth was also closely involved in working the Pottery, for he states: 'the Substance I am now possessed of and intitled to hath been in a great Measure acquired by the Labour and Industry of me and my Wife.' Elizabeth Butler in fact continued to operate the Works for a further two years after her husband's death.[18]

Wares 1745–65

The pots produced by Flint and the Butlers were presumably everyday wares made from the local yellow clays. The earliest documentary reference to pots being supplied from the Swinton Pottery is an invoice for 1757:[19]

The Marquiss Rockingham D^{r} to Ed^{w} Butler
Decr ye 15th 1757

	£
Two large Pitchers @ 9^{d} pr Pitcher	0.1.6
2 Stew Pots @ 9^{d} pr pot	0.1.6
$6\frac{1}{2}$ piece Dishes @ 3^{d} pr Dish	0.1.6
$6\frac{1}{3}$ at $1\frac{1}{2}$ p^{r} piece	0.0.9
To Paul Bower 12 puding pots at 2^{d} pr pot	0.2.0
To Jno Man one Large pot wth a Cover	0.1.6
	£0.8.9

13. L. Jewitt, op. cit., Vol. 1, p.495.
14. Borthwick Institute, University of York, probate records, Exchequer Court of York, Doncaster deanery, February 1766.
15. Wath-upon-Dearne parish registers, burials, 14 January 1763.
16. On the death of the 1st Marquis of Rockingham in 1750, his son Charles Watson-Wentworth (1730–82) assumed the title. He was twice prime minister, 1765–6 and 1782 until his death (the Rockingham Administration), and was much respected in South Yorkshire.
17. Borthwick Institute, University of York, probate records, Exchequer Court of York, Doncaster deanery, August 1763.
18. Elizabeth Butler was buried 3 October 1766. Wath-upon-Dearne parish registers.
19. Wentworth Woodhouse Muniments, London Household Vouchers.

To Sundry Pots delivered in Jn Evans Stewardship
as by Bill to Richard Gittins }
Rec^{d} June 24th 1758 by the payment of J^{n} Armitage
her
the Contents of this Bill by Eliz^{h} + Butler
mark

Jewitt states that a hard brown stoneware of Nottingham type was made, and illustrates a loving cup dated 1759 which was traditionally attributed to Swinton.[20] Excavations by the authors on the Pottery site have not produced sherds which can undoubtedly be dated to this period, although fragments of thickly potted red earthenware with a black, lead glaze and dishes decorated with trailed or combed slips may be of this date. A reference to Butler selling '13 cwt of Lead Ashes' on 26 September 1761 indicates that some of his pots were certainly lead glazed.[21]

William Malpass 1765–8

In 1765 the Pottery passed to William Malpass, who appears to have been a man of greater means than his predecessors, with numerous business interests in the locality, including rented property on nearby Kilnhurst Wharf. Fairbank's Map of Swinton[22] of 1776 shows that he held several houses from the marquis, one of which was situated immediately downhill from the Pottery, surrounded by land held by him (see map on page 24).

Wares 1765–8

Malpass's wares seem to have been of much the same type as those produced by the Butlers, common earthenwares such as porringers, pitchers and garden pots occurring in the invoices. This impression is supported by a letter written by him to the Wentworth Estate agent:[23]

Swinton Potworks March 21st 1768
S^{r} acording to your order Wey have Sent By
the Bearers Edward Scofield & tho^{s} Watson
2 Do^{z} of Pots Which i hoype Will Meet
With your aprobashon
the Remander of your halfpenne & part
of the 3 farthing garden pots are Ready
the Rest of your order Shall Be Completed
as Soon as Wey Posobly Can
Mr Robeson has Sent us an order to Stop

20. L. Jewitt, op. cit., Vol. 1, p. 495.
21. Wentworth Woodhouse Muniments, A–238.
22. Prepared for the 2nd Marquis of Rockingham and housed in the Muniment Room, Wentworth Woodhouse.
23. Wentworth Woodhouse Muniments, Bills for Parcels.

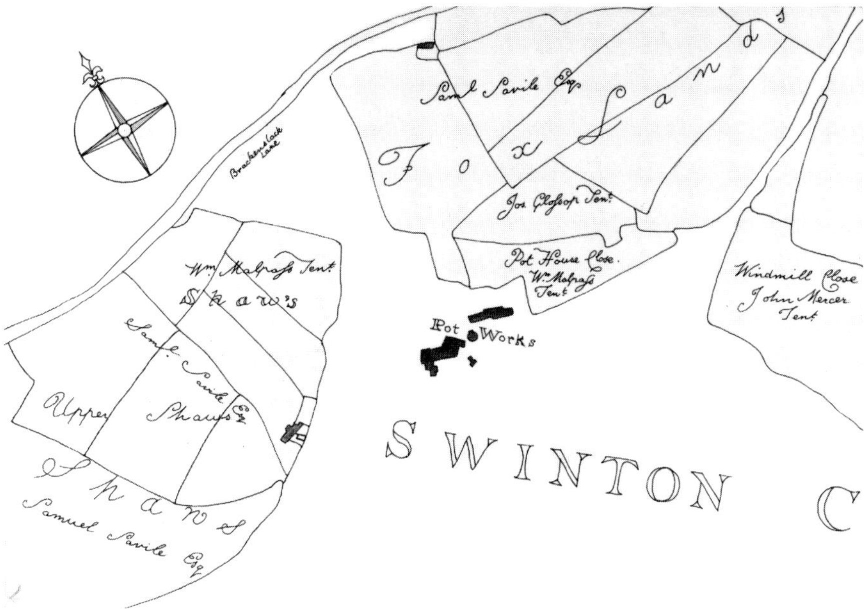

MAP showing the 'Pot Works' and part of Swinton Common. This drawing is closely based upon William Fairbank's preliminary sketch for his map of Swinton, dated 1776, prepared for the Marquis of Rockingham. This names his tenants, including William Malpass, who held 'Pot House Close' and other land and a house adjacent to the 'Pot Works'. *Original map in Sheffield City Library, Fairbank Collection, Wath 31L*

Makeing the Larg Sort Wey Now Wate for
his Comming over ...
i have Sent by order of Mrs Jennet a Larg Pot
& Cover if you Will be so Good as to order
the Men a Drink you Will oblidg
2 Do^{z} Pots—0.3.0   your Most Humble
1 Larg Pot   1.6   Sr^{t} W Malpass
& Cover

——
4.6

The documentary evidence suggests that to Malpass his wares were simply 'pots', large, small or garden, but in fact recent discoveries of sherds on the Pottery site which can with certainty be attributed to William Malpass show that he was producing very fine quality slip-decorated earthenwares in the Staffordshire tradition.

The majority of pieces recovered were parts of press-moulded dishes or chargers with notched edges, a number of which have two closely-spaced raised lines encircling the embossed letters WM in large capitals (for William

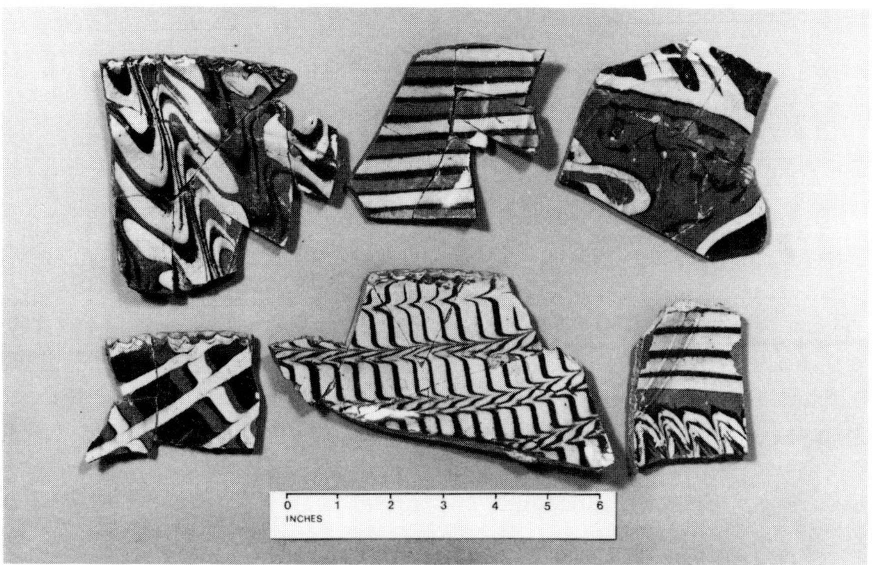

5. SLIPWARE SHERDS, *c.*1765–8. From the Swinton Pottery site, showing typical trailed and combed decoration. The sherd top right is embossed W M (mark 1), the initials of William Malpass. Length of scale 15.2 cm (6 in). *See pages 24–5*

Malpass) in the centre of the dish, and dating presumably to the period 1765 to 1768 when he worked alone (mark 1). The dishes are of a red or buff earthenware body, generally covered with a cream slip on to which the coloured clays in a semi-liquid state were trailed, typically chocolate-brown and a lighter ginger-brown, applied in many varied combinations. The upper surface is covered with a clear, lustrous, yellow glaze. Many of the trailed patterns were also combed to produce colourful abstract designs with considerable rustic charm. A selection of sherds of this type is shown in Plate 5.

Similar but earlier slipware chargers, chiefly of the period 1720 to 1740, decorated and marked in this manner, were made in north Staffordshire, associated in particular with the potter Samuel Malkin.[24] Curiously, members of a family with the surname Malkin are recorded in the Wath-upon-Dearne parish registers between the years 1763 and 1776, described as potters. It may be nothing more than a coincidence, but since the name is not a local one, it may possibly indicate one means by which the Staffordshire potting tradition came rather belatedly to Yorkshire.

24. See, for example, R.G. Haggar, *English Country Pottery*, London, 1950, pp.32–3.

2
Growth and Prosperity

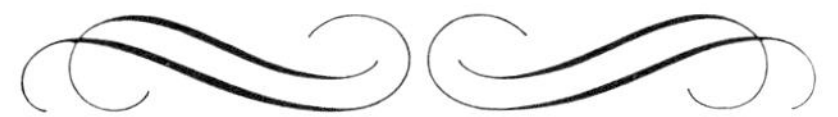

The production of coarse country pottery in Swinton under the first proprietors of the Pothouse might have been predicted, although perhaps one would not have expected that slipwares of such fine quality were being made by William Malpass. Similarly, whilst it was known that the Swinton Pottery began to produce finewares during the late 1760s, it was always assumed that nothing of note was manufactured until the association with the Leeds Pottery in 1785. Recent evidence has now made it necessary to reject this traditional view.

In Yorkshire the production of finewares began considerably later than in Staffordshire, where, during the first decades of the eighteenth century, refined earthenwares became lighter in colour with the introduction of white-burning clays and ground, calcined flint. When fired at temperatures in the range 1100°C to 1250°C and glazed with common salt thrown into the kiln during the final stages of firing, the product was a dense, white stoneware with a hard, pitted, vitreous glaze. The same constituents, however, when fired at somewhat lower temperatures resulted in what became known as cream-coloured earthenware, or creamware. Following the development about 1740 of liquid lead glazes, into which the porous, biscuit-fired pieces were dipped and then refired,[1] creamware with its soft, even, mellow glaze began to displace the stark, white stoneware as the standard English earthenware and was widely manufactured in Staffordshire, Yorkshire and elsewhere. The lead glaze could easily be coloured by the addition of metallic oxides, particularly those of manganese, iron and copper, to give rich browns and greens, or decorated with a range of on-glaze enamel colours to produce one of the most attractive of all ceramics.

Although creamware replaced salt-glazed articles in terms of popular appeal, the changeover was by no means rapid and during the 1760s and 70s considerable quantities of white stoneware continued to be made, many potters manufacturing the same range of items in both bodies—frequently from the same moulds.[2] Such was the case at Swinton well into the 1770s, the last reference to salt glaze in the factory invoices occurring in 1775.

1. Lead glazing had previously been accomplished by dusting powdered galena (lead sulphide) on to the article before firing.
2. I. Noël-Hume, 'The rise and fall of English white salt-glazed stoneware', Part II, *English Pottery and Porcelain* (ed. P. Atterbury), London, 1980, pp. 24–9.

William Malpass and William Fenney 1768–78; Bingley, Wood & Co. 1778–85

By February 1768, William Malpass had taken into partnership William Fenney, and with his arrival affairs at the Swinton Pottery took a very different direction. Fenney had been a glassmaker at Catcliffe,[3] near Rotherham, a member of a family which had long-established connections with the South Yorkshire glass trade and who had in fact supplied the 2nd Marquis of Rockingham with glass. In 1765 he had turned his attention to the manufacture of fine earthenwares and had been associated with John Platt at the Rotherham Pottery until 1767.[4] When this partnership was dissolved, he joined Malpass and from this time the real expansion of the Swinton Pottery began. Fenney lived in Swinton during the 1770s, renting from the marquis a sizeable property comprising a house, garden and croft near the marquis's racing stables.[5]

After 1776, Fenney's name no longer appeared on the invoices from the Pottery, and Malpass continued alone until 1778 when, being somewhat in arrears with his rents to the marquis, he too relinquished his interest in the Pottery.[6]

A new partnership trading as Bingley, Wood & Co. was founded in 1778 and held the Works until 1785.[7] Thomas Bingley was a local landowner and farmer with money to invest, while Willoughby Wood (b. 1732) was the Swinton schoolmaster.[8] Since neither man presumably had knowledge or experience of the pottery business, the management of the Works was left to others, very likely to John Brameld, whom Jewitt states was a partner at this time, and who was later to play such an important part in the Pottery's affairs.[9] Another partner mentioned by Jewitt was 'a person named Sharpe' of whom nothing further is known.

3. William Fenney commenced glass production at Catcliffe, near Rotherham, in 1740. The 60-ft-high Catcliffe glass-cone is Europe's oldest surviving example of its type (see G. D. Lewis, *The South Yorkshire Glass Industry*, Sheffield City Museums, 1973, p. 4).

4. A. J. B. Kiddell, 'John Platt of Rotherham Potter and Mason-Architect', *E.C.C. Transactions*, Vol. 5, Part 3, 1962, p. 172. See also J.V.G. Mallet, 'Rotherham Saltglaze: John Platt's Jug', *E.C.C. Transactions*, Vol. 9, Part 1, 1973, pp. 111–14.

5. William Fairbank's map of Swinton, 1776, Muniment Room, Wentworth Woodhouse. The 2nd Marquis was well known for his horse-racing interests.

6. Wentworth Woodhouse Muniments, A–255. Malpass had previously been in arrears with his rents to the marquis. An entry in the Estate Accounts for 1773 reads: 'Decr 30—William Malpass, allowed him all Rent and Arrears of Rent due Whitsun, Lammas and Martinmas 1773, in Consideration of his conveying all his Lands, Tenements and Premises, and all his Tenant rights and Interest of in and to three Cottages in Swinton to your Lordship £271:12:10.'

7. The Pottery, however, continued to trade as Bingley, Wood & Co. until 1787.

8. Willoughby Wood became the Swinton schoolmaster in 1754 and instructed 'Thirteen Poor Children Reading &c.' until at least 1769. A comparison of his signature on receipts for payment as schoolmaster (Wentworth Woodhouse Muniments, Household Vouchers) with that which appears on invoices from the Swinton Pottery leaves no doubt that it is the same person.

9. L. Jewitt, *Ceramic Art in Great Britain*, London, 1878, Vol. 1, p. 496.

Wares 1768–85

The introduction of more refined bodies at Swinton coincided with the arrival of William Fenney into the partnership in 1768. In view of his previous association with John Platt, the pots made at Swinton proved, as might be expected, to be very similar to those recorded in Arthur Young's account of his visit to the Rotherham Pottery in 1770: 'Besides the iron manufactory, they have a pottery, in which is made the white, cream-coloured (*Staffordshire*) and tortoiseshell earthen-ware.'[10] Our knowledge of these early Swinton finewares comes from invoices and from sherds excavated on the Pottery site, where deposits of white saltglaze and creamware dating to this period were found. The clay for these wares may have been the white-burning clay referred to in the Wentworth Estate Accounts where, for example, on 9 November 1768 there is a record 'received for pipe Clay sold from Swinton Common £2.'[11]

Salt-glazed Stoneware

In both body and quality, the Swinton white salt-glazed stonewares have proved, on the basis of present studies, to be indistinguishable from their contemporary Staffordshire counterparts.

The plate border-mouldings from dinner wares, for example, are chiefly the standard designs of the period (Plate 6), namely basket and diaper patterns in scroll-bordered panels; feather edge, the units consisting of seven barbs; and seed pattern within a Queen's shape border. Gadroon is found in two different versions, and the cockstail edge, unusual on salt-glazed items, occurs in a similar form on contemporary Swinton creamwares. Drawings of these plate edges are shown in Appendix I: Nos. 1–4, 10, 11. Several less common borders were also recorded.

Sherds of other dinner wares included small elegantly formed sauce boats with spiral fluting (Plate 6), raised flower-and-leaf designs, or panels of basket-moulded decoration. The factory invoices for 1771 include a reference to '6 White Boats 1/6', although in general the white saltglaze purchased from Swinton consisted of kitchen utensils, creamwares being preferred for tablewares at Wentworth.

The salt-glazed tea bowls and saucers recovered from the site were well formed and very finely potted. Some were enamelled in a characteristic style, one example (Plate 6) with a competently painted chinoiserie in black monochrome and a rococo border on the inside formed of scrolls and dot-and-diaper motifs. Only a few of the pieces recovered had enamelled or scratch-blue decoration.

Teapot shapes were mainly globular with the cover recessed into the body to

10. A. Young, *A Six Months Tour Through The North of England*, London, Salisbury and Edinburgh (2nd. edn., enlarged, 1771), Vol. 1, p. 116.
11. Wentworth Woodhouse Muniments, A–246.

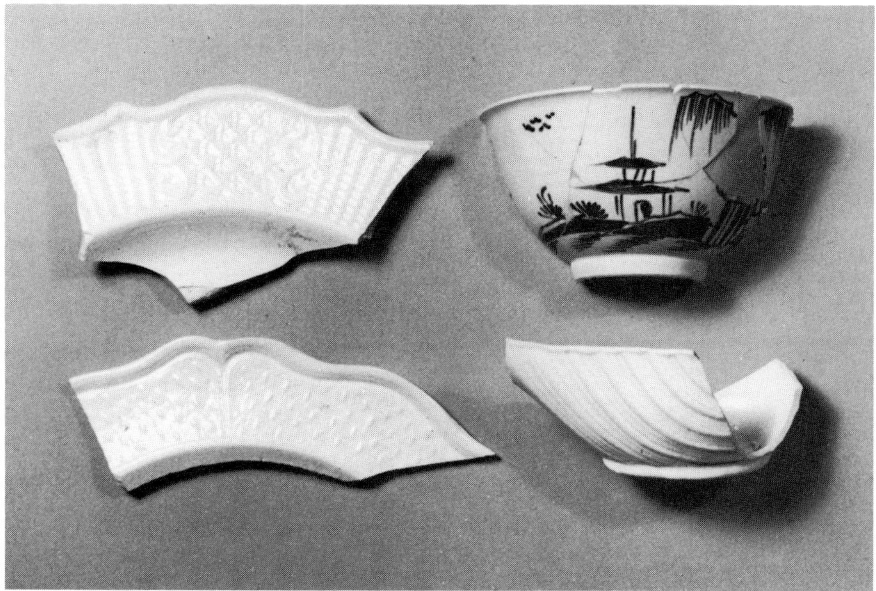

6. SALT-GLAZED SHERDS, *c.*1770–5. Basket-weave and seed pattern plate borders, a tea bowl enamelled in black and a small, fluted pap or sauceboat. From the Swinton Pottery site. Height of tea bowl 4.3 cm (1.7 in). *See pages 28–9*

give a smooth outline. One particularly interesting feature was the use of crossed, reeded handles with leafy terminals, of a type familiar on contemporary creamwares, but unknown on white saltglaze. Other teapots had galleries, and some were decorated with turned rings around the body. Spouts were straight and plain, crabstock, or curved and moulded, as shown in Appendix I: Nos. 15–17. Nos. 28–39 illustrate the forms of rounded and acorn finials, all known also from Staffordshire. Handle shapes were basically of strap or reeded type, single or crossed, usually with a pinched or curled lower end, typical of the period, and rarely with a flower or leaf terminal; crabstock handles were also used, to date associated only with teapots (Appendix I: Nos. 18, 22–4). Miniature teawares too were recovered, the tea bowls being about 2 cm (0.8 in) in height.

Parts of tankards or mugs were excavated, either straight-sided or slightly flared at the rim or base. The invoices from the Pottery sent to Wentworth House include in 1772 '12 White Muggs 2/-'. There are many references to kitchen and other household items in white salt-glazed stoneware such as patty pans, bowls, baking dishes and wash basins, and numerous fragments of such wares were found.

It is important to stress that all the items of white stoneware described here can be closely dated to the years 1768–75. There is a tendency in the literature to date such wares too early, and had the Swinton pieces not occurred in a well-defined archaeological context, their manufacture would, in all likelihood, have been assigned to the period *c.* 1750–60.

Sherds of brown Nottingham-type stoneware, notably a large piece of a tankard, were recovered from the site, but were uncommon. The only specific documentary references to this body occur in invoices of the Bingley, Wood & Co. period when, between 1778 and 1780, 'Brown Chamber potts' and 'Brown Quart Mugs' are mentioned.

Cream-coloured Earthenware

Fine quality creamwares were produced at Swinton from about 1768. An important documentary piece is the large teapot shown in Plate 7 bearing the following inscription enamelled in red:

ALL SORTS OF EARTH:
:ENWARE SOLD HERE
WHOLESALE & RETAIL
FROM SWINTON POTTERY.
BY RICH^{d} PATRICK 1773.

This was a display piece, intended to grace the window of an earthenware dealer's shop to advertise the products of the Swinton Pottery. Because of its unusual size, the potters evidently had some difficulties with the firing and attempted to disguise strain cracks around the base by over-painting them with leaves. The crossed, twisted handles are heavy and the spout too small for the body, but none the less as a documentary piece of Swinton creamware this teapot is an item of importance. It is painted on the reverse with red roses and other flowers and pale-green leaves, but has proved, however, to be rather uncharacteristic and by no means as well potted as the normal productions of this period. The whereabouts of Richard Patrick's shop is not known.[12]

Recently, a quantity of creamware sherds dating to the Malpass and Fenney partnership has been located on the Pottery site, greatly increasing our knowledge of their products. They include fragments of the whole range of useful wares and show that in general these early Swinton pots were of extremely fine quality, small elegant pieces, thinly potted and light in weight, dark cream in colour with a distinctly yellow glaze which is usually uncrazed.

In dinner wares, certain plate mouldings correspond with the white salt-glazed examples previously described, notably feather edge, cockstail and also gadroon. Conversely, batswing borders in at least two versions, and lobed plates with moulded fleur-de-lis devices are known in creamware only. Very similar examples of all these borders are recorded from other potteries; the Swinton plate mouldings are illustrated in Appendix I: Nos. 1, 2, 4–11.

Parts of sauceboats were found, including one small specimen delicately moulded with spiral fluting and elaborate rococo scrolls and shells framing a plain reserve on each side, and with gadroon borders. A large sauceboat of this type has been recognized (Plate 8), the crossed, reeded handles of which have

12. C. Bennett, 'The Richard Patrick Teapot', *Northern Ceramic Society Journal*, 1978–9, Vol. 3, pp. 149–50.

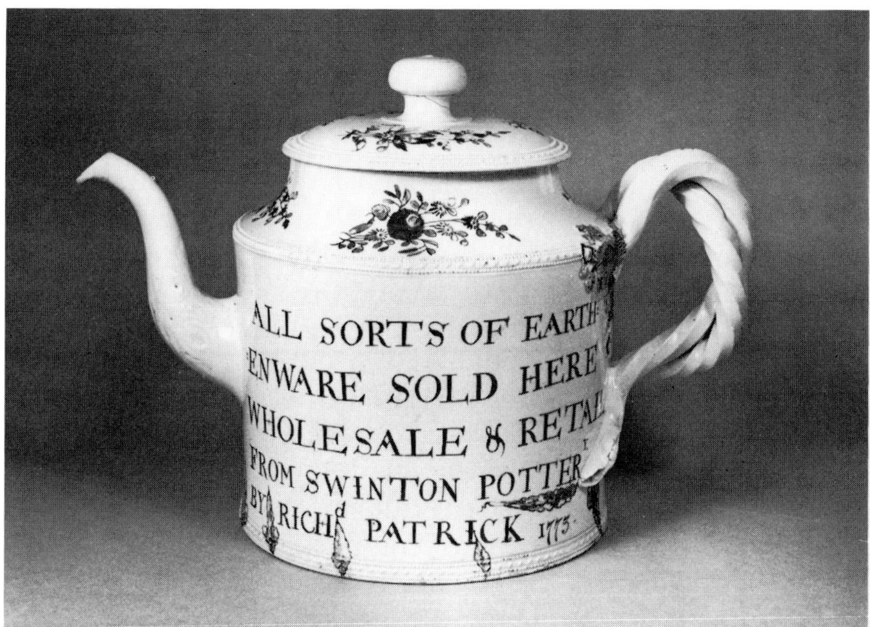

7. DOCUMENTARY TEAPOT. Creamware, deep cream, enamelled in red, black and green. Inscribed and dated 1773. Height 24.4 cm (9.6 in). *Mrs F. H. Hodgson and Clifton Park Museum, Rotherham.* *See page 30*

8. SAUCEBOAT, *c.*1770–5. Creamware, deep cream, decorated with green, brown and yellow glazes. Terminals, Appendix I: No. 45. Length 21 cm (8.3 in). *Victoria and Albert Museum, Crown Copyright.* *See pages 30–2*

characteristic Swinton flower-and-leaf terminals, and like many of the Malpass & Fenney creamwares, it is decorated with yellow, green and brown glazes. An entry in the invoices sent from the Pottery to Wentworth House in 1772 reads '4 large Cr^{m} Co^{r} Sauce Boats 3/-'. Parts of small round salts with leaf-moulded feet were found, and are listed in an invoice for 1775 '6 Cream Col^{r} Salts 1/-'. Similarly, fragments of a tureen with a gadroon edge (Appendix I: No. 2) were recovered, and as the invoices for 1771 record, such items were comparatively expensive '2 Large Cream Coler Turiens 15/-'.

The teawares from this period proved to be among the most characteristic and attractive of early Swinton products, three main types of teapot being recognized.

Jewitt illustrated a creamware teapot in the possession of the Brameld family which was said to be of Swinton origin.[13] This was cylindrical, enamelled with flowers and inscribed and dated 'Amelia Hallam 1773'. Since identically shaped teapots have now been recovered from the site, a date can be assigned to all the wares in this archaeological context. The most commonly found type, these cylindrical pots were small, very light in weight, occasionally plain, but more often with bands of beading, rouletting or bead-and-reel decoration around the base, shoulder and neck. They have crossed reeded or strap handles, with one of the distinctive Swinton terminals, while the spouts have an acanthus-leaf moulding. The covers are somewhat flattened with a button finial, or sometimes a button with a small protruding knop. Illustrated (Plate 9) is a teapot with a flower finial, identified as a Swinton product of this period by its characteristic terminals. The full range of known Malpass & Fenney creamware handles, spouts, finials and terminals is shown in Appendix I.

A second type of teapot recovered from the site is of a very unusual form, having a globular body with raised spiral fluting and rococo scrolls. The details of the moulded decoration are similar to those on the sauceboat illustrated in Plate 8. This teapot has a small plain foot, plain shoulder and a beaded border around the rim, while the handle is heavily ribbed, thickened at the top to form a thumbpiece and having a tripartite acanthus-leaf terminal at the base (see Appendix I: Nos. 19 and 20). The spout has indistinct acanthus moulding and the covers were presumably plain, since no fluted examples were found. A reference in an invoice of 1771 to '1 Tea pot Fluted 8^{d}' may refer to this shape.

Several variants of globular-shaped teapots were found, either quite plain, with the top recessed to take the cover, or of similar form but with a small shoulder and short upstanding neck, or with no shoulder but with a raised, pierced gallery. The associated spouts and handles were presumably the crabstock type which occurred in quantity on the site (see Appendix I: Nos. 17 and 24).

13. L. Jewitt, op. cit., Vol. 1, p. 510, Fig. 873.

A. JUG, 1774. Creamware, enamelled with flowers. Inscribed and dated 'H. Dyson 1774'. No mark. Height 15.5 cm (6.1 in) *See page 34*

B. DISH, *c*.1815–25. Pearlware, finely enamelled with a botanical study named on the reverse *Kalmia Glauca* (copied from Curtis's *Botanical Magazine*), and gilded. Probably by the artist George Collinson. Impressed BRAMELD + 1. Length 21.3 cm (8.4 in). *See page 78*

C. DISH, *c*.1820–42. Earthenware, transfer-printed in blue with the *Castle of Rochefort* pattern. Impressed BRAMELD + 1 and with a backstamp (mark 66). Length 48.3 cm (19 in). *See page 102*

9. TEAPOT, *c*.1770–5. Creamware, deep cream, enamelled in red and black. Spout, terminals and finial, Appendix I: Nos. 14, 41 and 44 respectively. Height 14.5 cm (5.7 in). *Yorkshire Museum, York.* *See page 32*

Fragments of globular teapots with large applied leaves and leafy terminals were recovered, colour-glazed all over in green, brown and deep yellow, reminiscent of Whieldon-type wares, and probably representing some of the earliest Swinton finewares.

Creamware tea bowls and saucers of the Malpass & Fenney period are, in general, elegantly shaped, the bowls slightly flared at the rim and standing on a small foot. One cup fragment had the base of a handle attached. Many such wares are described in the invoices, for example in 1771 '1 Doz. Cups & Saucers C^{m}. C^{r}. 3/-'. Sherds of miniature teawares were also recovered.

Tall, finely potted coffee pots were made, the example illustrated (Plate 10) having characteristic Swinton terminals and finial and a herringbone moulded spout. The decoration is in similar style to that on the 'Richard Patrick' teapot (Plate 7) which is dated 1773, but the treatment of the smaller flowers is noticeably different. In an invoice for 1773 there is a reference to '12 Coffy Cups & Covers 2/-', an unusual description in view of the covers unless the writer had caudle cups in mind.

Numerous barrel-shaped jugs were produced at Swinton, often with turned decoration around the body, and sometimes with raised bands of bead and reel or gadrooning around the rim and base. A face mask from beneath the lip of one such jug was found, while another type (Plate 11) has a lip in the form of a spirally-fluted cornucopia. The very decorative example illustrated (Colour Plate A), inscribed and dated 'H. Dyson 1774' is competently enamelled with coloured flowers by the painter of the 'Richard Patrick' teapot. It has the characteristic Swinton handle with a tripartite acanthus-leaf terminal (see Appendix I: Nos. 19 and 20). The painted scrollwork around the inscription appears on a similar smaller jug (Plate 11) inscribed 'Long live the Earl of Winchelsea 1774' in puce monochrome.[14] The invoices for 1773 record '2 two Quart Jugs, Covers & Grates 3/4'.

Reference has already been made to enamelled decoration on creamware. Sherds of teawares were painted mainly in red and black with attractive stylized flower designs, as on the teapot in Plate 9. The invoices of 1771 include '2 Teapots Inameled 1/4' while another reference in 1775 to '1 set blue & Cm cups & Srs' suggests that teawares were also blue-painted.

Manganese sponged decoration was much in evidence on sherds of all manner of items, especially plates and teawares, recovered during the excavations. This usually produced a purplish-brown colour, either sponged or streaked on to the surface, and which diffused into the glaze during firing. Sometimes patches of colour occur with this, usually green, yellow, or less commonly a smokey grey. These coloured-glaze effects are described as 'Tortoiseshell' in the factory invoices.

Other sherds were decorated with uniformly stained glazes, notably a clear bright-green or a rich brown, achieved by dipping into a liquid glaze. The brown teapots are described in the invoices as 'purple', or if combined with patches of yellow, as in 1770, the description is '5 large Teapots purple & Lemon Coler 5/-'. These purple examples were almost certainly the original brown-glazed 'Rockingham' teapots, the nineteenth-century versions of which were to gain such popularity, as discussed on pages 108–13.

Additional information from the factory invoices makes it clear that a wide range of items was produced. A list of wares sent to Wentworth House on 5 March 1774 specifically 'By Order of my Lord & Lady' includes the following:

4 Baskets & Stands @ 4/-	0.16.0
3 Sallad Dishes	0. 9.0

14. George Finch, 9th Earl of Winchilsea (1752–1826). The only connection with Swinton appears to be through the marriage of the 1st Marquis of Rockingham in 1716 to Mary, fourth daughter of Daniel Finch, 7th Earl of Winchilsea.

10. COFFEE POT, *c*.1770–5. Creamware, deep cream, enamelled in red and green, the flowers and leaves outlined in brown. Spout, finial and terminals, Appendix I: Nos. 13, 37 and 40 respectively. Height 22.5 cm (8.9 in). *Temple Newsam House, Leeds. See pages 33–4*

2 Doz Green plates	2. 2.0
2 Muffing plates & Cov^{r}	0. 3.0
6 Em^{ld} purple Teapots	0. 6.0
10 Setts of pierc'd Em^{ld} Chocalate Cups &c	21. 0.0

Decorative items were also supplied, as on 20 September 1775:

4 Large Vases Fluted	0.18.0

Listed in other invoices are cheese stands, custard cups, broth pots and venison dishes, porringers, bottles, pomade pots and more or less the whole range of domestic wares. Occasionally, the Pottery proprietors had difficulty keeping pace with the requirements of the great household at Wentworth, and William Fenney himself was sometimes moved to write a brief apology, as on 25 April 1772:

> . . . as we have not Large pichers at present to sute will take care to mak and send them on or before the 5th of May — I am for Selfes & partner Your Hb^{le} Servt Wm Fenney.

Clearly Fenney was reluctant to lose such important customers, and assurances were again the order of the day on 28 August 1773, when he wrote a terse note:

> Mad^{am}
> The Remander will com on Monday Next with out fail . . .

Fenney, it seems, was no more a man of letters than his partner William Malpass.

It has not proved possible to distinguish clearly between the wares of Malpass & Fenney and those of Bingley, Wood & Co., probably because the productions of the two periods were very similar. Evidence from factory invoices, however, suggests that blue-painted creamwares were becoming more popular during this later partnership, since many are listed, described as blue or 'Queen's blue'. Other items of interest in the Bingley, Wood & Co. invoices supplied between 1778 and 1785 include inkstands, a 'large Cullinder', 'Candlesticks & Extinguishers', char pots and a 'Round Compteer'.

Coarsewares

The manufacture of slip-decorated and black-glazed coarsewares at Swinton was continued alongside that of finewares until well into the nineteenth century. The excavated slipware jug (Plate 12) was recovered in the same context as creamwares which were undoubtedly made by Malpass & Fenney. This most attractive rustic jug is of a buff, porous earthenware, slip-decorated with chocolate-brown lines and blobs, fully glazed on the inside but only half-way down the outside. A feature of these Malpass & Fenney coarsewares is their very fine potting.

11. (*left*) JUG. Creamware, deep cream, enamelled in puce and inscribed 'Long live the Earl of Winchelsea 1774'. Handle and terminal, Appendix I: Nos. 19 and 20 respectively. Height 13.2 cm (5.2 in). *Fitzwilliam Museum, Cambridge. See page 34*

12. (*right*) JUG, *c*.1770–5. Slipware, buff earthenware body with trailed dark-brown slip decoration. Partially assembled from sherds excavated on Swinton Pottery site. Height 19 cm (7.5 in). *See pages 36–7*

Other sherds included parts of dishes, bowls and chamber pots of soft, red earthenware, slip-coated and lead-glazed on the upper surface only, and further decorated with trailed lines and blobs, or sponged manganese with patches of green glaze to produce a version of tortoiseshell ware.

An interesting bill recording the sale of waste for highway repairs perhaps sheds some light on the continuing manufacture of coarsewares alongside finewares:[15]

Mrs Jno Mercer & Sayles — Surveyors for the Highways of Swinton
1772 — to Wm Malpass & Fenney

	£ s d
127 Loads of Rubish from White Work at Sundries Times ... @ 6 ...	3. 3.6
46 Loads of D^{o} from the old Works @ 3^{d}	11.6
	£3.15.0

Rec^{d} Octe^{r} 17th 1772 the Contents in
Full for self & Partner

Wm Malpass

15. Swinton Parish Documents, Highways Accounts.

The reference to the 'old Works'[16] suggests that possibly the original buildings continued in use for coarsewares, whilst new ones were erected for the manufacture of saltglaze ('White Work') and creamware. Interestingly, the hard saltglaze waste was considered of greater value for road repairs than that from the old Works.

Very many similar bills from this and all subsequent periods survive recording the sale of sherds and other 'pothouse rubbish' for the repair of the local highways. They account for the relative scarcity of waste material on the Pottery site itself and explain why previous excavations failed to reveal significant quantities of early wasters.[17]

16. A similar reference occurs as late as 1805, 'To 2 Bundles of Bindings from Old Pottery'.
17. A. Cox and T. Lockett, 'The Rockingham Pottery, 1745–1842, a preliminary excavation', *The Connoisseur*, 1970, Vol. 173, No. 697, pp. 171–6. Details of the excavations carried out by the present writers were given in a paper entitled 'Recent Excavations at the Swinton Pottery: White Saltglaze and Creamware pre-1785' read to the English Ceramic Circle on 17 April 1982 and to be published in *E.C.C. Transactions*, Vol. 11, Part 3, 1983. See also Chap. 3, note 13.

3
The Leeds Partnership

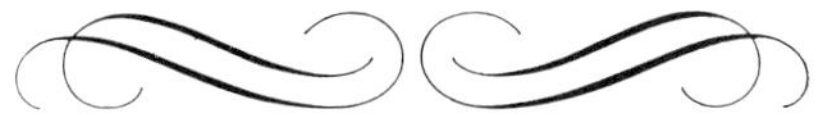

The realization that fine-quality creamwares and stonewares were produced at the Swinton Pottery under Malpass & Fenney, and later under Bingley, Wood & Co., makes necessary a complete revision of previous ideas about the next proprietors, Greens, Bingley & Co., who worked the concern from 1785 to 1806.

In 1785, John Green (1743–1805) of the Leeds Pottery, together with other partners,[1] took out a twenty-one years' lease on the Swinton Pottery, and thus began the relationship between these two establishments, although curiously the firm continued to trade as Bingley, Wood & Co. until 1787. The Leeds partners held a controlling number of shares in the Swinton Pottery and John Green, according to Jewitt, became the acting manager, thus ensuring a strong influence over the Swinton affairs.[2] The tendency has been to assume that this move in a sense rescued the Swinton Pottery from obscurity, when in fact the Leeds connection represented, if anything, a decline in the standards of wares produced at Swinton.

It is not known precisely why the two manufactories came to be linked in this way. In some respects the Swinton partners must have felt that an association with the large and thriving Leeds Pottery with its wide export trade would have certain advantages, and John Green was a wily, if not unscrupulous, businessman who would undoubtedly have put forward a proposition which sounded attractive.[3] Events were later to prove, however, that all the advantages were on the Leeds side.

John Green's relationship with the Swinton Pottery may have been closer than has been generally realized. Certainly his family lived in and around Swinton for many years,[4] and John Green himself may have been employed at

1. The names of all the partners are not known. The Swinton members included Thomas Bingley, John Brameld and his eldest son William, while among those associated with the Leeds Pottery were John Green, Ebenezer Green (probably John Green's cousin and one of the later partners), William Hartley and George Hanson. See L. Jewitt, *Ceramic Art in Great Britain*, London, 1878, Vol. 1, pp. 472, 497 and 500.

2. L. Jewitt, op. cit., Vol. 1, p. 497.

3. A portrait of John Green appears as the frontispiece in J. R. Kidson and F. Kidson, *Historical Notices of the Leeds Old Pottery*, Leeds, 1892.

4. Wentworth Woodhouse Muniments, A–1273. In this general rent roll of the estate in England and Ireland, compiled in 1723 with additions up to 1750, there is a reference to John

the Pottery during the Malpass & Fenney period. A bill for pots sent to Wentworth House probably in 1768 bears the signature of a John Green,[5] which corresponds closely with his manner of writing his name, as a comparison with his signature on documents concerning the Leeds Pottery shows, but although a strong possibility the evidence is not conclusive. The Leeds Pottery commenced in 1770 and John Green was in fact the only member of the early partnership to be described as a potter, which raises the interesting possibility that if he had worked previously at the Swinton Pottery and his knowledge was gained there, the early Leeds wares might well have much in common with Swinton pieces. Knowing the high quality of the Swinton products, once he was at Leeds he may have viewed the former concern as a serious rival, whose activities could best be controlled through an association of this type which in effect gave the upper hand to the Leeds partners.

Alternatively, a shrewd businessman whose first thought was always the financial objective, he perhaps realized the potential of the two concerns if worked together under his guidance. He knew well the advantages of Swinton, with its plentiful coal supplies and favourable position with regard to river and canal transport. His correspondence with Swinton was with John Brameld, who, as a practical potter and a man of some education, was in many ways the most important of the Swinton partners. In a letter dated 1788 from the Leeds Pottery, John Green notes, 'You have room now if you will but make neat goods and be observing to get money; but it will require a strict attention to keep every weelband in the nick.'[6] Perhaps in John Green's eyes the Swinton Pottery hitherto had not been working to maximum efficiency. Initially affairs within the new partnership seemed to be proceeding satisfactorily. In a letter to Earl Fitzwilliam[7] dated 16 October 1786, one of the Wentworth stewards, Richard Fenton, reported, 'The Pottery at Swinton goes on well and will be a good Work.'[8]

There is no doubt that the Greens, Bingley & Co. partnership was a time of expansion for the Swinton Pottery. A manuscript from the Swinton Parish Documents in the Doncaster Archives is entitled 'The dimensions of the Ground Plan of the Pottery taken the 30th Jan.ry 1788', and indicates clearly that as part of John Green's plans for the Works new buildings were being erected at this period.[9]

Green's colliery at Swinton. William Fairbank's map of Wath-upon-Dearne, 1775 (Muniment Room, Wentworth Woodhouse), shows an area of land near the Pottery annotated 'Coal got by Greens & Co.'.

5. Wentworth Woodhouse Muniments, Bills for Parcels, 1764–8.

6. L. Jewitt, op. cit., Vol. 1, p. 497.

7. William Fitzwilliam (1748–1833), 2nd Earl Fitzwilliam, succeeded in 1782, on the death of his maternal uncle, the 2nd Marquis of Rockingham, to the Wentworth family's estates in England and Ireland, but not to the title. After 1807 he was known as William Wentworth-Fitzwilliam.

8. Wentworth Woodhouse Muniments, F 106/141.

9. Swinton Parish Documents, P59/6/A4/3.

Unfortunately, the ground plan drawing which probably accompanied this is now missing, leaving a somewhat disembodied series of measurements. None the less, certain interesting facts emerge, such as the specific mention of new constructions as, for example, the dimensions of the 'New Slip House Hovel Inside' (13 ft 6 in) and 'Length of the Wall from the New Building to the Gateway' (181 ft 8 in). This particular building was 107 ft long, whilst the gateway was apparently provided with a gate 13 ft wide and flanked by pillars. Other buildings are named, including the 'Black Slip House' (22 ft by 22 ft 6 in), the 'Panchion Hovel' (45 ft by 36 ft), the 'Panchion Work', the 'Blue Ware Hovel' (17 ft 6 in long), and the 'Blue Bisc^{t} Workhouse & Hovel'. Certain of the original structures are referred to, such as the 'Old Slip House' (45 ft 8 in by 31 ft 6 in) and the 'Old Workhouse', whilst the existing 'Carpenter Shop' was extended. One rather curious set of measurements reads:

From the Gateway to the Elbow	77 ft 0 in
from the Elbow to the end of the Slip Kiln	24 ft 9 in

but without the original plan they are unlikely to be understood.

Clearly the association with Leeds involved a good number of changes at Swinton. Jewitt had in his possession letters from John Green written from Leeds to John Brameld at Swinton, dating to April and June 1788, and giving directions about the management of the concern in his usual business-like manner, and even offering a commission of 5% on all 'wearing apparell sould to your works'.[10]

The Swinton–Leeds relationship, however, was rarely a happy one, and towards the end of the twenty-one years' lease feelings on the Swinton side at least had become very bitter, mainly because the Pottery was not allowed to develop fully, but kept as a subsidiary of Leeds, as is explained in the following chapter.

During the period spanned by this partnership, south Yorkshire had become a nationally important area for the production of earthenware. In addition to the several potteries of the Leeds district, there were flourishing concerns in Castleford and Ferrybridge, and many smaller works including a number in the Swinton area at Mexborough, Newhill and Kilnhurst—all, like the Swinton Pottery, based on the twin advantages of coal and canals. In 1801 another large Pottery opened at the lower end of Swinton, the Don Pottery,[11] built beside the 'Long Cut' on the Don Navigation, and in fact founded by John Green after his personal financial difficulties in 1800 had caused him to withdraw from Greens, Bingley & Co., and from the Leeds Pottery.

This picture of local competition, in addition to that from north Staffordshire and elsewhere, provides an important background to the developments at the Swinton Pottery. The movement of workers is shown very

10. L. Jewitt, op. cit., Vol. 1, p. 497.
11. Swinton Parish Documents, Land Tax.

clearly in the Swinton Parish Documents, with skilled men being attracted from other centres of pottery manufacture, and Swinton potters in their turn migrating to other areas.

WARES 1785–1806

Until recent excavations on the Swinton Pottery site made possible the attribution of wares, the only information about the products of the Greens, Bingley & Co. period came from contemporary documentary evidence quoted by Jewitt, and from the invoices from the Pottery studied by the present writers. Jewitt implies that under the Greens, Bingley & Co. proprietorship, the items produced at Swinton were very similar to those of Leeds, since the same price lists were common to both concerns, with only the heading altered for use at Swinton. He quotes a list dated 1796 in his possession, which suggests that the Swinton Pottery at this period made a range of products comparable with those of most fineware potteries of the time.[12] He records that 'Greens, Bingley, & Co. Swinton Pottery, make, sell, and export wholesale, all sorts of Earthen Ware, viz., Cream-coloured, or Queen's, Nankeen Blue, Tortoise Shell, Fine Egyptian Black, Brown China, &c. Also the above sorts enameled, printed or ornamented with gold or silver.' The wares were further 'printed or enamelled with coats of arms, crests, cyphers, landscapes, &c.; also blue printed Nankeen patterns . . .'

This information from Jewitt and details of wares from Swinton Pottery invoices provide a good indication of the scope of its products. However, since no recognizable factory marks associated with this partnership are known, the actual identification of the wares produced here has been made possible for the first time entirely through a study of excavated material from the Pottery site. The sherds recovered in this way have enabled an outline to be given of the types of wares produced at Swinton,[13] and to show how they relate to their Leeds counterparts, by comparison either with marked examples, or with the Leeds *Pattern Books* and Drawing Books.[14]

Cream-coloured Earthenware

The Swinton creamware of this period is refined and pale in colour, no doubt due to the inclusion of china clay and china stone in the body. The glaze at this time has a slightly greenish tinge and shows little tendency to craze. The quality of the ware is good and will stand comparison with its Leeds equivalents. It must be said, however, that the 'neat goods' which John Green exhorted John Brameld to make at the Swinton Pottery have a somewhat mass-produced appearance when compared with the charming creamwares

12. L. Jewitt, op. cit., Vol. 1, p. 499.
13. A. and A. Cox, 'Recent Excavations at the Swinton Pottery: The Leeds Connection 1785–1806', *E.C.C. Transactions*, Vol.11, Part 1, 1981, pp.50–69.
14. Divided between Leeds City Libraries and the Victoria and Albert Museum. For details see D. Towner, *The Leeds Pottery*, London, 1963, pp.49–58.

produced there before the Leeds partners came on the scene. Sherds from dinner, dessert and tea services were recovered from the site, including fire-scorched and twisted biscuit wasters, which provided a clear indication that these were made at Swinton, not simply brought in from Leeds for decoration.

In dinner and dessert wares the following popular shapes were made at both concerns, the date given after each relating to the earliest reference in the invoices from the Swinton Pottery for goods supplied to Wentworth House: Royal (1789), Shell (1792), Concave (1792), Bath (1796) and Paris (1805). All these mouldings occur in identical form in the Leeds *Pattern Books*. The list quoted by Jewitt includes Queen's pattern, although curiously no sherds of this border moulding were found. Feather edge, which occurs in the list recorded by Jewitt, and also in the Leeds *Pattern Books*, was found on the site, but whereas it has been customary to attempt to attribute pieces with this border according to the number and spacing of the individual feather barbs, the situation regarding Swinton examples is complex, since seven-, eight- (in two versions), nine- and ten-barb units occur on flatware alone. Without exception, the Greens, Bingley & Co. feather edges differ from those of their predecessors at Swinton, but the nine-barb grouping is precisely the same as that used at Leeds.[15] Drawings of these border mouldings on plates are shown in Appendix II: Nos. 1–4.

Certain other plate borders have no known Leeds counterpart, and here one can begin to see differences between the productions of the two concerns. Interestingly, some of these had been used at Swinton by previous partnerships, although not in identical form. Of these, the gadroon edge occurs in two versions which are similar to those used by Malpass & Fenney. A variant of the cockstail border too was continued from this earlier proprietorship, and is distinguished from closely related designs on plates attributed to Melbourne in Derbyshire, and Rothwell,[16] south Yorkshire, chiefly by the alternately convex and concave radial lines regularly spaced around the border. The batswing moulding also continued in use, although the three Greens, Bingley & Co. variants differ from the two versions of this border used by Malpass & Fenney, and are different again from those recorded from Rothwell.[17] These distinctive Swinton plate edges are shown in Appendix II: Nos. 5–8.[18]

Two other Greens, Bingley & Co. moulded edges are unknown at Leeds and as yet have not been recorded from the earlier partnerships at Swinton. The diamond-beaded border occurred on sherds of octagonal plates and dishes, and the lobed border, with its simple scalloped outline, was found in quantity on plates (see Appendix II: Nos. 9 and 10). A similar design to the former has

15. P. Walton, 'An Investigation of the Site of the Leeds Pottery', *E.C.C. Transactions*, Vol. 10, Part 4, Plate 106b.

16. D. Towner, *Creamware*, London, 1978, p. 213, Figs. 2 and 4. Doubt has recently been cast on the existence of a pottery at Melbourne; for details see R. B. Brown, 'The Furnace Site at Melbourne', *Northern Ceramic Society Journal*, Vol. 3, 1978–81, pp. 95–9.

17. D. Towner, *Creamware*, Fig. 3.

18. Photographs of sherds from the Swinton site are included in A. and A. Cox, op. cit., Vol. 11, Part 1, 1981, Plates 22–32.

been noted on creamware wasters from Melbourne,[19] but the Swinton version is different, distinguished chiefly by the large diamond motif which is a prominent feature at every angle of the border.

The majority of dinner and dessert-ware sherds from the Swinton site were of plates or dishes. Tureens, sauceboats, and other such items were comparatively uncommon, and in every case their mouldings were those shared with Leeds, and not the distinctive Swinton types. Some were extremely close to their Leeds equivalents; parts of a small shell-edge sauce tureen, for example, appear to be identical to one in the Leeds *Pattern Book*.[20] The Swinton Pottery invoices sent to Wentworth House contain numerous references to such wares, as on 17 September 1801:

2 11 In Vegetable Dishes wth one partition 12/-

With teawares also, the more popular designs were made at both Leeds and Swinton, the most commonly found teapot shapes being plain or fluted globular, and plain or fluted cylindrical. These and their associated items, such as cups, saucers and sugars, in general, follow closely the illustrations in the Leeds *Pattern Books*.[21] Parts of tall coffee pots and miniature teawares were also found.

The close similarity between certain of the Swinton and Leeds products was emphasized by the discovery that the well-known Leeds flower-and-leaf finial, or rose knop,[22] occurs also at Swinton on creamwares only, and the recovery of a plaster mould from the Swinton Pottery site confirms that they were actually made here. Even the nick at the base of the stalk is present, previously believed to be a Leeds characteristic, and the two appear to be identical. The other commonly found finial was a rounded conical example which occurred on both creamwares and pearlwares. Drawings of these finials are reproduced in Appendix II: Nos. 17 and 18.

A comparison of teapot spouts showed one area where positive differences between Leeds and Swinton pieces may be recognized. The Swinton acanthus-moulded spouts proved to be quite different from any of the Leeds versions, and the teapot illustrated (Plate 13) has such a spout and on present evidence may be firmly attributed to Swinton. It has crossed strap handles with simple leaf terminals, and the flower-and-leaf finial, characteristics known at both factories. The glaze is of the greenish hue associated with Swinton creamware of this period, and is enamelled with festoons of flowers outlined in black and coloured red, pink, green and yellow. A Greens, Bingley & Co. invoice for 1790 records:

1 Large Enameld Tea Pott 1/6

19. D. Towner, *Creamware*, p. 213, Fig. 5.
20. See D. Towner, *The Leeds Pottery*, London, 1963, where the Leeds *Pattern Book* (c. 1814 edn.) is reproduced, dinner-ware shape No. 7.
21. Ibid., teaware shapes Nos. 1–4, 27, 28, 31 and 32.
22. The Leeds version of this finial is illustrated by P. Walton, op. cit., Vol. 10, Part 4, 1980, Plate 111a.

13. TEAPOT, *c*.1790. Creamware, pale cream, enamelled with festoons of flowers in red, pink, green, yellow and black. Spout, finial and terminals, Appendix II: Nos. 13, 18 and 22 respectively. Height 11 cm (4.3 in). *Pump Room Museum, Harrogate. See page 44*

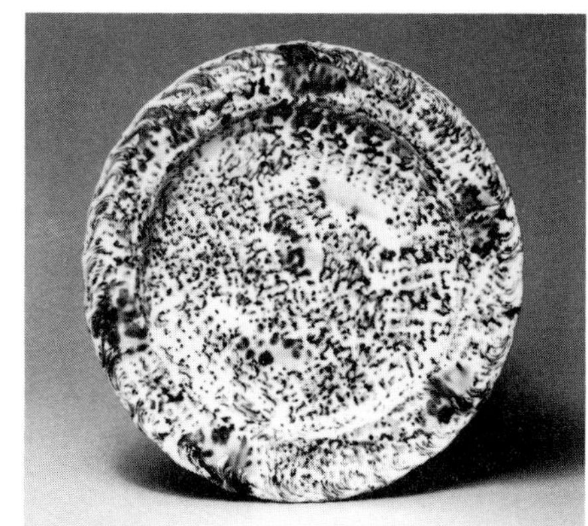

14. PLATE, *c*.1790. Creamware, the entire surface sponged with brown manganese and with areas of green and yellow glazes. Border moulding, Appendix II: No. 6. Diameter 24.1 cm (9.5 in). *Victoria and Albert Museum, Crown Copyright. See page 45*

Spouts, handles and terminals are shown in Appendix II: Nos. 13 to 15 and 19 to 23, some terminals like the Leeds 'classic' occurring at both concerns, others peculiar to Swinton.

Many creamware tea services and other wares were decorated with sponged manganese, the 'Tortoise Shell' of Jewitt's list of 1796. The teapots were small cylindrical or globular examples, with the rounded conical finial, single or crossed strap handles with simple leafy terminals, and the characteristic Swinton acanthus-leaf spout. The shade of brown varies considerably, although it tends to be paler than the dark, rich purplish-brown favoured during the Malpass & Fenney period, and often there are additional stripes or blotches of green or yellow (Plate 14).

Creamware from the Swinton Pottery was now also being supplied to visitors who stayed at Wentworth House. On 21 March 1789 '700 best Vine Leaf Enameld Tyles' costing £24.15.0 were ordered by the Rt. Hon. Lionel Damer, together with 1,730 'best Cr. Colour Square Tiles'. The enamelled tiles sold at 8½d each, the plain ones 3½d, and the whole order was sent to the Damer home in Dorset in three casks charged at 2/6 each, the price of the carriage and wharfage being 2/-. The tiles were ordered via Earl Fitzwilliam's steward at Wentworth House, and the letter which accompanied the bill for these is of interest because not only does it indicate how the wares were despatched, but also shows very well the deference with which the earl and his household were treated. The letter was addressed to Benjamin Hall, the steward.

Swinton Pottery March 23rd 1789

Sir

Annexd we beg leave to hand you Bill of the Tiles which you was pleased to order for the Rt Honble Lionel Damer, which are according to Order & do not doubt but the Quality will give Mr Damer entire satisfaction. They are directed for 'the Rt Honble Lionel Damer at Came near Blandford Dorsetshire to the care of Mr. Richd Moxon Hull and from thence to the Care of Gabriel Stewart Esqr Weymouth Dorsetshire', in 3 Casks & were sent from our Warehouse this Morning pr one of N. Robinsons Vessels Wm Willy Master for Hull marks L D C No 1, 2, 3.

We remain

with due Esteem
Sir
Your most obedient
and most humble servts
Greens Bingley & Co.

No doubt the Swinton Pottery at this period supplied such wares to other aristocratic households, but this is the earliest record known to the authors, apart from the invoices for the great quantities of items sent to Wentworth House.

Pearlwares

Pearlware, with a whiter body than creamware and a distinctly blue glaze, was first made at Swinton during the Greens, Bingley & Co. period, possibly from about 1790, and used alongside creamware for blue-painted and printed ware.

Swinton underglaze blue-painted decoration on pearlware also provides an interesting comparison with Leeds, and many examples were recently recovered from the Swinton site, mostly in the biscuit state with the decoration hardened on. Several teaware designs, including a pagoda pattern and a number of effective but simple borders (see Appendix II: 26–38) correspond

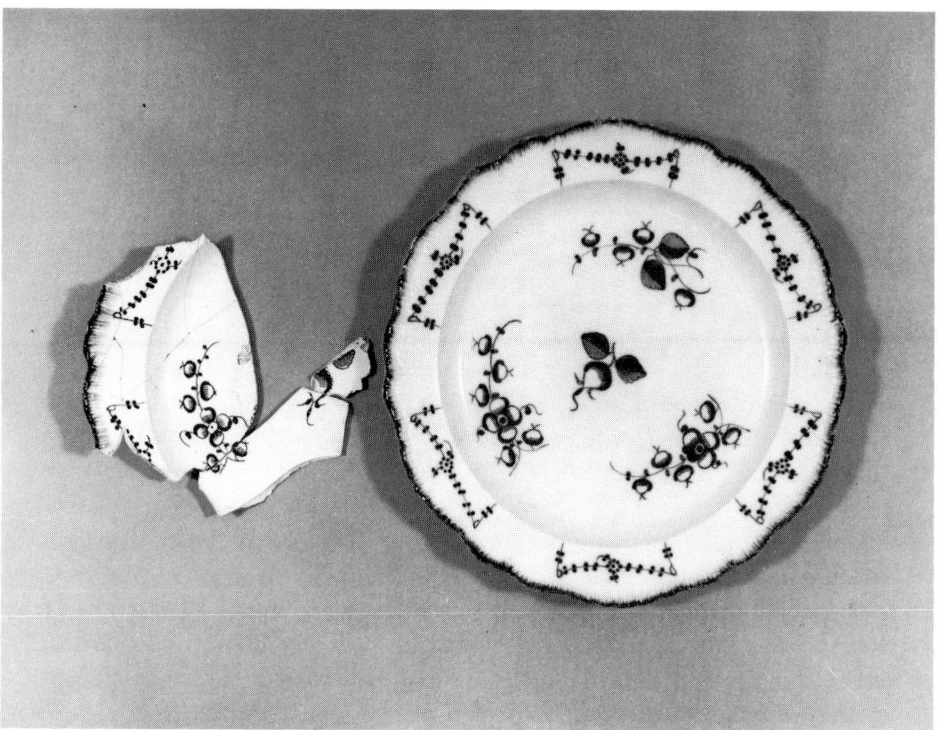

15. PLATE, *c.*1790. Pearlware, shell-edge border and underglaze-blue French sprig design. Matching sherds from Swinton Pottery site shown for comparison. Impressed with the letter I and a crescent (mark 3). Diameter 24.1 cm (9.5 in). *See page 47*

very closely with sketches in the Leeds New Tea Pot Drawing Book,[23] and yet are not known on authentic Leeds wares, nor on sherds from that site. It may be that these simple painted designs were executed at Swinton, leaving the more elaborate polychrome enamelling to be done at Leeds. Certain blue-painted teaware patterns which are not included in the Leeds New Tea Pot Drawing Book appear, on present evidence, to be exclusively of Swinton origin.[24]

Sherds of a blue-painted French sprig design, found on dessert and dinner wares, correspond exactly with the plate illustrated (Plate 15). Virtually the same decoration occurs in the Leeds Enamelled Table Service Book,[25] design No. 293, and versions of this pattern were popular at many potteries. An invoice for 1788 includes a reference to '1 doz Queens Blue Sprigg'd Oval Dishes 8/-', and in fact the design in the Enamelled Table Service Book is annotated 'Queens Blue'. Other painted designs include formal leaf borders in a style popular at Leeds and most other fineware potteries of the late eighteenth

23. Department of Prints and Drawings, Victoria and Albert Museum.
24. See A. and A. Cox, op. cit., Vol. II, Part 1, Plate 27b.
25. Print Room, Leeds City Libraries.

century. A pearlware jug with simple painted decoration is shown in Plate 16.

A limited range of transfer prints was in use at Swinton during this period, and the designs do not appear to relate to those known from the Leeds Pottery. They generally occur in blue on pearlwares, but black underglaze printing was used, and occasionally blue and black are found together on the same piece. The earliest documentary evidence for transfer printing at Swinton is an invoice for 1788:

July 14th To 2 Setts best Large Printed Cups & Srs 6/-

Several prints are relatively common on teawares; one of these, *Chinese Landscape with Two Figures*, depicts an oriental scene with figures in a white reserve, pagodas and islands. This was normally printed in blue, rarely in black, and also occurred rather unexpectedly in yellow on a glazed, brown, stoneware body, a type of ware which had not previously been associated with Swinton.[26]

A particularly attractive series of transfers is found on teawares, jugs and bowls, and was originally suggested by the authors to be derived from prints by Francesco Bartolozzi. The origin of these has recently been confirmed by Mr J.C. and Dr W.A.M. Holdaway. One, showing boys with a recumbent, garlanded goat, is taken from an engraving entitled *Children at Play* and signed 'F. Bartolozzi fecit'. Another, depicting cupids with arrows, is from a print named *Cupids at Play*, dated 1 November 1773 and further annotated 'G.B. Cipriani inv.' and 'F. Bartolozzi sculp.'. A third design in the series shows a naked boy in a landscape, but as yet the source of this particular example has not been recognized. Black is the usual colour (Plate 17), sometimes appearing greenish where the medium used in the transfer process has reacted with the glaze. These prints also occur in blue and black together with a blue border, as on the jug illustrated in Plate 18.

There is no evidence to suggest that on-glaze printing was used at Swinton at this period, even though examples are known on Leeds creamwares.

Dip-decorated Wares

Creamwares and pearlwares decorated with a thin layer of coloured slip seem to have been a popular product at Swinton in view of the quantities of sherds found, and this decoration was also used at Leeds. They were cheap, attractive, everyday wares, but relatively few intact specimens survive. The Swinton pieces included cylindrical or globular teapots, usually with the characteristic Swinton acanthus spout, many decorated with dark-brown or terracotta slip, often relieved with a band of chequered work, and with spouts, parts of covers and handles left cream. Some examples have applied cream festoons, occasionally tinged with green. The flower finial (Appendix II: No. 16) is

26. A. and A. Cox, op. cit., Vol. II, Part I, Plate 28d.

16. JUG, *c*.1790. Pearlware, enamelled in brown, blue, ochre and yellow, shown with matching sherds from Swinton Pottery site. Height 14.2 cm (5.6 in). *See page 48*

17. TEA BOWL AND SAUCER, *c*.1790. Pearlware, transfer-printed in black, the scene within the roundel, after Bartolozzi, *Children at Play*. A sherd from the Swinton Pottery site is shown for comparison. Diameter of saucer 12.3 cm (4.8 in). *See page 48*

18. JUG, *c*.1790. Pearlware, the border transfer-printed in blue, the sides and front with prints after Bartolozzi, *Cupids at Play* and *Children at Play* respectively, in black. Height 21.5 cm (8.5 in). *See page 48*

known in identical form at Leeds, where it is named 'Dasy knop' in the Drawing Book No. 4.[27]

Dip-decoration was perhaps used most frequently on mugs—tall, straight-sided vessels with strap handles and acanthus-leaf terminals. A record of the price of these occurs in an invoice for 1795:

2 Dzn. Dipp'd Mugs 5/-.

They were decorated with a plain covering of coloured slip, or with turned lines around the body to expose the creamware beneath, and typically there is a band of chequered decoration around the rim. A wide range of colours was used, principally black, brown, yellow, terracotta, orange, blue, speckled blue and mauve.

Variations of dip-decoration include very fine quality agate and marbled wares (Plate 19), and examples with an unusual sgraffiato decoration, where the slip is cut through in patterns to reveal the creamware body. Dip-decorated wares are known from many other sites, for instance, Leeds, Fenton Vivian in Staffordshire, and Coalport, and comparisons serve to emphasize the particularly fine quality of the Swinton examples.

Stonewares

Black basalt was produced at Swinton during the Greens, Bingley & Co. proprietorship, the 'Fine Egyptian Black' quoted in the list of wares in Jewitt's possession and referred to previously. The Leeds Blackware Drawing Book[28] contains a documentary reminder that connections between Leeds and Swinton were in some respects very close, since the designs include cross-references to the equivalent Swinton pattern numbers. For example, Leeds No. 4 is Swinton No. 5; Leeds No. 15 is Swinton No. 2, and so forth. Of the fourteen teapots illustrated and listed as having Swinton counterparts, eleven have simple engine-turned decoration and widow or spaniel finials on the covers. Three, however, have moulded classical motifs, one with swags, one with figures, and one with a vase and scrolling foliage. Curiously, the few sherds of basalt teawares recovered from the Swinton site do not correspond with these patterns, although a widow finial is identical to the Leeds version.

Red stonewares were also manufactured at Swinton, both glazed and unglazed, and decorated with a variety of engine-turned patterns. The Swinton Pottery invoices of this period refer to 'Red China Tea Pots', and the Leeds Drawing Book No. 1[29] shows very similar wares in 'terre rouge', which would render the products of the two factories difficult to distinguish.

The fine brown stoneware mentioned previously (page 48), which often occurs transfer-printed in yellow, does not seem to have been recorded at Leeds. It may possibly be the body referred to as 'Brown China' in the list of

27. Print Room, Leeds City Libraries.
28. Print Room, Leeds City Libraries.
29. Department of Prints and Drawings, Victoria and Albert Museum.

19. PLATE, *c.*1790. Creamware, pale cream, the border tinged with green glaze, the well marbled with red, brown, black and white slips. Border moulding, Appendix II: No. 6. Diameter 23.8 cm (9.4 in). *Victoria and Albert Museum, Crown Copyright.* *See page 50*

1796 quoted by Jewitt (see page 42). Alternatively, it could be identified with the term 'Devonshire Brown' as in an invoice of 1788:

6 Devonshire Brown Enameld Voasses	£2.5.0

or in 1790:

4 Devonshire Brown Sugar Cups	8.0

Coarse Earthenwares

Like their predecessors, the Greens, Bingley & Co. partnership continued the production of coarse everyday earthenwares alongside their finewares. Chiefly these comprised kitchen and other domestic items of a soft red or buff body, resulting from the use of local iron-rich clays, or a high-fired stoneware, partially coated with a thick brown or black glaze. Many large sections of black-glazed pitchers, pancheons and other thrown vessels were recovered from the site, which suggests they were made in quantity, possibly to supply a local demand. An invoice from the Pottery dated 1803 includes '2 Black Pitchers 1/8', and references to cheese pans, black jars and black bottles also occur at this period. Some of the coarsewares were of an impressive size, like the 3-foot high 'Chimney Pipes' supplied in 1787 at a cost of 5/- each.

Coarse plates and dishes with notched edges and decorated with combed or trailed coloured slips continued to be made. Although highly attractive, with a rustic appeal, they rarely achieved the quality of the similar items made earlier by William Malpass (see Plate 5).

4
The 1806 Crisis

In spite of the apparent success and prosperity of the Swinton Pottery in the early years of the nineteenth century, all was not well, and relations between the Leeds and Swinton interests in the Greens, Bingley & Co. partnership had become increasingly strained. The Leeds partners, it seemed, were using the association with Swinton to further their own ends at the expense of that concern, as has already been suggested. Charles Bowns, the Wentworth agent, wrote to Earl Fitzwilliam of 'the differences which frequently took place amongst the Copartners'.[1] By 1801, with five years of the lease left to run, John Brameld, whose capital was mainly invested in the Pottery, was feeling sufficiently desperate with the way affairs were going to offer to sell the Brameld shares to his partners at a loss, at £600 each, instead of their true value of £827. The offer was rejected, and it was becoming increasingly clear that the 'Leeds Gentlemen', as they are referred to in the contemporary correspondence, and who held the majority of the shares, intended only harm to the Swinton Pottery.

In 1801 John Green, their former partner, founded the Don Pottery in Swinton, and John Brameld may have wished, as the lesser evil, to withdraw from the Greens, Bingley & Co. partnership to join him there. Certainly the Bramelds held shares in the Don Pottery, and had close connections with that concern for many years.

By 1806 the Swinton Pottery had been run down to the point where production had virtually ceased and the unemployment of the workmen was becoming a real problem. On 1 January 1806, John Brameld wrote an eloquent letter to Earl Fitzwilliam, seeking his help in this seemingly impossible situation and making clear his personal and long-standing involvement with the Swinton Pottery:

> ... upwards of 50 Years of my Life have been spent in anxious & persevering Industry & in which I am now grown grey, every branch of my Family (a Wife & 6 Children) have too as their Years enabled them, contributed their Share towards that Fund of Earnings & Economy by which we hoped to

1. Wentworth Woodhouse Muniments, F 106/41, dated 16 March 1806.

raise ourselves to a decent degree of respectability & usefulness in the World, but alas! these Exertions have been counterbalanced by placing our little Property & our Confidence in the Power of Men whose System has prevented its acquiring those fair & considerable Profits which commercial Capital in general does acquire ...[2]

John Brameld believed, probably correctly, that his Leeds partners were restricting the development of the Swinton Pottery because:

... they feared that under the management of Men unconnected with any other Work of the Sort Swinton Pottery might establish a free Trade and become a formidable Rival to their favourite & more fortunate Work at Leeds.[3]

He felt the hopelessness of his situation all the more keenly because there was now no place in the manufactory for his two elder sons, William and Thomas, who had been forced unsuccessfully to seek work in Staffordshire.

It was John Brameld's hope that when the lease expired in 1806, he might purchase the partners' shares, but to do this and carry on the Works would need at least £12,000 to £15,000, which the Bramelds did not possess. Additionally, it would be necessary to build a flint mill, since it was unlikely that the Leeds Pottery proprietors would allow the Swinton Pottery to continue using the Leeds mill at Thorp Arch for the grinding of flint and material for glazes.[4] John Brameld writing to Earl Fitzwilliam on 1 January 1806 about his predicament continues:

The great Mr. Wedgwood has at his Works a Steam Mill and I think no place more suitable for one than Swinton Pottery so near to Coal.

John Brameld's hope was that the earl would purchase the eighteen shares of the other partners to enable the Brameld family to keep the Pottery going, assuring him that they had the experience and the will to work, but lacked only the funds. His tone was persuasive:

It is only support we want, it is only Money, we do not want Skill nor Industry ... for really my Lord I cannot see any impropriety in your Lordship carrying on your own Pottery in the midst of your Estate and working up the Raw Materials which it produces into a manufactured Article universally useful and which now makes a considerable figure in the Commerce and adds to the riches of the Country—I believe there are instances of Noblemen concerned in carrying on Works of various kinds on their own Estates ...

2. Ibid., F 106/40, dated 1 January 1806.
3. Ibid., F 106/40.
4. This mill still stands beside the river Wharfe about twelve miles from Leeds. For an illustration see J.R. Kidson and F.Kidson, *Historical Notices of the Leeds Old Pottery*, Leeds, 1892, Plate 4.

It is interesting that the close personal relationship which was to develop between the earl and the Brameld family was probably initiated by this letter from John Brameld.

It was likely that the earl would assist, since the closure of the Swinton Pottery would result in the unemployment of many local people. His initial reply, however, was not immediately encouraging in respect of financial help, but John Brameld was assured that his family would be given preference with regard to the tenancy. Charles Bowns, the Wentworth agent, who had consistently supported the Bramelds, informed the earl that he was sure the Leeds partners had no intention whatsoever of continuing with the Swinton Pottery, but that they were now employing delaying tactics with a view to harming that concern as much as possible. By May 1806 John and William Brameld were seriously worried:

> ... one great aim of theirs seems to be to ruin the Trade & Connexions of this place and Transfer them to Leeds Pottery; by holding it shut up in the manner now doing they will be able to effect it, even in the short space of 6 months unless some plan be devised and put in execution to prevent them.[5]

It would seem that in the interim between John Brameld's letter to the earl on 1 January 1806 and May of that year, some encouragement must have been given, for John Brameld goes on to put forward a scheme. The Bramelds would carry on the Pottery:

> ... on a reduced scale so as only to supply the British Trade, but yet so as to consume about 2000 Tons of his Lordship's Coal annually ...

This statement provides an interesting indication that during the Greens, Bingley & Co. period, the Swinton Pottery had evidently been trading abroad. However, it remained essential to rescue the Pottery's trade in the present situation, either by supplying customers with wares purchased elsewhere in Yorkshire or Staffordshire, or by renting the nearby Mexborough Old Pottery[6] until the Leeds partners could be removed from Swinton.

To achieve this, John Brameld requested an immediate advance of £2,000 from Earl Fitzwilliam to enable them:

> ... to counteract the nefarious designs of the Rulers of the Leeds Pottery, and in some measure to repair those injuries & avert those various evils which they have heaped, & are proceeding to heap on Swinton Pottery.[7]

These were strong words, but the views he expressed were echoed by Charles Bowns in a letter to Earl Fitzwilliam dated 19 May 1806:

5. Wentworth Woodhouse Muniments, F 106/43, dated May 1806.
6. Ibid., F 106/43. This Pottery was founded in 1800 by Robert Sowter and partners and stood immediately adjacent to the Don Navigation on the Swinton–Mexborough boundary. No trace of it now remains.
7. Ibid., F 106/43.

> I am sorry to inform your Lordship that the Leeds Pottery Comp^y refuse to deliver up the Premises at Swinton—they have ceased working, and I don't learn that they have any other motive for withholding the Possession than that of taking away the Trade, and injuring that Pottery as much as in their Power.[8]

The activities of the Leeds partners were becoming even more devious and were now directed against the earl himself, as Bowns, the Wentworth agent, further reported in the same letter:

> I have some reason to think that as the Pottery Works are erected upon the Waste,[9] the Comp^y are encouraged to try your Lordship's Title to them ...

There is no record of precisely what happened next, but in fact the Leeds partners withdrew, perhaps having failed to recognize that Earl Fitzwilliam would prove too powerful an adversary for them. The Bramelds received their £2,000 advance (see Appendix III) and were able to recommence production at Swinton without having recourse to the Mexborough project. All for the moment seemed favourable. Charles Bowns, who had long supported them, wrote to the earl on 2 June 1806:

> I have great confidence in their managing the Business with the utmost caution and prudence, and that they will not attempt to push it beyond their means ...[10]

This was to prove an unduly optimistic forecast, as subsequent events were to show, but for the moment the crisis was over and the Pottery's future was assured in the capable hands of John Brameld and his eldest son William.

8. Ibid., F 106/42, dated 19 May 1806.
9. Swinton Common.
10. Wentworth Woodhouse Muniments, F 106/44, dated 2 June 1806.

5
The Brameld Proprietorship

The information which exists about the Bramelds is slim compared with the details available for many potting families. There are no portraits, no diaries, only a few letters preserved in the Wentworth Woodhouse Muniments and such meagre facts as it has been possible to extract from wills, parish registers and other local documents.

The first member of the family of interest here is George Brameld, John Brameld's father. His gravestone in Wath-upon-Dearne churchyard provides the information that he was born in 1706, although it is not known whether he was in fact a local man. He was for many years a blacksmith in Swinton and a tenant of the Marquis of Rockingham, to whom he paid 10/- a year rent for 'a Smithy upon the waste', that is on Swinton Common.[1] The earliest documentary reference which the writers have found to George Brameld occurs in the Wath parish register, where the burial of a son George is recorded on 7 September 1732, and he and his wife Mary had at least twelve children, several of whom died in infancy. At this date the name Brameld is variously spelt, including Bramald, Brammald and Bramhall, all clearly referring to the same family.

John Brameld was born on 24 June 1741, the sixth son, although by the time of his father's death in 1785 only one elder brother, also named George, survived. George junior presumably had been intended to take over the blacksmith's business, and so it was that John Brameld took up a different trade and served his apprenticeship as a potter, probably at the Swinton Pottery, completing his time in 1762. The earliest documentary evidence of which we are aware for John Brameld working as a potter in Swinton occurs in 1779, when his name appears in a list of men liable for service in the local militia.

Certain of these details of early Brameld history are contained in a curious notebook which bears the name of John Brameld, but which was previously kept by one Joshua Hirst from 1748 and was added to at various times.[2]

1. Wentworth Woodhouse Muniments, A–222, Rental for 1751.

2. Science Museum Library, MS 1762: Special Collection. An interesting entry is 'John Brameld Loose November 1762', the word 'loose' being used here in the sense free from apprenticeship. We are indebted to Mr Ralph Boreham for very kindly drawing our attention to this notebook.

Described as an apothecary's notebook, it includes remedies for the treatment of illness in humans and animals, lists of payments for services and jottings about various family happenings.

One event considered worthy of note was that 'Geo^{r} Brameld Junior went to London September ye 21st 1763', and since he seems to disappear from the records after this point, it may be that he left home to seek his fortune there. He may have incurred his father's displeasure, for although the eldest son, he was left only £80 in the will of George Brameld senior, the greater part of the estate going to John Brameld.[3] George died in 1785 leaving to John 'my Lands, Tenements, Hereditaments, and Real Estate, And also all and singular my Goods, Chattels and Personal Estate'. His effects included bonds and securities and a 'Purse and Aparel' valued at £415; additionally he made bequests of £120 each to eight grandchildren and provided an annuity for a younger son Francis. George Brameld, therefore, by the time of his death was a man of some substance.[4]

There was little likelihood that John Brameld would take over the smithy, for by now he was a partner in the Swinton Pottery. His inheritance from his father coincided with the Swinton Pottery's association with Leeds in 1785, and as we know from his later correspondence,[5] he invested his money in the Company—hence his great concern when the Leeds partners attempted to run down the Swinton Pottery.

By the late eighteenth century the Brameld family lived in some style in Swinton. In 1795–6 John Brameld paid window tax on twenty windows, and his property consisted of a house, barn, stables, orchard, garden and land, which in 1826 was valued at £2,950.[6] The Swinton Parish Documents make it clear that the Bramelds were a respected local family, taking their turn in the administration of parish affairs. John Brameld was Surveyor of the Highways in 1780, Collector of the Land Tax in 1785, Warden of Swinton Chapel[7] in 1787 and Overseer of the Poor in 1802, posts which he was subsequently to hold again.

He had married Hannah Bingley, almost certainly one of the Bingley family who were associated in partnership with him at the Swinton Pottery, and they had six children, William (1772–1813), Ann (1775–1810), Sarah (1778–1822), Thomas (1787–1850), George Frederick (1792–1853) and John Wager (1797–1851). The sons too, as they came of age, played their part in the community.

3. Borthwick Institute, University of York, probate records, Exchequer Court of York, Doncaster deanery, March 1787.

4. George Brameld died on the 26 July 1785, aged seventy-nine, and was buried at Wath-upon-Dearne. His wife Mary, who died 30 May 1763, lies in the same grave. The gravestone was recently resited near the south doorway of the parish church.

5. Wentworth Woodhouse Muniments, F 106/40, dated 1 January 1806.

6. Swinton Parish Documents, Window Tax.

7. Swinton's medieval chapel was demolished *c.* 1816. Thomas Brameld, however, saved from destruction the chancel arch, and that of the south doorway, and had them erected in the grounds of the new parish church—see J. W. Brameld's note to this effect on the reverse of a sketch of the chapel, Swinton Parish Documents, P/59/10/32.

Thomas and William served in the militia—in the Wath Wood Company of the Rotherham Volunteer Infantry. All were involved at some time with the organization of the Poor Law: William was Overseer of the Poor in 1804, 1808 and 1812, and Thomas in 1825.

The Bramelds were a close family, serious, hard working and religious. As employers they took a personal and genuine interest in the well-being of their workers in a way one would not expect at this date, and when times were hard they often gave assistance to potters in distress.[8] Now and then a somewhat moral tone comes through in their correspondence. William, writing to Earl Fitzwilliam in 1810 requesting the building of workmen's cottages, writes that if the men originally taken on from the Leeds Pottery, temporarily closed in that year, are forced to return because of lack of accommodation 'we shall lose the labour & expense we have bestowed in making them better workmen as well as steadier men.'[9]

From about 1810 William and Thomas Brameld seem to have taken a leading part in the management of the Swinton Pottery. The ageing John Brameld was perhaps in poor health and unable to take an active interest, but the loss of his experience and good sense in business matters becomes apparent. He died in 1819,[10] and his will, made in 1812, stresses clearly all he had worked for, 'it being my most earnest wish and desire that my said four sons should continue to carry on the said Trade or Business jointly and entirely amongst themselves'.[11]

In spite of the success of the Pottery and his satisfaction at seeing it worked by his family, these were years of sadness for John Brameld. His eldest daughter Ann died in 1810 aged thirty-four; in 1813 William died aged forty-one, and a year later John's wife Hannah also died, aged sixty.[12] The loss of William must have been a severe blow, the management of the Works now becoming the responsibility of Thomas, then only twenty-six. His influence was to shape the future of the Swinton Pottery in a way that was to be significantly different from the development under his father and brother.

Thomas Brameld seems to have had a strong personality—artistic, imaginative, ambitious and persuasive—lacking the cautious realism of John and William. His younger brothers, George Frederick and John Wager, were partners with him in the Pottery, although it seems to have been Thomas who was the guiding spirit of the concern. George Frederick remains something of a

8. An account of working conditions in some of the north Staffordshire potteries during the first half of the nineteenth century, especially that of C. J. Mason, has been given given by R. Haggar and E. Adams, *Mason Porcelain and Ironstone 1796–1853*, London, 1977, pp. 89–98.

9. Wentworth Woodhouse Muniments, F106/11, dated 21 August 1810.

10. John Brameld died on the 12 June 1819, aged seventy-eight, and was buried at Wath-upon-Dearne in the same grave as his parents (see footnote 4).

11. Borthwick Institute, University of York, probate records, Exchequer Court of York, Doncaster deanery, August 1820.

12. Both William and Hannah Brameld, who died on the 29 August 1813 and 1 August 1814 respectively, are buried in the same grave as John Brameld and his parents (see footnotes 4 and 10).

shadowy figure. Not artistic, he would appear to have concerned himself with administrative matters, and spent some time on the Continent—notably in Russia—obtaining orders for earthenware. John Wager was reputed to be an accomplished artist,[13] but he probably had little time for exercising his abilities as a china painter, for he became the firm's traveller in Britain, and later was mainly concerned with running the Bramelds' London Warehouse.

It is sad that we know so little of the Bramelds as individuals. The impression one gains of the younger brothers is of three serious-minded men, fired with ideals, but always having to struggle. They were all well educated, possibly at the school in Swinton, and like their father and elder brother William, they could write eloquent prose, as their letters to the earls Fitzwilliam show. Just a rare personal touch of humour creeps in: on the reverse of a militia return for 1814 for Thomas and George Frederick is a pencilled note signed by Thomas and the young John Wager, stating 'G.F. Brameld exempt on the fair grounds of cowardice.'[14]

The Swinton Pottery 1806–26

The financial and moral support given by Earl Fitzwilliam in 1806 (see Appendix III) marked the beginning of the special and personal relationship between the Bramelds and the earl which was to assume an increasing importance over the years. Noted for his benevolence and less deeply involved in politics than his uncle the 2nd Marquis of Rockingham—who had twice been prime minister during the reign of George III—the earl devoted much time to his estates. He was always ready to assist local industries, and for the Bramelds, as well as financial aid, this help extended to the encouragement of visitors at Wentworth House to patronize the Swinton Pottery with orders.

In these early years the Bramelds were producing earthenwares only, which were not likely to recommend them in a great way to the wealthy, but at least one class of their wares rapidly found favour. These were the characteristically shaped brown-glazed Rockingham teapots named after the last Marchioness of Rockingham, which are described on pages 108–9. No less a person than the Prince of Wales, later George IV, purchased a number of these pots after seeing and admiring them at Wentworth House when on a visit to Earl Fitzwilliam in 1806.[15] A bill to Wentworth from the Swinton Pottery dated 26 February 1807 records:

> To Tea Pots for His Royal Highness the Prince of Wales agreeable to order rec[d] from Mrs Crofts and according to Bill of particulars sent with them 19/6.

13. See page 202 where details are given of his known works.
14. Swinton Parish Documents, militia records.
15. L. Jewitt, *Ceramic Art in Great Britain*, London, 1878, Vol. 1, p. 499. Jewitt, however, in this account tends to confuse Rockingham teapots with Cadogans.

To gain the custom of the Prince of Wales so soon after taking over the Pottery was undoubtedly an achievement for the Bramelds, and the success of their Rockingham teapots was assured.

In spite of this promising start, however, there was little chance that the Bramelds might pursue any ambitious plans during the first years after 1806. The advance from the earl, although sufficient to rescue them from their immediate difficulties, gave them very little scope for expansion or improvement. To increase their working capital they soon began the unsatisfactory practice of borrowing small sums from local tradesmen, and then paying interest on these loans for many years, gradually accumulating sizeable debts. One such loan was from John Watson, a carpenter of Ardsley, near Barnsley, who lent £30 in 1806, and a further £30 in 1807, on which the Bramelds paid interest of 30/- per annum, and continued to do so until their bankruptcy in 1825.[16] This hand-to-mouth existence is confirmed by a comment in a letter written by William, the eldest son, in 1810: 'We are just able to carry on, but without a Guinea to spare ...'[17] He was at this time engaged partly in travelling to obtain orders, while Thomas remained in Swinton with his father.

Their limited resources meant that they could not always produce sufficient earthenwares to supply demands, and Thomas at the Pottery was kept busy. He wrote on 23 April 1809 to William on his travels in East Anglia, 'You will conceive we are doing pretty well with your orders—as we draw 4 Gloss & 3 Blue Kilns pr Week and have constantly employed all the three Packers.'[18] The wares went from Swinton Wharf via the Don Navigation waterway to Hull and from there to other areas of Britain.

Moreover, since the country was still at war with France, most able-bodied men at the Pottery were liable for militia service, and the Bramelds could ill afford to lose even temporarily any of their skilled potters. Thomas wrote to William, 'I am making all the exertion I am able to avoid being any injured by the Local Militia going out—and I trust we shall not suffer any material inconvenience.'[19] However, they could not easily avoid their turn in supplying labour for repairing the roads in Swinton, and in early 1810 alone no fewer than twenty-nine working days were involved for Pottery workmen.[20]

Since any delay in meeting orders provided an excellent chance for their competitors to take advantage, the temptation of expanding beyond their means was great. In the years after 1806 when the Leeds Pottery was in trouble

16. Wentworth Woodhouse Muniments, F 127/197 and F 127/198, the latter dated 4 September 1827.
17. Ibid., F 106/11, dated 21 August 1810.
18. Ibid., MD/182, dated 23 April 1809.
19. Ibid., MD/182. Thomas may have been alluding to the incident in 1805 when Volunteers from the Sheffield and Rotherham areas rallied to the cry 'French have landed' and marched as far as Doncaster before realizing it was a false alarm. See W. White, *History, Gazetteer and Directory of the West-Riding of Yorkshire*, 1837, Vol. 1, pp. 52–3.
20. Swinton Parish Documents, Disbursements of the Surveyors of the Highways.

and temporarily closed, the Bramelds could not resist the opportunity of reclaiming some of the customers Swinton had lost to Leeds in the latter years of the Greens, Bingley & Co. partnership and of taking on experienced Leeds workmen. The immediate result of this was that they were unable to pay their rent, and their debts continued to mount.

To all appearances, however, the Pottery seemed to flourish, the range of wares gradually improved and extended, and more buildings were erected on the site. Earl Fitzwilliam had advanced a total of £7,500 between December 1811 and June 1816 for the construction of a flint mill, workmen's cottages and a house for the Bramelds near the Pottery.[21] However, in spite of this apparent prosperity, the Bramelds could not come to terms with their financial problems, and by 1825 matters had deteriorated to such an extent that bankruptcy was inevitable. William Newman, Earl Fitzwilliam's solicitor, and Mr C. D. Faber, who had examined the books and accounts of the Pottery, reported to the earl that in their view the causes of the Bramelds' financial failure were occasioned by their substantial foreign trading losses and the continual borrowing at unfavourable rates of interest — 12 to 15% per annum — to maintain a working capital to offset these losses.[22]

The Bramelds had in fact agreed in 1806 to give up overseas trade, but following the peace in Europe after 1815, when the home trade was greatly depressed, they had again looked to foreign markets. George Frederick Brameld had spent some time in St. Petersburg, Russia, promoting the sale of their wares.[23] However, finding buyers was one thing, securing payment from them was quite a different matter, and by 1825 their losses through foreign debtors were in the region of £22,000 — an incredibly large sum.[24] In addition,

21. See Appendix III and Wentworth Woodhouse Muniments F106/11. It is uncertain precisely where the Brameld family lived during the late eighteenth and early nineteenth centuries. A letter in the Wentworth Woodhouse Muniments (MD/182) written by Thomas Brameld and dated 23 April 1809 is headed 'Hill-top', whilst one of 29 November 1842 was written from 'The Cottage'. Since a new house was built for the Bramelds *c.* 1811–6, this may well have been 'The Cottage'. John Guest (*Historic Notices of Rotherham*, 1879, p. 620) includes the following note about one section of a local 'Roman Ridge' or 'Rig' (actually an Iron Age linear earthwork): 'Swinton Park lies south of it. Directly after it emerges from Wath wood it passes on the north side of Brameld's cottage.... Brameld's cottage was the residence of Mr Brameld, the occupier of the Rockingham pottery, on Swinton Common. The position of the cottage under the Roman Rig is pretty and secluded and the grounds appear to have been laid out with taste; but the cottage is now rather dilapidated and the grounds at the time of our visit were somewhat overrun with weeds. On the east side of the kitchen garden is a fence of hornbeam, which we examined.' This house stood immediately north-west of the Pottery on rising ground. No trace of it now remains, as the site is occupied by a dwelling of comparatively recent construction.

After the closure of the Rockingham Works in 1842, the family moved into another residence. An entry in the Wentworth Estate Annual Account for 1842–3 reads, 'June 30 1843 — Mr Brameld sundry Bills paid for Repairs at the House now occupied by him near the Pottery £95.5.0.' The authors are unaware of documentary details relating to this house.

22. Wentworth Woodhouse Muniments, F 106/48, undated but *c.* 1826.

23. L. Jewitt, op. cit., Vol. 1, p. 502.

24. Wentworth Woodhouse Muniments, F 106/48.

their arrears in rents and interest on loans owed to Earl Fitzwilliam had grown from £749 at about the time of John Brameld's death in 1819 to the alarming figure of £4,148 on 1 May 1825, as revealed in the Annual Accounts of the Wentworth Estate. The three Brameld brothers were declared bankrupt on 21 December 1825.[25]

The news of this distressing situation broke in Swinton at Christmas 1825 and was likely to have had a significant effect on the local population, for the Bramelds' dealings at home also left much to be desired. Their policy of borrowing from local people meant that they owed much money in the neighbourhood, and many stood to lose by their bankruptcy. In the Wentworth correspondence is a letter of appeal to the earl written on 13 April 1826 by some twenty of the Bramelds' creditors who had loaned sums between £13.6.0 and £905.8.9.[26]

Indeed, the earl seemed the only hope of salvation, as the threat of the Pottery closing with the resulting unemployment of some 270 persons would mean much hardship.[27] Furthermore, not only would the Bramelds' Works suffer, but also the nearby Don Pottery, worked by John and William Green, the sons of John Green.[28] This was closely linked with the Bramelds, who had held shares in it since it opened in 1801, and was likely to suffer the same fate.

On Boxing Day 1825 William Newman wrote to the earl:

> Mr Green one of the owners and Partners in the Don Pottery has been with me in a State of the most poignant distress—they are so connected with the Bramelds in this odious System of drawing and accepting Bills for the accommodation of each other that the Failure of the latter must involve both concerns in one Common Ruin. I really feel quite un-manned when I contemplate the scenes which I have witnessed within the last Week, and the misery which awaits so many Families.[29]

If events were to take this inevitable course, he estimated that the total of those who would lose their employment would not be less than 500 or 600, a very considerable number for that area.[30]

Earl Fitzwilliam was particularly likely to be influenced in any decision to give assistance by the argument that the continuation of the Swinton Pottery was for the general good of the neighbourhood, where many of the inhabitants were in fact his tenants. Moreover, there was already much distress in the

25. Date given in a deed dated 2 February 1831 in the Muniment Room, Wentworth Woodhouse.
26. Wentworth Woodhouse Muniments, F 106/46, dated 13 April 1826.
27. Ibid., F 106/46.
28. John Green snr. of the Greens, Bingley & Co. partnership, and of the Leeds Pottery, died in 1805. He had been declared bankrupt in 1800 (see the *Leeds Mercury* for 26 April 1800).
29. Wentworth Woodhouse Muniments, F 107/159, dated 26 December 1825.
30. In 1821 the population of Swinton was 1,050 (Swinton Parish Documents, Census data). Not all the Pottery workers necessarily lived in Swinton.

country, especially in the north of England, as *The Times* reported in May 1826:

> Owing to the unparallelled stagnation of trade and the consequent want of employment in the manufacturing districts of Lancashire and Yorkshire, the greatest distress has for some time prevailed, and apprehensions were long entertained of some serious disturbance.

In fairness to the Bramelds, then, it must be conceded that in spite of their lack of financial ability, it was a difficult period for those in trade, and they were not the only Wentworth tenants in debt at that time.[31]

Nor was Swinton the only pottery in difficulties. In Yorkshire the Leeds Pottery was also in trouble again; the concern closed in 1826 causing much hardship, as one of their Overseers of the Poor reported to his Swinton counterpart:

> ... the Leeds Pottery has been Set down a long time, which throws a great weight on our Town and we have asked them if any prospect of beginning again presents itself—but they cannot tell when.[32]

The Castleford Pottery too had been discontinued in 1820, leaving David Dunderdale, one of the principal partners, much in debt, and the Ferrybridge Pottery was also troubled by continual financial crises. The same problems affected north Staffordshire as well. A letter to the Swinton Overseers of the Poor in 1824 from Samuel Astbury, who had moved on to work for Bourne, Baker and Bourne in Fenton, stated that:

> ... I have a Wife now at down Lying and a Family to maintain and Myself but a very Indifferent place of Work as Indeed the potters have in a general way...[33]

Probably there was little doubt that Earl Fitzwilliam would assist the Bramelds to continue in business, and whilst William Newman, the earl's solicitor, agreed with this course of action, he felt that the decision to give financial aid should not apparently be given too readily. It seems that he had astutely assessed their characters as he remarked to the earl:

> I have no reason certainly, to doubt the Integrity or the Industry of the Messrs. Bramelds, but their dispositions are [of] too sanguine a Nature.[34]

It can only have been their misguided optimism that affairs would improve that can have allowed them to continue borrowing as they had done from local people with little hope of repayment. After the bankruptcy a dividend of only 3s 4d in the pound was paid, and many lost their savings in this way (see

31. Wentworth Woodhouse Muniments, G 47/5, dated 23 May 1826. Several companies extracting minerals on the Wentworth Estate were also unable to pay their debts to Earl Fitzwilliam.

32. Swinton Parish Documents, Poor Law correspondence, letter dated 3 April 1826.

33. Ibid., 15 March 1824.

34. Wentworth Woodhouse Muniments, G 47/4, dated 6 February 1826.

Appendix III). A letter exists from John Watson, the carpenter previously mentioned, who wrote to Earl Fitzwilliam of his personal tragedy, that his wife 'had sixty Pounds Bequeath'd Her by a Relation & had the Misfortune to put it into the Hands of Brameld & Co of Swinton & has Lost the whole save only 3s 4d per £.'[35]

However, money was advanced to the Bramelds, their stock in trade and effects to stand as security, with the earl having the power to seize all their possessions at any time. They were not to embark on foreign trading again, nor to resort to their former methods of raising capital or obtaining credit. To ensure that they were keeping within the set bounds, they were to render annual accounts to the earl's agents and allow their books to be inspected when required.[36]

Some indication of the extent of the Pottery at this time is shown in the engraving (Plate 1) and in the advertisement which appeared in the *Leeds Mercury* on 11 March 1826, when the concern was to let. There were two large biscuit ovens, five glazing ovens, hardening kilns for six printers, three enamelling kilns, seven throwing wheels, large green rooms and a sliphouse for up to fifty tons of clay per week. The entire advertisement is included in Appendix IV. Of particular interest is the statement that it is suitable 'for the Manufacture of China and Earthenware, on a very extensive Scale'. The year 1826 has normally been given as the one in which porcelain production commenced, and there is a traditional tale of how Thomas Brameld produced specimens of his porcelain at a meeting of creditors and so impressed Earl Fitzwilliam that he agreed to support the new venture.[37]

All the evidence, however, shows that porcelain production had begun before the bankruptcy of 1825, since in fact decorative china is included in an invoice sent to Wentworth House dated 15 August 1825, and porcelain is mentioned in the stock for sale in the advertisement of March 1826. The commencement of an ambitious new scheme involving expensive alterations to the buildings and the preparation of moulds and other equipment necessary for the production of porcelain would hardly have been undertaken during early 1826, when the Works were being run by assignees. Jewitt[38] may well have been correct when he stated that costly experiments in porcelain production contributed towards the bankruptcy, and are reflected perhaps in the rapidly mounting debts between 1819 and 1825. When Earl Fitzwilliam's support was given to the Bramelds on 14 April 1826, it was 'to carry on the Works at Swinton Pottery as a Porcelain and Earthen Ware Manufactory.'[39] It is certain, therefore, that porcelain production on a commercial scale must have commenced in 1825.

35. Ibid., F 127/198, dated 4 September 1827.
36. Ibid., F 106/47, dated 14 April 1826.
37. L. Jewitt, op. cit., Vol. 1, pp. 501–2.
38. L. Jewitt, op. cit., Vol. 1, p. 501.
39. Wentworth Woodhouse Muniments, F 106/47.

The Rockingham Works 1826–42

The manufacture of porcelain was Thomas Brameld's overriding ambition, but probably he was unable to devote much time and effort to his favourite project until after the death of his father John Brameld in 1819. Possibly John, of all the family the most realistic and cautious, disapproved of so ambitious a scheme in view of their straitened circumstances. Porcelain wasters excavated on the site in conjunction with shaping tools dated 1818 suggest that experiments were in progress at or soon after that date. Thomas lacked his father's caution, but he had an enthusiasm and a belief in his work that was infectious and convinced others against their better judgement that he could succeed.

His ambition was to produce the best of fine porcelains, of a standard which would attract the custom of the aristocratic and wealthy visitors to Wentworth House, whom the earl obligingly brought to visit the Pottery, which became something of a show-place on the Wentworth Estate. To emphasize their special relationship with the earl, a new factory mark was adopted for porcelain which included the griffin crest of the Wentworth family, and the Swinton Pottery at this time was renamed the Rockingham Works.

A local writer, Ebenezer Rhodes, who visited the Works late in 1826, commented:

> The forms of the various wares manufactured by the Messrs. Bramhelds are generally good, in many instances peculiarly elegant, and sometimes new. Their gold ornamental work is extremely rich in colour, and finely finished. In fact, the tea, table, and dessert services manufactured at this place are not surpassed in quality, design, and execution, in any part of the kingdom. ... The shew-rooms at these works contain many excellent specimens of richly-enamelled china, and beautiful flower painting. ... This establishment is liberally patronized by Lord Milton and the Wentworth family; and as it appears to be under the direction of both taste and talent, it can hardly fail to be successful.[40]

Rhodes was much impressed by what he saw and felt that the new Rockingham porcelains represented a strong challenge to the old established concerns.

The porcelains bearing the factory's red griffin marks, manufactured between 1826 and 1830, are probably the Bramelds' finest. Enthusiasm for the new venture was high, care and attention was lavished on the decoration of the wares, and as yet financial problems were kept at bay. The family at Wentworth gave costly orders for porcelain for themselves and to despatch to relatives and friends elsewhere, and brought Rockingham wares to the attention of aristocratic and even royal customers. In 1827, Augustus, Duke of

40. E. Rhodes, *Yorkshire Scenery*, London, 1826, pp. 153–4. The title Lord Milton devolved upon the eldest son of the earls Fitzwilliam.

Sussex, younger brother of George IV, visited the Works, an event reported in the *Sheffield Iris* on 6 November:

> His Royal Highness the Duke of Sussex arrived last week at Wentworth House, where he now remains. On Friday last his Royal Highness, accompanied by the Right Honourable Earl Fitzwilliam, Lord and Lady Milton, and a large party of Distinguished friends from Wentworth, visited the Rockingham Works. In going through the Manufactory, his Royal Highness remarked upon the many improvements over the foreign China Works, and expressed himself most decidedly of the opinion that Yorkshire porcelain is superior to any he has seen—His Royal Highness many times complimented Messrs Brameld on the beauty and originality of their productions, and gave a liberal order for an elegant breakfast service for Kensington Palace.

The relationship between the Bramelds and their aristocratic patron is unparallelled in the history of English ceramics, although similar instances may be found on the Continent. The influence of the earl was of the greatest importance to them, for he was a powerful and much respected figure, and when in 1827 the Bramelds opened a shop in York, the meeting place of the county families of the north of England, they were careful to stress the patronage of the Fitzwilliam family. The following advertisement appeared in the *Yorkshire Gazette* on 24 March 1827:

> The Nobility, Gentry, and Inhabitants of the City and County of York, and the North of England, are most respectfully informed that a Handsome selection of Superior PORCELAIN and EARTHENWARE of their own Manufacture, will in future be kept in the City, by BRAMELD & CO. of the ROCKINGHAM WORKS, near Rotherham, who, until they can meet with a suitable Situation, have furnished the Masonic Hall, in Little Blake Street, with as large a STOCK of Elegant and Useful Breakfast, Dinner, Dessert, Tea, Coffee, and Toilette Services, and Ornamental Ware, as the short Time they have had Possession of it would permit.
>
> The Rockingham Works are carried on under the immediate Patronage of the Right Hon. Earl Fitzwilliam, and Lord and Lady Milton.
>
> B & Co will feel much obliged to those who honour them with a call.
>
> York March 19th 1827

The appearance of this advertisement caused an immediate reaction from a long-established York china dealer, William Pomfret, who sold what he regarded as the best of English and Continental china, and who in an advertisement of his own in the *Yorkshire Gazette* the following day stated:

> As for Yorkshire made China, he must confess he is no Dealer in any but of such as he can himself recommend, and by the sale of which he can expect future support.

Nothing daunted and full of confidence, the Bramelds thereafter boldly headed their advertisements YORKSHIRE CHINA, and must have felt a degree of satisfaction when William Pomfret was declared bankrupt in 1829. By May 1827 the Bramelds had moved to 17 Coney Street,[41] opposite the Black Swan coaching inn, and from then until the closure of the shop in 1833 the business at York seems to have flourished, with Haigh Hirstwood, better known as a china painter at the Pottery, acting as manager.

In Doncaster the Bramelds hired rooms for the duration of the Races, and they had outlets in Leeds and Scarborough, also possibly on a temporary basis, and some kind of establishment in Newcastle.[42] A London shop proved a great asset to their trade, initially a wholesale warehouse at 13 Vauxhall Bridge Road from 1828; and in addition to this, from 1832 to 1834 they leased part of 174 Piccadilly, presumably as a retail outlet. There is no record of a shop in 1835 and 1836, but in 1837 they took premises at 3 Titchborne Street and 56 Great Windmill Street, possibly one building with two entrances. Tallis's *Street Views of London* (*c.* 1839) shows 3 Titchborne Street with a large griffin over the doorway and the words 'BRAMELD & CO,. Rockin^{m}. China, Glass & Pottery Warehouse'. John Wager Brameld was manager of their London affairs for much of the period up to 1842, the year in which the Rockingham Works ceased trading.[43] All the evidence suggests that the factory's wares became fashionable in London and sold well.

The culmination of the Bramelds' success was the commission which they gained in 1830 to manufacture a dessert service for William IV. Thomas Brameld's aim was to produce a service which would amaze by its richness and originality of form, and in this he certainly succeeded. The royal service gave the Bramelds prestige and publicity, and they could now style themselves 'Manufacturer to the King', the words included in a new puce griffin factory mark used on their porcelain. Other orders for impressive services for the aristocracy were received, but the royal service took them too long to produce and cost too much, putting a considerable strain on their already unstable finances (see page 134).

Their annual accounts submitted to Earl Fitzwilliam began to show a deficit from 1831, and marked the beginning of steadily mounting debts.[44] By August 1832 Thomas Brameld was writing an apologetic letter to Wentworth House describing his feelings as 'excessively harassed' and regretting that they could not pay their rents.[45] External factors were once more against the success of

41. The Bramelds' advertisement in the *York Courant* for 22 May 1827 referring to these premises includes '... some splendid vases to be seen today, just arrived from the Manufactory.'
42. R. C. Bell, *Tyneside Pottery*, London, 1971, p.49, where there is a reference to Brameld & Co., Folley Wharf, Sandgate in 1824.
43. T. A. Lockett, 'The Bramelds in London', *The Connoisseur*, 1967, Vol.165, No. 664, pp.102–3. Also D.G.Rice, *The Illustrated Guide to Rockingham Pottery and Porcelain*, London, 1971, pp.127–31.
44. Wentworth Woodhouse Muniments, G47/8a; 8b; 9 and 10, balance sheets to 31 December 1827 (profit £1,537.17.3); to 28 February 1829 (profit £1,043.13.2); to 3 April 1830 (profit £1,121.8.2) and to 8 October 1831 (loss £996.2.8) respectively. No further balance sheets appear to have been submitted to the earl.
45. Ibid., G 47/11, dated 28 August 1832.

trade:[46] in fact, the *Quarterly Review* for this period hints at political unrest in the country and the fear of revolution, while the new threat of cholera was claiming many victims and badly affecting trade in general. It was no wonder that John Wager Brameld on his journeys around the country had been finding a reduced demand for wares.

Thomas, however, was optimistic that if a loan of £2,000 were to be advanced by the earl to pay the workmen's wages until they could complete and receive payment for the king's service, the Pottery would soon prosper. As he wrote to Fitzwilliam in August 1832:

> ... we know very well that we can Manufacture as good an article for the Market as any other House, and by the Means of reduced expenditure in every way, We can afford to sell at Market prices, & ensure business.[47]

The initial reply from Wentworth House was not encouraging, but after a personal interview with the persuasive Thomas, the Bramelds were given their loan in weekly payments over a three-month period commencing on 29 September 1832 (see Appendix III).

Information for the years after 1832 is somewhat incomplete. There were apparently no further requests to Wentworth for money—possibly it had been made clear to Thomas that they could look for no further assistance from that quarter. At the same time, by the terms of the 1826 agreement, they were unable to borrow from any other source. The Brameld brothers it seems were not businessmen, and where shrewder men might have succeeded they failed entirely, their debts continuing to mount year by year.

Thomas Brameld believed that the reason for their problems was that because they never had sufficient capital to run the Works to their full extent, they could not make the quantity of ware they required. Later, he wrote to Earl Fitzwilliam:

> ... our China really sells so well to the Trade, in fact, <u>has such a preference in the Market</u>—that the quantity which could be produced would be sure to meet with a ready sale.—This is no fancied estimate but founded on the fact that we have always had great difficulty to produce <u>sufficient for our orders</u>;—and that, had the Works been capable of turning out more, we could readily have disposed of it to safe people.[48]

Admittedly, times were hard, and the Bramelds were not the only potters to run into difficulties. In 1835 John and William Green of the Don Pottery, after unsuccessfully appealing for help to Earl Fitzwilliam, were declared bankrupt and the Pottery was advertised for sale.

The Bramelds, for the moment at least, were more fortunate. The 3rd Earl

46. *The Times* for 2 January 1832 reported that in the West Riding of Yorkshire many firms were 'working what is called "short time"—that is not more than 8, 9, or 10 hours per day'.
47. Wentworth Woodhouse Muniments, G 47/11.
48. Ibid., G 47/18, dated 29 November 1842.

Fitzwilliam, who had succeeded to the title in 1833,[49] had previously, as Lord Milton, encouraged the Bramelds. Like his father he had brought their wares to the notice of important customers, including Princess Victoria, who was staying at Wentworth House in 1836. The *Sheffield Mercury* for 30 January of that year records the following:

> Earl Fitzwilliam's presents of porcelain, manufactured at the Rockingham Works, near Rawmarsh, tendered by his Lordship to the Duchess of Kent and the Princess Victoria, when on their visit at Wentworth House, were sent to the Palace at Kensington last week; they consist of a set of vases, with original views of his Lordship's extensive domains in Yorkshire, a statue of the Marchioness of Abercorn, and baskets with exquisite wreaths of raised flowers, and the letter V, formed by delicately pencilled red and white roses, lilies of the valley and forget-me-nots.[50]

Possibly, like so many others, these distinguished visitors were taken on a tour of the Rockingham Works. The following year Victoria succeeded to the throne, and Jewitt states that Thomas Brameld submitted new specimen plates for the royal dessert service appropriate to the new queen.[51] The cost would have been £1,700, but since the service had not been used during the lifetime of William IV, it is hardly surprising that Victoria did not consent to this proposal. However, by 1838 the Bramelds styled themselves on their bill heads 'China Manufacturers and Potters to the Queen and Royal Family', and an exquisitely decorated cup and saucer with a VR monogram (Plate 87) is possibly part of a service commissioned by Queen Victoria,[52] although the puce griffin mark on their wares which includes the words 'Manufacturer to the King' remained unchanged. Griffin marks with the legend 'Manufacturer to the Queen' are occasionally encountered. These were, however, not used by the Bramelds, but by Isaac Baguley, who worked as an independent decorator on the site after the closure of the Rockingham Works in 1842 (see pages 200–1).

By the late 1830s it seems possible that the Bramelds had become totally disillusioned by the vicious circle in which they found themselves. Unable to produce enough of the wares which they knew they could sell because of insufficient capital, they could not recoup the profits from a healthy trading situation. At the same time, they were unable to increase their capital by borrowing, and so in effect their hands were tied.

This, together with accumulating debts in unpaid dues to Earl Fitzwilliam, can be the only explanation for the fact that in its final years an alarming state of chaos reigned at the Rockingham Works. A letter to Thomas Brameld in September 1839 from Richard Shillito, the general overlooker in charge of the

49. Charles William Fitzwilliam (1786–1857), son of the 2nd Earl Fitzwilliam.
50. A Rockingham porcelain basket, octagonal in shape, and decorated in precisely this manner was sold at Christie's, 13 October 1980, lot 42, illustrated in the sale catalogue. It was marked with a puce griffin.
51. L. Jewitt, op. cit., Vol. 1, fn. p. 514.
52. L. Jewitt (op. cit., Vol. 1, p. 514) refers to 'the breakfast service prepared for Her Majesty'.

earthenware department of the Pottery, suggests that the situation had become entirely out of hand:

> One half of the men are doing little or nothing and yet have money to spend and get drunk with.[53]

Wages were paid to workmen who had spent the day drinking, or even to those who had left the Pottery altogether. Work was not being done, and what was done was often done badly:

> In the hovels there is not half work done for the wages. Our Biscuit [kiln] which we formerly set in two days with two Men now takes five or six the same time.

It seems incredible that such waste and inefficiency could be tolerated, and the only explanation seems to be that the Bramelds were now entirely dispirited and had little heart for keeping a close watch on matters at the Pottery. As Shillito comments:

> ... if such things be allowed no wonder you are in such straights for Money.... My life is quite miserable to see such villany and imposission for the last 2 or 3 Months I have been out of all manner of patience to see the little work done for the money....

In addition to the internal disorganization, it appears also that they had suffered to a great extent from theft and vandalism, for the Pottery was situated on the outskirts of Swinton and was not enclosed as, for example, was the nearby Don Pottery. In 1810 William Brameld had requested cottages to be built to serve as lodge gates (Plate 4), but this does not seem to have helped.[54] When Thomas Brameld was hoping to reopen the Works in 1842, he was anxious to have a wall built around the buildings 'for that we have always been most grievously robbed to a very serious extent, there is no doubt whatever'.[55]

Their disillusionment with Swinton led the Bramelds to look elsewhere. Jewitt records a letter dated 1 June 1840 in which they were negotiating with L. L. Dillwyn for the use of the Glamorgan Pottery, Swansea, for the manufacture of porcelain.[56] With their roots so firmly in Swinton, only dire circumstances could have made them consider moving to another area. In the event, nothing came of the scheme.

The Bramelds' advertisements in the last years of the Pottery's existence lack the confidence and enthusiasm of earlier days. One (page 72) which appeared in the *Yorkshire Gazette* on 19 December 1840 includes useful wares only.

The Wentworth Estate Accounts reveal the steadily worsening debts which the Bramelds had no hope of repaying. Earl Fitzwilliam could not be expected to tolerate this state of affairs indefinitely, and the stark wording of the note of

53. Wentworth Woodhouse Muniments, MD182, dated 6 September 1839.
54. Ibid., F 106/11, dated 21 August 1810.
55. Ibid., G 47/18, dated 29 November 1842.
56. L. Jewitt, op. cit., Vol. 2, p. 439.

ROCKINGHAM WORKS
Near Rotherham
A LARGE and VARIED ASSORTMENT OF BREAKFAST,
DINNER, DESSERT, TEA and TOILET SERVICES
in China, Earthenware, kept constantly in
Stock with every Article useful to the Housekeeper
SERVICES MADE TO ORDER.
Crests Painted, or Engraved and Printed at a
moderate charge, if required.

distraint from the bailiff, Edward Lancaster, sent to the Bramelds on 21 December 1841, left little doubt as to his intentions:[57]

> To Messieurs Thomas Brameld, George Frederic Brameld and John Wager Brameld
> TAKE NOTICE, That I have this day, by the Order and for the Use of Earl Fitzwilliam Your Lordlord taken and distrained the several Stock in Trade, Fixtures and all other matters and things, Goods and Chattels ... in and upon the Potteries, Warehouses, Flint Mill and other Erections, in the Township of Swinton, and in the Parish of Wath upon Dearne in the County of York which you rent and hold of and under the said Earl Fitzwilliam....

The earl was thus exercising his right to seize all that the Bramelds possessed in view of their continued failure to keep their part of the bargain entered into in 1826. A telling entry in the Wentworth Estate Accounts on 30 June 1842 indicates the extent of the Bramelds' debts in rents and other dues to the earl:

> Swinton—Brameld Messrs their Arrears being irrecoverable £13,180.0.10

The earl's patience was exhausted, but Thomas Brameld, optimistic to the last, made one final plea to him in a letter of 29 November 1842:

> ... to be allowed the chance of carrying on our own favourite trade, the Manufacture of China—and that you will Kindly let us have the whole of the Works, and the use of the Fixtures, Models and other utensils:—for—in such case we feel confidently that we can find friends in the form of partners, or otherwise, to furnish us with the money we should consider necessary to enable us to go on, in the circumscribed way we have laid down to ourselves, without ever thinking of asking pecuniary aid from your Lordship on account of the Manufactory.[58]

Thomas, however, must have realized that there could be virtually no possibility of the Rockingham Works reopening as he envisaged. Instead he had to content himself with running the flint mill, together with his brother

57. Wentworth Woodhouse Muniments, MD 182.
58. Ibid., G 47/18.

George Frederick, and ironically even in this venture they could not keep their affairs in order and were soon in debt again.[59] John Wager was now living in London and took little part in events in Swinton.[60]

On 10 June 1842 the Works was advertised to let in the *Doncaster Nottingham and Lincoln Gazette*,[61] but this seems to have created no real interest, and the concern was in fact never to open again for the manufacture of porcelain. The high rents, the dilapidated state of some of the buildings and a demoralized work force meant that the Pottery was unlikely to prove an attractive proposition to any prospective tenant.[62] There is a sad note about the advertisement of the final sale of wares which appeared in the *Sheffield Iris* on 31 December 1842:

ROCKINGHAM WORKS
NEAR SWINTON
SALE OF CHINA AND EARTHENWARE
The whole of the extensive Stock is now on
Sale at the Works, at very Reduced Prices.
Wholesale and Retail Dealers may be
supplied, as well as Private Families.

Subsequently, all remaining stock and some items of the Bramelds' household effects and furniture were auctioned on the 1, 2 and 4 May 1843. Details are recorded in an auction book of Lancaster & Sons of Barnsley, who conducted the proceedings.[63]

The following month, part of the Works was reopened by two former workmen, Isaac Baguley and his son Alfred, who decorated porcelains and earthenwares which they bought from other manufacturers.[64] They specialized in brown-glazed wares of Rockingham type, and the fact that they used versions of the Rockingham red griffin mark has sometimes caused confusion.[65] Isaac Baguley died in 1855 and in 1865 Alfred transferred his decorating activities to nearby Mexborough.

A firm of earthenware manufacturers, P. Hobson & Son, used part of the site for a while from 1852,[66] but gradually the buildings fell into a ruinous condition. When Jewitt visited Swinton during the 1870s, he found the Works 'a sad and desolate-looking wilderness.... and in the area, where but a few

59. Ibid., A–399, Annual Estate Account for 1846–7. The debts steadily mount over successive years.
60. See footnote 43.
61. We are indebted to Mr F. Fowler for bringing this advertisement to our attention.
62. Wentworth Woodhouse Muniments, G 47/18, a letter to Earl Fitzwilliam in which Thomas Brameld requests financial help to repair the ruinous buildings.
63. A copy may be seen in the Rotherham Library, Department of Local History.
64. Occasionally the printed anchor mark of Sampson, Bridgwood & Son, of Longton, Staffordshire, may be noted on Alfred Baguley's later wares.
65. Details of marks used by the Baguleys are given on page 228.
66. L. Jewitt, op. cit., Vol. 1, p. 507.

years ago all was life, activity and bustle in the execution of a royal order, "weeds and briars grow".'[67] The Brameld brothers did not live to see the final decay of the Works. Thomas died on 23 November 1850 and George Frederick on 30 June 1853. Both are buried in Swinton on the north side of the church. John Wager died in 1851 and is presumably buried in London.

The history of the Bramelds' proprietorship is a somewhat depressing account of recurrent financial failure. Yet in considering Thomas Brameld's achievements, one must admire his determination and the single-mindedness of his aim, for certainly he succeeded in producing porcelain that in its day was universally admired. Jewitt saw him as a man of integrity, and indeed he had many fine qualities, but in his financial dealings he can only be described as irresponsible. There is little doubt that without the continued assistance of the earls Fitzwilliam, the life of the Rockingham Works would have been considerably shorter.

67. L. Jewitt, op. cit., Vol. 1, p. 507.

6
Brameld Earthenwares

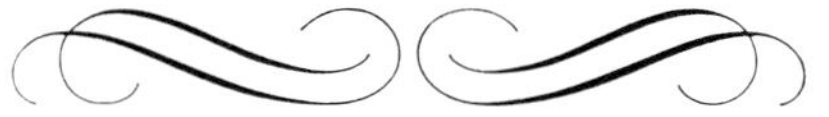

The first Brameld earthenwares were probably little different from those manufactured by Greens, Bingley & Co., since the Bramelds' restricted budget, initially at least, gave little scope for innovation. According to Jewitt, the old price lists continued in use, with merely the name of the former partners erased and 'Brameld & Co., Swinton Pottery' substituted.[1]

The identification of early Brameld wares is not always easy, since excavations on the Pottery site showed clearly that impressed BRAMELD marks were rarely used before about 1820. In general, few products of the years 1806 to 1820 have been hitherto recognized, whilst those marked wares which have previously been described and illustrated in the literature for the most part belong to the period *c.*1820 to 1842.

Information about the pre-1820 Brameld wares comes chiefly from excavated material, factory invoices, and to some extent from Thomas Brameld's recipe book for bodies and glazes which he kept from about 1808 (see Appendix VI).

Cream-coloured and Enamelled Earthenwares

Creamware was still the main body in production after 1806, and the factory invoices show clearly that it was in fact made throughout the Brameld period. This was not necessarily the fine creamware of the eighteenth century, but often a darker body with a thin covering of cream-coloured slip, probably what Thomas Brameld referred to in 1809 as 'common C.C. Ware'.[2]

The invoices sent to Wentworth House list not only the wares purchased for the use of the family, but the whole range of domestic and utilitarian items required for a household where it is recorded that seventy people sat down every day to dine in the servants' hall alone.[3] Large quantities of earthenware were required for their everyday needs, and were in general supplied by the Swinton Pottery. Surprisingly, perhaps, tableware shapes such as Bath, Royal, Paris and Concave were being ordered right up to 1842. After 1825, however, there is a noticeable decrease in the quantity of creamware supplied, most items being of the common dairy and domestic kind, including in 1831 a '26 In Child

1. L. Jewitt, *Ceramic Art in Great Britain*, London, 1878, Vol. 1, p. 501.
2. Wentworth Woodhouse Muniments, MD/182, dated 23 April 1809.
3. A. Bryant, *The Age of Elegance 1812–1822*, London, 1950, p. 289.

Bath' which cost £2.2.0. Such ordinary items were used and broken and have rarely survived. Few were marked—of the many thousands of excavated fragments of creamware from the early Brameld period, only three pieces were impressed BRAMELD.

A fine-quality pierced creamware plate is illustrated (Plate 20). The piercing corresponds exactly with that on the plate shown in the Leeds *Pattern Book*, page 11, design No. 43, 'Shell Edge Pierced Desert Plates, from 6 to 10 Inches', proving that the old punches were still in use in the early Brameld period.[4] Other marked specimens known include a melon tureen on a fixed leaf stand and a toast rack in the Yorkshire Museum, York, and in a private collection a jelly mould with a peacock design,[5] and a bidet complete with mahogany stand and cover.

The recent excavations at Swinton revealed an extensive range of previously unrecognized early Brameld pearlwares, mostly teapots, tea cups or bowls and saucers, finely potted and painted in a limited but colourful palette of brown, orange, ochre, yellow, blue and pale green. The decoration consisted chiefly of delicate formal borders, and painted sprigs or blue stars scattered across the surface were also popular. More elaborate designs included a colourful basket of flowers, reminiscent of New Hall decoration, and a naively-painted exotic bird amidst sponged green foliage. Many references to enamelled teawares occur in the invoices, as in June 1818:

6 pair Enameled Cups & Saucers 4/-
2 Enameld Oval T Pots 5/-

Probably now rare survivors, these early Brameld pearlwares have not been recognized.

The Bramelds were soon experimenting with improved earthenwares, and one such, listed in Thomas Brameld's recipe book under 'Bodies used by T B May 1808', was chalkware (see Appendix VI). Jewitt describes this as 'a remarkably fine white earthenware ... but, owing to its costliness through loss in firing, [it] was made only to a small extent, and is now of great rarity.'[6] Thomas Brameld notes beside the glaze ingredients 'All these Materials ground very fine—the finer the better', suggesting it required particular time and attention to produce.

Chalk body is frequently mentioned in the invoices between 1812 and 1828, and clearly it was used for the better enamelled and gilded earthenwares. On 24 July 1820 is recorded:

To 6 7^{In} Chalk En^{d} Plates French Sprigs 5/-

and such pieces, light in weight and very white, are known (Plate 21). Mostly, however, this body was used for teawares which were often enamelled with

4. The Leeds *Pattern Book* (*c.*1814 edn.) is reproduced in D. Towner, *The Leeds Pottery*, London, 1963, pp. 59–141.
5. A. and A. Cox, *The Rockingham Works*, Sheffield, 1974, Plate 3.
6. L. Jewitt, op. cit., Vol. 1, p. 501.

20. PLATE, *c.*1806. Creamware, pale cream, with shell-edge border and pierced decoration. Impressed BRAMELD. Diameter 20.7 cm (8.1 in). *See page 76*

21. DISH, *c.*1810–20. Chalkware, the border with basket-weave moulding. Enamelled in green, blue and iron-red, the edge outlined in blue. Impressed BRAMELD + (?). Length 25.8 cm (10.2 in). *See pages 76 and 114*

sprigs, and occasionally more elaborate decoration and gilding. Pattern books were evidently in use as the following entry for 12 May 1823 shows:

> 18 Pairs Chalk En^{d} H^{d} Teas London Nr 374 13/6

The teapots were round, oblong or oval, the cups 'London' or 'Irish'. Such teawares have not been recognized.

Other references of interest in the invoices sent to Wentworth House include '6 Pairs Chalk En^{d} Chocolates & S^{rs}', a 'honey hive', a 'Chalk En^{d} & Gold

Toast Rack N^{r} 571' and a 'Chalk Blue lined Egg Stand 4 Cups'. Chalk ware is no longer mentioned in the invoices after 1828, by which time it had probably been replaced by porcelain for the finer tea and dessert wares.

The Bramelds also produced tablewares of a good quality earthenware body with a slightly bluish glaze, as distinct from the fine, white chalk body. Sometimes impressed BRAMELD, they were probably made during the years 1815 to 1825 when their competent enamelling and gilding provided a partial substitute for porcelain. They are rare survivors. In this body, dessert plates, oval or square-shaped dishes and oval tureens are known decorated with simple gilt bands and enamelled with accurately reproduced botanical specimens and flowers named in script on the reverse, usually in Latin, more rarely in English. Temple Newsam House, Leeds, has an exquisitely painted small tureen,[7] a plate is in the collections of the Victoria and Albert Museum, and several pieces (Plate 22 and Colour Plate B) are known in private collections.[8]

The quality of the enamelling is very fine, most probably the work of George Collinson, whom Jewitt describes as the best flower painter at the Swinton Pottery.[9] The plants were copied from botanical publications of the eighteenth and nineteenth centuries, including Curtis's *Botanical Magazine*—the competently painted study of *Cytisus laburnum* (Plate 22) is from this source and appears as print number 176 in Vol. 5, published in 1796. Jewitt dates these wares around 1810 to 1815, but the earliest documentary reference to Collinson in Swinton is 1820.

Similarly shaped plates and dishes were enamelled with landscapes (Plate 23), romantic rather than actual views, either freely painted across the well of the piece, or enclosed within a plain gilt band.[10] George Collinson may also have decorated these, since a contemporary reference describes him as a landscape painter (see page 216). One example has also been recorded of a shaped dish with a realistic study of birds in a landscape; it is impressed BRAMELD + 1.[11]

Earthenwares painted with relatively simple designs were apparently made in quantity throughout the Brameld period, like the pierced basket and stand shown in Plate 24, but are now uncommon. Plates identical to those produced in porcelain with moulded C-scrolls are found with the scrolls picked out in colour, and the plate centre with loose sprays of flowers of the type referred to in the factory's Pattern Books for porcelain tablewares as 'flowers by girls'. An unusual earthenware plate in the collections of the Rotherham Museum is

7. P. Walton, *Creamware and Other English Pottery at Temple Newsam House, Leeds*, Bradford and London, 1976, item no. 867, illustrated.
8. See also L. Jewitt, op. cit., Vol. 1, p. 508.
9. Ibid., Vol. 1, p. 509.
10. G. A. Godden, *An Illustrated Encyclopaedia of British Pottery and Porcelain*, London, 1966, Plate 495.
11. A. A. Eaglestone and T. A. Lockett, *The Rockingham Pottery* (new revised edn. 1973), Plate IXa.

22. DISHES, *c.*1815–20. Pearlware, with gilded borders and enamelled botanical studies of, *left to right*: *Cytisus laburnum, Melaleuca nodosa* and *Dillenia speciosa.* All impressed BRAMELD + 1. Lengths 27 cm (10.6 in) and 23.1 cm (9.1 in). *See page 78*

23. PLATE, *c.*1815–20. Creamware, with central enamelled landscape within gilt bands. Impressed BRAMELD within a floral wreath (mark 30). Diameter 23.5 cm (9.3 in). *See page 78*

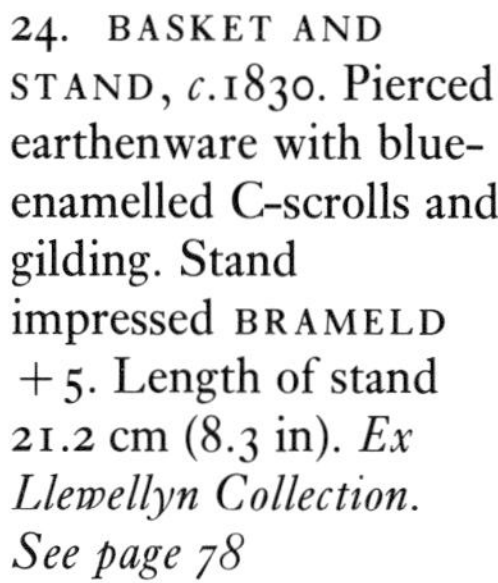

24. BASKET AND STAND, *c.*1830. Pierced earthenware with blue-enamelled C-scrolls and gilding. Stand impressed BRAMELD + 5. Length of stand 21.2 cm (8.3 in). *Ex Llewellyn Collection.* *See page 78*

decorated in underglaze blue with an exotic dragon which extends over the edge of the plate to the underside (Plate 25). The large dish illustrated in Plate 26 is from a dinner service painted in blue with an attractive formal flower-and-leaf design.

Relatively uncommon are earthenware plates marked with a printed red griffin (mark 52) and the impressed word KAOLIN. They have a moulded border with a raised design of elaborate scrolls and flowers, similar to the versions used on Nantgarw and Coalport porcelains. They are decorated in the manner of porcelain, each with a flower painting in the centre, and with further flower sprays normally appearing around the border. Specimens may be seen in the Sheffield City Museum and in the Yorkshire Museum, York.

A documentary teapot in a private collection, enamelled with flowers on one side and inscribed 'Ann Thompson 1827' within a floral wreath on the other, is particularly important since it is the only dated piece of Brameld earthenware known to the authors. Of 'London' shape with brown outlined edges and impressed BRAMELD + 11, it is identical in form to the example shown in Plate 44.

A number of other everyday items such as jugs were occasionally elaborately enamelled, like the magnificent creamware specimen with cricketing scenes illustrated by Dr Rice.[12] More usually, jugs are simply decorated to emphasize moulded details (Plate 64). Many toilet articles supplied to Wentworth House were enamelled and the descriptions in the invoices seem to refer to a Pattern Book. For example, on 12 May 1823:

6 Pair Enameld Ewers & Basons Nr 49 £3.4.0

and in September 1838, '4 pairs Ewers & Basins No 1 End Ivy Leaf Border' were supplied, together with matching soap boxes and trays. Chambers with Greek key or green oak borders were also mentioned, although few such Brameld wares survive.

Decorative Earthenware

In his account of earthenwares, Jewitt states '... the Swinton Pottery produced many vases and other objects of a high degree of excellence, both in design, manipulation, and in decoration, and were, indeed, far in advance of most of their competitors.'[13] There are few references to such decorative pieces in the factory invoices, and no fragments of these wares were recovered during excavations on the Pottery site. Further, it seems that Brameld ornamental earthenwares were generally unmarked, and in many cases can only be identified from Jewitt's drawings or descriptions.

There is no doubt that he was correct in his attribution of the largest and most famous of the Bramelds' earthenware vases, the dragon vases. The one

12. D. G. Rice, *The Illustrated Guide to Rockingham Pottery and Porcelain*, London, 1971, Plate 38.

13. L. Jewitt, op. cit., Vol. 1, p. 509.

25. PLATE, *c.*1815–20. Pearlware, with a dragon in underglaze blue. Impressed BRAMELD + 1. Diameter 21.3 cm (8.4 in).
Clifton Park Museum, Rotherham. *See page 80*

26. DISH, *c.*1815–20. Pearlware, painted with stylized flower-and-leaf design in blue, the edge outlined with ochre. Impressed BRAMELD + 1. Length 48.4 cm (19.1 in). *See page 80*

example recognized by the authors (Plate 29)[14] from a line drawing by Jewitt[15] is decorated with the familiar Brameld transfer-print known as *India*, the name occurring in backstamps on dinner wares which have this pattern. The decoration thus confirms the origin of this impressive piece, which stands 1 m 2 cm (3 ft 4 in) high. It is colourful in appearance, the blue-printed design over-painted predominantly with blue and red enamels; the lotus leaves at the neck are orange on a deep-blue ground, while the dragon finial, serpent handles and dolphin feet are each coloured green, blue and red. Two miniature dragon vases have been illustrated, 15.2 cm (6 in) high, basically of the same design, but without covers.[16] Another form of vase has been recognized (Plate 27) from its having serpent handles identical to those on the dragon vases, and being decorated with the Brameld *Rose Jar* print.

Jewitt is the only source of information for the attribution of certain other Brameld ornamental earthenwares, and whilst he is normally reliable, he is not infallible, as is shown in the case of a particular class of brown-glazed wares (see page 112). The so-called lotus vases were said by Jewitt to have been made at Swinton.[17] No marked examples are known, but a green-glazed pair in the collections of the Victoria and Albert Museum are unmistakably of the curious

27. (*left*) DRAGON VASE, *c.*1820–40. Earthenware, transfer-printed with the *Rose Jar* pattern in blue and further coloured in red and green. No mark. Height 29.8 cm (11.7 in). *See pages 82 and 100*

28. (*right*) VASE, *c.*1820–40. Earthenware, finely moulded in the form of the keep of Conisborough Castle, decorated with a clear, green glaze. No mark. Height 25.4 cm (10 in). *See pages 83–4 and 114*

14. A. and A. Cox, 'New Light on Large Rockingham Vases', *Connoisseur*, Vol. 173, No. 698, 1970, pp. 238–43.
15. L. Jewitt, op. cit., Vol. 1, Fig. 877.
16. J. G. and M. I. N. Evans, 'Brameld Ornamental Earthenware', *Northern Ceramic Society Journal*, Vol. 2, 1975–6, p. 100 and Plate 40.
17. L. Jewitt, op. cit., Vol. 1, p. 509.

29. DRAGON VASE, *c.*1820–40. Earthenware, transfer-printed with the *India* pattern in blue and coloured with blue and red enamels.
No mark. Height 1 m 2 cm (3 ft 4 in). *Present whereabouts not known.* *See pages 82 and 98*

design illustrated by Jewitt, formed of overlapping lotus leaves and further ornamented with moulded butterflies and insects. Similarly, the green-glazed vases in the form of the keep of the local landmark, Conisborough Castle (Plate 28), were also stated by Jewitt to have a Swinton origin.[18] Made in at

18. Ibid., p. 510.

least two sizes, the design varies slightly, some examples having turrets, others plain battlements. However, a Brameld attribution should not automatically be assumed for these, or for the lotus vases, as the moulds for both subsequently passed to the nearby Mexborough Rock Pottery,[19] although the crisp moulding and bright-green glaze on the vase illustrated suggests it was made at the Swinton Pottery. Of the very few decorative items in earthenware mentioned in the invoices sent to Wentworth House, possibly the most interesting was a green-glazed piece supplied on 12 May 1823, namely:

1 Green Glazed Scent Jar 12.0

A further decorative item illustrated by Jewitt is 'one of a pair of remarkably fine *pot-pourris*' in earthenware, said to be the work of Thomas Brameld.[20] These were 45.7 cm (18 in) high, globular in form, with lion-mask handles and a lion couchant finial. Painted with chinoiseries, they must have been striking pieces, but no examples have since been recorded.

Certain Brameld earthenware vases may be recognized because they occur in well-known porcelain shapes and are sometimes decorated in an ornate manner more typical of that body as, for example, the hexagonal vases illustrated in Plate 30. Similarly, an unmarked trumpet-shaped vase in the Newmane Collection is of the same form as its porcelain counterparts and is printed with the *India* pattern in blue.[21]

An unusual Swinton piece in a private collection is a two-handled cup and stand in biscuit earthenware, the cup glazed inside. Impressed BRAMELD+ followed by an indistinct number, it is identical to pieces made by Wedgwood and was perhaps intended for amateur decoration.[22]

The figures shown in Plate 31 are of particular interest, since although the Rockingham Works was noted for its porcelain models, only this one pair in earthenware has been recorded. Impressed BRAMELD+4, these versions of the well-known cobbler and wife would probably be attributed to Staffordshire in the absence of a factory mark. The quality of the moulded detail and decoration is unusually fine for earthenware figures.

An interesting group of Swinton decorative wares is marked in a distinctive way with the name 'Brameld' in red script (mark 33) and a painted number within the presently known range 2000 to 2021 on earthenwares. These include two covered vases of baluster shape, a small vase with dragon-head handles,[23] and a cylindrical vase,[24] all finely decorated with painted designs in a curious

19. Ibid., p. 510. At the closure of the Rock Pottery in 1883, the model for the Conisborough Castle vases passed to the Kilnhurst Pottery. See O. Grabham, 'Yorkshire Potteries, Pots and Potters', *Annual Report of the Yorkshire Philosophical Society for 1915*, York, 1916, p. 78.
20. L. Jewitt, op. cit., Vol. 1, Fig. 871.
21. A caneware vase of this shape is described on p. 108.
22. B. Hillier, *Pottery and Porcelain 1700–1914*, London, 1968, Plate 88.
23. J. G. and M. I. N. Evans, op. cit., Plates 41 and 43.
24. D. G. Rice, op. cit., Plate 52.

30. HEXAGONAL VASES, *c.*1825–30. A rare pair in earthenware, the body panels alternately rich blue with gilding, and white with naturally-coloured, enamelled flowers. Gilt edges and monkey finials. No marks. Height 43.3 cm (17 in). *See page 84*

31. COBBLER AND WIFE, *c.*1820. Extremely rare pair of earthenware figures, attractively coloured in green, brown, fawn, grey, white and black. Impressed BRAMELD +4. Height of cobbler 17.8 cm (7 in). *Newmane Collection.* *See page 84*

mixture of oriental and classical styles, and numbered 2000, 2002, 2003 and 2017 respectively. A vase with similar decoration, but in porcelain, and marked in the same way is illustrated in Plate 65. Useful wares also occur with this marking, as, for example, the creamware tureen in the Temple Newsam Collection, Leeds, enamelled with botanical studies and described on page 78, which bears the number 2006. Finally, the dish shown in Plate 39 is numbered 2021, although it is impressed BRAMELD + 1 rather than with a painted script mark. The precise significance of these pieces and their curious high numbers is not clear, since it is most unusual to find painted numbers in any form on either useful or decorative Brameld earthenwares.

Dale's Patent Furniture

On 28 February 1838, the Bramelds signed an agreement with William Dale of Shelton to buy his patented invention 'for the manufacture of China, Ironstone China or Earthenware Pillars, Columns, or Rails &c., for Bed-Posts, Window-Heads, &c., &c.' and employed Dale to superintend their production.[25]

The columns and posts were moulded in hollow sections held together by a rod which passed through their entire length. All examples which have come to the writers' attention have been of a substantial earthenware body, rather than porcelain. Jewitt describes items including a table, and had in his possession 'several of the original drawings of designs for beds, window cornices, lamps, candelabra, tables &c.' A window cornice 2 m 54 cm (8 ft 4 in) in length with the Dale's patent griffin (mark 46) may be seen in the Yorkshire Museum, York, and a torchère, possibly not in its original form, is in the Rotherham Museum. A pair of unmarked bed posts transfer-printed with the *India* pattern is in the Victoria and Albert Museum and a remarkable four-poster bed with similar posts has been illustrated.[26]

These items achieved a certain prominence, although they were made in the years when the Bramelds' financial problems were increasing and the work force becoming less than efficient. Drake's *Road Book of the Sheffield and Rotherham Railway*, 1840, records that the Bramelds:

> ... have lately introduced a novel article in china bedsteads, which is stated to be under the immediate patronage of her present Majesty.[27]

Nevertheless, these wares did not become best-sellers, and are now largely forgotten.[28]

25. Agreement quoted in full by L. Jewitt, op. cit., Vol. 1, p. 505.
26. L. Jewitt, op. cit., revised version, London, 1972, p. 234.
27. We are indebted to Mr John Griffin for drawing this to our attention.
28. Further details are given by J. G. and M. I. N. Evans, 'Rockingham—the Final Fling', *Northern Ceramic Society Journal*, Vol. 1, 1972–3, pp. 63–7.

Printed Earthenwares

A wide range of transfers was used at the Swinton Pottery during the Brameld period. The early prints occur on pearlware, the later ones on the various earthenware bodies. Certain backstamps include the words 'granite china' or 'stone china', and although some of the wares are of a comparatively dense earthenware, they are generally not so vitrified as the Staffordshire ironstones.

The earliest Brameld transfer-prints are known chiefly from excavated sherds, as marks were infrequently used before about 1820. After this date, the impressed BRAMELD mark was stamped on a high proportion of pieces and the name of the transfer is sometimes included in a printed backstamp. Occasionally, prints are named in the factory invoices.

Blue was by far the most popular colour, although black, grey, and green also occur, and very rarely fawn and an overglaze brick-red. The quality of the Bramelds' transfer-prints is somewhat variable, some excellent and attractive, others quite poor, unlike the high standard and imaginative designs used at the neighbouring Don Pottery at this period—for example, in their Sicilian scenes.

Transfer-printed decoration may be found on almost any of the Bramelds' wares. Dinner services were one of the main products, and an invoice sent to Wentworth House includes an interesting description of a 276-piece dinner service supplied on 30 December 1823:

1 full Size Blue Printed Service Peasant Pattern
consisting of the following articles viz
34 Dishes 10–20 Inches
2 Gravy Dishes
2 Fish Drainers
16 dozn. Plates & Soups
12 Bakers
2 Soup Tureens furnished
6 Sauce do do
8 Coverd Dishes
4 Drainers to fit Do
8 Pickles to fit Do
2 Cheese Salvers
2 Salad Bowls
2 Ash Dishes £16.11.0

This service is decorated with the *Peasant* pattern, possibly that nowadays referred to as 'Woodman', and is described as 'full size', but the composition could be varied to suit the customer's requirements. For example, larger meat dishes up to 66 cm (26 in) have been recorded; the Sheffield Museum possesses a particularly long, narrow dish, possibly for salmon, and asparagus dishes were made. The invoices to Wentworth detail items such as that on 14 September 1826:

12 Blue Printed Ov Pott^{y}. Pots larg for Moor Game £3.4.0

Tureens were supplied complete with covers, stands and ladles, and some types had built-in food warmers. Other printed items from the invoices include mustards, pepper castors and gravy argyles.

Brameld printed teawares are now rare, but the factory invoices reveal that they were produced in quantity. Earthenware cups and saucers were purchased by the dozen, with teapots, cream jugs, slop bowls and sugars supplied as optional extras. Coffee cans (Plate 44) recorded in an invoice for 1823, are uncommon, as are coffee pots. Printed breakfast cups and saucers were made, as were toast racks and egg cups.

Other transfer-printed wares include a range of jug shapes—*Cottage*, *Dutch*, *Barrel*, *Burton* and *Perth*—and also mugs, punch bowls and basins. In toilet wares one finds footbaths (Plate 43), soap boxes, ewers and basins, chamber pots and bidets. Further interesting items recorded in 1827 are:

1 Blue Printed Supper Service complete	£1. 8.0
1 Mahogany Tray	1. 6.0
	2.14.0

and there are references also to '1 Sett Blue Printed Flower Jarrs' in 1820, and in 1838 '30 Blue Printed Ink Stands' ordered by Lady Charlotte Fitzwilliam.

Transfer-prints *c.*1806–20

Excavated material has made possible the identification of several new early Brameld transfer-prints.

One of these, *Shepherd* pattern, is a delightful, naive, blue print which, to judge from the quantity of sherds, was relatively common on teawares. The design shows a shepherd and shepherdess in an extensive landscape, with sheep and a small dog (Plate 32). A floral print, *Peony*, has a continuous pattern of stylized leaves and flowers (Plate 33), not unlike Wedgwood's pattern of this name. It occurs in blue or brown on teawares. Brown transfer-prints are not known on post-1820 Brameld earthenwares, but interestingly Thomas Brameld's recipe book (see Appendix VI) contains a reference to a glaze for brown-printed wares used by him in 1811. Excavations have shown that a version of the design known as *Pea Flower* on dinner wares was also used on teawares, probably at a slightly earlier date. Oblong teapots, sucriers, tea cups or bowls and saucers were found, printed in blue with this all-over pattern of flowers and tendrils, and a roundel of pea pods in the centre of the saucers. Another rather curious print depicts three *Chinese Fishermen* and a strange pig-like creature in a stylized landscape with a pagoda and other buildings of

32. SAUCER DISH, *c.*1810. Pearlware, transfer-printed in blue with the *Shepherd* pattern. No mark, identified by sherds from site of Swinton Pottery. Diameter 21.2 cm (8.3 in). *See page 88*

33. TEA BOWL AND SAUCER, *c.*1810. Pearlware, transfer-printed in brown with the *Peony* pattern, the rims edged in red-brown. Shown with a matching sherd from the Swinton Pottery site. No mark. Diameter of saucer 13.3 cm (5.2 in). *See page 88*

somewhat gothic appearance. Printed in blue or brown, it has been identified on a small cream jug in a private collection.

Fragments of other blue transfer-prints were found, including a landscape pattern; a horseman with a sack in front of him; a distinctive early *Willow* design noticeably different from the later print of this name used by the Bramelds; an unusual border pattern of large foxglove flowers and shamrock leaves; and several attractive chinoiseries.

In addition to these blue or brown transfer-prints, the black underglaze prints described below were also recovered, mainly on teawares, which are probably those frequently referred to in the invoices between 1815 and 1820 as 'vignette'. For example, on 8 July 1816:

> 12 pairs Vignette Han[d] Irish Cups & Saucers 6/-

A series of *Romantic Landscapes*, somewhat idealized scenes of country life, with rustic cottages, churches, shepherds tending sheep amidst gothic ruins or contemplating churchyard memorials, were made. In contrast, urban scenes occasionally occur in the same series and a design including a pottery with smoking kilns. The prints are found on teawares of the shapes shown (Plate 34), of which only the principal pieces normally bear an impressed BRAMELD mark. Marked plates are also known.

Comparable in date and style to the romantic scenes is an attractive series of animal prints (Plate 35), recognized from excavated sherds. They are mainly foreign creatures shown in appropriate landscapes, each named in minute script hidden in the foliage at the bottom of the scene. Names of the animals include *Ferret*, *Squirrel like Opsum* (*sic*), *Panglin*, *Dalmatian* and *Golan Sheep*. Others with the name missing or indistinct appear to be roe deer, zebra, hyaena and wallaby. The source of the prints is not known. Three factory-marked plates with similar animal prints, although not apparently from the same series, have been illustrated.[29] It should be stressed that other manufacturers at this date produced wares of this type.

Another rare transfer named in script, almost certainly by the engraver of the animal series, is one depicting the *Badsworth Hunt* in pursuit of a fox (Plate 36). The Badsworth, Yorkshire's oldest hunt, was founded in 1720.

The above are all underglaze-black prints on items with a distinctly blue glaze. Although Thomas Brameld entered in his recipe book a means for 'Printing upon the Glaze', bat-printing is to date not known either on excavated sherds, or on authentic Brameld wares.

TRANSFER-PRINTS *c.*1820–42

The identification of Brameld transfer-prints in use after about 1820 presents few problems in view of the more regular use of factory marks. It is possible to ascertain from the invoices sent to Wentworth House the approximate dates

29. H. Lawrence, *Yorkshire Pots and Potteries*, Newton Abbot, 1974, p. 69.

34. Part TEA SERVICE, *c.*1815–20. Pearlware with a distinctly blue glaze, transfer-printed in black with *Romantic Landscapes*. Teapot impressed BRAMELD +3 (*in private possession*), cream jug impressed BRAMELD +1. Length of teapot 24.5 cm (9.6 in). *Clifton Park Museum, Rotherham.* *See page 90*

35. CUP AND SAUCER, *c.*1815–20. Pearlware with a noticeably blue glaze, transfer-printed in black with *Animals*, that on the cup named in the print *Squirrel like Opsum (sic)*. A sherd from the Swinton Pottery site is shown for comparison. No mark. Diameter of saucer 13.9 cm (5.5 in). *See page 90*

36. TWO-HANDLED CUP and PLATE. *c.*1815–20. Pearlware, transfer-printed in black with the *Badsworth Hunt* named in the print. Cup inscribed 'JOSEPH KITSON ECCLESFIELD', with a modelled frog inside. No mark. Plate impressed BRAMELD +3. Diameter 25.2 cm (9.9 in). *Ex Llewellyn Collection.* *See pages 90 and 96*

when certain patterns were in fashion, and since normally each is found on particular shapes, one can begin to see a chronological order for transfer-printed earthenwares.

Pea Flower, for example, is the first pattern to be named in the invoices in 1818, followed by *Peasant* in 1823. Both transfers occur on dinner services with octagonal plates and dishes, and square, shallow vegetable tureens. The plates are without moulded detail, but the prints include gadroon or dentil borders. *Castle of Rochefort* is first mentioned in 1825 and has plates which are lobed without an edge moulding.[30] This print continued in favour with the Fitzwilliam family at Wentworth until 1842, a reminder that designs could always be re-ordered.

Flower Groups and *Parroquet* are found with shell and gadroon-moulded borders, not unlike the porcelain shapes of the period 1826–30. *Floral Sketches* occurs on pieces with a rococo moulding similar to that on the Brameld KAOLIN plates, which are marked with the red griffin and therefore belong to the period 1826–30. A slightly later date may be given to *India* and *Don Quixote*, which are found on ornately moulded rococo shapes, often gilded, and this is borne out by the invoices, where the only reference to both these patterns occurs in 1840.

Brameld transfer-prints may be divided into the following groups for ease of description. Backstamps which accompany a number of them are reproduced in Chapter 11.

30. It was near Rochefort that Napoleon Bonaparte on 15 July 1815 boarded a British warship *en route* for St. Helena where he was exiled.

37. DISH, *c.*1820–30. Earthenware, transfer-printed on-glaze in red with the *Peasant* pattern. Impressed BRAMELD within a floral wreath (mark 30). Length 23.8 cm (9.4 in). *See pages 92 and 96*
TUREEN, *c.*1820–30. Earthenware, transfer-printed in blue with *Pea Flower*. Impressed BRAMELD +1 and with a printed backstamp (mark 67). *See pages 92 and 93*

39. *(right)* DISH, *c.*1820–5. Earthenware, transfer-printed with *Exotic Flowers* coloured in pastel shades. Impressed BRAMELD +1 and with black-painted marks STONE CHINA/ ※ /2021. Length 23.6 cm (9.3 in). *Newmane Collection.* *See page 94*

38. *(left)* PLATE, *c.*1820–30. Earthenware, transfer-printed in blue with unnamed botanical subjects and coloured over, and dark-blue border gilded. Impressed BRAMELD within a floral wreath (mark 30). Width 24.9 cm (9.8 in). *See page 93*

Floral Prints

Pea Flower is found on octagonal dinner plates and associated pieces (Plate 37) and consists of an all-over pattern of pea flowers, leaves and tendrils on a darker-blue ground. A similar version occurs on teawares (see page 88). In the factory invoices sent to Wentworth House, the following appears for 16 June 1818:

6 Blue Printed Bowls Pea Flower 2/-

Also relatively early are octagonal dinner or soup plates, transfer-printed in blue with *Botanical Flowers*, often over-painted and within dark-blue borders, sometimes gilded. The example illustrated (Plate 38) shows bittersweet (woody nightshade), whilst other specimens recorded are narcissus and tulip.

40. PLATE (*left*), *c.*1830. Earthenware, transfer-printed in blue with *Flower Groups*. Impressed BRAMELD +(?) and with a printed backstamp (mark 61). Diameter 26.9 cm (10.6 in). *See pages 94 and 98*
PLATE (*right*), *c.*1825. Earthenware, transfer-printed in blue with *Indian Flowers*. Impressed BRAMELD. Diameter 26 cm (10.2 in) *See page 98*

These prints resemble the Wedgwood botanical series, although somewhat less fine.

A very rare floral pattern (Plate 39) consists of a bold *Exotic Flowers* design extending across the surface of the piece, the transfer coloured-in with subtle and attractive shades.

Other prints include pleasingly spaced sprays of English garden flowers with full-blown roses predominating. *Flower Groups* (Plate 40) is one such, comprising several similar studies of flowers and foliage with butterflies, printed in a light blue. These prints occur on earthenware plates with gadroon-moulded borders and on matching tureens with elaborate shell handles and finials. They have also been noted on jugs and bidets. The name of this relatively uncommon pattern, found only in blue, is known from printed backstamps.

Floral Sketches (Plate 41) is somewhat similar in its use of English garden flowers. Recorded only in blue, it consists of several designs of baskets or vases of flowers in landscapes, and has a printed shell and gadroon border. It occurs on dinner wares moulded with unusual floral scrolls.

Unnamed groups of garden flowers and butterflies are printed in green on earthenware teawares of rococo form (Plate 42) and they are extremely rare survivors. More commonly, similar patterns are found in blue, green or grey on dinner wares within a border of small printed berries known as *Llandeg's*

41. TUREEN, LADLE AND STAND, *c*.1830. Earthenware, transfer-printed in blue with *Floral Sketches*. The stand impressed BRAMELD + I and with a printed backstamp (mark 59). Height 11 cm (4.3 in). *See page 94*

42. TEAPOT AND STAND, *c*.1830. Earthenware, transfer-printed in green with a floral pattern. The stand impressed BRAMELD + I. Height 17.8 cm (7 in). *See page 94*

43. FOOTBATH, *c.*1825–35. Earthenware, transfer-printed in blue with *Boys Fishing*. Impressed BRAMELD +(?). Overall length 52.8 cm (20.8 in). *Courtesy of Bryan Bowden. See pages 88 and 96*

blackberry border. This border design occurs also on porcelain (Plate 85) as do other floral patterns more usually seen on earthenwares, such as the *Flower and Hop* motifs around the foot of the 'Joseph Kitson' loving cup (Plate 36) which also occurs on porcelain teaware pattern 728. The use of earthenware prints on porcelain was, however, not widespread at Swinton.

Romantic Scenes

Peasant pattern (Plate 37), named in an invoice for 1823 (page 87), is almost certainly the Bramelds' name for 'Woodman', showing a wood cutter returning to his cottage. This attractive scene occurs on octagonal shapes, where it is found normally in blue, very rarely in black or overglaze red—not bat-printed.

A particularly decorative pattern is *Boys Fishing* (Plate 43) noted on jugs, mugs, punch bowls and toilet articles. This depicts two boys fishing in a river watched by a seated woman. Curiously, some prints are extremely rare, for example, *Girl with a Parrot* illustrated in Plate 44; *Apple Gatherers* (Plate 45) showing a girl and two boys picking apples; *Bo-Peep* which is an unsophisticated scene of a shepherdess with a dog but without her sheep;[31] *Packhorse* which includes a laden horse in a landscape;[32] *Fishermen* with rather foreign-looking figures standing beside a river bank, one with an oar over his

31. A. Cox and T. Lockett, 'The Rockingham Pottery, 1745–1842, a Preliminary Excavation', *Connoisseur*, Vol. 173, No. 697, 1970, pp. 171–6, Plate 3.
32. H. Lawrence, op. cit., p. 70.

44. COFFEE CAN and TEAPOT, *c.*1820. Earthenware, transfer-printed in blue with a slightly indistinct print of *Girl with a Parrot*. Teapot impressed BRAMELD +6. Length of teapot 24.3 cm (9.6 in). *See pages 80, 88 and 96*

45. MINIATURE PLATES, *c.*1820–30. Earthenware, transfer-printed. *Top, left to right: Children with a Kite, Oriental Figures in front of a Pagoda. Bottom, left to right: Burns Cotter, Apple Gatherers.* Blue-printed, except for *Oriental Figures* which is black and enamelled in red, blue, green and yellow. All with impressed BRAMELD marks, except *Apple Gatherers.* Diameters 11 cm (4.3 in). *See pages 96, 100, 102 and 104.*

46. PLATE, *c*.1820. Earthenware, transfer-printed in blue with the *Camel* pattern. Impressed BRAMELD + II. Diameter 21.6 cm (8.5 in). *See page 98*

shoulder, a tall building on a hill in the near distance, the whole within a border of flowers and draped nets;[33] and *Camel* (Plate 46) which shows a man with the kneeling animal in an Eastern landscape.

Certain late transfers are known from excavated sherds, for example, *Peacock* pattern, a blue print of a peacock on an urn filled with flowers and known on an unmarked breakfast cup and saucer in a private collection.[34]

Oriental

A further range of transfer-prints may be described as oriental or exotic. The most commonly found is the pattern named 'Twisted Tree' in the recent literature, but more correctly known as *India*, as it is so termed in the factory invoices and in the Bramelds' backstamps which frequently accompany this print. Consisting of a gnarled tree with spreading branches full of exotic flowers, birds and insects (Plates 29 and 47), it occurs in blue, green and grey,[35] and is often coloured over the glaze to give a bright and attractive design on dinner wares, decorative items and toilet articles. It is found most frequently on later rococo shapes, sometimes gilded.

Indian Flowers is the Bramelds' name for a rather delicate blue transfer of branches with leaves, flowers, birds and nests. This extremely uncommon pattern is known on dinner wares (Plate 40), a feeding boat and on an unmarked saucer in the Sheffield City Museum with the words 'SHEFFIELD MECHANICS INSTITUTION' printed in the well.[36]

Parroquet is one of the finest Brameld transfers, with the birds perched among large oriental flowers. It occurs on dinner wares with crisply-moulded

33. We are indebted to Terence Lockett for drawing our attention to this print.
34. Sherds deposited in the Sheffield City Museum.
35. At the closure of the Rockingham Works, the copper plates for this pattern passed to the Rock Pottery, Mexborough.
36. An educational institution established in 1832 in George Street.

47. SOUP TUREEN, LADLE AND STAND, *c.*1835–40. Earthenware, transfer-printed in blue with the *India* pattern. Enamelled in red, pink and green and gilded. No mark, but from a service with impressed BRAMELD marks. Height 30.5 cm (12 in). *See page 98*

48. DISH, *c.*1830. Earthenware, transfer-printed in blue with *Parroquet*. Impressed BRAMELD +1 and with a printed backstamp (mark 63). Length 54.7 cm (21.5 in). *See page 98*

49. PLATE (*left*), *c.*1830. Earthenware, transfer-printed in blue with *Broseley*. Impressed BRAMELD within a floral wreath (mark 30) and printed in error with the backstamp *India* (mark 60). Diameter 24.8 cm (9.8 in). *See page 100*
PLATE (*right*), *c.*1830. Earthenware, printed in blue with *Oriental Figures with an Urn*, enamelled in red, yellow, green and orange. Impressed BRAMELD. Diameter 21.6 cm (8.5 in). *See page 100*

gadroon borders (Plate 48), printed in blue and occasionally coloured in enamels.

Willow is recorded in the invoices sent to Wentworth House in 1825, and although at other potteries it is one of the most common prints, it is found only infrequently on marked Brameld wares. The *Broseley* pattern (Plate 49) is also uncommon, recorded on dinner wares and rarely on porcelain teawares. It is mentioned on an invoice for 1842.

Four transfers include Chinese figures in oriental settings. *Oriental Figures with an Urn* is printed in blue, with men in front of a giant flower-filled urn and a bridge crossing to a pagoda (Plate 49). A very uncommon design, it may be found lightly coloured. Another equally rare pattern is *Chinese Figures on a Terrace*, printed in fawn on octagonal plates with a girl at an open window of a pagoda-like building. An example is in the Yorkshire Museum, York. The Bramelds' names for these two transfers are not known, but the third of this type has the name *Rose Jar* in backstamps. This blue-printed design, normally coloured over the glaze, shows an oriental figure with a fan in one hand and a leafy branch in the other, standing in a stylized garden (Plate 27). In addition to decorative earthenwares, this pattern is known on dinner wares and on porcelain teawares, where it is pattern number 642. A most attractive miniature plate illustrated in Plate 45 has a print of *Oriental Figures in Front of a Pagoda*, a restrained and pleasing scene coloured with enamels.

50. PLATE, *c.*1820–5. Earthenware, transfer-printed in black with *Exotic Pheasant*, coloured over in yellow, orange, blue and green. Impressed BRAMELD. Diameter 18.6 cm (7.3 in). *See page 101*

51. DISH, *c.*1820. Earthenware, transfer-printed in blue with a view of the *Swinton Pottery*, printed in reverse. The inscription on the scroll reads *North-west view/ of the Earthenware Manufactory at/ Swinton, near Rotherham, in Yorkshire./ Established in the year 1745*. Impressed BRAMELD. Diameter 32.3 cm (12.7 in). *See page 101*

Found on both earthenware and porcelain is a transferred *Imari* pattern, usually over-painted in a bright palette.[37] An equally rare print shows an *Exotic Pheasant* with leaves, flowers, branches and a butterfly within a Greek-key border (Plate 50), printed in black and painted in bright colours over the glaze.

Topographical

Representations of actual views on Brameld earthenware are uncommon, only two named prints having been recorded. An extremely rare example is a view of the *Swinton Pottery* before it was renamed the Rockingham Works (Plate 51),

37. A. A. Eaglestone and T. A. Lockett, op. cit., Plate XIIb.

52. SOUP TUREEN AND STAND, *c.*1825–42. Earthenware, transfer-printed in blue with *Castle of Rochefort, South of France*. Tureen impressed BRAMELD with 13 beneath, the stand impressed BRAMELD +6. Height 35.8 cm (14.1 in).
See pages 92 and 102

which appears on large dishes. It is reproduced in reverse on the actual pieces, presumably because the copper plate was intended for the production of prints on paper rather than on pottery.[38] The other named view is *Castle of Rochefort, South of France*, commonly found on dinner wares (Plate 52 and Colour Plate C) and often referred to in the factory invoices, as on 7 October 1825:

24 Printed Dishes Rochefort £3.5.8

The name of this pattern is known from backstamps.

LITERARY

Only two subjects in this category have been recorded to date. One very rare example is *Burns Cotter* showing a peasant arriving at his cottage door and being welcomed by his wife and children. The inspiration for this transfer comes from Robert Burns's poem *The Cotter's Saturday Night*, written in 1785, in which lines 14 to 22 describe accurately the scene depicted.[39] The print is named in a backstamp on a saucer in the collection of the Sheffield City Museum. It is also known on a tall coffee pot, teawares and miniature plates (Plate 45).

38. A dish in the Sheffield City Museum decorated with this transfer is impressed TWIGG'S, a mark of the Kilnhurst Old Pottery, which the Bramelds held from 1832 to 1839, when it passed to the Twigg brothers.
39. J. Kinsley (ed.), *The Poems and Songs of Robert Burns*, Oxford, 1968, Vol. 1, p. 146.

53. DINNER SERVICE, *c.*1835–42. Earthenware, transfer-printed in green with *Don Quixote*. Comprising 165 pieces, this shows the range of shapes in a neo-rococo service. Many pieces impressed BRAMELD + 1, but other numbers also occur, as do printed backstamps (mark 62). Height of soup tureen on stand 29.2 cm (11.5 in) *See page 103*

The adventures of Cervantes' knight *Don Quixote* form the basis of a sequence of well-known transfer-prints on Brameld dinner wares.[40] Unlike most patterns on services where the same design was used on all pieces, the *Don Quixote* series consists of some eighteen different ones, all of which are associated with the same backstamp. It is known in blue, green and black; a large dinner service printed in green is illustrated in Plate 53. The shapes are in the late revived rococo style.

COMMEMORATIVE

One Brameld commemorative print only is known to date. This depicts *Queen Caroline* (Plate 54), the unfortunate and much maligned wife of George IV, shown wearing a characteristic plumed hat, and it is a more attractive portrait of her than most contemporary versions. It can be dated fairly closely, since George IV was proclaimed king on 31 January 1820 and Caroline died on 7 August 1821. Queen Caroline seems to have won much popular support in the Sheffield region. White's *Directory*[41] records that in 1820 a dutiful address welcoming her return to England, and signed by 10,600 females of Sheffield, was presented to her.

40. A. A. Eaglestone and T. A. Lockett, op. cit., p. 92, attribute this series of prints to the works of T. Stothard.
41. W. White, *History, Gazetteer and Directory of the West-Riding of Yorkshire*, Sheffield, 1837, Vol. 1, p. 61.

55. (*right*) PLATE, *c*.1820. Earthenware, printed in blue with the *Lord's Prayer*, the border moulded with fruiting vine. Impressed BRAMELD +7. Diameter 13.5 cm (5.3 in). *Newmane Collection. See page 104*

54. (*left*) COMMEMORATIVE PLATE, *c*.1820. Earthenware, transfer-printed in black with a named portrait of *Queen Caroline*, the border moulded with oak leaves and acorns. Impressed BRAMELD +(?). Diameter 21.2 cm (8.3 in). *See page 103*

NURSERY

Certain Brameld transfer-prints were obviously intended for children. Small dishes and plates in a private collection show children at play with a kite (Plate 45) and a see-saw. These are printed in light blue within a vermicelli border.

A very attractive series of small pearlware plates for the nursery was produced at Swinton. They have crisply-moulded relief borders of leaves and flowers, or oak and acorn designs, and are occasionally enamelled in bright colours over the moulded detail. The centres of the plates are decorated with black transfer-prints including 'FOR SAMUEL' with a boy on a rocking horse;[42] 'FOR MARTHA WHAT PRETTY TOYS' showing two boys playing with toys; 'FOR HENRY' with a stage coach and horses;[43] and simply 'FOR WILLIAM' on an unglazed waster from the Pottery site. A most unusual nursery plate has a blue-printed roundel in the centre enclosing the *Lord's Prayer* (Plate 55).

MISCELLANEOUS

Other transfer-prints include *Paris Stripe*, a light-blue or green chintz-type pattern, the name known from backstamps. It occurs on dinner wares and sometimes other items such as jugs (Plate 64) and footbaths, where the design also incorporates bands of printed flowers. The *Blue Shamrock* pattern,

42. A. and A. Cox, *The Rockingham Works*, Sheffield, 1974, Plate 6.

43. We are indebted to the owner of this plate, and to Mr D. Cavill, for kindly drawing it to our attention.

56. PLATE, *c.*1830–42. Earthenware, transfer-printed in black with a scene depicting a coaching inn, inscribed the 'Green Man Hotel & Tavern'. Impressed BRAMELD. Diameter 25.6 cm (10.1 in). *See page 105*

commonly called 'Union', found on earthenware and porcelain dinner and teawares, consists of roses, thistles and shamrocks. It is mentioned in an invoice sent to Wentworth House dated 4 December 1829:

4 EW Bakers Blue Shamrock &c 14/-

Two further transfers named in the invoices, *Blue Drapery* in 1833 and *Grove* in 1842, have yet to be identified.

A rare print showing the steamship *Forfarshire* appears on a dish in the Dundee Museum and was presumably intended for use on the ship.[44] The *Forfarshire* was wrecked off the Farne Islands on 7 September 1838, a tragedy made famous by the young heroine Grace Darling, who aided the rescue of survivors.

Another specially commissioned transfer occurs on a plate in a private collection with the floral border which accompanies the *Don Quixote* scenes, printed in black. The centre of the plate shows a coaching inn, the *Green Man Hotel & Tavern* inscribed over the door with the name of the innkeeper, Thomas Whitmarsh (Plate 56).[45]

44. T. A. Lockett and A. A. Eaglestone, 'Royal Rockingham Porcelain—a re-assessment', *Connoisseur*, Vol. 162, No. 653, 1966, pp. 172–5, Plate 1.

45. A Rockingham copper plate in private possession is engraved with the names of several establishments for which wares were presumably produced. They include John Louder, Grey Hound Inn, Scoulthorpe; Ipswich Union; Henry Kirton, Tea Dealer, West Street, Boston; and Norwich Workhouse.

Stonewares

Only one piece of marked basalt has been recorded, a small plaque with an applied amorino in redware.[46] Curiously, this was impressed ROCKINGHAM, a mark which must be regarded as somewhat suspect except when it occurs on certain Brameld brown-glazed teawares (see pages 108–13). The present whereabouts of this plaque is not known.

Both documentary and excavated material shows, however, that black basalt was produced, but it seems to have been a ware with which the Bramelds experienced some difficulties. Thomas Brameld's notebook (see Appendix VI) contains several recipes for Egyptian black, gathered from various sources and tried in turn to find a satisfactory body. They include Keeling's, Harvey's, Jas. Burnett's, Hollins's and J. Meyer's. Two unnamed recipes have 'useless' written against them, whilst Meyer's is annotated 'Blisters'.

Egyptian black is listed in the bodies used by Thomas Brameld in 1808, and in a letter to his brother William dated 1809 he mentions black basalt and states that they could do more in this line.[47] The invoices sent to Wentworth House record the following

16 August 1816: 1 Egyptian Black oval Cream 1/-
15 August 1825: 4 Egyptian oval T Pots 4/-

Excavated material includes engine-turned wares, and many fragments from rather tall teapots with a band of moulded ivy leaves around the shoulder and a fine, thin, fluted body. Pieces were found from a large oblong teapot with rose, thistle and shamrock devices and *Tria Juncta in Uno* motifs.[48] No marks were noted on any black basalt sherds from the site.

The Bramelds produced a fine, cane-coloured stoneware, usually decorated with applied figures, flowers, fruiting vine and other motifs. The 'sprigged' work may be cane-coloured, white, blue, brown, or sage-green to contrast with the body. The inside of hollow ware is usually glazed.

Jugs are probably the best known of these products, in particular the distinctively shaped 'Grecian Pitchers' (Plate 57), the handles of which are curiously formed as a horse's tail at the upper end, whilst the lower section is modelled as its leg and hoof. The applied figures on these pieces are finely modelled child musicians within borders of applied Grecian wave and anthemion pattern. At least four sizes are known, and a mug of similar form is in the collections of the Victoria and Albert Museum. A splendid jug and bowl set of this type in a rather dark caneware was kindly brought to the writers' attention by Mr B. Bowden. Both pieces were decorated with white applied figures and were marked with the word BRAMELD on a white cartouche

46. M. H. Grant, *The Makers of Black Basaltes*, 1910, Plate LXXXIX, Fig. 4.
47. Wentworth Woodhouse Muniments, MD/182, dated 23 April 1809.
48. A. A. Eaglestone and T. A. Lockett, op. cit., Plate X, where a complete example is shown.

57. JUG (*left*), *c*.1820–30. Caneware, with applied blue figures of child musicians. Marked BRAMELD on a blue cartouche (mark 31). Height 14 cm (5.5 in).
JUG (*right*), *c*.1820–30. Caneware with applied Bacchic figures in sage green. Marked BRAMELD on a green cartouche (mark 31). Height 15.8 cm (6.2 in).

58. BREAKFAST CUP AND SAUCER, *c*.1820. Caneware, with applied white figures. Cup impressed BRAMELD +7, the saucer impressed BRAMELD. Diameter of saucer 16.5 cm (6.5 in). *See page 107*
COMPORT, *c*.1820–30. Caneware, with applied white flower and fruiting-vine motifs. Impressed BRAMELD +7. Height 9 cm (3.5 in). *See pages 107 and 108*

(mark 31). The bowl had a diameter of 34.3 cm (13.5 in).

A second type of caneware jug is of baluster shape with a loop handle (Plate 57), usually found with applied Bacchic figures and a border of stylized leaves. A curious and rare variant of this jug has a false spout formed as a serpent's head, its tail encircling the piece and extending into a handle. An example in the Warrington Museum has brown applied work. Other types of caneware jugs include one with moulded cockle shells of precisely the same shape as that shown in Plate 64, and another with moulded daisies at the top and ribbed lines beneath, sometimes found with a cover.

Breakfast and tea wares are occasionally seen in caneware, the cups of 'London' shape (Plate 58) accompanied by saucers, saucer dishes and other main pieces.[49] The applied figures on these wares are of dogs and sheep, together with trees, bushes and stylized flowers, some of the motifs corresponding with those on Wedgwood jasper ware. A cylindrical mug with applied figures is in the collections of the Sheffield City Museum.

Plates, shaped dishes and comports from dessert services occur in caneware, but are rare. The dishes have a continuous band of leaf-and-flower applied decoration around the inside, and realistic fern leaves under the outside edge, or applied figures of infants and animals. A square comport is illustrated in Plate 58, and as with teawares it is impressed BRAMELD rather than with an applied cartouche mark as found on jugs and mugs.

Decorative items in caneware include trumpet-shaped spill vases with applied cane-coloured classical figures. A similar piece is described in the Wentworth invoices for 22 June 1824:

2 Stone party coloured spill pots 3/-

Candlesticks are mentioned in the invoices on 12 May 1823:

2 Stone Party coloured Candlesticks 7/-

although no actual specimen has been recorded. Small caneware posy baskets are known, described in the invoices as violet baskets.

Colour-glazed Ware

One achievement for which the Swinton Pottery is widely known is the rich brown glaze stained with manganese and iron and commonly referred to as a 'Rockingham' glaze.[50] This type of decoration was developed at Swinton as early as about 1770, as is proved by excavated sherds, and was extensively used after 1806. So popular did this glaze become that rival manufacturers quickly followed on the Bramelds' success, some even marking their wares with a version of the Rockingham factory mark. That the Bramelds were aware of their imitators is shown by the wording of an advertisement of 1827 in which they describe themselves as 'original Inventors, and sole Manufacturers of the genuine Royal Rockingham Teapots &c., to be had here, at the Manufactory and at Mortlock's, London'.[51]

The brown glaze is especially associated with Rockingham teapots, the tall baluster-shaped pots (Plate 59), often now incorrectly termed coffee pots, but clearly originally intended for tea since they occur with gilt inscriptions to this effect, such as those in an invoice for 12 May 1823:

6 Rockingham T Pots Burnishd Gold Letterd Black & Green 3 Sizes 15/-

49. A caneware teapot was in the Llewellyn Collection, sold at Sotheby's, 23 January 1973, lot 75.

50. L. Jewitt, op. cit., Vol. 1, p. 498, describes it as 'one of the smoothest and most beautiful wares that has ever been produced at any place'.

51. *York Courant*, 22 May 1827.

59. ROCKINGHAM TEAPOT, COVERED SUGAR AND CREAM JUG, *c.* 1830. Earthenware, brown-glazed and decorated with gilt chinoiseries. All pieces impressed ROCKINGHAM (mark 36), the sugar additionally with C..5 in gilt. Height of teapot 18.9 cm (7.4 in). *Ex Llewellyn Collection. See pages 108–9*

They were made by the Bramelds from the earliest years of their proprietorship; in fact, their first invoice sent to Wentworth House in 1807 lists Rockingham teapots. A Pottery bill-head of the 1830s includes the words 'Original Makers of their Teapots to the late Marchioneſs of Rockingham'. Since Mary, the last marchioness, died in 1804, the Bramelds clearly refer to an earlier product. Whilst in the eighteenth-century invoices there is no mention of Rockingham teapots as such, frequent references to 'purple' teapots occur, and the matter is clarified by an invoice of 5 August 1816 sent to Wentworth House:

8 Rockingham or Purple Tea Pots 2 sizes 12/-

Thus the term 'purple' refers to brown-glazed wares, first supplied in 1770 during the Malpass & Fenney partnership. This class of ware was clearly popular with Lady Rockingham who, in one request alone placed in October 1780, ordered from the Swinton Pottery eighteen 'Purple Tea Potts', which probably explains how they acquired the name 'Rockingham'.

In 1807 Rockingham teapots were ordered by the Prince of Wales (see page 60). These brown-glazed pots may be simply decorated with gilt bands, or gilded more elaborately with chinoiseries, floral patterns or competently enamelled. Matching cream jugs and covered sugars also occur (Plate 59). A somewhat less common type of brown-glazed teapot has a more rounded shape with an acanthus-moulded spout and a strap handle—an example may be seen in the Rotherham Museum. In addition to an impressed factory mark, a Cl mark (page 229) may be present on these wares.

Cadogan pots, or unspillable lidless pots, are normally brown-glazed. Based on a Chinese wine-pot original, they were, according to Jewitt, intended for use as coffee pots.[52] They are filled through a tube in the base and must have been almost impossible to clean. A large Cadogan lettered 'HOT WATER' (Plate 60) suggests a more likely use for these items, although the very small ones were probably sold as novelties. They are first mentioned in the invoices sent to Wentworth House in September 1826, and further references show that they were made until the closure of the factory. Cadogans were made in at least six sizes and are decorated in much the same manner as are Rockingham teapots. Several contemporary factories produced these curiosities, Spode, and Copeland and Garrett examples being the most common. Of the many potters who throughout the nineteenth century manufactured brown-glazed wares, few succeeded in achieving the same attractive glaze effects as did the Bramelds. Their wares, mostly unmarked, have nevertheless often acquired a Rockingham attribution.

Far more confusing, however, are certain brown-glazed items with a Rockingham mark, but with characteristics not normally associated with this factory. In an attempt to clarify the situation, the authors have determined the composition of the glaze on a number of such pieces using the technique of X-ray fluorescence spectroscopy. Brief details of this method are given in Appendix VII. Specimens with impressed 'Brameld' or 'Rockingham' marks were examined, as were twenty-five brown-glazed sherds recovered from various areas of the Swinton site. For comparison, wares bearing impressed marks of the Spode, Copeland and Garrett, and Wedgwood concerns were also analysed.

The composition of the glaze on sherds from the Brameld period varies relatively little and matches that on the tall Rockingham teapots and more rounded teapots previously described, covered sugars, sparrow-beak jugs and covered hot-water jugs (Plate 61)—all teawares. These items, when marked, are impressed ROCKINGHAM (mark 36), the length of the mark being 2.24 cm (0.88 in). There is no doubt whatsoever about the authenticity of these pieces.

Two differently shaped Cadogans bear marks which, taken at face value, indicate a Swinton product, namely BRAMELD and ROCKINGHAM. Of the examples analysed, *only* those impressed BRAMELD in its various forms (several different stamps were used, see pages 220–1) have a glaze which denotes a Swinton origin. Further support for this contention is that the writers are unaware of Cadogans with a ROCKINGHAM mark (37 or 38) *and* a Cl mark, whereas many such pots impressed BRAMELD have this additional distinguishing feature. Brown-glazed wares with the uncommon imprints MORTLOCK'S/CADOGAN and MORTLOCK'S/ROYAL/ROCKINGHAM have been shown to be authentic Swinton products; they were manufactured specifically for the London retailer John Mortlock of Oxford Street, London.

52. L. Jewitt, op. cit., Vol. 1, p. 499.

60. CADOGAN POT (*left*), *c.*1840. Earthenware, brown-glazed. Impressed ROCKINGHAM (mark 38), but apparently not made at Swinton. Height 17.2 cm (6.8 in). *See page 110*

CADOGAN POT (*right*), *c.*1820–40. Earthenware, brown-glazed and further ornamented with gilt, including the inscription 'HOT WATER'. Impressed MORTLOCK'S/ CADOGAN (mark 44). Height 20.1 cm (7.9 in). *See page 110*

61. COVERED JUG, *c.*1830. Earthenware, brown-glazed with flower-and-leaf decoration in gilt. Impressed ROCKINGHAM (mark 36) and C.3 in brown. Height 19.5 cm (7.7 in) *See page 110*

Well-modelled toby jugs[53] clearly impressed ROCKINGHAM (marks 37 or 38) have a glaze inconsistent with a Swinton attribution, as do jugs decorated in relief with men smoking and drinking,[54] which bear mark 38. Similarly, two jugs illustrated by Dr Rice would seem not to be of Swinton origin.[55] One, of low circular shape with an arc handle, has a glaze identical to that used by Wedgwoods *c.* 1840; it is prominently impressed ROCKINGHAM (mark 39).[56] The other has concentric rings around the base and neck, an angular handle, and is pale brown in colour, possibly due to its being dipped once only in a liquid glaze.[57] It bears mark 41. Two further examples are in the Yorkshire Museum, York.

It might be argued that the Bramelds used more than one recipe for their brown glaze. Whilst this cannot be refuted, it should be stressed that the glaze on all sherds of this ware from the Swinton site varies relatively little. In addition, no fragments of toby jugs, nor of any of the pieces upon which doubt is cast, have been recovered during excavations. Moreover, if a Swinton origin is claimed for Cadogans impressed ROCKINGHAM, one has to explain why the Bramelds not only changed the compositon of the glaze but also altered the shape—compare that of the Cadogan on the left in Plate 60 with the shape of the pot on the right, which is of undoubted Swinton manufacture—and chose to mark them differently. The simplest explanation is surely that they were made elsewhere. Further research is required on this subject.

Little doubt now surrounds the tall, baluster-shaped teapots with a rounded conical finial,[58] and jugs with crossed strap handles,[59] impressed 'Rockingham' in script (mark 40), said by Jewitt to be 'the earliest used by these works ... a mark of great rarity'.[60] The composition of the glaze on these pieces matches that on wares with SPODE and COPELAND &/ GARRETT marks, and significantly fragments of wares bearing this Rockingham script mark have been excavated on the Spode factory site,[61] thus supporting the analytical evidence and refuting Jewitt's statement.

Problems frequently arise with the attribution of those Wedgwood pieces, commonly teapots, prominently impressed ROCKINGHAM (mark 39) in

53. D. G. Rice, op. cit., Plate 1.
54. We are indebted to Miss C. Bennett for permitting the glaze to be analysed on the example in the Rotherham Museum.
55. D. G. Rice, op. cit., Plates 8 and 15.
56. This jug is in the Sheffield City Museum. The glaze was analysed by kind permission of Miss M. Pearce.
57. We wish to thank Mr B. Bowden for allowing the glaze on this jug to be examined whilst it was in his possession. L. Jewitt, op. cit., Vol. 1, p. 498, states that the Bramelds' brown-glazed ware was dipped and fired no fewer than three times.
58. D. G. Rice, op. cit., Plate 6.
59. G. R. P. Llewellyn, 'Rockingham Ware and Porcelain: Its Marks', *The Connoisseur Year Book, 1962*, pp. 140–6, Plate 3.
60. L Jewitt, op. cit., Vol. 1, p. 515.
61. We are indebted to Mr Robert Copeland and Mr Paul Holdway for providing information about this excavated material.

large capital letters, since the word WEDGWOOD in small capitals is often obscured (intentionally?) by the thick glaze, or may indeed be absent. They occur in various shapes, often with round or 'widow' finials, and sometimes with wheel-engraved decoration. The Wedgwood glaze differs markedly from that used by the Bramelds. A rather squat teapot with an arc handle in the Victoria and Albert Museum is almost certainly a Wedgwood product, in spite of its Rockingham mark.[62] An identically shaped brown-glazed teapot, beautifully decorated with gilt chinoiseries in the manner used by the Bramelds, is impressed both ROCKINGHAM (mark 39) and WEDGWOOD/ETRURIA, the latter used over the limited period *c.* 1840–5.[63] The price lists issued by Wedgwood's during the 1870s, and possibly earlier, enumerate 'Rockingham' tablewares, and a list for 1877 includes the note 'Rockingham ware decorated with flowers &c. made in great variety.'[64] These are late products, but nevertheless they are a source of confusion.

Clearly, brown-glazed wares impressed with a ROCKINGHAM mark should be attributed with care, and on the evidence cited here only those bearing mark 36 should be accepted *without doubt* as authentic products of this factory.

Several pieces decorated with a dark-blue glaze have come to our attention, notably a baluster-shaped teapot similar to the Rockingham teapots (Plate 59), but with distinct differences in moulded detail, elaborate gilding and a pierced, flattened knop—a feature most uncharacteristic of Swinton. Furthermore, it is impressed ROCKINGHAM (mark 38), a mark which occurs on certain brown-glazed items of doubtful origin. Unmarked blue Cadogan pots are known, identical in shape to the one shown on the left in Plate 60, which also bears mark 38, as do small jugs decorated with figures in relief. Only the mark suggests a Swinton attribution for these pieces—an unreliable guide, as was pointed out in the case of certain brown-glazed wares. Significantly, no blue-glazed items appear in any of the factory invoices we have examined.

Earthenwares with a green glaze were manufactured in quantity at Swinton, mainly in the form of dessert services (Plate 62) with distinctive shapes and an all-over glaze which ranges from a good bright green to a relatively dull hue. Its quality is by no means as consistently high as the factory's brown glaze.

The most common form of service includes plates moulded in the form of over-lapping vine leaves. Comports, tureens (Plate 63) and leaf-shaped dishes are known; rarely the outlines of leaves were gilded to produce a most pleasing effect. Of the few green-glazed items purchased for use at Wentworth House, the following are recorded on 3 August 1821:

2 5 In Green Glazed Leaves 8d

62. D. G. Rice, op. cit., Plate 9.
63. G. A. Godden, *Encyclopaedia of British Pottery and Porcelain Marks*, London, 1964, mark 4085. Mr David Wilby most kindly drew our attention to this teapot.
64. Miss Gaye Blake Roberts of the Wedgwood Museum, Barlaston, very kindly provided this information.

A basket-weave design is the basis of a second type of service, reminiscent of that used for mid-eighteenth-century salt-glazed wares. These pieces may indeed originate from moulds used for the production of such wares, but the details do not correspond with those on sherds of salt-glazed flatware recovered from the Swinton site. Matching tureens and diamond-shaped dishes are recorded, but are uncommon. This same moulding occurs on the chalk-body dish shown in Plate 21.

A third variety of service has plates with a moulded basket-weave centre and a border consisting of stylized leaves. Once again the principal pieces are rarely seen (Plate 63).

Other useful wares include rustic-handled jugs with a moulded design of primrose leaves forming the lower part and flower heads around the neck. Authentic green-glazed Cadogan pots are known, but are rare—an example may be seen in the collections of the Victoria and Albert Museum. No factory-marked decorative pieces with this glaze are recorded, although Jewitt attributes lotus vases and Conisborough Castle vases (Plate 28) to Swinton (see pages 82–4).[65]

A yellow glaze was used by the Bramelds, but not to any extent. There is one mention only in the invoices sent to Wentworth House on 20 July 1838:

11 Yellow Hand Bowls 9/2

A yellow-glazed covered jug impressed BRAMELD has been illustrated, the body moulded with an all-over diamond pattern.[66] Another covered jug similarly marked (Plate 64) has the yellow surface boldly over-painted in dark blue to emphasize the moulded detail and produce a striking, if gaudy, effect.

Other Bodies and Types of Decoration

Dip-decorated ware in which the body of the piece is covered with a coloured slip was produced with many forms of decoration at most potteries during the late eighteenth and early nineteenth centuries. Often the pot was turned on a lathe to produce bands of contrasting colour, or chequered patterns, resulting in colourful everyday items.

Dip decoration was used extensively in the Greens, Bingley & Co. period, and was still popular with the Bramelds. Marked specimens are not known, but sherds excavated at Swinton reveal that banded wares in brown with chequered designs were produced after 1806. Certainly other colours were tried, as Thomas Brameld lists the following range of dips in his recipe book: orange, olive-green, chocolate, blue, flesh colour, and the somewhat unhappily named 'flesh colour spotted'.

Mocha ware, produced by the chemical action of a dark, acid colorant as it

65. L. Jewitt, op. cit., Vol. 1, pp. 509–10.
66. J. Jefferson Miller, *English Yellow-Glazed Earthenware*, London, 1974, Plate XXXVII.

62. PLATES AND DISH, *c.*1820–42. Earthenware, green-glazed. *Left*, plate with basket-weave decoration, impressed BRAMELD + 13; *centre*, dish with moulded vine leaves, impressed BRAMELD +(?); *right*, plate with basket-weave and stylized leaves, impressed BRAMELD +4, diameter 21 cm (8.3 in). *See page 113*

63. TUREENS, *c.*1820–42. Earthenware, green-glazed. *Left*, with moulded vine-leaf decoration, no mark; *right*, with basket-weave and stylized leaves, impressed BRAMELD +8, height 17.2 cm (6.8 in). *See pages 113–4*

64. JUG (*left*), *c.*1830. Earthenware, printed in green with *Paris Stripe*. No mark. Height 19.1 cm (7.5 in). *See page 104*
JUG (*right*), *c.*1830. Earthenware, yellow ground, the moulded detail picked out in dark blue, Impressed BRAMELD beneath which is the figure 8. Height 18 cm (7.1 in). *See page 114*

diffused over the surface of a coloured, alkaline slip to create fern-like patterns, was made by many potters. There is a reference in the factory invoices for 10 August 1811 to:

4 Mocha Flower Jars 1/3

and sherds from the Swinton site reveal the Brameld mocha to be of excellent quality.

Lustre decoration was certainly used at Swinton and the following items were supplied to Wentworth House between 1818 and 1824:

6 Drab Lustre Mugs 2/6
6 Lustre Cans 2/-
4 Lustre Horns 1/8
2 Lustre Spill pots 1/-

Sherds of copper, silver and pink lustre have been recovered from the Pottery site and details for producing 'Metallic Lustre' occur in the Brameld recipe book. No marked examples have been recorded.

Several other fine earthenwares were produced, although not all have been recognized. Listed in the 'Bodies used by TB—May 1808' (see Appendix VI) is 'Chalcedony or Orange', and there is a further recipe for a white slip to coat the inside of this ware. Fragments of an orange-coloured body are known from the Swinton site, and the following occurs in the factory invoices for 6 August 1807:

6 Chalcedony Enamel^d lined Jugs 19/6

The same list of bodies used by Thomas Brameld includes a reference to 'Cottage', elsewhere described as 'Brown or Cottage Body' and also intended to be lined with a white slip. 'Cottage jugs' are mentioned several times in the factory invoices of this period, but no examples have been recorded.

Other finewares for which details are given in Thomas Brameld's recipe book have not been recognized, and indeed may never have been produced. He includes notes for making blue and white jasper, for example, and a 'Delph Glaze'. In 1808, when many of the notes were written, Thomas Brameld would have been twenty-one, not long out of his apprenticeship, and no doubt keen to gather information for possible future use.

Of the more substantial bodies there is a reference in 1831 to

4 31 Inches Stone Marble Bird Pots £14.14.0

having been delivered to Wentworth House. These large garden pieces were probably made of a durable stone-china body.

Fireproof wares are known only from sherds excavated from the factory site. Made of a glazed, buff-coloured earthenware, they are impressed with the curious mark FIRE PROOF/ BRAMELD/ DEEP MINE/ IMPROVED, and as purely utilitarian pieces it is unlikely that many have survived. On 8 August 1829 Wentworth House was supplied with:

6 Fire Proof Ewers & Basons 9/-

although why toilet items should need to be fireproof is not immediately obvious.

The Bramelds were primarily known as fineware manufacturers, but they still found it worthwhile to continue the production of coarse earthenwares. The traditional black-glazed items—porringers, chamber pots, pitchers and jars—were still being made until at least 1813, and the manufacture of coarse garden pots went on until the closure of the Works.

7
Rockingham Useful Porcelain

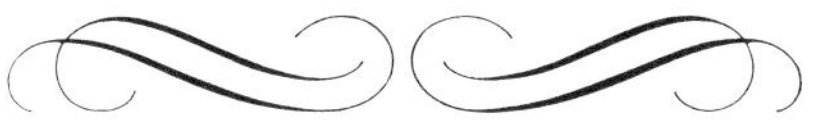

The Rockingham Works quickly became renowned for its bone china. The production of this ware was an ambitious step for Thomas Brameld, although something which he had been considering for several years, since he was recording recipes for porcelain from as early as 1808 (pages 246–8).

Experiments seem to have started at least by 1818 (page 66), and it is perhaps possible to recognize certain of these early porcelain pieces. One such vase (Plate 65) decorated with a painted pattern which combines oriental and classical features, is of a very different body from that normally associated with Rockingham, rather hard and grey in appearance due to its low bone-ash content,[1] and with a markedly blue glaze. It is of similar design to certain earthenware vases discussed on pages 84 and 86, and like those it is marked with the painted name 'Brameld' and the number 2030. It is possible that there may be experimental porcelain counterparts of all this class of earthenwares. Jewitt records two trial pieces which were in the possession of one of Thomas Brameld's sons, a pair of small leaves of salmon colour with gold veins,[2] and interestingly a salmon colour is a prominent feature of the vase illustrated.

Once the porcelain body had been perfected, it seems to have been used with little modification throughout the years of production, something quite unusual in a ceramic world where most of the large concerns were constantly experimenting and changing the paste in use, or using several simultaneously. X-ray fluorescence analysis of a range of samples of both decorative and useful porcelain made throughout the period of porcelain production has proved this consistency,[3] and it has even been possible to show which of the recipes noted by Thomas Brameld was the one selected for the large-scale manufacture of bone china. Described simply as 'Another Porcelain Body', the raw materials are by weight:

1 Blue Clay
1½ Cornish Clay
1 Cornish Stone
2½ Calcined Bones

1. As revealed by X-ray fluorescence analysis.
2. L. Jewitt, *Ceramic Art in Great Britain*, London, 1878, Vol. 1, p. 511.
3. A. Cox, 'The Analysis of Rockingham Porcelain in the Light of Thomas Brameld's Notebook and a Comparison with Some Other Examples of Nineteenth Century Bone China', *Northern Ceramic Society Journal*, Vol. 3, 1978–9, pp. 25–39. See also Appendix VII.

65. VASE, *c.*1820–5. Porcelain, possibly experimental. Enamelled decoration in salmon, orange, blue, red, green and pink, with gilding. Neck not original. Painted *Brameld* mark in red (mark 47) and 2030/※ Height 17.6 cm (6.9 in). *See pages 86 and 118*

and interestingly the resulting porcelain, with a bone-ash content of about 45%, assuming that best English calcined bone was used, has a composition close to that of modern bone china. Although the Bramelds enticed some of their foremost artists and modellers from Robert Bloor's Derby factory, and were initially influenced to a certain extent by the products of this concern, connections with it were stylistic only, for their porcelain bodies are quite different. The perfection of this body at Swinton was probably the achievement of Thomas Brameld himself, since in his recipe book he generally names his source if the information came from elsewhere. Documentary evidence too supports the use of one porcelain body at Swinton. In a letter to Earl Fitzwilliam in 1842 proposing to recommence the manufacture of porcelain, Thomas Brameld states his intention 'To make some of the old superior Sort of China, as hitherto;—but, also to introduce from our Formula a Common & cheaper Sort of China—at such prices as will be likely to ensure a free sale.'[4]

In appearance Rockingham porcelain is white and, although quite translucent, is surprisingly substantial. The glaze generally fits badly and is commonly characterized by minute crazing, resulting in the wares being susceptible to staining. The different appearance of certain items of early red-period porcelain, which 'ring' when struck and do not craze, is probably to be attributed to a change in the composition of the glaze and to somewhat different kiln conditions during the biscuit firing, since the paste is that normally

4. Wentworth Woodhouse Muniments, G 47/18, dated 29 November 1842.

associated with this factory.[5] Information about the source of some of the Bramelds' raw materials for the manufacture of porcelain occurs in a note written by Lord Milton in 1829.[6] The Cornish clay was obtained from the St. Stephen's China Clay & Stone Co. near St. Austell, and from the Meledor China Clay Co., St. Columb, the cost being 70/- per ton in ½-ton casks, put on board a ship for Hull, and it was supplied through George Malcolm & Sons, wharfingers and shipping agents of 22 High Street, Hull. Clay was also obtained from Wareham, Dorset, and flint from Ramsgate, Sandwich, Shoreham and other areas of Kent and Sussex.[7]

Porcelain production on a commercial scale began in 1825, for it is clear that when Earl Fitzwilliam's financial support was given after the bankruptcy of that year, the Pottery was already established as a china works. It was towards the end of 1826 that the name 'Rockingham Works' was first used and the griffin factory mark from the Wentworth family crest adopted. Late in August of that year, the local newspapers were still using the name Swinton China Works,[8] and the first invoice which bears the name Rockingham Works dates to some time after 30 November 1826. By early 1827 the elaborate bill head (Plate 68) incorporating the engraving of the Works was in use.

The griffin mark also probably dates from late 1826. A porcelain hexagonal vase (Colour Plate H) in the Hurst Collection at the Yorkshire Museum, York, is marked 'Brameld' in puce script (mark 48), suggesting that it was made before the renaming of the Pottery and the introduction of the new mark. Similarly, a porcelain cup in the Rotherham Museum dated 1826 is inscribed *Rockingham/China Works/Swinton* (mark 49).[9] One of the earliest pieces to be marked with the griffin is the rhinoceros vase (Plate 98) which is dated 1826, now in the Rotherham Museum, and which was described by Ebenezer Rhodes as having just been completed when he visited the Works in December of that year.[10] Interestingly, it is marked with the uncommon circular red mark (mark 51) including a griffin statant, an incorrect version of the Wentworth crest, which is believed to have been used for a brief period only before being replaced by the heraldically accurate griffin passant which appears in the more usual red mark (mark 52). The griffin was probably adopted as an acknowledgement of Earl Fitzwilliam's assistance, and was symbolic of the special relationship between the earl and the Bramelds. The name Rockingham Works may have had slightly more commercial undertones, perhaps deriving

5. Bone china is biscuit-fired at about 1280°C, the glost firing being some 200°C lower. The temperature within a kiln varies with position and the precise control of firing conditions during the early nineteenth century was impossible.

6. Wentworth Woodhouse Muniments, G 83/94, dated 10 September 1829.

7. H. de la Beche and T. Reeks, *Catalogue of Specimens of British Pottery and Porcelain in the Museum of Practical Geology*, London, 1855, p. 167.

8. *Sheffield Iris*, 29 August 1826, where an account occurs of the artist George Collinson rescuing a drowning boy.

9. A.A. Eaglestone and T.A. Lockett, *The Rockingham Pottery*, Rotherham, 1964, Plate IVa.

10. E. Rhodes, *Yorkshire Scenery*, London, 1826, p. 154.

from the brown Rockingham teapots which had found favour with the Prince Regent, and were so much a household word that by 1828 Mortlock's could simply describe them as 'Rockinghams'.[11]

In 1826, with financial affairs at least temporarily on an even keel, Thomas Brameld could devote himself to his main interest and, as Jewitt records, he determined 'to make his porcelain at least equal to any which could then be produced'.[12] When Ebenezer Rhodes visited the Works in late 1826, he found a thriving porcelain manufactory and was impressed by the range and quality of the wares:

> The porcelain works of Worcester, Derby, and Staffordshire, have here a formidable rival; and it is highly gratifying to behold so important an establishment founded and flourishing amongst us.[13]

In the early years of porcelain production there was a sense of optimism and enthusiasm which only the rising tide of debt could gradually destroy.

Dinner and Dessert Services

The Bramelds produced far more earthenware than porcelain dinner services. Such porcelain dinner wares as are known have the same plate mouldings as the dessert services, but the tureens, now extremely rare, differ in form (Plate 66).

66. SOUP TUREEN, *c.*1826–30. Porcelain, from a dinner service, with green ground and gilding. Painted crest and motto '*Simplex Munditiis*'. No mark. Height 28 cm (11 in). *See page 121*

11. *The Times*, 16 June 1828.
12. L. Jewitt, op. cit., Vol. 1, p. 502.
13. E. Rhodes, op. cit., p. 154.

The decoration tends to be fairly simple, with a plain ground colour, gilt bands or transferred union motifs—roses, thistles and shamrocks—in green or blue, whilst others are painted with small moss roses or a crest. The size of a dinner service could be varied according to requirement, but might typically consist of table or dinner plates, soup plates, serving dishes of various sizes, vegetable dishes and covers, sauce tureens and stands, soup tureens and stands, a fish drainer and salad bowl.

An unusual dinner plate is illustrated in Plate 67, distinctively enamelled in a *famille verte* palette over an oriental-style print, with even the paste tinted a greyish colour in imitation of hard-paste Chinese porcelain. The authors are not aware of any large dishes or tureens associated with this shape of plate.

The Bramelds lavished the greatest care and attention on their dessert services, which were as much for display as they were functional. A contemporary, somewhat satirical comment, occurs in Granville's *Catechism of Health* (1832), 'A dessert is an unnecessary display of twenty dishes of fruit, cakes, biscuits, and preserves, symmetrically arranged on a polished mahogany table, or one covered with a damask table-cloth, after a profuse dinner.' Porcelain dessert wares were intended to be impressive, the Rockingham service for William IV being the outstanding example; but many lesser services are also extremely decorative. The most splendid were undoubtedly those made during the red-griffin period, 1826–30, when much care was given to rich ground colours, elaborate gilding and competent enamelling.

A wide range of ground colours was in use, including claret, imperial blue, lilac, pale pink, rose pink, a deep raspberry colour, dark green, mid green, apple green, orange, apricot, yellow, turquoise and a very beautiful overglaze matt blue which, unfortunately, proved susceptible to staining.[14] The ground colours were sometimes left plain, or they might be further decorated with painted reserves, or gilded with flowers, leaves, scrolls and other decorative motifs.

The enamelling of the early period is particularly fine, with views (occasionally named), birds, fruit, butterflies and other insects.[15] Most popular were flowers, especially full-blown roses and tulips, poppies, auriculas, vetches and convolvulus. Named botanical studies, figures, sea shells, feathers and garden scenes are rare.

14. This shade of blue was used on the royal dessert service and was known as 'Brunswick blue'.

15. The Yorkshire collector W. T. Freemantle of Greasborough, near Rotherham, recorded in 1909 that he was offered a red griffin-marked plate decorated with insects, each named on the reverse and further inscribed 'Insects of India by Donovan' (The Freemantle File, Rotherham Library, Department of Local History). Some forty pieces of Rockingham porcelain from the Freemantle collection, many of considerable importance, were sold to the Sheffield City Museum in 1910.

67. PLATE, *c.*1830. Porcelain, transfer-printed and decorated in a *famille verte* palette. Puce griffin, mark 58. Width 24.7 cm (9.7 in). *Ex Llewellyn Collection.* *See page 122*

Less expensive wares were transfer-printed, usually with floral designs, sometimes painted over in colour. At this same end of the price scale there were simple gilt patterns, which also served to emphasize the whiteness of the porcelain.

The gilding of the red period is very lavish. It may be at its simplest in the form of a rich coppery-gold line, or in complex arabesques, or beautifully defined bands of delicately formed flower and leaf motifs. Rarely the gilding is raised and tooled.

At this time the Bramelds, away from the mainstream of porcelain production, were still unknown, for as the York china-dealer William Pomfret scornfully maintained, who had ever heard of Yorkshire china?[16] The market they sought was primarily the aristocratic and well-to-do, and in this their relationship with Earl Fitzwilliam proved invaluable. Wealthy visitors to Wentworth House often ordered expensive wares, as on 25 January 1827, when

16. *Yorkshire Gazette*, 25 March 1827.

one of the services described in the invoice shown in Plate 68 was supplied to the Hon. Mrs J. Dundas through Earl Fitzwilliam. The details of this service, which appear beneath one of the Bramelds' elaborate bill-heads, read as follows:

1 Porcelain Deſsert Service N°. 409 consisting of the following articles (viz) — 63.0.0
24 Plates. 8 Fruit Dishes. 2 elevated end
Dishes & Stands. 1 Centre Piece & Stand.
2 Cream Bowls complete.[17]
Cask & Package — 0.6.0

Sent p Waggon from
Doncaster to the Hon. M^rs^. J.Dundas
Carlton near Richmond.

A dish decorated with this pattern—the lowest dessert pattern number known to the authors—is illustrated in Plate 69 and the superb quality is representative of the best of early wares. The painting is almost certainly the work of John Creswell. A special cask was provided, since the journey by waggon must have been a perilous one, and in fact the production of such crates became quite a local industry. A second, less expensive dessert service, pattern 421, consisting of the same number of pieces, is also included on this invoice, destined for Mrs Robert Cooke of Owston.

In dinner and dessert services normally only the plates bear the factory mark, but occasionally the printed griffin occurs on dishes and tureens.

The dessert-ware shapes in use during the red griffin period, 1826–30, are quite distinctive, and with one exception are unlikely to be confused with those of other factories. They are based either on silverware shapes or natural forms. The former consist of a series of gadroon borders, referred to in the factory invoices sent to Wentworth House as Gadroon A, B, C and so on, as on 10 February 1829:

1 China Table Service Gadroon C Nr 488 B — £33.19.7
for Mrs Wharton Gilling Vickery near Richmond

Probably the earliest of these shapes, and one of the rarest, is the *anthemion and gadroon* border on plain circular plates, sometimes bearing the uncommon early red circular griffin mark. The superb-quality dish with this

17. Now commonly referred to as tureens; they were, however, originally intended to contain cream to serve with dessert.

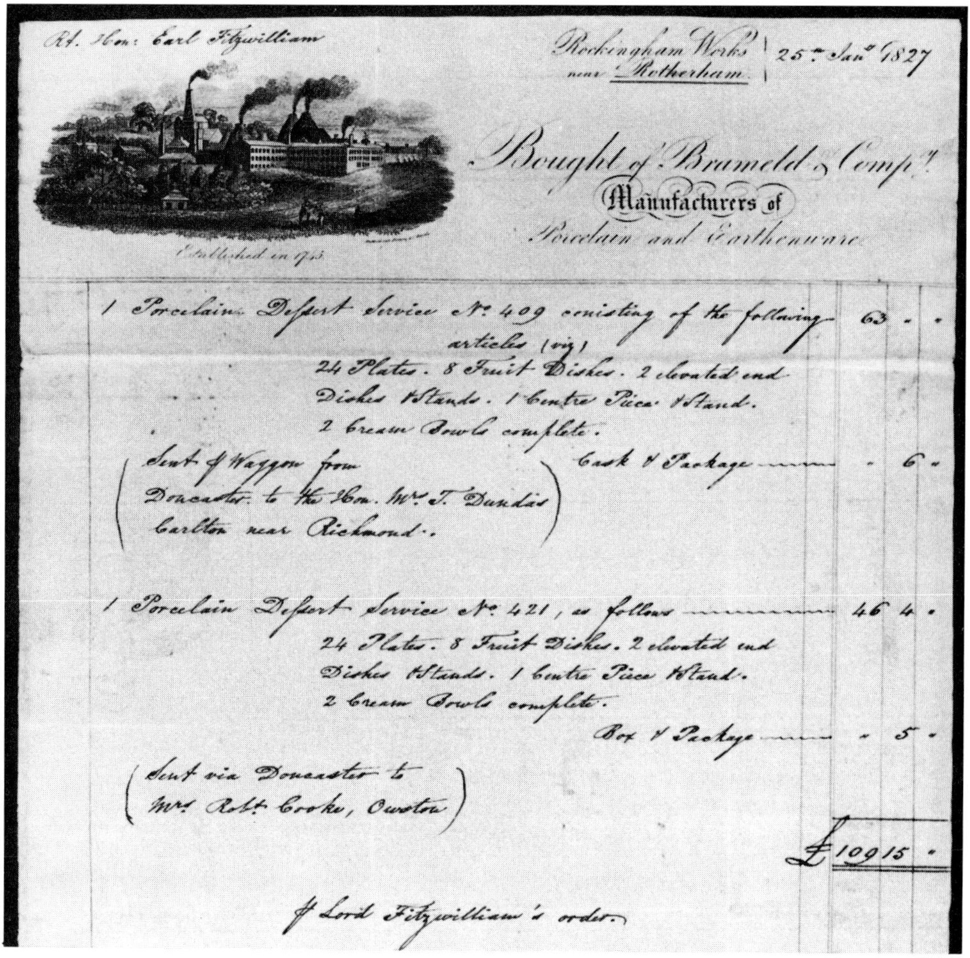

Rt. Hon: Earl Fitzwilliam

Rockingham Works near Rotherham | 25th Jany 1827

Bought of Brameld & Compy.
Manufacturers of
Porcelain and Earthenware

Established in [illegible]

	£	s	d
1 Porcelain Dessert Service No. 409 consisting of the following articles (viz)	63	.	.
24 Plates. 8 Fruit Dishes. 2 elevated end Dishes & Stands. 1 Centre Piece & Stand. 2 Cream Bowls complete.			
(Sent p Waggon from Doncaster to the Hon. Mrs. T. Dundas Carlton near Richmond.) Cask & Package	.	6	.
1 Porcelain Dessert Service No. 421, as follows	46	4	.
24 Plates. 8 Fruit Dishes. 2 elevated end Dishes & Stands. 1 Centre Piece & Stand. 2 Cream Bowls complete.			
Box & Package	.	5	.
(Sent via Doncaster to Mrs. Robt. Croke, Owston)			
	£109	15	.

p Lord Fitzwilliam's order.

68. INVOICE. Dated 25 January 1827, detailing two dessert services supplied by the Bramelds, one of pattern 409. A dish with this pattern is illustrated in Plate 69. *Trustees of the Fitzwilliam (Wentworth) Estates and Sheffield City Libraries. See page 124*

69. DISH, *c.*1826. Porcelain, *anthemion and gadroon* moulding, finely enamelled, probably by John Creswell, and richly gilded. Red griffin, mark 51, and pattern number 409. Width 21.5 cm (8.5 in). *See Plate 68 and page 124*

70. DISH, *c*.1826. Porcelain, *anthemion and gadroon* moulding, with claret ground and lavish gilding, the enamelled decoration probably by John Creswell. Red griffin, mark 52. Length 25.4 cm (10 in). *Godden Reference Collection*. *See page 126*

moulding shown in Plate 70 may well also be the work of John Creswell. A very similar moulding was produced at Coalport on closely related comports, plates and dishes.[18]

Another gadroon design found relatively commonly has a *shell and gadroon* border, is essentially octagonal in outline, and is characterized by small protrusions on each side of the large moulded shells around the edge. Plates (Plate 72), elevated comports or centrepieces (Plate 71) and matching dishes of oval, square and shell shape formed parts of such services, in addition to small tureens with shell finials. This moulding continued in use after 1830.

Gadroon with acanthus-leaf and shell moulding is another version and may also be found with either red or puce griffin marks. The plates are basically twelve-sided and less angular than those of the previous design. The plate illustrated (Plate 72) is from a well-known series with a rose-pink ground colour around the border, enamelled in the centre with a named Yorkshire scene *Byland Abbey*. The views are taken from various sources, including Ebenezer Rhodes's *Yorkshire Scenery* published in 1826.

The *shark's-tooth and S-scroll* moulded borders occur on basically round plates, and are best known as the type included in William IV's dessert service

18. G.A. Godden, *Coalport and Coalbrookdale Porcelains*, London, 1970, Plates 138 and 139.

71. DISH, CENTREPIECE AND TUREEN WITH STAND, *c.*1826–30. Porcelain, from a dessert service of *shell and gadroon* moulding, with an apple-green border and flower sprays in reserves. The accompanying plates with red griffins, mark 52, and pattern number 465. Height of centrepiece 18 cm (7.1 in). *Courtesy of Sotheby's.* *See page 126*

72. PLATE (*left*), *c.*1826–30. Porcelain, *shell and gadroon* border, matt over-glaze blue ground with unnamed botanical study.
Red griffin, mark 52, and pattern number 511. Diameter 24.5 cm (9.6 in).
See page 126
PLATE (*right*), *c.*1826–30. Porcelain, *acanthus-leaf, shell and gadroon* moulding. Rose-pink ground and enamelled view, named on reverse, *Byland Abbey*. Red griffin, mark 52. Diameter 24.1 cm (9.5 in). *See page 126*

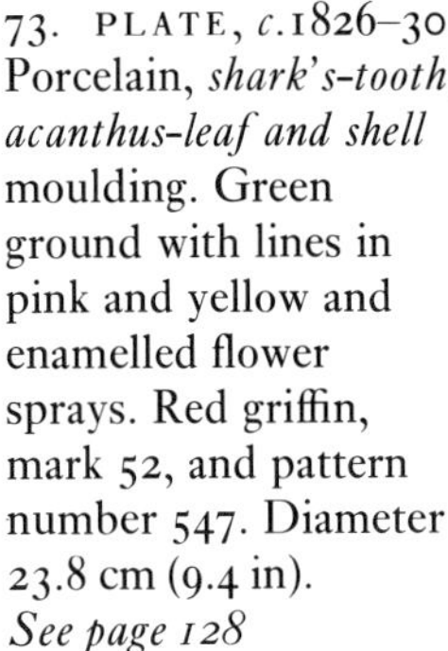

73. PLATE, *c.*1826–30. Porcelain, *shark's-tooth, acanthus-leaf and shell* moulding. Green ground with lines in pink and yellow and enamelled flower sprays. Red griffin, mark 52, and pattern number 547. Diameter 23.8 cm (9.4 in).
See page 128

(Colour Plate D). Plates with this border may be marked with the red or puce griffin and the decoration is often very fine. Circular, oval, shell-shaped and square dishes are found with this moulding, and tureens, covers and stands, rounded in form, the tureens with heavy rustic handles and oak and acorns moulded in high relief. The latter items are comparatively rare survivors from any dessert service.

Similar are the uncommon plates with *shark's-tooth, acanthus-leaf and shell* borders (Plate 73) which also occur with either the red or puce griffin mark. The matching dishes are of the same shapes as those described immediately above, but with this variant of the moulding. Tureens have not been recorded. It is worth noting that very often the shapes of items in services might be 'mixed', possibly at the customer's request.

Dessert shapes which follow natural forms are rare. The best-known design has plates with borders moulded as a wide band of overlapping and realistic *primrose leaves*, left white (Plate 74), or coloured, for example, in two shades of grey. Usually the plate centres are enamelled with flowers. The comports and tureens are composed entirely of moulded leaves with plain reserves at the sides for painted decoration (Plate 74). They have been recorded with both the red and puce griffin marks.

Equally rare is a border consisting of small, elaborately moulded *flower heads and leaves* in a wide continuous band. Illustrated (Plate 75) is a very fine plate with a green ground and charming figure study *The Broken Pitcher*, probably the work of George Speight. A tureen with this moulding in the Newmane Collection is of unusual angular form, with a claret ground colour and flower paintings in reserves. It has a distinctive acorn finial.

74. PLATE, *c.*1826–30. Porcelain, *primrose-leaf* moulding, the centre with a flower group on a buff ground. Red griffin, mark 52. Diameter 24.8 cm (9.8 in). *Private Collection.* *See page 128*

TUREEN, COVER AND STAND, *c.*1826–30. Porcelain, *primrose-leaf* moulding with enamelled flower sprays. No mark. Height 27.9 cm (11 in). *Sheffield City Museum.* *See page 128*

75. PLATE, *c.*1826–30. Porcelain, *flower-head and leaf* moulding. Green ground and richly gilded border, the centre with a figure study named on the reverse *The Broken Pitcher*, probably by George Speight. Red griffin, mark 52. Diameter 24.8 cm (9.8 in) *Courtesy of Christie's.* *See page 128*

76. PLATE (*left*), *c*.1830–42. Porcelain, *C-scroll* moulding, enamelled with a poppy on a grey ground. Puce griffin, mark 55, and pattern number 750. Diameter 23.2 cm (9.1 in). *See page 130*
PLATE (*right*), *c*.1830–42. Porcelain, *C-scroll* moulding, the light-green border overlaid with a gilt scale pattern. Enamelled crest of the Harcourt family and motto '*Le Bon Temps Viendra*'. Puce griffin, mark 55. Diameter 23.2 cm (9.1 in).
Ex Llewellyn Collection. *See page 130*

An unfortunate characteristic of red-period dessert wares—and teawares also—is that they tend to suffer badly from strain cracks, caused partly by the thick sections of some of the wares, especially near footrings.

Only three plate mouldings appear to belong exclusively to the puce griffin period, 1830–42. One is the very commonly found *C-scroll* border (Plate 76) used extensively during the eighteenth century at Sèvres, in which the plate edges are slightly lobed to follow the line of the scrolls. This moulding is not unique to Rockingham amongst the English porcelain manufactories, as a similar version was in use at Derby, for example, and unmarked pieces should be regarded with caution. The tureens accompanying these services are oval, with rustic handles and moulded oak and acorns, but are rarely seen. The dish forms are illustrated in Plate 77.

A second type, rarely found, follows the same basic *lobed* shape, but without the raised C-scrolls. The example shown (Plate 78) is finely enamelled with an ornithological study and has the same raised lattice gilding as does the royal dessert service.

In the later years of the puce griffin period, comports and tureens of different shapes from those described above were supplied with C-scroll plates. Those of the type illustrated (Plate 79) were often finely decorated, but another version with a strawberry finial to the tureen is rarely of the quality of the earlier productions, and decoration tended to comprise coloured-over transferred flower sprays. They appear to be authentic Brameld products, not pieces bought in from elsewhere, but they represent the declining standards of the later years.

77. PLATES AND DISHES, *c.*1830–42. Porcelain, *C-scroll* moulding, enamelled with colourful birds in the style of John Randall. Puce griffins, mark 55, and pattern number 700. Diameter of plates 22.9 cm (9 in). *Courtesy of Christie's. See page 130*

78. PLATE, *c.*1830–42. Porcelain, *lobed* edge. Raised-gilt lattice border and enamelled ornithological study, named on reverse *The Green Toucan*. Puce griffin, mark 55. Diameter 23.5 cm (9.3 in). *Courtesy of Christie's. See page 130*

79. TUREEN, COVER AND STAND, *c.*1835–42. Porcelain, late rococo shape. Transfer-printed with grey floral design, gilded and with enamelled landscapes. No mark. Height 19.4 cm (7.6 in). *See page 130*

Another extremely rare moulding, *rococo scrolled-leaf* with trailing tendrils extending into the border of the plates is illustrated (Plate 80). This exceptionally fine piece is enamelled with a named bird subject *Bernicle Goose* (*sic*). Only puce-marked examples are known; the matching dishes and tureens have not been recorded.

The forms of decoration on dessert wares of the post-1830 period are many and varied. The neo-rococo style was pre-eminent at this time, and the plain, coloured borders were giving way to elaborate feathery scrolls together with fine floral and leafy traceries in gilt, which sometimes ignored the moulded detail altogether. Coloured scrolls or panels of irregular shape, often in grey or in pastel colours, were favoured. Painted landscapes, flowers and other subjects now tended to be fanciful rather than realistic, and enclosed by delicate scrolling rather than a solid gilt band. Applied sea-shell motifs in lilac-coloured paste were also used after 1830 on dessert and teawares.

With any dessert service, ice pails could be ordered as separate items. An invoice sent to Wentworth House on 13 October 1838 includes:

2 China Ice Pails £13.13.0

evidently splendid specimens in view of their cost. A plain ice pail with simple gilt decoration, perhaps more suited to a dinner service, is in the collections of the Rotherham Museum and has unusual lion-head and -paw handles.

One reason why occasional rarities or unusually shaped wares are found is that from time to time the Bramelds undertook special commissions. A very expensive service supplied to Wentworth House on 16 April 1831 illustrates this point and underlines the importance of the Fitzwilliam family's patronage to the Pottery—this particular service was ordered by Lord Milton:

To one China Diſsart Service got up to patterns consisting of 72 Plates 20 Comports & 4 Ice pails including the taking disigns for same	£295. 4.8

Similarly, the Bramelds might on occasion match existing services if required, as on 8 August 1829:

To 3 China Compotiers to match Chelsea	£2. 6.6
towards Expenses Modelling, Moulds making &c	3.12.0

The moulds for such items might well be used again and the piece griffin-marked as though it were a normal production.

Unmarked wares of undoubted Swinton origin are sometimes found with untypical decoration and this may often be explained by the sale of wares in the white to independent decorating establishments. The plate illustrated (Plate 81) has an unmistakable Rockingham moulding—compare with Plate 72—but it bears the name of the Worcester decorators Doe and Rogers. The gilding with its raised jewelling is out of character with that normally used at Swinton.

80. PLATE, *c.*1835–42. Porcelain, *rococo scrolled-leaf* moulding, enamelled with flower sprays and an ornithological study of *Bernicle Goose (sic)* named on the reverse. Puce griffin, mark 55. Diameter 24.1 cm (9.5 in). *Courtesy of Christie's.* *See page 132*

81. PLATE, *c.*1827–30. Porcelain, *acanthus-leaf, shell and gadroon* moulding. Overglaze matt-blue ground, burnished and jewelled gilding and an enamelled view of *York*, named on the reverse. Rockingham porcelain, externally decorated. From the print *South West View of the City of York* drawn by G. F. Gibson, engraved by W. Woolner, published 24 June 1827. Mark *Doe & Rogers/ 17 High St/ Worcester* in red script. Diameter 25.8 cm (10.2 in). *See page 132*

The Royal Dessert Service

Perhaps the most notable achievement of the Rockingham Works is the remarkable dessert service prepared for William IV and ordered in 1830, when the king ascended the throne.[19] Services were also commissioned at this time from the Worcester factory and from Davenport's, among others, but the Bramelds as relative newcomers on the porcelain scene seem to have determined to outshine their rivals in producing a service of extraordinary richness and unusual design.

Jewitt possessed the sketches for this service entitled 'Original Designs for His Majesty's Dessert, 12th Nov., 1830, per J. W. B.' (John Wager Brameld), and twelve specimen plates were duly submitted to the king.[20] Many of these plates still exist in private and public collections, all having the royal arms in the centre, but with different borders, some with rich ground colours such as pink, orange, red and green, overlaid with tooled gilding, others naturalistically painted.[21] The king chose a light matt-blue ground—described at the time as 'Brunswick blue'—enriched with a lattice-work of raised gilt with the oak-and-acorn motifs which had been his own suggestion. There is an inner border with red and white roses, thistles, shamrocks and leeks which, like the royal arms in the centre, are painted in minute detail (Colour Plate D).

The designs for the comports were also presumably submitted for the king's approval, and work on the service was well in hand by 1832, since many of the plates are so dated. On 14 April of that year, the *Yorkshire Gazette* reported:

> Swinton Pottery—At this very extensive establishment a dessert service value 3,000 guineas, is being prepared for the King. We understand the articles are of the most excellent workmanship, under the direction of the following artists, The Royal Arms by Mr Speight, jun, the flowers and ornaments by Messrs Bretnell, Bayley, Pedley, &c., modeller Mr Griffin.

Jewitt gave the value of the service as £5,000, and indeed it seems that the Bramelds entirely underestimated both the cost and the time it would take to complete the work.[22] In fact, its production did much to undermine their already precarious finances, and by September 1832 they were having to borrow money from Earl Fitzwilliam to pay their workmen's wages (see Appendix III).

It was some time shortly before May 1837 that the service was finally ready, packed into specially made mahogany boxes and sent off to London with,

19. For a detailed description see A. and A. Cox, 'The Rockingham Dessert Service for William IV', *Connoisseur*, Vol. 188, No. 756, 1975, pp. 90–7.
20. L. Jewitt, op. cit., Vol. 1, pp. 505 and 514.
21. Two specimen plates were donated to the Victoria and Albert Museum by the 5th Earl Fitzwilliam, one with a blue border, the other green. D. G. Rice, *The Illustrated Guide to Rockingham Pottery and Porcelain*, London, 1971, illustrates three other specimen plates as Colour Plates IV, V and VI.
22. L. Jewitt, op. cit., Vol. 1, p. 513.

tradition has it, a mounted escort.[23] Almost as soon as it was delivered, the long-suffering William IV was prevailed upon to lend it back to the Bramelds for public exhibition at their London showroom, The Griffin, Piccadilly, and the service was still there when the king died on 20 June 1837. Jewitt states that it was first used at Queen Victoria's coronation.[24]

The service undoubtedly created much interest. The *York Courant* for 13 July 1837 describes it as:

> A porcelain dessert service of the most magnificent and unique design, and surpassing in splendour any specimen in this branch of art ever before the public.... It was manufactured by order of his late Majesty, who a short time before his lamented demise, inspected and expressed his admiration of it.... It has also excited the attention and admiration of artists and amateurs, as well as of other persons of all ranks in society, particularly the higher classes.

John Timbs in his *Curiosities of London* recorded the exhibition of the service and the admiration it received.[25] The designs may now appear over-elaborate, but Jewitt, writing in the 1870s, when ornate pieces were still popular, described the service as 'truly gorgeous', and 'one of the finest produced in this or any other country'.[26]

When seen as a whole, the service is indeed quite magnificent and is still used, largely for display on state occasions. When supplied it consisted of 144 plates and 56 principal pieces, of which 119 plates and 54 main items now remain. The plates were only considered acceptable if absolutely perfect and several unfinished examples are known, rejected at an early stage because of some minor blemish.

The main pieces of the royal service, designed by Thomas Brameld,[27] were certainly most unusual and are illustrated in Colour Plate E and Plates 82, 83 and 84. They include four 'double' and eight 'triple dress plates' for pastries, eight 'grand baskets' for fruit with stems modelled as realistic oak branches supporting an open basket, and also for fruit four 'mulberry baskets', the stems formed of mulberry leaves and fruit. Among the most impressive are the four very accurately modelled 'pine baskets' and the eight 'tropical comports' with stems of sugar cane supporting a wreath of exotic fruit, each named beneath the rim. There are four 'single dress plates' formed of wheatsheaf stems supporting a pierced basket, and four unusual 'shell comports' for conserves. Perhaps most impressive of all are the eight 'ice cellars' very ornately gilded and enamelled, the stems of holly and berries, modelled from nature.[28]

23. One such box lettered 'PEACH BOWL' survives in a private collection.
24. L. Jewitt, op. cit., Vol. 1, p. 514.
25. J. Timbs, *Curiosities of London*, 1855, p. 606.
26. L. Jewitt, op. cit., Vol. 1, p. 513.
27. Ibid., p. 513. This apparently contradicts Jewitt's previous statement (Vol. 1, p. 505) where he noted that the original sketches were 'per J. W. B.' i.e. John Wager Brameld.
28. The names of the pieces are those which occur in the contemporary description of this service in the *York Courant* for 13 July 1837.

82. COMPORTS FROM THE ROCKINGHAM ROYAL DESSERT SERVICE, *c.*1830–7. DOUBLE AND TRIPLE DRESS PLATES. Enamelled with figures and landscapes, richly gilded and encrusted with applied 'Dresden' flowers. Both with elaborate royal griffin mark 56. Height of triple dress plate 62.2 cm (24.5 in). *Reproduced by gracious permission of Her Majesty the Queen.* *See page 135*

The bases of all the comports are decorated with two named views, often chosen to suit the purpose of the piece, for example, the 'tropical comports' have colonial scenes such as *Mausoleum of Safter Jung, Delhi* and *Spring Garden Estate, St. George's Jamaica*; the 'shell comports' seascapes; and the 'ice cellars' snow scenes. Others have English views, for example, *Rydal Water, near Ivy Cottage, Westmorland* on a 'triple dress plate', or country seats of the gentry, castles and other buildings such as *Haddon Hall, Derbyshire.* The 'single dress plates' are painted in the centres with groups of roses, thistles, shamrocks and leeks, and many items are encrusted with 'Dresden' flowers, some gilded, others naturally coloured.[29]

Even before the king's service was completed, its reputation was already considerable, bringing expensive orders from the nobility. On 23 October 1830, the Duchess of Cumberland ordered a 54-piece service similar to the king's, the plates to be enamelled with sea and landscapes, birds, shells and fruit instead of arms, but the comports were to be identical and 'to be shewn to her as they are prepared in turns for the King to see'.[30] In November 1833 the Duke of Sussex gave a liberal order, and commissions were received from the Duke of Sutherland, the Duke of Cambridge, and the King of the Belgians.[31] One wonders whether any of these elaborate services were realistically costed by the Bramelds, the price quoted to the Duchess of Cumberland, for example, being 250 guineas.

29. The Bramelds' term for applied leaf-and-flower decoration.

30. L. Jewitt, op. cit., Vol. 1, p.504.

31. This service is apparently no longer in the Belgian royal household. We are indebted to Monsieur C. De Valkeneer, Conseiller au Cabinet du Roi, for providing this information.

D. ROYAL DESSERT PLATE, 1832. Porcelain, finely enamelled with the arms of William IV and with raised and tooled gilding. Marked with an elaborate royal griffin (mark 56) and dated 1832 in gilt. Diameter 23.4 cm (9.2 in). *Reproduced by gracious permission of Her Majesty the Queen.* *See pages 128 and 134*

E. ROYAL WINE COOLER, *c.*1830–7. Porcelain, from William IV's dessert service. Enamelled and richly gilt. Marked with an elaborate royal griffin (mark 56). Height 37.6 cm (14.8 in). *Reproduced by gracious permission of Her Majesty the Queen.* *See page 135*

83. COMPORTS FROM THE ROCKINGHAM ROYAL DESSERT SERVICE, *c.*1830–7. MULBERRY BASKET (*left*). The stem moulded with fruit and leaves. The enamelled landscape on the base depicts *Pembroke*. GRAND BASKET (*centre*). Supported on a gnarled oak branch, with applied flowers beneath the rim. In the centre is a stand formed of the leaves and fruit of the guava. The enamelled scene on the base named *Lyme Regis, from the Sidmouth Road, Devon*. PINE BASKET (*right*). The modelled pineapple shows an extraordinary degree of realism. The landscape on the foot named *Inverary Castle, & Dun-y-quaich*. All pieces with elaborate royal griffin mark 56. Height of pineapple comport 26.7 cm (10.5 in). *Reproduced by gracious permission of Her Majesty the Queen.* *See page 135*

84. COMPORTS FROM THE ROCKINGHAM ROYAL DESSERT SERVICE, *c.*1830–7. SHELL COMPORT (*left*). Modelled as a limpet shell supported on a stem of red coral. The views on the base are seascapes, the example shown entitled *A Breeze*. TROPICAL COMPORT (*centre*). The border of the stand formed of carefully modelled tropical fruit, each named in script beneath the rim, the stem formed of twisted sugar cane. The scene on the foot is named *Matlock High Tor, Derbyshire*. SINGLE DRESS PLATE (*right*). The stem formed as a wheatsheaf entwined with pink convolvulus. The open basket painted with Union flowers in the centre, the landscape on the base named *Bamborough Castle, Northumberland*.
All pieces with the elaborate royal griffin mark 56. Height of single dress plate 22.9 cm (9 in)
Reproduced by gracious permission of Her Majesty the Queen. *See pages 135 and 202*

Orders were also given by Queen Adelaide, albeit of a modest kind, items having been recorded from a breakfast service of basket-weave moulding, and dinner plates with C-scrolled borders, all decorated quite simply with a gilt dentil edge and a crowned AR monogram.[32]

The prestige of producing a service for the king was considerable. However, it cost the Bramelds too much and took them too long to prepare, but they had the satisfaction of the undoubted impression which it created and it earned them the right to incorporate the words 'Manufacturer to the King' in their factory mark. In many circles Rockingham porcelain had now become the fashionable ware to own.

Teawares

Until comparatively recently, almost any unmarked tea service in the neo-rococo style was attributed to Rockingham, in the mistaken belief that the factory's wares were usually unmarked. In fact quite the reverse is true, particularly after 1830 following royal patronage when the griffin mark was used with confidence, and perhaps a certain pride. Thomas Brameld claimed, not entirely without prejudice, that 'at Piccadilly we could always sell our own Tea, B[rea]kfast & Dessert China much more readily than that we had from 4 or 5 other Manufactories.'[33]

A tea and coffee service typically consisted of twelve tea cups, twelve coffee cups and twelve saucers, a teapot, cover and stand, a covered sugar, cream jug, slop bowl and two bread-and-butter plates. Side plates occur but rarely, although small 'cup plates' were available in all the standard teaware shapes. Services could be made up to suit the customer's requirements, and might be ordered without coffee cups, or with tea cups and saucers only, for use with a silver teapot, jug and sugar bowl. The following service, with no coffee cups, was supplied to Wentworth House on 28 July 1832:

1 China Royal Tea Sett 33 pieces Nr 766
with Dresden T Pot Sugar & Cream £7.4.8

The red or puce griffin mark normally occurs on saucers only—and not always on all the saucers in a service. Completely unmarked sets do occur, but are uncommon. Generally a pattern number was painted on all pieces, but again exceptions do occur.

Teawares are described below, although one cannot be dogmatic about the matching of cups and saucers, or indeed the shapes of main pieces associated with a given cup and saucer, as they may vary, resulting in some unusual

32. A breakfast cup and saucer is in the collection of the Sheffield City Museum. *The Royal Kalendar* includes the Bramelds as suppliers to the queen's household in 1832. See J. G. and M. I. N. Evans, 'More About Rockingham Teawares', *Antique Collecting*, Vol. 14, No. 11, 1980, pp. 28–30.

33. Wentworth Woodhouse Muniments, G 47/18, dated 29 November 1842.

85. Part TEA AND COFFEE SERVICE, *c.*1830–42. Porcelain, *figure-seven handle.* Transfer-printed in blue with Llandeg's blackberry pattern. Puce griffins, mark 55, and pattern number 802. Height of teapot on stand 16 cm (6.3 in). *See pages 139, 140 and 207*

combinations. Pairings made at a later date are generally obvious.

The red-griffin period teawares, 1826–30, show the same characteristics of decoration as are found on contemporary dessert wares, with the use of rich ground colours which may be further ornamented. Sometimes bold colour combinations were used, such as deep-blue and apricot, or pink and green, to give striking effects. The subject matter of the enamelling is also similar; named views on teawares, however, are very rare. Landscapes and romantic scenes in autumnal colours are often enclosed in round or square gilt surrounds (Plate 90). Flower groups too were very popular.

The gilding may be quite intricate and is sometimes in a band low down inside a deep coffee cup, which must have been extraordinarily difficult to execute. Enamelled decoration is usually more profuse within cups, and hence was lost to view when they were in use, but was most impressive in a display cabinet. On red-period wares, the outsides of cups are normally decorated with a plain ground colour, or a continuous band of gilt leaves and tendrils, or other simple devices.

Less expensive wares were decorated with plain bands of gilt (Plate 88), and were popular, to judge by the numbers surviving today. Transfer-printed services also appealed to the less wealthy (Plate 85), and include flower designs and some charming chinoiseries.

Even when unmarked, Rockingham teawares may be recognized by their characteristic shapes or handle-forms as described below. Although some were introduced in the red-griffin period, they all continued in use later and thus

86. Part TEA SERVICE, *c.*1826–42. Porcelain, *square handle*. Blue ground with apricot-coloured leaf decoration. Marks not known, pattern number 612. Height of teapot on stand 17.3 cm (6.8 in). *Courtesy of Henry Spencer and Sons, Retford.*

may also be found with the puce mark. Examples of the more unusual cup shapes are shown in Plate 96.

The *figure-seven handle* is probably the earliest Rockingham teaware shape (Plate 85); it occurs on a documentary cup dated 1826 decorated with painted butterflies (page 120). The cups have bell-shaped bodies with handles resembling a curved figure seven, and occur with plain, round saucers with a deep well and correspondingly deep footring. This is one of the few handle shapes which is not unique to Swinton, but was used in slightly different forms at several contemporary factories—for example, Davenport, Coalport and Spode.[34] During the puce period, a plain circular saucer with no well commonly accompanied cups with this handle. The usual cup shape has a slight ridge around the body approximately where the lower part of the handle joins. A rare variant is known, apparently introduced after 1830, which lacks this ridge and the cup is somewhat less flared (Plate 96).

The teapot and sucrier which accompany cups with this handle are circular in section with no moulded detail, but they have a pronounced shoulder and a dome-shaped finial (Plate 85). The cream jug is of similar form with a bridge over the lip.

Teawares with a *square handle* are very similar to a design used by Ridgway's with the same fluted body form and slightly scalloped rims to the cups.[35] The teapot and sugar (Plate 86) have a shoulder of angular form, and covers with upright, stylized flower-bud finials, whilst the matching sugar has two small

34. M. Berthoud, *H. & R. Daniel 1822–1846*, Wingham, 1980, Plate 134, where several contemporary versions of this handle are shown.

35. G. A. Godden, *The Illustrated Guide to Ridgway Porcelains*, London, 1972, Plate 55 and Colour Plate IV.

87. TEA CUP AND SAUCER, *c.*1837–42. Porcelain, primrose-leaf moulding with Queen Victoria's monogram surrounded by a wreath of Union flowers. Puce griffin, mark 55. Dimensions not known. *Courtesy of Christie's.* *See pages 70 and 142*

88. Part TEA AND COFFEE SERVICE, *c.*1826–30. Porcelain, *crossed rustic handle.* Primrose-leaf mouldings with gilt borders. This service includes cup plates, one shown under the coffee cup. Red griffins, mark 52, and pattern number 655. Height of teapot on stand 20.4 cm (8 in). *See pages 139 and 142*

handles moulded as shells on projecting supports. The clearest distinction between the products of the two factories is in the saucers, the Rockingham examples having an exceptionally deep footring. Unlike the Rockingham versions, the Ridgway matching creamers do not have a bridged spout. The coffee cup handles tend to be set high up on the Ridgway pieces and low down on the Rockingham ones. Pattern numbers if present are a useful guide (page 230); the Ridgway services with this handle will normally have a high fractional pattern number.

The foregoing are the most frequently seen red-period shapes; the following are uncommon.

The *crossed rustic handle* is associated with cups formed of moulded, overlapping primrose leaves and saucers with a similar band of leaves around the border (Plate 87). The main pieces of these services, now extremely rare, are among the most curious designs which the Bramelds ever produced (Plate 88). Generally, the decoration is of simple dentil gilding, but examples are known where the moulded leaves are coloured, as in pattern 873, with two shades of green.

Equally rare and entirely different in concept are the *French Empire* style pieces (Plate 89), which are relatively simple and classical in form. The cups are waisted beneath the rim, and the handles formed as a horse's tail which becomes a hoof and leg at its lower end. The saucers are plain and circular with a deep footring. The teapot and jug with their phoenix spouts are particularly striking. They are usually described as French shapes, but the immediate inspiration may have come from Derby, as teaware pattern 684 in the Rockingham Pattern Book (see page 230) seen by the authors is described 'Gold hoops to match French cups sent by Cocker from Derby', a pattern well known on this Rockingham shape. Occasionally, Empire pieces are elaborately decorated, but the more usual plain gilt bands seem more appropriate to the style. Very rarely, this shape occurs with the crossed rustic handle.

Round fluted cups and saucers occur in conjunction with the square handle, the saucers being deep, without a well, and may be marked with either the red or the puce griffin. A cup of this type is shown in Plate 96. The main pieces to such services are extremely rare; the only item known to the authors is a red-period baluster-shaped covered sugar with a splayed circular foot and the flower finial used on teapots and sugars associated with the square handle. It is 14.3 cm (5.6 in) in height and is decorated with pattern 653—an apricot and blue ground overlaid with gilt leaf and pendant-drop motifs.

Rarely, round fluted cups have a simple rustic-loop handle (Plate 96), as occurs on teawares with the basket-weave moulding. Applied lilac-coloured shells and paterae may decorate such pieces.

Bucket-shaped cups with straight sides tapering towards the base have the figure-seven handle and plain circular saucers with a deep well (Plate 90). They may bear the red or puce griffin mark and are rare. No main pieces to match this cup shape have been recorded.

89. Part TEA AND COFFEE SERVICE, *c.*1826–30. Porcelain, *French Empire* style. Plain white porcelain, gilded. Red griffins, mark 52, and pattern number 680. Height of teapot 18.9 cm (7.4 in). *See page 142*

90. TEA CUP, COFFEE CUP AND SAUCER, *c.*1830–5. Porcelain, *bucket shape*. Green ground with wide gilt bands and landscape decoration on cups. Puce griffin, mark 55, and pattern number 714. Diameter of saucer 15.2 cm (6 in). *Sheffield City Museum.* *See pages 139 and 142*

The new Rockingham teawares of neo-rococo type which were introduced during the puce griffin period, 1830–42, are of very different appearance. Shapes were now more curving, with scrolled and leafy mouldings, the decoration became lighter, the rich ground colours and gilding giving way to delicate traceried patterns in abundance.

However, Rockingham shapes are restrained in comparison with those of some of their contemporaries, which can be ungainly and overdecorated. The Rockingham handle forms are eminently practical, unlike certain of the clumsy

91. Part TEA AND COFFEE SERVICE, *c.*1830–42. Porcelain, *basket-weave* moulding. Green and yellow ground with enamelled flower groups. The saucers with puce griffins, mark 55, and pattern number 832. Height of teapot on stand 18.0 cm (7.1 in). *Yorkshire Museum, York.* *See page 144*

and awkward scissor-bow types favoured, for example, by Daniel, Spode and Coalport.

The quality of decoration is often superb, with great attention to detail—for instance in the application of gilded motifs—even on relatively simple wares. At the same time, some Rockingham tea services were sparsely and somewhat unimaginatively decorated, pattern 1170 being a case in point, with its meagre grey C-scrolls and gilding. However, cost was always the governing factor, and a plain pattern brought a Rockingham service within the reach of those unable to afford the more splendid productions. Grey in fact was to prove immensely popular on tablewares during this period and innumerable services were decorated with this colour in a wide variety of patterns.

It is probably worth restating at this point that all teaware shapes introduced before 1830 continued in production during the puce griffin period, although the revived rococo forms were doubtless more fashionable.

Possibly the first of the new puce griffin teawares are those characterized by a *basket-weave* moulding on the outside of cups and the underside of saucers. There are centrally-placed reserves on either side of the cups and the handle is a simple rustic loop. The rims of the cups and saucers are scalloped. Often the style of decoration relates more to the red than to the puce period, with rich ground colours such as claret, green and blue (Plate 148). The teapot, sugar and cream-jug shapes (Plate 91) are the same as those in the three-spur services (see below), but with rustic handles, a crabstock spout to the teapot and rustic loop finials to the covers, although examples also occur with the crown finials normally associated with the three-spur handle.

F. TEAPOT AND STAND, *c*.1830–42. Porcelain, three-spur handle, with matt overglaze-blue decoration and gilding. Accompanying saucers with puce griffins (mark 55). Pattern number 2/75. Height 19 cm (7.5 in). *See page 145*

G. URN-SHAPED VASE, *c.*1826–30. Porcelain, enamelled with flowers, probably by the artist John Creswell, and gilded. Red griffin (mark 52) and Cl 12 in gilt. Height 26.7 cm (10.5 in). *Sheffield City Museum.* *See page 158*

92. Part TEA AND COFFEE SERVICE, *c.*1830–42. Porcelain, *three-spur handle.* Enamelled green sprigs and gilding. Puce griffins, mark 55, and pattern number 1309. Height of teapot on stand 19.2 cm (7.6 in). *See pages 144–5*

93. Part TEA SERVICE, *c.*1830–42. Porcelain, *rustic single-spur handle.* Applied lilac shells and gilt bands. From a service with puce griffins, mark 55, and pattern number 591. Height of teapot 17.5 cm (6.9 in). *Sheffield City Museum.* *See page 146*

Probably the most common Rockingham teaware shape is that with the instantly recognizable *three-spur handle*, both cups and saucers having moulded C-scroll decoration around the edges. The teapots and sugars (Plate 92) have bulbous, low-bellied bodies standing on four small scrolled feet. The teapot spouts are moulded with acanthus leaves at the base usually picked out in gilt, and the covers surmounted by a very distinctive crown finial, presumably in recognition of royal patronage (see Colour Plate F). The cream

94. TEAWARES, *c.*1838–42. Porcelain, *single-spur handle*. Teapot with grey ground overlaid with seaweed gilding. No mark, pattern number 1139. Height 19.4 cm (7.6 in). Sucrier with dark-blue stylized leaves and transfer-printed flower sprays coloured with enamels and gilded. No mark, pattern number 1476. Tea cup and saucer with grey 'bulrush' decoration. Puce griffin, mark 55, and pattern number 1423. *See page 146*

jugs occur in two forms, a small, squat, sparrow-beak type, and a taller helmet-shaped version. The full range of neo-rococo decoration may be found on these wares.

Extremely rare is the *rustic single-spur handle* shape consisting, as its name implies, of a looped, gnarled twig with a pronounced vertical spur. Cups with this handle are flared at the lip and have a sharp ridge slightly below the point where the lower part of the handle joins the cup (Plate 96). The teapot and covered sugar (Plate 93) also have rustic handles and large star-shaped flower finials to the covers.

Perhaps the latest of the Rockingham teaware shapes are those with the *single-spur handle*. The tall teapot (Plate 94) is somewhat ungainly in form, with its solid heavy base consisting of rococo scrolls, and the decoration is often less fine than on the earlier wares. The handles on all the main pieces and cups have a flattened, projecting thumbpiece and are unique to the Rockingham factory. The finial to the covers is a flower bud positioned on its side accompanied by leaves and normally gilded. A suggestion that these shapes were bought in from elsewhere for decoration is untenable in view of the discovery of deformed wasters of this shape on the Swinton site (sherds in the Sheffield City Museum), and analysis of the porcelain body shows it to be of the usual Rockingham composition.[36] More convincing, however, and of great importance, is the fact that the saucer shape which invariably accompanies cups with the single-spur handle appears in the factory's Pattern Books. Illustrated (Plate 95) is a page from a Rockingham Pattern Book, which we have been permitted to examine, where teaware pattern 1441 is shown

36. A. Cox, op. cit. (see footnote 3 above). See also Appendix VII.

95. PAGE FROM A ROCKINGHAM PATTERN BOOK, *c.*1838–42. This shows a saucer decorated with pattern 1441 and directions for the artist. These patterns are finely painted in watercolours. *See pages 146–8*

consisting of three brightly coloured birds amongst branches. The outer border of the saucer is clearly delineated and leaves no doubt that it is of the single-spur type. The directions written beside the drawing—which is in watercolour—reads '2 Birds in Cup/3. Saucer', and beside the leafy motif in the lower left is annotated '2 Sprigs Outside Cup'. Interestingly, the handle shown on the lower right is of the three-spur variety, and although as previously stated various unusual combinations of cups and saucers do occur, no example is known to the authors of a cup with a three-spur handle being paired with a saucer from a single-spur service.[37]

The high pattern numbers which feature so regularly on single-spur teawares signify their late date of manufacture, and although standards did decline towards the end of the factory's life, some remarkably fine services of this shape were, nevertheless, still produced.

Certain other teawares have been recorded, but so infrequently that they may not have been standard Rockingham productions. The explanation may be the matching of a service from another factory, or even of wares bought in for decoration when stocks of biscuit porcelain were low and urgent orders had to be met.

For example, teawares of the shape traditionally termed 'London' are known from both the red and puce griffin periods, enamelled and gilded, or transfer-printed, one piece with the *Broseley* pattern in blue (Plate 96). Similarly, cups and saucers of unusual size occur, smaller than the standard products, yet larger than miniatures. One of the most curious of all is a complete service in private possession of unmistakable H. & R. Daniel forms and style of decoration, and yet with the saucers all clearly marked with authentic puce griffins.[38] Such unusual pieces are, however, rarely encountered.

The standard teaware shapes may also be found in the form of breakfast services with the same mouldings, but with considerably larger cups and saucers. Coffee cups in breakfast services are uncommon, although they are listed in an invoice to Earl Fitzwilliam dated 8 August 1829:

To China Breakfast Service, Royal Plants and
Flies consisting of
24 Pairs Bowls & Saucers, 24 Pairs Breakfasts
24 Pairs Breakfast Coffees & Saucers
8 Muffins—8 Dishes, 6 Butter Tubs fixed St[s]
2 Honey Pots fixed St[s] 4 Slop Bowls extra large
12 Milk Jugs diff[t] Sizes, 2 Coverd Do
24 Egg Cups fixed Stands, 6 Sugar Bowls & Covers
1 Roll Tray large, 6 Breakfast Bowls without handles
6 Dejenue Creams.—72 Plates £162.3.0

No tea or coffee pots were provided with this service, perhaps because metal urns were more suitable for the requirements of a large household. A plate from a breakfast service almost certainly of the same pattern as that described in the invoice is shown in Plate 97. In addition to the items mentioned above, toast racks also occur—a puce-marked example from a service made for the Earl of Radnor is in the Rotherham Museum.

37. We express our grateful thanks to the owner of this Pattern Book for most kindly providing the photograph reproduced here.
38. For the shapes see M. Berthoud, op. cit., Plate 51, 2nd Gadroon shape, *c.* 1826–36.

96. SELECTED ROCKINGHAM TEA CUPS, *c.*1826–42. *Top row, left to right:* the *figure-seven handle* cup shape (Height 5.4 cm (2.1 in)); a variant of this cup form; a *round fluted* cup with a square handle. *Bottom row, left to right*: 'London' shape cup; the *rustic single-spur* type; *round fluted* cup with a rustic-loop handle. With the exception of the cup shown top left, these are relatively rare examples. All accompanying saucers are griffin marked. *See pages 140–8*

97. PLATE, *c.*1826–30. Porcelain, from a breakfast service, enamelled with butterflies and a botanical study named on reverse *Mirabilis Jalapa*. Red griffin, mark 52. Diameter 21.1 cm (8.3 in). *See page 148*

Cabaret, or 'dejenue' services as the Bramelds called them, were made at the Rockingham Works. One such service is described in an invoice for 20 September 1829:

To 1 Dejenue China Service consisting of a Tray 1 Pair Cups & Sr 1 Pair Coffee & Saucers 1 Tea Pot 1 Sugar 1 Cream & 1 Slop Bowl	£8.9.0

These were often exquisitely decorated, as the example supplied to Wentworth House on 8 August 1829:

1 Dejenue Tray with Birds and
Landscapes Miss Fitzwilliam £11.11.0

The price indicates that this must have been an extremely fine piece. A cabaret set in Rotherham Museum has the basket-weave moulding and is decorated with roses and all-over 'seaweed' gilding. The cups are of normal size, the teapot, sugar and cream jug smaller than standard productions.

8
Rockingham Decorative Porcelain

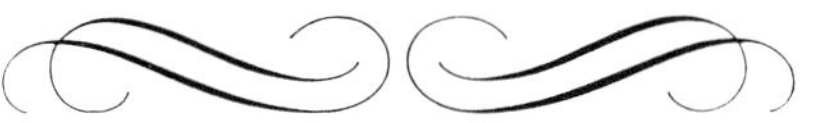

Much adverse criticism has been directed against Rockingham decorative porcelain in particular, and as a result it has acquired an undeservedly bad reputation over the years. In several earlier general works on ceramics one may read of its poor shapes, overloaded with applied decoration, and epitomizing the worst in nineteenth-century taste. In all such points of criticism there is often an element of truth and a degree of exaggeration. One must remember that during the 1820s the emerging style of the period was to be reflected in highly decorated neo-rococo wares, and the Bramelds, like any others in a strictly competitive business, reacted to popular demands. Contemporary accounts of those most ornate of Rockingham productions, the rhinoceros vases and the royal dessert service, make it clear that in their day they were considered the ultimate in fashion and good taste.

However, taste is ephemeral, and the formerly much admired wares of the 1830s and 1840s, particularly the neo-rococo pieces, came to be regarded as extravagant and overdecorated. Admittedly, some extremely bad neo-rococo items were made, but the worst examples were not products of the Rockingham Works. They are in what has come to be known as the 'Rockingham style', but from potteries producing less tasteful wares and using no recognizable factory mark. Since Rockingham ornamental items are usually marked, it came to be assumed that almost any unmarked piece of neo-rococo type originated from the most familiar source, and the Bramelds took the blame for many debased decorative items made elsewhere. During the early twentieth century, the understanding of Rockingham porcelain reached its nadir, as is well exemplified by Mrs Willoughby Hodgson's book *Old English China*, 1913, where, of the eleven pieces of 'Rockingham' illustrated, only one is a genuine product of this factory. In recent years, following a study of previously unpublished design books, it has been realized that most major porcelain factories at this period were fashioning wares in the 'Rockingham style'.

Authentic Rockingham ornamental pieces of the period 1826 to 1830, when the red griffin mark was in use, show the same characteristics of decoration as do useful wares, with fine enamelling, a preference for rich ground colours and lavish gilding. The change to neo-rococo shapes coincides with the introduction of the puce griffin mark in approximately 1830, although it was not a complete break and many of the old forms continued in use. These later wares are characterized mainly by the use of encrusted flower decoration, and although this style came to be particularly associated with the Rockingham Works, there is no evidence to suggest that it originated at Swinton.

Rockingham wares in the revived rococo taste, with few exceptions, are comparatively restrained in form and not over-embellished with encrusted work. The applied flowers are delicately and carefully fashioned and generally coloured in pastel shades, with pale-greens, pinks and yellow predominating, quite unlike the heavy and sometimes harshly coloured applied work on the wares of some of their contemporaries. The Coalport and Minton Design Books indicate quite clearly the origin of certain of the more unfortunate vase shapes and other decorative items.[1]

The two rhinoceros vases (or pot-pourri jars) in particular have served to strengthen the impression that Rockingham porcelain was clumsy in shape and overornamented. The mistake has been the assumption that they were typical products of the factory, whereas one, if not both, were actually made as show pieces.

The vase now in the Rotherham Museum (Plate 98) is dated 1826, and it was said to be the largest object in porcelain to have been fired in one piece in England at that time, in itself a remarkable achievement for a firm which had so recently embarked on the manufacture of china.[2] The overall height with the cover in position is 1 m 14 cm (3 ft 9 in). Admittedly, the design is somewhat bizarre to modern eyes, with the body resting on three paw feet, and amply provided with oak leaves and acorns which surround large paintings positioned between three gnarled handles. The enamelled scenes from Cervantes' *Don Quixote* are reputedly the work of the youngest Brameld brother, John Wager (see page 202). The neck of the vase is pierced with hexagonal openings, rather like a honeycomb, with modelled bees. The domed cover is crowned with a gilded rhinoceros and to date the choice of this unlikely beast has defied explanation, and it does not in fact appear on what seems to be a preliminary sketch for the vase by Thomas Brameld on a letter dated 26 September 1826.[3]

To those who saw it in the mid-1820s, the vase evoked none of the horror which it struck in the hearts of later observers. A local writer, Ebenezer Rhodes, who visited the Rockingham Works in late 1826, saw this vase soon after its completion and had nothing but praise for its magnificence.[4] Llewellynn Jewitt writing in the late 1870s could still describe this scent jar as 'of surpassing beauty'.[5]

1. See, for example, G. A. Godden, *Coalport and Coalbrookdale Porcelains*, London, 1970, Plates 177–95 and 220–6. Also G. A. Godden, *Minton Pottery and Porcelain of the First Period 1793–1850*, London, 1968, Plates 88–127.
2. L. Jewitt, *Ceramic Art in Great Britain*, London, 1878, Vol. 1, p. 512.
3. A. and A. Cox, 'New Light on Large Rockingham Vases', *The Connoisseur*, Vol. 173, No. 698, 1970, pp. 238–43.
4. E. Rhodes, *Yorkshire Scenery*, London, 1826, p. 155.
5. L. Jewitt, op. cit., Vol. 1, p. 512.

98. RHINOCEROS VASE, dated 1826. Porcelain, of massive proportions, lavishly gilded and enamelled with scenes from Cervantes' *Don Quixote*. Red griffin, mark 51. Height 1m 14 cm (3 ft 9 in). *Clifton Park Museum, Rotherham.* *See pages 152–4*

Its true function, however, as previously mentioned, was as a show piece, a point not known to previous authors. It stood in a special display case at the Pottery, where it was probably intended to amaze and impress visitors to the Works by the striking impression which it would create, the superb quality of its decoration and the considerable technical achievement which it represented. The reason for its over-ornate appearance may be explained by the fact that it attempts to demonstrate all the various aspects of ornamentation in use at that time. The following entry occurs in the Wentworth invoices for 1842 after the closure of the Works:

> Sent to Wentworth House April 12th
> by order of Mr Newman
> The large China Rockingham Scent Jar—Adventures of Don Quixote &c &c—& the Case in which it stands.

No charge was made, for it seems that the vase and other choice items from the showroom were taken to Wentworth House as part payment of the Bramelds' debts to Earl Fitzwilliam.

The rhinoceros vase in the Victoria and Albert Museum is basically of the same design, although some 17.8cm (7in) smaller. It is decorated with finely painted flowers, traditionally the work of Edwin Steele. Possibly this vase was originally intended to grace another of the Bramelds' showrooms, perhaps that in Piccadilly, London. In 1868, the *Illustrated London News* for 29 August published an engraving of the vase which at the time was included in the National Exhibition of Works of Art opened in May of that year by the Prince of Wales. It was stated to be in the possession of Mortlock's, the Oxford Street China Dealers, who subsequently sold it to the Victoria and Albert Museum.

A more accurate assessment of the qualities of Rockingham ornamental porcelain may be gained from their normal productions. A wide range of decorative items can be shown to be authentic products of the factory and most in fact bear a mark, contrary to a still-current belief that much Rockingham is unmarked. The manufacture of such a large variety of ornamental wares within a relatively short period can hardly have been a sensible commerical proposition and must have contributed to the early closure of the Works.

Cabinet Pieces

Some of the finest items were doubtless intended as cabinet pieces. With plates, however, it is sometimes difficult to recognize those which were made solely for display, since often examples which appear too elaborate for use were indeed made as functional wares. However, plates which bear the signature of an artist were almost certainly intended to be purely decorative. The very fine plate illustrated (Plate 99) showing young women bathing in a wooded landscape is inscribed on the reverse '*The Enchanted Stream/Speight Pinx*t'. George Speight was a talented Swinton-trained artist whose work is well-documented. He is recorded as having painted the coats of arms on the king's dessert service (page 134), and certainly this signed plate shows the same remarkable attention to detail.

The very uncommon puce griffin-marked plates with borders encrusted with large flowers can only have been intended as decorative items. The Bramelds occasionally described wares specifically as cabinet pieces, as in an invoice for 4 August 1842:

1 Mahogany Case with 12 Cabinet Plates

It seems likely that these had been displayed in the showroom at the Pottery and were sent to Wentworth House after the Works closed. A reference to a plate which was evidently a cabinet piece occurs in an invoice for 18 October 1839:

1 China Plate Harcourt Pattern view of Wentworth House—sent to the Hble Wm (?) Wodehouse—being a present from the Hble George Fitz m

£3.0.0

Similarly, plaques—'tiles' or 'slabs' as they were called—were intended as decorative items, showing the best work of the factory artists and sometimes bearing their signatures. They were sold unmounted, and it was customary to display them in heavy gilt frames. Plaques were relatively expensive, but the wealthy found them ideal gifts, as an invoice for 24 July 1828 indicates:

99. CABINET PLATE, *c.*1826–30. Porcelain, *shark's tooth and S-scroll* border. Enamelled with a scene of women bathing, inscribed on reverse 'The Enchanted Stream/Speight Pinx[t].' Red griffin, mark 52. Diameter 24.1 cm (9.5 in). *See page 154*

To 3 China Tiles presented by Earl F to the young Ladies £13.13.0

Lord Milton also purchased plaques from the Rockingham Works, as on 16 April 1831:

to 2 China Slabs painted Fruit & Flowers £4.4.0

In a Christie's sale of Rockingham held on 12 and 13 February 1830, when presumably some of the Bramelds' old stock was being cleared to make way for wares in the revived rococo style, there are several references to 'tiles', the subject matter including flowers, named views, Shakespearian scenes, fruit, marine views and gardens.[6] When the Pottery closed in 1842 plaques from the showroom were sent to Wentworth House, the subjects listed as landscapes, fruit, 'Dead Game' and 'Young Recruit'. Several signed plaques from the red-

6. D. G. Rice, *The Illustrated Guide to Rockingham Pottery and Porcelain*, London, 1971, pp. 132–8.

griffin period are illustrated in Chapter 10, where details of artists are given.

Certain teawares seem to have been intended for display rather than for use and should be considered as cabinet pieces. One rare type is shown here (Plate 100), a matching teapot, sucrier and cream jug in the Godden Reference Collection, finely enamelled with bright butterflies on pale-green foliage and birds on the reverse. The teapot was originally shown as a sketch by Jewitt, and stated by him to be in the possession of a Mr Manning.[7] Matching cups and saucers have not been recorded. Unlike the standard productions, the main pieces in these cabinet services were sometimes marked.

Several types of cabinet cups were made and the bucket-shaped example illustrated (Plate 101) shows all the characteristics of early Rockingham porcelain, with a rich, smooth, claret ground and lavish gilding. The view, *Attingham House, Shropshire*, is named on the base and the flower-filled cornucopias on either side of the painting are of finely chased gilt, while the scrolling leaves above and below it are applied with the very finest of brushes, or 'pencils' as they were known. On the reverse of the cup is a scene in slightly raised matt gold of a girl in a landscape holding a lamb, with a sheep by her side. Both chased and raised gilding are uncommon forms of decoration at Rockingham and were reserved for the finest pieces.[8]

Caudle cups are of similar bucket shape with entwined rustic handles and usually a cover and stand. The particularly fine piece illustrated (Plate 102) is enamelled with a fruit study which seems very likely to be the work of the notable artist Thomas Steel (see pages 210 and 212). A similar caudle cup, cover and stand formerly in the possession of Mr B. Bowden was decorated with named botanical studies and insects. Other forms of cabinet cups are known with scrolled handles which rise above the level of the rim, and an unusual porcelain loving cup painted with flowers and fruit has been recorded.[9]

Another type of cup is modelled as a shell with a bright-red coral handle, the saucer moulded in the form of a scallop shell. Some are delicately coloured in shades of pink and blue (Plate 103) while others are enamelled with flower sprays. The saucers may be marked with either the red or puce griffin.

The first piece of porcelain known to have been supplied to Earl Fitzwilliam at Wentworth House was:

1 China End. Gold burnd. Cabinet Cup & Std. 10/6

7. L. Jewitt, op. cit., Vol. 1, p. 511 and Fig. 875.
8. The gilt on Rockingham porcelain was applied by the process known as mercury gilding, whereby a gold–mercury amalgam was brushed on to the ware and the mercury subsequently driven off by a low temperature firing. The thin layer of gold was then either lightly sanded to a relatively dull polish, or more commonly burnished with a hard stone, such as agate, to bring out its lavish brilliance. Alternatively, the gilt was applied over a raised area built-up from composition and would then not normally withstand being burnished, but could be lightly tooled, or chased, with a metal point. The royal dessert service probably provides the best example of raised and tooled gilding on Rockingham porcelain.
9. A. A. Eaglestone and T. A. Lockett, *The Rockingham Pottery* (new revised edn. 1973), Plate XVIa.

100. CABINET TEAWARES, *c.*1830. Porcelain, finely enamelled with plants and butterflies. No marks. Height of teapot 17.8 cm (7 in). *Godden Reference Collection.* *See page 156*

101. (*left*) CABINET CUP, *c.*1826–30. Porcelain, with claret ground and rich chased gilding. Enamelled with a named view *Attingham House, Shropshire.* Red griffin, mark 52. Height 8.6 cm (3.4 in). *See page 156*

102. (*right*) CAUDLE CUP AND STAND, *c.*1826–30. Porcelain, with finely enamelled studies of fruit in the manner of Thomas Steel. Red griffin, mark 52. Overall height 9.8 cm (3.9 in). *See page 156*

103. CABINET CUP AND SAUCER, *c.*1826–30. Porcelain, of shell form. Coloured in pink, blue, mauve and brown with a red coral handle. Red griffin, mark 52. Overall height 7.9 cm (3.1 in). *Hurst Collection, Yorkshire Museum, York.* *See page 156*

This reference occurs in an invoice dated 15 August 1825, a year earlier than that previously accepted for the commencement of porcelain production on a commercial scale at the Rockingham Works.

Vases

Compared with that of many contemporary porcelain manufactories, the range of vase shapes produced at the Rockingham Works was not extensive. A study of marked pieces makes this clear, and also shows that the extravagantly ornate neo-rococo vases with flamboyant asymmetrical scrolls and overloaded with applied decoration bear little resemblance to the genuine products of the Pottery, which are often restrained examples of their type. As with almost all Rockingham, there is a distinction in style between the earlier pieces and those introduced after about 1830.

The rare and handsome Empire vases of urn shape (Colour Plate G) were among the earliest of Rockingham vases and closely resemble their Derby counterparts. Classical in form, with simple upswept handles, they display the best of red-period decoration, usually with rich ground colours and elaborate gilding. They show some of the most competent of Rockingham flower and fruit painting, including the distinctive styles of John Creswell and Thomas Steel. A superb vase of this shape in a private collection has a green ground with a fine study of green and black grapes, peaches, plums and strawberries. Like all examples of this type it bears the red griffin mark.

Equally rare, the Empire vases of amphora shape (Plate 104) are elegant and restrained in outline and typical of the red period to which they belong, with their strong ground colours and lavish chased gilding. Excellent specimens may be seen in the Rotherham Museum and in the Yorkshire Museum, York.

The tall, impressive, hexagonal vases (Colour Plate H) are perhaps one of the Bramelds' most pleasing designs, the inspiration for these clearly being oriental. Their covers, which have a long neck that fits inside the vase, are surmounted by either a monkey or a rose. They are often decorated with ground colours, either in panels alternating with enamelling, or with the whole body coloured green or blue, for example, sometimes with reserved flower sprays. They were supplied singly, in pairs, or in garnitures, and an important set of seven pieces, including two matching flared beakers is in the Newmane Collection. A very fine garniture of five, most attractively decorated in Imari-style, the tallest being 43.2 cm (17 in) in height, is in the collection of Lotherton Hall, Leeds City Museums.[10]

Hexagonal vases may have been among the first porcelain ones produced at Swinton, since the specimen illustrated in Colour Plate H has the very rare early mark 'Brameld' in puce script (mark 48). Most belong to the red griffin period, but puce-marked examples are known, and in addition to the griffin

10. Formerly in the Llewellyn Collection and illustrated in *The Connoisseur Year Book, 1962*, p. 142, Plate 6.

104. AMPHORA-SHAPED VASE, *c*.1826–30. Porcelain, matt blue ground, enamelled with a flower group in the style of John Creswell and lavishly gilded. Red griffin, mark 52, and Cl. 14 in gilt. Height 34.8 cm (13.7 in). *Hurst Collection, Yorkshire Museum, York.* *See page 158*

there may be a small moulded pad of concentric rings on the base. Hexagonal vases were also produced in earthenware, although the pair shown in Plate 30 are decorated very much in the manner of porcelain.

Probably the most commonly found Rockingham vase is of trumpet shape with a plain circular foot, which lends itself to a wide variety of decoration. On the earlier pieces this usually takes the form of a gilt-outlined panel enclosing a painting of a landscape, birds, flowers, fruit or figures. An extensive range of ground colours were used. The example illustrated (Plate 105) has a rare turquoise ground, with a study of fruit and flowers within a gilt-bordered reserve. On the finest examples the gilding surrounding the enamelled panel may be ornately chased. In contrast, other trumpet vases are quite simply decorated, some with no more than a plain ground colour with gilt bands around the base and rim. Puce-period pieces are frequently left white and enamelled with a landscape or birds without any surround, or alternatively enclosed within light rococo gilt scrolls. Trumpet vases may be marked with the red or puce griffin and, as with all vase shapes introduced before 1830, those manufactured after this date appear never to have been subsequently produced with applied flowers.[11] They range in size from miniatures to 19.1 cm (7.5 in) in height. This very common vase shape was produced by many potters throughout the nineteenth century and unmarked specimens should be carefully compared with the one shown in Plate 105 before a Rockingham attribution is assumed.

Somewhat similar in concept are the vases with an overhanging-lip, which are basically cylindrical, flared at the base and neck and distinguished by a broad everted rim. The usual decoration consists of a painted reserve within a band of ground colour, or a continuous garland of flowers, as on the example shown in Plate 106. They are found with red or puce griffin marks and in sizes ranging from miniatures up to 21.5 cm (8.5 in), as single vases, pairs or garnitures of three or more. An unusual variant of this shape with a slightly raised inner collar is in the Doncaster Museum.

Possibly the simplest of all vases produced at the Rockingham Works were the cylindrical spill holders, straight-sided, rather narrow pieces (Plate 107) with a slightly spreading circular foot. They are often decorated with a continuous landscape or flower painting, although pleasing flower sprays are also known, as on the pair illustrated. Since vases of a similar appearance were produced elsewhere, for example at Minton's about 1815, unmarked specimens of this type should be attributed with care. In the writers' experience, when a Rockingham mark is present it is the puce griffin, but Dr Rice records a red-marked piece.[12]

One of the rarer forms, the eagle-handled vase, sometimes occurs with matching cylindrical spill holders (Plate 107). Straight-sided on a square base

11. D. G. Rice, op. cit., p. 54, records, however, a pair of trumpet-shaped vases covered all over with tiny applied mayflower heads, except for two reserves enamelled with flowers.
12. D. G. Rice, Ibid., Plate 121.

H. HEXAGONAL VASE, *c.*1826. Porcelain, with unusual orange ground colour, enamelled flower sprays and gilding. Rare early mark *Brameld* in puce script (mark 48). Height 48.4 cm (19.1 in). *Hurst Collection, Yorkshire Museum, York.* *See page 158*

I. BASKET, *c.*1830–42. Porcelain, encrusted with modelled flowers. Named on the border *Exeter from Exwick Hill.* Puce griffin (mark 55). Length 23 cm (9.1 in). *Yorkshire Museum, York. See page 166*

J. FIGURE, *c.*1826–42. Porcelain, one of the Continental peasant series, named around the base *Paysanne du Canton de Zurich.* Impressed griffin (mark 53). Height 18.5 cm (7.3 in). *Yorkshire Museum, York. See page 188*

105. (*left*) TRUMPET VASE, *c*.1830–42. Porcelain, rare turquoise ground, enamelled with fruit and flowers. Puce griffin, mark 55, and Cl. 4 in red. Height 14.2 cm (5.6 in). *See page 160*

106. (*right*) OVERHANGING-LIP VASE, *c*.1826–30. Porcelain, matt blue ground, enamelled with a continuous band of flowers. Red griffin, mark 52, and Cl. 9 in gilt. Height 14 cm (5.5 in). *See page 160*

107. GARNITURE OF VASES, *c*.1830–42. Porcelain, eagle-handled vase flanked by two of cylindrical shape. Enamelled with flower sprays and gilded. Cylindrical vases marked Cl. 2 in red. Height of central vase 10.9 cm (4.3 in). *See pages 160–2*

and with an outcurving rim, it has handles modelled as eagle heads, each with a ring in its beak. The shape appears to be Regency in spirit, yet all recorded examples belong to the puce period. Similar vases were made by Flight, Barr and Barr, Worcester, about 1815, but are rather slimmer than the Rockingham versions.

Perhaps the most original of the Bramelds' designs for vases, the stork-handled type (Plate 109) belong exclusively to the puce period, and yet are still restrained in concept and far removed from the excesses which certain of their contemporaries achieved. The characteristic features are the realistically fashioned stork-head handles, sometimes with chased-gilt feathers. A wide range of decorative effects was obtained, those made soon after 1830 having rich ground colours with fine paintings in square reserves. An interesting garniture of three in the Rotherham Museum has unusual continuous landscapes depicting Lakeland scenes. Other examples have flower sprays or exotic birds in the style of John Randall surrounded by light rococo scrolls in gilt. Occasionally the vases were more ornately decorated with applied work, like the one shown in Plate 109 which has encrusted flowers framing a Sussex view. They were produced in several sizes from 11 cm (4.5 in) to 37.2 cm (14.6 in) in height. A rare variant in a private collection is mounted on a square base.

A most curious pair of vases of related design with swan handles is illustrated in Plate 108. These are not characteristic Rockingham forms, and the piercing around the rim is a very unusual feature on wares from this factory. However,

108. PAIR OF SWAN-HANDLED VASES, *c.*1835–42. Porcelain, very rare shape with pale-blue ground, enamelled with birds on one side and encrusted with flowers on the other. Puce griffin, mark 55, on each piece. Height 16 cm (6.3 in). *Courtesy of Tennant's, Richmond.* *See pages 162–4*

109. STORK-HANDLED VASE, *c.*1830–42. Porcelain, one of a pair. Rare lilac ground with white encrusted flowers and enamelled view of *New Church, Brighton* named in red under the base. Puce griffin, mark 55. Height 37.2 cm (14.6 in). *Yorkshire Museum, York. See page 162*

110. (*left*) DOUBLE-LIPPED VASE, *c*.1830–42. Porcelain, one of a pair, decorated with coloured applied flowers and an enamelled bird study. Puce griffin, mark 55. Height 21.1 cm (8.3 in). *Fitzwilliam Museum, Cambridge. See page 164*

111. (*centre*) SCROLL-HANDLED EWER, *c*.1830–42. Porcelain, with coloured applied flowers and a view of *Radford Folly*, named in red script on the base. No mark. Height 21.6 cm (8.5 in). *Sheffield City Museum. See page 164*

112. (*right*) SNAKE-HANDLED EWER, *c*.1830–42. Porcelain, with coloured, applied flower decoration and gilding. Puce griffin, mark 55, and Cl. 2 in gilt. Height 23.1 cm (9.1 in). *Courtesy of Tennant's, Richmond. See pages 164 and 166*

the applied work is typical and both are in fact printed with an authentic puce griffin mark. It may be that these vases were bought in from elsewhere for decoration, but on balance it seems likely that, as with certain of the dessert and teawares described previously, they are products of the Rockingham Works made in the last years of the factory's life.

A relatively rare shape, often encrusted with white or coloured flowers, the double-lipped vases represent one of the more obviously neo-rococo forms in use at the Rockingham Works. The example shown in Plate 110 demonstrates well the very fine quality of the Bramelds' applied decoration of the puce griffin period to which they belong. Three sizes have been recorded, the tallest being 29 cm (11.4 in) in height. Although not strictly within this category, scroll-handled ewers (Plate 111) are occasionally matched with double-lipped vases as a garniture. The body shape is the same with a single scrolled handle, but the neck is modelled as an ewer. They are invariably of the puce period, and the standard of the enamelled decoration on both these types is often extremely high. They occur in three sizes, the largest being 21.6 cm (8.5 in) in height.

It is appropriate to mention here the rare snake-handled ewers (Plate 112), which have somewhat narrow bodies moulded with acanthus, applied flowers

113. CAMPANA-SHAPED POT-POURRI VASE, *c*.1830–42. Porcelain, enamelled with shells on one side, a romantic landscape on the other, and encrusted with coloured flowers. Ornately gilded. Puce griffin, mark 55, and C..3 in gilt. Height 34 cm (13.4 in). *Formerly in the Llewellyn Collection.* *See page 166*

and with a sinuous handle in the form of a snake. A stopper shaped as a flower accompanies these pieces which appear to have been produced in two sizes, 16 cm (6.3 in) and 23.1 cm (9.1 in). All date to the puce period.

Large pot-pourri vases with pierced covers are among the more ornate and imaginative items made at the Rockingham Works. Perhaps the most handsome are the campana-shaped examples (Plate 113), usually enamelled on each side with landscapes, flowers, fruit or, less commonly, shells, surrounded by encrusted flowers. The elaborate moulding is picked out in gilt. They were introduced in the puce griffin period and are known in at least two sizes, 26.7 cm (10.5 in) and 34 cm (13.4 in) in height. Two related types of pot-pourri vases or jars were produced, both with bulbous bodies and entwined rustic handles, but one has three small feet and a body identical in shape to that of the teapot shown in Plate 100, whilst the other, illustrated in Plate 114, has four feet. Both pot-pourris have pierced covers with elaborate, flower-encrusted finials, and are decidedly uncommon. As might be expected, they were introduced after 1830.

In addition to the standard productions described above, unusually shaped vases are occasionally encountered. The curious overhanging-lip and swan-handled vases have already been mentioned and a further baluster-shaped variety of simple profile is shown in Plate 115. Only two examples of this previously unrecorded design are known to the authors, unmarked apart from the painted Cl 3 which appears on both pieces. The decoration would suggest that they belong to the red-griffin period.

Baskets

Among the most attractive of Rockingham decorative items are ornamental baskets, the majority of which were produced after 1830 and can be of superb quality.

The best known of the shallow baskets is the elongated, octagonal type (Colour Plate I and Plate 116) which occurs in several sizes ranging from 16.5 cm (6.5 in) to 34.3 cm (13.5 in) in length. They have crossed rustic handles and around the edge is a moulded border of primrose leaves, generally with applied flower-and-leaf decoration, carefully formed, and characteristically coloured in pinks, yellows, greens and sometimes blue and bright orange. The centres are often painted with named views, frequently of Sussex coastal towns,[13] but romantic landscapes, flowers, fruit or shells are also found. Some, like the example in Plate 116, have plain-white applied flowers, the view in this case being of *Wentworth House*, the seat of Earl Fitzwilliam, patron of the Pottery. All such baskets date to the period after 1830.

Less common are the shallow, round baskets on four small, scrolled feet, with crossed rustic handles and encrusted decoration (Plate 117). The larger

13. G. A. Godden, *An Illustrated Encyclopaedia of British Pottery and Porcelain*, London, 1966, Colour Plate XI.

114. (*left*) BULBOUS POT-POURRI VASE, *c*.1830–42. Porcelain, encrusted with coloured flowers and with an enamelled view *In Denby Dale*, named on the base. Puce griffin, mark 55. Height 25.4 cm. (10 in). *Courtesy of Sotheby's.* *See page 166*

115. (*right*) BALUSTER-SHAPED VASE, *c*.1830. Porcelain, rare form with matt blue ground and enamelled flower group. Mark Cl. 3 ·.· in red. Height 19.2 cm (7.6 in). *See page 166*

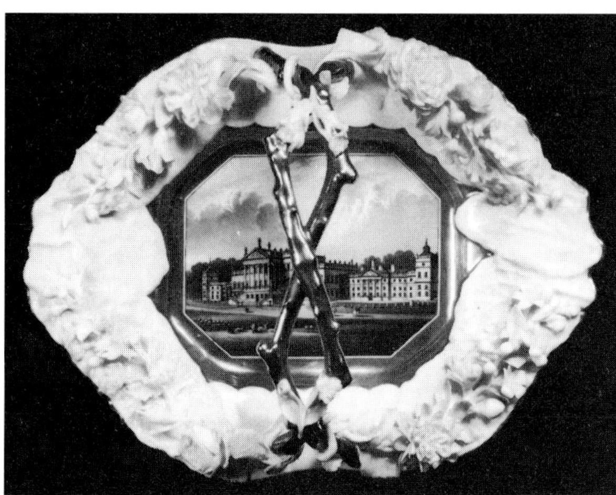

116. ELONGATED OCTAGONAL BASKET, *c*.1830–42. Porcelain, white applied flowers and enamelled view of *Wentworth House, Yorkshire, the seat of Earl Fitzwilliam*, named on the reverse. Puce griffin, mark 55. Length 22.9 cm (9 in). *Courtesy of Christie's.* *See pages 166 and 168*

117. CIRCULAR BASKET, *c*.1830–42. Porcelain, with coloured applied flowers and a gilt motif in the centre. No mark. Diameter 16 cm (6.3 in). *See pages 166 and 168*

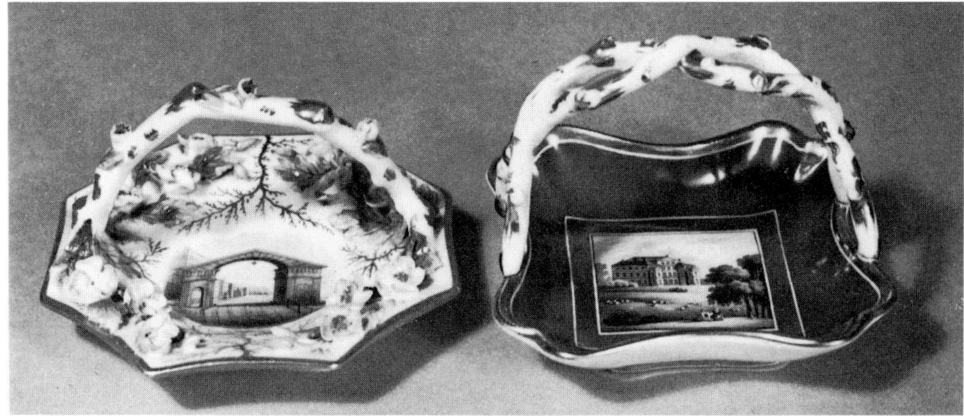

118. OCTAGONAL BASKET, *c.*1830–42. Porcelain, encrusted with coloured flowers and enamelled with a named view of *E. Lodge. St. Leonards.* Puce griffin, mark 55. Diameter 9.7 cm (3.8 in). *Hurst Collection, Yorkshire Museum, York.* *See page 168*
SQUARE BASKET, *c.*1830–42. Porcelain, green ground and enamelled view, named on reverse, *Tong Hall, Yorkshire, Colonel Plumbe.* Puce griffin, mark 55. Width 9.2 cm (3.6 in). *Yorkshire Museum, York.* *See page 168*

ones may have pierced covers and were evidently intended for pot-pourri: the largest examples are 21.6 cm (8.5 in) in diameter. When marked, they invariably bear a puce griffin.

Certain shapes are found rarely—for example, small octagonal baskets (Plate 118) with a single rustic handle, and square and oblong baskets (Plate 118) with shaped sides, indented corners and crossed twig handles. A very rare, large variety is basically square with ornately moulded borders and projecting leafy scrolls at the corners, identical in outline to the dish illustrated in Plate 119. The collection of the Yorkshire Museum, York, includes several of these more unusual pieces.

It is typical of the Rockingham Works that although they produced a relatively small range of standard shapes, there are a number of curious rarities with perhaps only one example recognized to date, thus making it difficult to assess fully the range of their wares. Similarly, familiar forms were subtly altered to create something quite different—a cup with primrose-leaf moulding, for example, might be given basket handles and a cover to produce a most unusual pot-pourri container,[14] and the larger baskets were sometimes made without handles to provide dishes for decorative or useful purposes, as shown in Plate 119.

Deep, circular baskets with outcurving rims and a single rustic handle are relatively common. The larger ones (Plate 120) generally have pierced covers and were for pot-pourri. The sides may be enamelled, but more often simply have a delicate band of gilded tracery. Small examples are usually without

14. J. G. and M. I. N. Evans, 'Rockingham Ornamental Porcelain Inkstands and Related Items', *Antique Collecting*, Vol. 11, No. 9, 1977, pp. 29–31.

119. DISH, *c*.1830–42. Porcelain, with border of moulded flower heads and elaborate acanthus-leaf corners. Green ground and enamelled flower group of a type described in the Rockingham Pattern Books as 'Flowers by Girls'. Puce griffin, mark 55. Length 31.2 cm (12.3 in). *See page 168*

120. DEEP POT-POURRI BASKET, *c*.1830–42. Porcelain, decorated with coloured applied flowers and a band of gilding around body. Puce griffin, mark 55, and C. 3 in red. Height 14.4 cm (5.7 in). *See page 168*

121. HELMET-SHAPED BASKET, *c*.1830–42. Porcelain, elaborately encrusted with realistic flowers, the body decorated with gilt stripes. Puce griffin, mark 55. Height 20.3 cm (8 in). *Formerly in the Llewellyn Collection. Courtesy of Sotheby's.* *See pages 169–70*

covers and may be plain or encrusted, an unusual piece (Plate 131) having single moulded flower heads around the outside of the body. The flower-encrusted specimens bear the puce griffin mark, but plainer, red-marked examples occur, normally with a rich ground colour. They vary in diameter up to about 13.5 cm (5.3 in).

Other baskets are helmet-shaped with a loop handle. The decoration may be of a uniform or striped ground colour with gilding, or encrusted (Plate 121) to appear full of flowers. All belong to the puce-griffin period. The example illustrated shows very well the quality of the flower modelling at the Rockingham Works.

Inkstands and Desk Pieces

It is doubtful whether all the various inkstands produced at Swinton were ever intended to be primarily functional, but they are extremely decorative, and that was perhaps the main requirement.

The large examples are most handsome, one type with a rectangular bulbous body resting on paw feet being Regency in inspiration; yet the specimen in the collections of Sheffield City Museum is in fact puce marked.[15] Another variety of desk inkstand (Plate 122) is more rococo in form, being of serpentine shape with acanthus-leaf moulding at the corners extended to form feet. It has compartments in the top for a taperstick and ink container, and is beautifully decorated.

Small inkstands were termed 'portable inks' by the Bramelds. A curious example introduced during the red period is modelled as a cockle shell, with shell feet and winkle-shell pen holders—one has been recorded with its sea-urchin cover intact.[16]

More common are the cylindrical inkstands with a flared rim and moulded lion masks at opposite sides of the body (Plate 123). They have a central container for ink which should be complete with a small cover. Three symmetrically arranged holes accommodate quills and they are usually decorated in the characteristic manner of the red period to which they belong, typically with a ground colour which may include reserved panels of enamelled flowers. Novelty pieces produced at this period were inkstands formed as miniature shoes, and doubtless others await recognition. The small inkstands introduced after 1830 are rococo in style, bulbous in form (Plate 123) and sometimes have applied flowers for additional decoration.

As opposed to inkstands, one occasionally finds ink-trays with matching, but removable, pots. A particularly fine and expensive example of this type was supplied to Wentworth House on 2 May 1839:

> 1 China Ink Tray. Green Ground Birds
> Gold Traced emboss'd Flowers } £12.12.0
> 2 China Inks with Glass linings

A similar set has been illustrated by Geoffrey Godden, the tray also decorated with birds.[17]

15. D. G. Rice, *Rockingham Ornamental Porcelain*, London, 1965, Plate 71.
16. J. G. and M. I. N. Evans, op. cit., Fig. 67.
17. G. A. Godden, *The Illustrated Guide to British Porcelain*, London, 1974, Plate 473. For illustrations of further inkstands see D. G. Rice, 'Rockingham Porcelain Inkstands', *Collectors Guide*, March 1976, pp. 74–7.

122. DESK INKSTAND, *c.*1830. Porcelain, with removable ink-well and taperstick. Enamelled with flower groups and gilded. Puce griffin, mark 58, and CL..4 in red. Length 23.5 cm (9.3 in). *Courtesy of Christie's.* *See page 170*

123. INKSTAND, *c.*1826–30. Porcelain, pink ground, the reserves painted with flowers. Moulded lion masks with gilded detail. Red griffin, mark 52. Height 5.5 cm (2.2 in). *See page 170*

INKSTAND, *c.*1830–42. Porcelain, of rococo form, the moulded scrolls outlined in grey and with flower sprays and gilding. No mark. Height 5.6 cm (2.2 in). *See page 170*

Pen trays, or quill holders, were also made and although essentially rectangular, they took several different forms. The most common one from the red period has straight, out-curving sides with extended ends moulded with flowers in low relief. Basically the same shape was used in the puce period, but adapted to the neo-rococo taste with leafy C-scrolls along the border and at the ends to form protruding handles. Both varieties stand on a flanged foot and are approximately 26.6 cm (10.5 in) in length. Frequently the scrollwork is picked out in gilt, enhancing any enamelled decoration, to produce most attractive items. Much less common are the quill holders standing on four small paw feet which sometimes terminate in lion masks. As would be expected, they date to the red period, but may have continued in production into the years immediately after 1830. The curious, attractive pieces realistically modelled as a standing elephant with a miniature castle on its back (an example is in the Sheffield City Museum) have been described as inkstands, but are in fact quill holders, and again these were introduced during the red-griffin period.

Other desk pieces included card racks for holding cards or letters (Plate 124). Rectangular in form, tapered towards the base, and standing on four scrolled feet, they are usually encrusted with flowers and painted with a named view or a flower spray. All date to the years after 1830. The example illustrated is finely decorated with an enamelled view of *The Seat of H. Firth Esq*[r]., a gentleman's residence situated within a few miles of the Pottery at Rose Hill, Rawmarsh, and one of the most local scenes depicted on Rockingham porcelain.

Small tapersticks for melting wax for seals were sometimes supplied with inkstands, or could be purchased separately; they normally have a plain circular foot and may have a ring handle in the form of a dolphin (Plate 131). A reference to tapersticks occurs in an invoice sent to Wentworth House on 10 October 1835:

1 China small cat and 2 small tapers taken in the carriage by Lady Anne	5/6

On 2 May 1839, the Bramelds supplied the following:

2 China Hexagon Tapers	£3.3.0

No examples of this type have been recognized.

Several varieties of chambersticks too are known, one with a saucer-like base moulded with C-scrolls and a handle as used on three-spur cups. Another has a square-shaped base with a leaf-and-gadroon edge, and a third has a leaf-shaped drip tray. An unusual piece of this type in the Rotherham Museum has flowers around the foot of the nozzle, which is modelled as a thistle. Chambersticks appear to belong mainly, if not entirely, to the puce period.

Full-sized candlesticks were also made after 1830. One variety with a rococo scrolled base, slim baluster stem and an acanthus-moulded top (Plate 125) is light and attractive. The other more common design is less successful, being somewhat squat and heavy in appearance, with raised leaves and tendrils.

124. CARD RACK, *c*.1830–42. Porcelain, green ground, coloured applied flowers and a view, named on the underside, *The Seat of H. Firth, Esqr. Rose Hill, Yorkshire*. No mark. Length 12.6 cm (5 in). *See page 172*

125. CANDLESTICKS, *c*.1830–42. Porcelain, with acanthus-leaf moulding, rococo-scrolled bases and applied flowers. Puce griffins, mark 55. Height 26.4 cm (10.4 in). *Newmane Collection*. *See page 172*

126. COTTAGE, *c.*1830–42. Porcelain, formed as a spill vase and naturalistically coloured. Puce griffin, mark 55. Height not known. *Courtesy of Bryan Bowden.* *See page 174*

127. PASTILLE BURNER, *c.*1830–42. Porcelain, with coloured, applied flower decoration and gilding. Puce griffin, mark 55. Height 10.2 cm (4 in). *Courtesy of Tennant's, Richmond.* *See page 174*

Pastille burners were manufactured at the Rockingham Works, although not the numerous cottages and castles which for many years were attributed to this factory. Only one authentic cottage, marked with the puce griffin, has ever been recorded (Plate 126), and that was a flat-backed type, apparently intended as a spill container and quite different from the more usual cottages which generally have a Coalport or Staffordshire origin. The most common form of Rockingham pastille burner has a bulbous body with moulded flames at the top, the whole on a small circular stand. Examples from the puce-griffin period are often flower-encrusted, like that illustrated in Plate 127. Other shapes are known, notably one in the form of a chalice with a pierced conical cover, mounted on a cylindrical pedestal and dating to the years after 1830.

Scent Bottles

Large numbers of scent bottles were produced at the Rockingham Works; in fact one of the first pieces of porcelain supplied to Wentworth House on 15 August 1825 was such an item:

1 China En^{d} Gold burn^{d} Lavender Bottle 4/-

128. SCENT BOTTLES, *c*.1830–42. Porcelain, showing three types, *left to right*: tapered, diamond-shaped and long-necked, all with applied coloured flowers and additional gilding. The tapered bottle bears the puce griffin, mark 57, and C.3 in red. The diamond-shaped and long-necked examples have the puce griffin, mark 55, and Cl. 2 in red and gilt respectively. Height of long-necked bottle 12.6 cm (5 in). *See pages 175–6*

Perhaps more decorative than functional, they made suitable presents, as an invoice for 25 January 1840 records:

> Ordered by Lady Charlotte Fitzwilliam & sent to Lady Louisa Cotes by Mail 8th Jan.
> 2 China Eau de Cologne Bottles No. 5, Dresden White Flowers & Gold Crest £7

From the description and relatively high price, they were probably large examples of the pear-shaped type with long tapering necks and elaborate stoppers (Plate 128), specimens of which may be up to 30.5 cm (12 in) in height. More common are scent bottles in a number of sizes with a flattened, bun-shaped body, a long neck of uniform diameter, and a plain or encrusted stopper (Plate 128). Several rarer shapes survive, all of which date to the years 1830 to 1842, such as those with a bulbous, almost spherical body and a slight moulded ridge below the neck—a very unusual variant of this type (Plate 129) lacks this shoulder and has a somewhat longer neck. Similarly, scent bottles occur which are diamond shaped (Plate 128); hemispherical on a flat base (Plate 129); and

129. SCENT BOTTLES, *c.*1830–42. Porcelain, showing two rare forms: a previously unrecorded bulbous shape and a hemispherical example, both with coloured encrusted flowers and gilding. Puce griffins, mark 55. Heights 9.9 cm (3.9 in) and 8.6 cm (3.4 in) respectively. *Hurst Collection, Yorkshire Museum, York.* *See pages 175–6*

hexagonal—all with short necks. They are found in a number of sizes and may be decorated with encrusted or 'Dresden' flowers, sometimes modelled as tiny mayflower heads covering the entire surface of the body. Doubtless, other types await recognition.

Perhaps more strictly in the category of 'toys' are small scent sprinklers, shaped like a watering can with perforations in the end of the curved spout (Plate 130). Rare examples are known in a uniformly tinted lilac paste with white applied flowers.

Miniature Decorative Pieces

A wide range of miniatures (Plate 131) was made at the Rockingham Works, attractive items, particularly suitable for ladies to give as presents to each other. These include ring holders, formed as a small saucer with a raised column in the centre, and pin trays which occur in two shapes, both of which were introduced in the red-griffin period. Essentially square in shape, one has corners in the form of concave shells, the other has an acanthus-leaf and gadroon edge. They are often miniature works of art, beautifully enamelled and gilded, whilst others with encrusted flowers must surely have been more decorative than useful. Unusual dressing-table items are the small porcelain boxes with covers in the form of butterflies, painted and gilded to enhance the insect's wings and body. An invoice dated 8 December 1837 and sent to Wentworth House records:

7 China Drop Boxes for Lady Anne 14/3

130. MINIATURE TEAPOT, *c.*1830–42. Porcelain, with coloured applied flowers. Puce griffin, mark 55, and Cl. 2 in red. Height 6.4 cm (2.5 in). *See page 177*
MINIATURE SCENT SPRINKLER, *c.*1830. Porcelain, encrusted with coloured flowers. Puce griffin, mark 57, and Cl. 2 in gilt. Height 9.7 cm (3.8 in). *Sheffield City Museum. See page 176*

and may refer to the small, circular, covered boxes which are occasionally found. Single flower models were made, though few have survived; one is mentioned on 1 November 1834:

1 Dresden Single Flower p. Lady Charlotte 7/-

Items for personal adornment were produced, such as studs, though none are known to the authors. In 1831 '8 Setts China Studs' were purchased by the Hon. Miss Fitzwilliam, and on 17 October 1832:

24 China Studs Cl 4 Pencilled Foxes Heads In front
& In back £1.10.0

On small objects of this type there would be no room for the griffin mark and the Cl-mark alone would be the clue to their origin (see page 229).

Other miniatures which made popular presents were tiny vases, some no more than 4.5 cm (1.75 in) in height, scaled down versions of the larger originals, trumpet and overhanging-lip shapes having been recorded—examples of the former are in the Yorkshire Museum, York. In spite of their diminutive size, the decoration is exquisite. Similarly, one finds a range of small-scale teawares (Plate 130), often flower-encrusted, and violeteers in the form of a small teapot without a cover, but with an open grille across the top. Buckets, watering cans and basins and ewers are known. Particularly attractive are miniature slippers with a trodden-down heel (Plate 131). The range of these wares seems to have been extensive, and doubtless others await recognition. It was probably fashionable to make a collection of these pieces, hence the variety.

There are several references to small animal figures, including dogs and rabbits, and some of the known examples are quite tiny, as mentioned on page 190. They also perhaps found their way into ladies' collections, or in some cases were gifts for children. The '1 China Dogs Head Whistle 1/6' in an invoice for 15 August 1829 was maybe for a child. All these miniatures were relatively inexpensive, although the actual work involved in their production and decoration must in some cases have been considerable.

Miscellaneous

There are certain other pieces of Rockingham which may be classed as decorative wares, although they have a useful function.

Punch bowls at their best represent some of the finest of the Bramelds' porcelains. The example illustrated (Plate 132) is enamelled with hunting and shooting scenes in elaborately gilt-bordered reserves on a rich green ground. This plain, round bowl is marked with the red griffin, but another type belonging to the puce period has shallow fluting and stands on four leafy feet with a single applied leaf between them. The Yorkshire Museum, York, has a very unusual large bowl beautifully painted with flower groups and with an out-curved rim moulded with a wave pattern. It bears the red griffin mark.

Cache-pots were made, although only one pair of these beaker-like pots has so far been recorded.[18] Of tapering cylindrical form, they are decorated with panels of flowers divided by painted and gilded columns. They belong to the puce griffin period.

Trays were among the most impressively decorated pieces of Rockingham porcelain. Some of the larger ones seem to have been treated almost like plaques, to show off the finest specimens of an artist's work. One such tray in private possession has an enamelled portrait of *Earl Strafford occupied in dictating his defence to his secretary*. It is marked with the red griffin and signed by George Speight who, tradition has it, copied the scene from an original reputedly by Van Dyck at Wentworth House. Two similar, fine examples are in the Rotherham Museum, one painted with fruit by Thomas Steel, the other with a naked cupid reclining against a red curtain—both bear the red mark.

Smaller card trays were made in the puce-griffin period, rectangular in shape with rustic handles, generally with a narrow, coloured border and a named

18. Formerly in the Llewellyn Collection, sold Sotheby's 21 November 1972, lot 98, illustrated in the catalogue. Now in the Rotherham Museum.

131. MINIATURE DECORATIVES, *c.*1830–42. Porcelain, showing: scent bottle marked Cl. 2 in red; basket with puce griffin, mark 55, and Cl. 2 in gilt; taperstick with CL, 4 in gilt; and slipper with puce griffin, mark 57, and Cl. 2 in red. Height of basket 8.8 cm (3.5 in). *See pages 169, 172 and 176–8*

132. PUNCH BOWL, *c.*1826–30. Porcelain, green ground, with finely enamelled hunting and shooting scenes in reserves and elaborately gilded. Red griffin, mark 52. Diameter 27.2 cm (10.7 in). *Clifton Park Museum, Rotherham.* *See page 178*

133. CARD TRAY, *c.*1830–42. Porcelain, green ground, the centre finely enamelled with a view of *Newstead Abbey, Nottinghamshire, the Seat of the late Lord Byron*, named on the reverse. Puce griffin, mark 55. Length 29.2 cm (11.5 in). *Sheffield City Museum*. *See pages 178 and 180*

view within a gilt band in the centre. The fine example illustrated (Plate 133) is enamelled with a prospect of *Newstead Abbey*. Other types of tray made in the later years were encrusted with flowers and painted and gilded in the neo-rococo style. These sometimes formed the base for inkstands, cabaret sets or for miniature tea services.

Several forms of highly decorative jugs were made during the early years of porcelain production (Plate 134), usually of somewhat angular shape. The enamelling, generally of flowers and insects, and the gilding, are both frequently of a very high order. They are relatively uncommon, and curiously sometimes have raised concentric rings on a small pad on their base, in addition to the red griffin mark. One of the most common types of jug produced after 1830 has a bulbous shape, not unlike a three-spur teapot body with a rustic handle (Plate 135). The decoration is often elaborate and they are occasionally commemorative, with a date and name or initials. Other jugs from this period have a scrolled handle with a thumbpiece and a generous lip, whilst others with primrose-leaf moulding around the lower part, flower heads around the upper body and a substantial crabstock handle, are frequently decorated with strong ground colours and gilded. Identical jugs occur in earthenware covered with a green glaze.

134. JUG (*left*), *c*.1826–30. Porcelain, enamelled with a named botanical study *Papaver*, and insects. Red griffin, mark 52. Height 16 cm (6.3 in).
JUG (*right*), *c*.1826–30. Porcelain, enamelled with a flower group. Red griffin, mark 52, and Cl. 3 in gilt. Height 14.0 cm (5.5 in). *Newmane Collection.* *See page 180*

135. JUG, *c*.1830–42. Porcelain, claret ground with additional detail in yellow, gilded, and with a monogram GS in gilt script. Puce griffin, mark 55. Height 12.7 cm (5 in). *See page 180*

136. MUG, *c.*1830–42. Porcelain, with horse's-hoof and tail handle. Green vertical stripes, enamelled flower groups, and inscribed in gilt 'Mary Anne Moody'. Puce griffin, mark 55. Height 6.5 cm (2.6 in). *Formerly in the Llewellyn Collection.* *See page 182*
RHYTON, *c.*1826–30. Porcelain, moulded as a fox mask, with a gilt collar. Red griffin, mark 52, and Cl. 1 in red. Length 11.4 cm (4.5 in). *See page 182*

Rockingham porcelain mugs are normally straight-sided with handles which have the top part moulded in the form of a horse's tail, the lower part its leg and hoof (Plate 136). They are attractive pieces and apart from one very grand example with a rich claret ground and a portrait of the Duke of Wellington in a reserve, much in the style of William Corden,[19] they are generally more simply decorated with flower sprays. They occur in several sizes and it is not unusual to find them inscribed, like the example illustrated, which bears the name 'Mary Anne Moody'. Bucket-shaped beakers without handles are also known and there is a reference in an invoice for wares sent to Wentworth House on 14 September 1838 to:

1 China Water Leaf Beaker 4/6

but nothing matching this description is known to the writers.

Porcelain hunting cups, or rhytons, are rare survivors. They are formed as well-modelled hound or fox masks (Plate 136) and are normally undecorated, except for a band of gilt around the moulded collar. They are known from both the red- and puce-griffin periods, and an example is recorded in a factory invoice for 3 September 1828:

1 China Fox Head Present to Miss Edmonds 4/6

19. Formerly in the Llewellyn Collection and illustrated in *The Connoisseur Year Book, 1962*, p. 144, Plate 9.

All items of furniture such as curtain poles and bed posts which the writers have seen have been of earthenware and are described on page 86. One exception occurs in an invoice sent to Wentworth House for goods supplied on 3 September 1828:

1 China Garden Seat £16.16.0

Presumably of the Chinese barrel-shaped type, it commanded a very high price. No example has so far been recorded.

Clearly, for such a relatively short-lived porcelain manufactory a wide range of decorative items was produced, many in such strictly limited numbers that the cost of making moulds can hardly have been justified. This totally unbusinesslike approach is typical of the Brameld brothers and doubtless one more contributory factor to the early closure of the Rockingham Works through insolvency.

9
Porcelain Figures

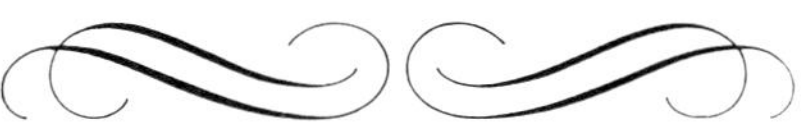

In common with several English manufactories of the early nineteenth century, the Rockingham Works produced figures and busts, now of considerable rarity, in the same bone-china body as was used for the factory's other decorative and table wares. Biscuit (unglazed) and enamelled figures were issued, the former having a fine, white, granular appearance, quite unlike Derby biscuit porcelain of either the Duesbury or Bloor periods.

Rockingham figures are generally well modelled, and the animals in particular are among the finest issued by the nineteenth-century English factories. Models of humans tend to have somewhat posed attitudes, lacking in life and movement, the result, as will be shown, of many having been closely based on contemporary engravings.

Contrary to the statements of previous authors, figure production at Swinton did not cease in 1830. This erroneous belief arises from the fact that only the red griffin, or an impressed version of this mark, occurs on figures. The factory invoices, however, show that figures were supplied to the Fitzwilliam household until the closing years of the Works—for example, on the 19 October 1839:

1 Pair China Bis^t French Shepd & Shep^s [1]	11/-
1 Pair ,, Flower Boy & Girl[2]	9/6
ordered by Confectioner to be used as ornaments for dress plates for Desserts	

The use of figures for table decoration at this date is surprising, since this is usually regarded as an eighteenth-century practice. Further evidence for the continued production of figures is provided by the fact that excavated fragments of them were found on the Swinton site in association with porcelain wasters of the puce griffin period, 1830–1842. Finally, at least one example is impressed with the griffin mark and ROYAL/ ROCKINGHAM WORKS/ BRAMELD and must therefore post-date the commission for the royal dessert service given in 1830.

1. Almost certainly the pair model number 35.
2. Probably the pair model number 48.

A link with the Derby factory can be plainly discerned in the case of figures. The similarity between certain models from these two manufactories is remarkable, several having almost identical counterparts as indicated in the list of Rockingham porcelain figures (pages 195–9). Various theories have been advanced to account for these similarities, but it is only through a close study of the Swinton Parish Documents and excavated material that a satisfactory explanation can now be given.

Rockingham figures are mounted on a variety of bases—for example, square, circular, rocky, scrolled in a rococo manner—but they are rarely, if ever, totally solid as are certain Bloor Derby bases. In general, they are hollow and enclosed on the underside except for a hole about 1 to 3 cm in diameter (0.4 to 1.2 in). The only exceptions to the above which have come the the writers' attention are the bases of the 'flat-backed' figures which are concave and without a hole.[3] A factory mark is commonly present, as is an incised model number, normally prefixed by the abbreviation 'No.' On glazed examples a Cl mark may also occur (see page 229). It should be stressed, however, that neither the construction of the base, nor the way in which the model number is incised, is unique to Rockingham.

The models which attract the greatest attention are undoubtedly the theatrical personalities. These are based on roles made famous by the celebrated actor John Liston (*c.* 1776–1846) in plays first produced in London during the early nineteenth century—characters such as Lubin Log (No. 11) from *Love, Law and Physic* produced at Covent Garden in November 1812, or Simon Pengander (No. 7) in *Twixt Cup and Lip*, staged at the Haymarket Theatre in June 1826.[4] Only enamelled versions of theatrical personalities have so far been recorded, and like almost all Rockingham standing figures they have a support in the form of a post, or some other means to prevent collapse during the firing process. They occur on simple, unornamented bases on which the name of the character is sometimes written in gilt script, and not capitals as is the case with their Derby equivalents. Several theatrical figures also have written around the base a humorous catch-phrase associated with the role; for example, Paul Pry (No. 9) illustrated in Plate 137, a character in the play of that name produced at the Haymarket in September 1825, bears the gilt inscription 'I hope I don't intrude'. These figures were based on published prints, the model of Paul Pry being remarkably close to J. W. Gear's engraving of John Liston in this role, as may be seen in Plate 138.

The model shown in Plate 137 of *Madam Vestris* (No. 6) singing 'Buy a Broom', a song particularly associated with her, may represent the actress

3. D. G. Rice, *Rockingham Ornamental Porcelain*, London, 1965, p. 53 fn., records two most unusual figures on oval bases which are concave on the underside.
4. A full account of the career of Liston, and of the many plays in which he appeared, is given by L. Stephen and S. Lee (eds.), *The Dictionary of National Biography*, London, 1917 (reprinted 1949–50).

137. THEATRICAL FIGURES, *c.*1826–30. Porcelain (*left to right*): John Liston as Billy Lackaday, red griffin, mark 52, incised No. 8, height 15.5 cm (6.1 in). John Liston as *Madame Vestris* lettered 'Buy a Broom', red griffin, mark 52, incised No. 6, height 16 cm (6.3 in), *formerly in the Llewellyn Collection.* John Liston as Paul Pry, lettered 'I hope I don't intrude', red griffin, mark 52, incised No. 9, height 14.5 cm (5.7 in), *formerly in the Llewellyn Collection. Courtesy of Christie's.* *See pages 185 and 188*

138. ENGRAVING entitled *Mr. Liston as Paul Pry* and sub-titled 'I hope I don't intrude; Just called to ask you how your tooth is'. Drawn and engraved by J. W. Gear *c.*1826. Compare with the Rockingham figure of this subject shown in Plate 137. *Victoria and Albert Museum, Crown Copyright.* *See page 185*

139. CONTINENTAL PEASANT FIGURES, *c.*1826–42. Biscuit porcelain (*left to right*): *Paysanne de S^t. Angelo*, impressed griffin, mark 53, incised No. 120, height 19.8 cm (7.8 in). *Paysanne des environs de Bayonne*, impressed griffin, mark 53, incised No. 114, height 22.4 cm (8.8 in). *Paysan Piemontais de la Vallee d' Aoste*, impressed griffin, mark 53, incised No. 57, height 19.1 cm (7.5 in). *See page 188*

140. ENGRAVING of *Paysanne de S^t. Angelo, Roy^me. de Naples*. No. 38 in a series of prints by Hippolyte Lecomte entitled *Costumes des Différentes Nations*, 1817–19. Compare with the Rockingham figure of this subject shown in Plate 139. *See page 188*

herself,[5] but equally well it could be Liston impersonating this artiste, as he is known to have done. To date, the model number of Tristram Sappy has not been ascertained and this figure, therefore, appears at the end of the list of known Rockingham figures.

The modeller of the Rockingham theatrical subjects remains unidentified. Samuel Keys jnr. is known to have been responsible for the closely related figures produced at Derby,[6] and it is tempting to speculate that he might have spent a short time in Swinton, or even have supplied the Bramelds with models, but documentary evidence is lacking to link Keys with the Rockingham factory.

A series of Continental peasants wearing regional costume was modelled at Swinton (Colour Plate J and Plate 139) of which sixteen have so far been recognized. The authors have been able to show[7] that they are based on works by the French artist–lithographer Hippolyte Lecomte (1781–1857)[8] who, between 1817 and 1819, issued a numbered series of prints in the form of a book, apparently untitled, but now variously known as *Costumes des Différentes Nations, Costumes Européens* or an anglicized version of such titles which, in general, were given by later cataloguers such as Lipperheide[9] or Colas.[10] Variants of this book are recorded in which the number of plates varies between 86 and 90, and also their subject matter.[10] Clearly the Bramelds had access to Lecomte's work, since with few exceptions, the figures are faithful representations of the lithographs as shown in Plates 139 and 140, where the Rockingham figure of *Paysanne de St. Angelo* and the published source are compared. In certain instances the figures differ slightly from the print where the modelling of some delicate feature was impracticable, such as the double-handled vessel balanced on the head of *Paysanne des environs de Bayonne* and which, in the actual figure (Plate 139), is replaced by a sturdy basket of fruit, whilst other parts of the figure are accurately copied from the print. However, in the case of the previously unrecorded peasant *Montferrine des environs de Casal*, an example of which may be seen in the City Museum and Art Gallery, Birmingham, the print upon which it is based does not occur in the copy of Lecomte's work in the Library of the Victoria and Albert Museum. Nevertheless, it is the authors' belief that it probably does appear in one of the variant copies of this volume, for even the idiosyncratic Brameld brothers would hardly have drawn on more than one source for this unusual and attractive series of figures.

5. Madame Vestris (1797–1856), born Lucia Elizabeth Bartolozzi in London, married Auguste Armand Vestris in 1813. For details of her career see L. Stephen and S. Lee, op. cit.
6. J. Haslem, *The Old Derby China Factory*, London, 1876, p. 181.
7. A. and A. Cox, 'Hippolyte Lecomte and the Rockingham Peasant Figures', *Connoisseur*, Vol. 195, No. 785, 1977, pp. 195–200.
8. Born at Puiseux and exhibited at the Paris Salon between 1804 and 1847. For further details see E. Bénézit, *Dictionnaire Critique et Documentaire des Peintres, Sculpteurs, Dessinateurs et Graveurs*, Paris, Nouvelle Édition 1948–55 (réimprimé 1959–62).
9. F. J. von Lipperheide, *Katalog der Freiherrlich von Lipperheide'schen Kostümbibliothek*, Berlin, 1896, No. 52.
10. R. Colas, *Bibliographie Générale du Costume et de la Mode*, Paris, 1933, no. 1806.

As may be seen from the list of figures, four separate groups of Continental peasants are presently known. It might be deduced that the gaps within the groups possibly represent further examples of peasants awaiting discovery, and this is almost certainly the case. Fragments of figures and parts of master models have recently been excavated on the Rockingham site, and so closely are the models based upon Lecomte's work that identification of many of the sherds is immediately possible. There is thus direct evidence that the following figures, previously unrecorded, were produced:

Plate number in Lecomte's work	*Name of figure*
1	*Femme du Canton de Lucerne.*
7	*Paysan du Canton de Berne.*
10	*Paysanne de la Vallee de Bas-Inn en Tirol.*
18	*Paysanne du Canton de Zug en habite de Fête.*
23	*Paysan Valencien.*
28	*Femme des environs de Bilbao.*
30	*Matelot Catalan.*
54	*Chef de Tartares de la Crimée.*
59	*Paysan des environs d'Utrechk.*
60	*Laitiere des environs d'Harlem.*
73	*Habitant de l'Istrie des environs de Pola.*
77	*Habitant de Constantinople.*

In addition, a previously unknown, named solid base from a master model was excavated: this fortunately, has an incised model number:

138 *Laitiere des environs d'Harlem.*

Of great interest and importance, this base bears the incised inscription 'by T. Griffin/ July 15th 1830'. Not only does this reveal that Thomas Griffin, previously foreman of the figure department at Derby (see page 214), was responsible for modelling the Continental peasants, but No. 138 becomes the highest recorded model number of a Rockingham figure.

It can now be confirmed that model No. 13, an unnamed biscuit figure, discovered by Dr Rice, of a young woman carrying a basket of flowers on her left arm belongs to the group of Continental peasants, and is in fact *Femme de la Vallee de Tésino en Tyrol*,[11] and appears on Plate 13 in Lecomte's work. Conversely, the pair *Swiss boy* and *Swiss girl* (both No. 23), the Turks (No. 3 and No. 25), the Russian peasant (No. 37) and the Continental shepherd (No. 58) are not members of this series.

In the past, it was customary to attribute to the Rockingham Works virtually all porcelain animals manufactured in England during the first half of the nineteenth century whose real origin was in doubt, especially those with a coat consisting of applied, shredded strands of porcelain. As a result, countless

11. D. G. Rice, 'Rockingham Porcelain Figures', *Collectors Guide*, September 1974, p. 79, Plate 7.

numbers of sheep and poodles passed as Swinton products on grounds which can only be described as traditional. Fortunately, research based upon attention to marked specimens and excavated sherds, has enabled the authentic products to be recognized and the reputation of the Rockingham factory to be enhanced. Animals produced here are now known to be uncommon and, contrary to former belief, no poodles in any form, nor sheep with applied fleecy coats, were made at Swinton. They are largely of north Staffordshire origin—for example manufactured by Samuel Alcock & Co.—and in general were produced after the closure of the Rockingham Works. Recumbent ewes and rams were certainly made by the Bramelds, but all known models have moulded and not applied fleeces (see Plate 141).

Cats and dogs are possibly the animals most frequently seen. A cat with an imperious expression sitting on a tasselled cushion (No. 77) was issued in three sizes, also a seemingly dozing cat (No. 104) and a playful cat with kittens (No. 107). Of the several studies of dogs, a particularly fine, long-haired spaniel (No. 91), its head resting on one leg, is superbly modelled, as is evident from examples left in the biscuit state. Exceptionally, the modeller was less successful, as with the previously unrecorded figure of a dove (No. 112) with outstretched wings standing on a rocky base, to be seen in the collection of the Yorkshire Museum, York. This Museum has the most comprehensive display of Rockingham figures which is on view to the public. Of the other animals that were issued, special attention should be drawn to the elephant (No. 69) and the diminutive rabbits, squirrels and dogs (Nos. 70 to 74) which were probably created with children in mind. A squirrel (No. 73) is illustrated in Plate 141.

Animal figures were purchased by the Fitzwilliam family and the invoices sent to Wentworth House show that on 30 November 1826 the following were supplied:

4 China Biscuit rabbits £1.2.0

and on 10 October 1835:

1 China small cat & 2 small tapers
taken in the carriage by Lady Anne 5/6

Once again, the Rockingham–Derby connection with respect to figure production can present difficulties in the absence of distinguishing factory marks, and careful attention is required when attributing ewes and rams (Plate 141) and stags and does. It should be noted too that Chamberlain's and Grainger's, both of Worcester, produced animal figures in the Rockingham style.

During recent excavations on the Swinton factory site fragments of several previously unrecorded animal figures were recovered, the most notable of which possibly represents a horse.[12]

12. A horse was modelled at Derby *c.* 1820 (see J. Twitchett, *Derby Porcelain*, London, 1980, Plate 346).

141. ANIMAL FIGURES, *c*.1826–42. Porcelain (*left to right*): Small squirrel, white with gilt collar, marked Cl. 1 in red, incised No. 73, height 3.8 cm (1.5 in). Ram, white with a red patch, sitting on a grassy mound, impressed ROCKINGHAM/ WORKS/ BRAMELD, Cl. 1 in red, incised No. 108, length 6.9 cm (2.7 in). Rabbit, fawn on a dark-red base, impressed ROCKINGHAM/ WORKS/ BRAMELD, Cl. 2 in red, incised No. 106, length 6.1 cm (2.4 in). *Yorkshire Museum, York. See pages 189–90*

142. ROMANTIC FIGURES, *c*.1826–42. Biscuit porcelain (*left to right*): Girl sewing with a cradle by her side, impressed griffin, mark 53, incised No. 28, height 12.7 cm (5 in). Boy with a bird on his hand, impressed griffin, mark 53, incised No. 30, height 12.3 cm (4.8 in). Boy with a broken pitcher, impressed griffin, mark 53, incised No. 26, height 13.5 cm (5.3 in). *See pages 191–2*

A somewhat unrelated group of figures may be described as romantic, some of which are close in spirit to models produced during the eighteenth century—in particular a piping shepherd with a dog at his side and a shepherdess feeding a sheep (both incised No. 4). This pair and the *Swiss boy* and *Swiss girl* (both No. 23) are perhaps the most attractive of this group. Two further pairs in this category are a boy writing and a girl sewing (both No. 28), and a boy with a broken pitcher and a girl with a jug (both No. 26) (see Plate 142). Not only do both pairs have Derby equivalents, but the latter pair was also produced by Minton's, numbered 38 and 39 respectively.[13]

13. The boy with a pitcher is illustrated in G. A. Godden, *Minton Pottery and Porcelain of the First Period 1793–1850*, London, 1968, Plate 148.

Two other figures, a girl with a lamb and a boy with a dog (both No. 35) have Derby counterparts, as does the cobbler whistling to his caged starling (No. 39), modelled by George Cocker at Derby and based upon an earlier original.[14] This modeller's presence at Swinton in 1831, and possibly as early as 1829, must surely account for these remarkable similarities. Recent evidence reveals that he produced twenty-nine figure models for the Bramelds (see page 214), but precisely which ones can at present only be surmised. Interestingly, Cocker was also associated with the Minton factory, which may provide an explanation for the Rockingham–Minton connection.[15] Yet a further link with Derby is provided by the hitherto unrecorded pair of biscuit figures (both No. 48) of a seated girl holding a garland of flowers, and a boy sitting on an upturned basket in a similar pose, his hat resting on his knees. A rare and particularly striking figure of a shepherd accompanied by a sheep and a dog (No. 58) is notable for the quality of the modelling.

Totally different in concept are a child sleeping (No. 63) and the child awakening (No. 64), both after marble originals by Sir Francis Chantrey. A second sleeping child (No. 65, but see footnote 25) and yet a third (No. 66) reveal a curious preoccupation with this subject—the last mentioned, previously unrecorded, may be seen in the Yorkshire Museum, York. Also recorded here for the first time is the enamelled figure of a boy with a wreath of flowers on his head and holding a basket of flowers, possibly representing *Spring* from a set of *Seasons*. This model, currently on loan to the Sheffield City Museum, bears a griffin mark but no model number. Equally rare is the attractive figure of a boy with a bird on his raised hand (No. 30) illustrated in Plate 142.

Falling into none of the previous categories are a drunkard, or toper (No. 1), lettered in script around the base 'Stea-dy-La-ds'; a pair of previously unrecorded miniature Turks (both No. 3), and a larger version of the male (No. 25); and a bearded Russian peasant (No. 37). With the exception of theatrical personalities, full-length studies of notables of the day were rarely issued at Rockingham, and thus the model of *Napoleon* (No. 42), who died in 1821, is unexpected.

The rare two-dimensional figures with a flat back and mounted on a rectangular base are unusual, partly on account of their simplicity. Two different subjects are known, namely a pair of greyhounds—one standing, the other lying down—and two boys boxing (Plate 143). They are decorated only in gilt and do not bear a model number. The Minton factory also made models of this type.[16]

The standard of enamelled decoration on Rockingham figures is not especially notable, and with few exceptions the relatively sombre palette, with large areas left white, are almost distinguishing features. Pastel shades applied

14. F. B. Gilhespy, *Derby Porcelain*, London, 1961, p. 45 and Plates 65 and 66.
15. G. A. Godden, op. cit., p. 113.
16. G. A. Godden, op. cit., p. 82 and Plates 128–33.

143. FLAT-BACK FIGURE, *c.*1826–30. Porcelain, a rare figure of boy boxers, glazed and gilded. Red griffin, mark 52, and Cl. 1 in red. Height 9.2 cm (3.6 in). *Hurst Collection, Yorkshire Museum, York.* *See page 192*

144. BUST OF GEORGE IV, *c.*1826. Biscuit porcelain. Incised with the very rare mark 'Brameld & Co's/ Rockingham Works/ near Rotherham/ Yorkshire' (mark 50). Height 17.5 cm (6.9 in). *Courtesy of Mrs D. Murray.* *See pages 193 and 223*

in broad washes are also commonly found. As would be expected, animals, when enamelled, are naturalistically coloured, but many have gilt decoration only. Some figures of humans do, however, wear eye-catching dress—green waistcoats, yellow trousers, red skirts—and a few are decorated with patterned clothing. This tends to be prominent on figures with low model numbers, for example a Milkmaid (No. 2), in the Yorkshire Museum, and theatrical personalities. Exceptionally, one notes a style of enamelling more associated with contemporary Minton figures, typified by finely patterned clothing in bright colours with additional gilding, clearly the work of one particularly talented artist.

In biscuit porcelain, a limited range of busts of distinguished personages of the day was published. The usual mark is an impressed griffin (mark 53), but exceptions are known—as, for example, the fine study of *George IV* (1762–1830) (Plate 144) with its unique incised inscription. The presence of fire-cracks and kiln dirt on this piece suggest an early date of manufacture. His brother, Frederick Augustus, *Duke of York* (1763–1827) appears in two versions. Recollecting that the Bramelds were commissioned by William IV to supply a dessert service for the royal household, it is likely they would produce a bust of this monarch, and although no fully authenticated example has been recorded, busts of him with Rockingham characteristics are known. Similarly, in recognition of the support given to the Bramelds by the second *Earl Fitzwilliam* (1748–1833), the three known busts of their patron must surely be authentic Swinton products in spite of the absence of factory marks—examples are in the Rotherham, Sheffield and York Museums. Jewitt[17] attributes them to Rockingham, stating that the modeller was William Eley, who 'executed some admirable works'—presumably other busts. *Lord Henry Brougham* (1778–1868), the orator and advocate of Queen Caroline, also appears in the form of a bust, and is shown wearing a long wig. These personalities normally stand on a circular base, whereas two others, *William Wordsworth* (1770–1850) and *Sir Walter Scott* (1771–1832), occur either simply cut off at the shoulders, or mounted on a socle. An indication of the cost of these decorative items is provided by an invoice sent to Wentworth House for goods supplied on 4 October 1831:

4 China Biscuit Busts £3.12.0

Jewitt records a full-length statue of *Lady Russell* after Chantrey's original, but this has not been recognized, nor has the statue of the *Marchioness of Abercorn*,[18] friend and confidante of Princess Victoria (the future queen), mentioned in a list of presents given by Earl Fitzwilliam to the princess when she visited Wentworth House in 1836 (see page 70).

17. L. Jewitt, *Ceramic Art in Great Britain*, London, 1878, Vol. 1, p. 515.
18. Second daughter of the 6th Duke of Bedford.

Rockingham Porcelain Figures and Busts

Listed below are the porcelain figures and busts which have been recorded to date, together with the principal dimension of the models. Thus the height is normally given, but in the case of recumbent figures their length (l) is stated. The dimensions quoted should be regarded as approximate, since the size of a figure depends upon the way in which it was assembled from its component parts and the degree of shrinkage which took place during firing. Those marked with an asterisk (*) were also produced at Derby, some in almost identical form.

Model number		*Height* cm	in
1	A drunkard, 'Stea-dy-La-ds'.	14.0	5.5
2	A milkmaid, a pail in her right hand.	18.5	7.3
3	A miniature Turk on a scrolled base.	7.6	3.0
3	A miniature female Turk on a scrolled base.	7.6	3.0
4	A piping shepherd wearing a plumed hat, a dog by his side.	20.3	8.0
4	A shepherdess feeding a sheep by her side.	16.5	6.5
*6	*Madame Vestris* (or John Liston impersonating her) singing 'Buy a Broom'.[19]	16.0	6.3
7	John Liston as Simon Pengander.	17.5	6.9
8	John Liston as Billy Lackaday.[20]	15.2	6.0
*9	John Liston as Paul Pry.	14.7	5.8
10	John Liston as Moll Flaggon.[21]	16.0	6.3
11	John Liston as Lubin Log.	17.8	7.0
13	Continental peasant *Femme de la Vallee de Tésino en Tyrol* (see page 189).	18.5	7.3
14	Continental peasant *Paysanne de Schlier en Tirol.*	19.8	7.8
15	Continental peasant *Paysanne du Mongfall en Tirol.*	18.5	7.3
*16	A pug dog seated.	7.1	2.8
*16	A pug bitch seated.	7.1	2.8
18	Continental peasant *Paysanne du Canton de Zurich.*	18.5	7.3
19	Continental peasant *Montferrine des environs de Casal.*[22]	19.4	7.6

19. See pages 185 and 188 for comments on this figure.
20. A character in the play *Sweethearts and Wives*. See pages 185 and 188 for details of Liston in other roles.
21. A character in the play *Lord of the Manor*.
22. We are indebted to Miss Emmeline Leary for bringing this previously unrecorded figure to our attention.

Model number		Height	
		cm	in
21	Continental peasant *Paysanne des environs de Bilbao.*	not known	
22	Continental peasant *Paysanne de Sagran en Tirol.*	17.8	7.0
*23	*Swiss boy.* A boy wearing a straw hat, a knapsack by his left side.	21.1	8.3
*23	*Swiss girl.* A girl wearing a straw hat, a basket in her left hand, a bundle of faggots in the other.	19.1	7.5
*25	A Turk on a shell base.	9.7	3.8
*26	A boy clasping a broken pitcher which rests on a rocky pile.	13.5	5.3
*26	A girl holding a lamb, a pitcher in her right hand.	14.7	5.8
*28	A boy writing seated on a drum.	12.2	4.8
*28	A girl sewing seated on a stool.	12.7	5.0
*29	A grotesque man, his hands on his generous stomach.	9.7	3.8
30	A boy with a bird on his left hand.	12.3	4.8
31	A girl holding a basket of flowers over her head.	22.4	8.8
32	A boy Bacchus, scantily clad, a cup in his right hand.	14.7	5.8
*35	A girl standing on a pierced scroll base holding a lamb.[23]	14.7	5.8
*35	A boy standing on a pierced scroll base holding a dog.[23]	14.7	5.8
36	A beggar boy carrying a basket of apples.	12.7	5.0
36	A beggar girl stirring a bowl held in her left hand.	12.7	5.0
37	A bearded Russian peasant, a knapsack on his back.[24]	16.5	6.5
*39	A seated cobbler whistling to his caged starling.	14.0	5.5
40	A girl kneeling playing with a kitten.	9.7	3.8
40	A boy kneeling feeding a dog.	10.2	4.0
42	*Napoleon* in military uniform, a scroll in his left hand.	20.3	8.0
44	A boy kneeling on his left knee feeding a rabbit.	14.0	5.5
44	A seated girl, a lamb under her right arm, a bowl in her left hand.	9.7	3.8
*48	A girl seated holding a garland of flowers.	10.2	4.0

23. Possibly the pair known as the 'French shepherd and shepherdess' (see page 184). An almost identical pair of this name was produced at Derby *c.* 1830, where they are model numbers 57 (see J. Twitchett, op. cit., Plate 342).
24. Modelled also at Gardner's factory near Moscow.

Model number		Height cm	Height in	
*48	A boy seated on an upturned basket holding a garland, his hat on his knees.	10.2	4.0	
49	Continental peasant *Chef de Tartares Noguais.*	18.6	7.3	
50	Continental peasant *Paysan de la Vallee de Ziller en Tirol.*	19.9	7.8	
53	Continental peasant *Paysan du Canton de Zurich.*	19.1	7.5	
57	Continental peasant *Paysan Piemontais de la Vallee d'Aoste.*	19.1	7.5	
58	A Continental shepherd with a sheep and a dog.	19.9	7.8	
63	A child sleeping, its head on a basket of fruit.	12.7	5.0	(1)
64	A child awakening, its right arm outstretched.	12.2	4.8	(1)
65	A child sleeping.[25]	10.2	4.0	(1)
66	A child sleeping, its right arm across its chest.	12.5	4.9	(1)
69	A standing elephant.	3.8	1.5	
70	A miniature group of a rabbit and young.	2.5	1.0	
71	A miniature of a dog sitting on a rocky base looking to the left.	2.5	1.0	
72	A miniature of a rabbit.	1.3	0.5	
73	A miniature of a squirrel eating from its front paws (two sizes).	5.1 3.8	2.0 1.5	
74	A miniature of a dog sitting on a circular base looking to the left.	3.6	1.4	
76	A pug dog sitting on a rococo base (two sizes).	6.9 5.3	2.7 2.1	
77	A cat sitting on a tasselled cushion (three sizes).	6.4 5.8 4.6	2.5 2.3 1.8	
*80	A recumbent stag.	7.1	2.8	(1)
*80	A recumbent doe.	8.4	3.3	(1)
83	A dog in running attitude.	7.4	2.9	
84	A dog standing drinking from a bowl.	8.4	3.3	
87	A dog lying down with head raised.	9.7	3.8	(1)
89	A dog standing watching a mouse.	8.9	3.5	
*91	A recumbent long-haired spaniel with its head			

25. Model No. 65 was first listed by A. A. Eaglestone and T. A. Lockett, *The Rockingham Pottery*, Rotherham, 1964, p. 119, but later doubted by them in the revised edition, 1973, p. 144, of this book. It has subsequently been reported by Dr D. G. Rice, op. cit. (footnote 11 above), p. 82. An example of model No. 65, sold at Sotheby's on 8 May 1973, lot no. 23, and illustrated in the sale catalogue, appears to be identical to the figure incised No. 63 in the Yorkshire Museum, York, depicting a sleeping child. The authors have not seen an example of No. 65.

Model number		*Height* cm	in	
	resting on its left leg.[26]	7.1	2.8	(1)
92	A recumbent hound, its head raised.	9.7	3.8	(1)
93	A hound running.	5.8	2.3	
94	A recumbent long-haired dog with its head slightly raised, its tail curled to the left.	10.9	4.3	(1)
94	As above, but modelled in reverse.	10.9	4.3	(1)
99	A swan.	5.8	2.3	
100	A recumbent sheep, its left front leg outstretched.	7.6	3.0	(1)
101	A seated hound, its head raised.	7.6	3.0	
102	Two children lying entwined kissing.	16.5	6.5	(1)
*104	A recumbent cat with head raised, its tail curled around to the left.	7.1	2.8	(1)
106	A crouching rabbit.	6.1	2.4	(1)
107	A cat with three kittens.	10.2	4.0	(1)
*108	A recumbent ram, its head turned to the left.	6.9	2.7	(1)
*108	A recumbent ewe, its head turned to the right.	6.3	2.5	(1)
109	A small recumbent sheep, its head turned to the right.	3.9	1.5	(1)
110	A crouching hare eating.	7.4	2.9	(1)
*111	A bushy-tailed squirrel eating from its front paws.	5.8	2.3	
112	A dove with open wings on a rocky base.	7.6	3.0	
113	Continental peasant *Homme du Peuple à Valence.*	18.5	7.3	
114	Continental peasant *Paysanne des environs de Bayonne.*[27]	22.4	8.8	
115	Continental peasant *Paysan Basque des environs de Bayonne*	20.3	8.0	
119	Continental peasant *Femme d'Andalousie.*	19.1	7.5	
120	Continental peasant *Paysanne de St. Angelo.*	19.8	7.8	
136	A peacock with upright fanned tail.	9.9	3.9	
138	Continental peasant *Laitiere des environs d'Harlem* (see page 189).	not known		

The model numbers of the following are not known:

		cm	in	
	John Liston as Tristram Sappy[28] (possibly No. 5 or No. 12).	18.5	7.3	

26. An almost identical dog signed by the Derby modeller William Coffee is illustrated in H. G. Bradley (ed.), *Ceramics of Derbyshire 1750–1975*, London, 1978, Plate 42.

27. *Paysanne Basque des environs de Bayonne* is recorded by D. G. Rice, *Rockingham Ornamental Porcelain*, London, 1965, p. 92. The title of the engraving upon which this figure is based does not include the word 'Basque'.

28. A character in the play *Deaf as a Post.* No fully authenticated example is known to the authors.

Model number		*Height*		
		cm	in	
A cat sitting on an oval rococo base.		5.8	2.3	
A youth wearing a loin cloth holding a basket in front of him—possibly symbolic of *Spring*.		10.2	4.0	
A flower boy and girl (see pages 184 and 192, possibly No. 48).		not known		

The following two-dimensional 'flat-backed' figures are known, neither of which bears a model number:

		cm	in	
Two boys boxing.		9.2	3.6	
Two greyhounds, one standing, the other reclining.		7.4	2.9	(1)

The following busts and statues are known, or have been recorded, none of which bears a model number:

		cm	in
The Duke of York.[29]		18.5	7.3
George IV.		17.5	6.9
The Duke of York (second version).		16.5	6.5
William IV.[30]		17.8	7.0
Lord Brougham.[31]		16.5	6.5
Earl Fitzwilliam.		38.1 34.3 30.5	15.0 13.5 12.0
Sir Walter Scott.	height unmounted	19.1	7.5
William Wordsworth.	height unmounted	20.3	8.0
A statue of the *Marchioness of Abercorn* (see page 194).		not known	
A statue of *Lady Russell* (see page 194).		not known	

29. A similar bust was made by Chamberlain's, Worcester.
30. Attributed to Rockingham by Dr Rice on the basis of paste and style.
31. A similar bust was issued by Mintons.

10
Artists and Other Workpeople

Since virtually all business documents relating to the Swinton Pottery are lost, our knowledge of the artists employed there to decorate porcelain and earthenware is much less complete than for most important factories of comparable date. Apart from those artists named by Jewitt and the few signed pieces recorded, information about these Swinton workpeople has been obtained from a wide variety of documentary sources.

Certain names appear in the surviving factory Pattern Books, but many more have been traced in the Swinton Parish Documents. Most significant of these were the militia lists, drawn up annually from 1779 to 1832 to record the names, ages and occupations of all men aged between eighteen and forty-five who were liable for service in the local militia.[1] The early years are incomplete, but from 1820 to 1832 most lists survive, thus giving a good indication of the artists present in the first years of porcelain production, and a record of those who served their apprenticeship at the Swinton Pottery. Obviously, the names of older artists are missing, and also of any who happened to live outside the Swinton boundary. Additional information comes from local parish registers and other documents such as bastardy orders, and Poor Law returns and correspondence.

China Painters

JOHN BAGLEY (b. 1810)
A china painter named in the 1831 militia list.

ISAAC BAGULEY (1794–1855)
Baguley's presence in Swinton as early as 1826 is shown by reference to him in a deed.[2] Formerly a Derby artist, he was one of a number of experienced painters the Bramelds managed to entice from elsewhere. A factory document of 1829 states that he had 'charge of all the painting and gilding department in china and enamel earthenware'.[3] Jewitt's comment that Baguley was one of their best painters and gilders,[4] and Chaffers' statement that he was a painter

1. Ages and occupations were, however, not always stated exactly.
2. Registry of Deeds, Wakefield, Vol. IZ, 1827, p. 600, No. 574.
3. L. Jewitt, *Ceramic Art in Great Britain*, London, 1878, Vol. 1, p. 503.
4. L. Jewitt, op. cit., Vol. 1, p. 506.

of birds[5] cannot be substantiated, since signed specimens of his work are not known. He evidently remained at the Works until its closure, his name occurring in the 1841 Census together with those of his sons Alfred (1821–91) and Edwin who were apprentice china-painters there. After the Works closed in 1842, Isaac and Alfred continued working on the site as independent decorators purchasing wares largely from north Staffordshire (see pages 73 and 228).

WILLIAM WILLIS BAILEY (b. 1806)

Bailey was one of the most talented artists at the Rockingham Works, his name occurring in the militia lists between 1828 and 1831. In 1832 he was included in an account of artists engaged on the royal dessert service which appeared in the *Yorkshire Gazette* for 14 April of that year (see page 134). White's *Directory of Sheffield* for 1833 lists him as 'Bailey Wm. Ornamental Painter'.

He seems to have been a most versatile artist, Jewitt describing him as 'the principal butterfly painter, and who also painted landscapes and crests'.[6] In the Pattern Book (see p. 230) seen by the writers, dessert pattern 478 is annotated 'Landscape Bailey. Maroon band. Lose gilding under maroon'. Dr Rice illustrates a documentary plaque of a dog chasing game,[7] and two further unmarked plaques *The Clyde from Erskine Ferry* and *Sunset—View on the Welsh Coast*.[8]

At some time during the 1830s, Bailey became an independent decorator at nearby Wath-upon-Dearne. A magnificent dessert service of unknown manufacture with many pieces signed by Bailey and inscribed 'Wath', or 'Wath China Works', as he called his decorating establishment, was sold by Messrs Christie's.[9] The scenes are taken from contemporary paintings and literature of the 1830s, all showing figures in landscapes, and are reminiscent of some of the scenes on the large and elaborate wine coolers (Colour Plate E) in the royal dessert service. Items from the Wath service may be seen in the Rotherham Museum. A plaque sold at Phillips[10] depicts a view of *Windsor Castle*, 'from a drawing by P. Dewint, Esqr., W. W. Bailey, Pinx^{t}, China Works Wath'.

SYLVANUS BALL (b. *c.*1795)

Included in the militia lists for 1828 as a potter and 1831 as a painter. In the 1841 Census he is described as a china-painter living in Swinton, and his association with the factory was therefore a long one.

5. W. Chaffers, *Marks and Monograms on Pottery and Porcelain* (15th revised edn. 1965), Vol. 2, p. 180.
6. L. Jewitt, op. cit., Vol. 1, p. 515.
7. D. G. Rice, *Rockingham Ornamental Porcelain*, London, 1965, Plate 98.
8. D. G. Rice, *The Illustrated Guide to Rockingham Pottery and Porcelain*, London, 1971, Plates 147 and 148.
9. 19 November 1973, lot 4, illustrated in the sale catalogue.
10. 22 July 1981, lot 188, illustrated in the sale catalogue.

John Wager Brameld (1797–1851)

Although better known as one of the three partners who controlled the Rockingham Works during the period of porcelain manufacture, John Wager Brameld was a skilful artist. Jewitt recorded 'Mr. John Wager Brameld, like his brother [Thomas], was a man of pure taste. He was an excellent artist, and some truly exquisite paintings on porcelain by him have come under my notice. He was a clever painter of flowers and of figures, and landscapes.'[11]

Ebenezer Rhodes, who visited the Works in 1826, noted that John Wager painted the scenes from *Don Quixote* on the rhinoceros vase (Plate 98) which is now in the Rotherham Museum.[12] Jewitt further states that he had seen a snuff box decorated with a painting of *The Politician* and signed 'J. W. Brameld', but the present whereabouts of this piece is not known. It seems probable that John Wager Brameld's artistic talents were not used to the full, for he spent much time as the firm's traveller, and later was involved with managing the Bramelds' London shop and warehouse.

After the closure of the Works in 1842 he stayed in London, residing at 7 Coburg Place, Bayswater, and entered several pieces of Rockingham porcelain in the 1851 Exhibition. In the Catalogue he fancifully described himself as 'Manufacturer', but most probably the items were decorated (possibly by him) before 1842 and he simply had them in his possession at the time of the Exhibition.

Thomas Brentnall (*c.*1801–*c.*1869)

Brentnall was previously at Derby, Haslem[13] stating that he 'excelled as a flower painter', although his work at Derby has not been recognized. In 1821 he moved to Coalport and was there until at least 1824. He is first recorded in Swinton in the 1831 militia list as a china-painter, aged thirty. White's *Directory of Sheffield* for 1833 names Brentnall as a flower-painter, and the Wath-upon-Dearne parish registers include the baptism of twin sons in May 1837. By June 1841 he was in Staffordshire.[14]

Brentnall was one of the artists employed on the dessert service for William IV, and he is the only artist specializing in flower painting mentioned in the *Yorkshire Gazette* for 14 April 1832 (see page 134), where the service is described. Therefore, he may well have painted the distinctive flower groups in the centre of certain of the royal comports (Plate 84). No signed examples of his work are known.

11. L. Jewitt, op. cit., Vol. 1, p. 502.
12. E. Rhodes, *Yorkshire Scenery*, London, 1826, p. 155.
13. J. Haslem, *The Old Derby China Factory*, London, 1876, p. 111.
14. G. A. Godden, *Coalport and Coalbrookdale Porcelains*, London, 1970, p. 105.

JOSEPH BULLOUGH (b. 1796)

The first reference to Joseph Bullough occurs in the Swinton militia list for 1828, where he is described as a china-painter, then aged thirty-two. Jewitt,[15] quoting a document of about 1829, describes him as a 'sorter of biscuit ware', but the Swinton parish register for that same year recording the baptism of his son gives his occupation as china-painter.

HENRY CARR (1811–33)

The presence of this artist at the Rockingham Works is known from a bastardy order dated 22 February 1832 requiring that Henry Carr, china-painter of nearby Rawmarsh, should maintain his illegitimate daughter.[16] Since the child was then six weeks old, Carr must have been in the area from at least the spring of 1831, presumably employed at the Rockingham Works during this period. He was still working for the Bramelds in March 1833 when he was in trouble with the Overseers of the Poor for failing to pay maintenance money, and with characteristic generosity the Bramelds paid it for him.[17] The Rawmarsh parish registers record the burial of Henry Carr, aged only twenty-two, in September 1833.

THOMAS COLCLOUGH (b. 1789)

Described as a china-painter in the 1831 Swinton militia list. He is also mentioned in the Rockingham Pattern Book seen by the writers, where teaware pattern 935 is annotated 'Colclough Pattern from 776'.

WILLIAM CORDEN (1797–1867)

Both Jewitt[18] and Haslem[19] record the presence of this Derby-trained artist at Swinton, Haslem stating that he worked on the royal dessert service. Corden's work is known on Derby, and signed Coalport plaques are recorded.[20] Painting in his style, notably portrait decoration, occurs on Rockingham,[21] but there are no known contemporary references to link Corden with the factory.

WILLIAM COWEN (1797–1860)

Cowen was a well-known Rotherham artist who exhibited at the Royal Academy. According to Jewitt,[22] he was employed as a decorator at the

15. L. Jewitt, op. cit., Vol. 1, p. 503.
16. Swinton Parish Documents, Poor Law.
17. Ibid., Poor Law correspondence.
18. L. Jewitt, op. cit., Vol. 1, p. 515.
19. J. Haslem, op. cit., p. 113.
20. G. A. Godden, op. cit. (footnote 14 above), p. 108, refers to the sale of porcelain blanks for outside decoration.
21. A mug finely decorated in this artist's manner with a portrait of the Duke of Wellington is illustrated in *The Connoisseur Year Book, 1962*, p. 144, Plate 9.
22. L. Jewitt, op. cit., Vol. 1, p. 515.

Rockingham Works, although there is no evidence for this. More probably, prints taken from his local and other views were used by factory artists in decorating wares as, for example, a plate illustrated by Dr Rice[23] finely enamelled with a *Northern View of Rotherham*. This is taken from a print which appears in Ebenezer Rhodes' *Yorkshire Scenery*, 1826, where, opposite page 65, appears *Northern View of Rotherham* drawn and etched by Wm. Cowen.

JOHN CRESWELL (b. 1801)

Jewitt possessed the original agreement dated 17 November 1826 between Creswell and the Bramelds, stating that he would work five years for them.[24] The Swinton parish registers include an entry dated June 1826 for the baptism of a son, where Creswell is described as a china-painter, the first time this occupation appears in any of the local documents. He is further recorded in the militia lists for 1828 and 1829. Jewitt, who describes Creswell as 'an excellent painter', quotes from the articles of agreement the wages that Creswell was to receive—'7s. 6d. a day for the first three years; 9s. 3d. a day for the fourth year; and 10s. 6d. a day for the fifth year.' It seems that Creswell was also employed at Wentworth House, as an invoice from the Pottery dated 14 December 1829 shows:

> To John Creswells Wages in painting Plants &c
> at Wentworth House £5.5.0

It is not known where Creswell worked before coming to Swinton, but he seems to have been one of the most notable artists employed at the Rockingham Works during this period. His style may now be recognized, since a Rockingham plaque shown in Plate 145, bears on the reverse the inscription 'Creswell, Pinx: N° 15', suggesting that it was one of a numbered series. Interestingly, the following plaque, or 'slab', was supplied to Wentworth House on 3 September 1828, destined to be a gift from the earl:

> 1 China Slab N° 15 present to Miss Edmonds £1.14.6

and may be the one illustrated. Creswell's work is very similar to that of Edwin Steele and would probably have been attributed to that artist. This plaque serves as a reminder that there is always a tendency to assign painting to the well-known names in a factory, whereas many of the less well-documented artists could produce very creditable work. The contemporary spelling of this decorator's name is Creswell and not Cresswell, as given by Jewitt and later authors.

HAIGH HIRSTWOOD (1774–1854)

Jewitt states that Hirstwood 'was a clever painter of flowers, &c., and was considered the best fly painter at the Rockingham works. In 1826 he copied, for

23. D. G. Rice, op. cit. (footnote 8 above), Plate 74.
24. L. Jewitt, op. cit., Vol. 1, pp. 503–4.

145. PLAQUE, *c.*1826–30. Porcelain, enamelled with flowers and fruit in a basket by the artist John Creswell. Red griffin, mark 52, and painted inscription 'Creswell, Pinx: N°. 15'. Length of plaque 17.5 cm (6.9 in). *See page 204*

use in the decoration of the Rockingham china, upwards of five hundred insects at Wentworth House, which had been arranged by Lady Milton.'[25] The earliest documentary reference to his presence in Swinton occurs in the will of William Brameld which he signed as a witness on 10 February 1813.[26] He is recorded in the 1821 Census and in the 1822 militia list, but he moved to York some time between 1827 and 1830 to manage the Bramelds' shop there until its closure in 1833.[27] He then opened his own shop and china decorating business in York which seems to have flourished.

No signed work by Haigh Hirstwood is known. Jewitt states that he was one of the artists who were employed in decorating the royal dessert service, but since by 1830 he was in York, this seems improbable.

25. Ibid., p. 462.
26. Borthwick Institute, University of York, probate records, Exchequer Court of York, Doncaster deanery, March 1814.
27. For details of the Bramelds' York shop and Hirstwood's activities in that city see A. and A. Cox, *The Rockingham Works*, Sheffield, 1974, pp. 119–24.

JOSEPH HIRSTWOOD (1813–31) and WILLIAM HIRSTWOOD

Sons of Haigh Hirstwood, they were both apprentice china-painters at the Rockingham Works. Nothing is known of William, but Joseph is recorded in the Swinton militia list for 1831. The parish registers note his burial, aged nineteen, in September 1831.

An interesting plaque (Plate 146), previously in the possession of the Hirstwood descendants, is said to have been the work of Joseph, and if so he was an exceptionally talented young man.[28] Although unmarked, the plaque with its fine flower group is painted on the back of a factory waster, the reverse transfer-printed in blue with the Rockingham *Union* pattern which was used on tablewares.

WILLIAM HOPKINS (b. 1795)

A china-painter recorded in the Swinton militia lists between 1826 and 1831. The next reference to him occurs in the 1841 Census, and it seems likely, therefore, that he was in Swinton throughout the 1830s.

WILLIAM JONES (b. *c.* 1806)

A china-painter included in the 1828 Swinton militia list.

WILLIAM LEYLAND (1807–53)

Jewitt describes Leyland as 'a clever painter, gilder, and enameller, and understood well all the practical details of the potter's art'.[29] He is recorded in the Swinton militia lists between 1825 and 1831, first as an apprentice, then as a china-painter. The Swinton parish registers record the baptisms of his children between 1829 and 1833, and another child was baptized at Wath in 1837. He left the Rockingham Works in 1839 to work as a china-decorator for his father-in-law Haigh Hirstwood in York. Although he worked for the Bramelds for at least fourteen years, his style has not been recognized on Rockingham wares other than on a plaque attributed to him by Oxley Grabham decorated with a hollyhock, a full-blown tulip and other flowers.[30]

WILLIAM LLANDEG (1809–36)

Described by Jewitt[31] as 'a charming fruit and flower painter', Llandeg is included in the Swinton militia lists for 1829 and 1831. His burial in October 1836 is recorded in the Swinton parish registers, and a tombstone marks his grave in the churchyard. His name, variously spelt Llandeg, Landeg or Llandegg, occurs frequently in the Rockingham Pattern Book seen by the writers. In dessert wares:

28. O. Grabham, 'Yorkshire Potteries, Pots, and Potters', *Annual Report of the Yorkshire Philosophical Society for 1915*, York, 1916, p. 109 and Plate 103.
29. L. Jewitt, op. cit., Vol. 1, p. 462.
30. O. Grabham, op. cit., p. 109 and Plate 104.
31. L. Jewitt, op. cit., Vol. 1, p. 515.

146. PLAQUE, *c.*1830. Porcelain, enamelled with a flower group attributed by family tradition to Joseph Hirstwood. No mark, but painted on the back of a waster printed with the Rockingham *Union* pattern. Length of plaque 17 cm (6.7 in). *See page 206*

561 Landeg's groups 4 on plate.
682 Apple blossom in centre by Llandegg.
695 Hawthorn blossom on a crome green leaf crimson ground. Gilding as 675. by Llandegg.

In teawares:

742 Wild flowers by Llandeg.
927 Groups of flowers by Llandeg.
931 Printed Green raseberry, a Group of flowers in Centre & 3 Sprigs around Cup & Saucer. Stenceled by Llandegg.

The raspberry, or blackberry border (Plate 85), a closely-patterned transfer-printed design of tiny berries usually blue, green or grey, is associated with Llandeg, and sometimes used as a border for his own paintings, or with simple flower sprays as in dessert pattern 607 'Flowers by girls—olive blackberry border'. This transfer-printed design is also found on earthenwares.

JOHN LUCAS (1811–33)
Haslem states that John Lucas came to Swinton shortly after completing his apprenticeship under his father Daniel at Derby.[32] His stay at the Rockingham Works was brief, since the record of his burial in the Swinton parish registers on 7 May 1833 gives his place of abode as Derby. Presumably his work on Rockingham must be rare and has not been recognized. Haslem says that 'he painted somewhat after the manner of his father, but his execution was more refined', and he refers to two Rockingham plaques by Lucas, *The Plains of Waterloo* and *View of Chatsworth.*

JOSEPH MANSFIELD (b. 1803)
Mansfield came to the Rockingham Works from Coalport[33] during the 1820s and became, according to Jewitt, 'the principal embosser and chaser in gold'.[34] He is recorded in the Swinton parish registers following the death of his daughter in February 1827, and is described as a china-painter in the militia lists between 1828 and 1831. The Wath-upon-Dearne registers include the baptism of a son in April 1837, and in William White's *History, Gazetteer & Directory of the West Riding of Yorkshire* for 1838 he is described as a 'chaser and gilder'.

GEORGE MERT (b. 1802)
A china-painter included in the 1829 militia list.

JOSEPH MILLS
The baptism of Mills' son is recorded in the Swinton parish registers in November 1833, and this is the only such entry where the artist's occupation is specifically given as china-gilder. Another son was baptized in 1835, Mills then being described as a china-painter.

WILLIAM OSBORN
The Wath-upon-Dearne parish registers include the baptism of Osborn's daughter in March 1839, his occupation given as china-painter.

PEDLEY (first name not known)
Pedley's name is included in a list of Rockingham artists who were working on the dessert service for William IV (see page 134), and clearly he must have been an artist of note. Unfortunately nothing more is known of him.

32. J. Haslem, op. cit., p. 122.
33. G. A. Godden, op. cit. (footnote 14 above), p. 117.
34. L. Jewitt, op. cit., Vol. 1, p. 515.

JOHN RANDALL (1810–1910)
Apprenticed to his uncle Thomas Martin Randall, a ceramic-decorator at Madeley near Coalport, he went on to Rockingham probably after 1831. His stay there was short for by 1835 he was in Coalport after having also worked briefly in Staffordshire.[35] The only contemporary reference to the time he spent in Swinton occurs in White's *Directory of Sheffield* for 1833. The colourful birds associated with Randall and well known on Coalport, are certainly in evidence on Rockingham porcelain of the puce-griffin period (Plate 77). However, work should be attributed to him with caution since another Swinton artist, Russell, was at the same time painting birds which are similar in appearance to those by Randall, if somewhat less competently executed (Plate 148).

JOHN RAYNER (b. 1797)
References to this artist occur in the militia lists, land tax returns, and Swinton parish registers between 1823 and 1838. He is described as a painter of earthenware from 1823 to 1828, a china-painter between 1829 and 1834, and thereafter as a potter.

JAMES ROSS (b. 1811)
An apprentice china-painter recorded in the Swinton militia lists for 1829 and 1831. In the Rockingham Pattern Book seen by the writers, dessert pattern 640 is annotated 'A bunch of fruit in centre by James Ross'. A marked and signed example of his work dated 1829 is shown in Plate 147, where a plaque with a finely painted study of black grapes is illustrated. This is of particular interest in view of the fact that any Rockingham fruit painting, especially if it includes grapes, is usually attributed to the more famous Thomas Steel. Since the term of Ross's apprenticeship at Swinton would include the years 1829 to 1831, it is possible that he may have been taught by Steel, as these dates correspond closely with the period of time which this notable fruit-painter spent at the Rockingham Works.

RUSSELL (first name not known)
The only references to Russell occur in the Rockingham Pattern Book seen by the writers, where several patterns are assigned to him, for example in dessert wares:

643 Printed as 857. Russells flying birds in centre.
644 Printed as 643. Russells birds in Centre.

Examples of pattern 644 are in the Rotherham and Sheffield Museums; they

35. G. A. Godden, op. cit. (footnote 14 above), p. 122.

have a green-printed border of *Landeg's blackberry pattern* (see pages 94 and 207). In teawares, the following patterns occur:

881 Russells birds.
888 Russells birds.
916 Russells birds flying.
918 Russells birds.

A Rockingham tea cup and saucer decorated with pattern 888 is illustrated in Plate 148, and these colourful, exotic birds have much in common with those normally attributed to John Randall.

JOHN SHELDON (b. 1803)
A china-painter recorded in the Swinton militia lists for 1826 and 1828.

GEORGE SPEIGHT (1808–79)
One of the better-known Rockingham artists, George Speight came from a Swinton family of potters. His baptism is recorded in the parish registers on 16 June 1808, and since his father William was a pot-painter and his grandfather Godfrey was a potter in Swinton, George Speight was therefore continuing a family tradition when he served his apprenticeship at the Rockingham Works. His name appears in the militia lists and parish registers between 1826 and 1839, during which period six children were baptized. He left Swinton in 1839, or soon after, and by 1841 he was working for Ridgways.[36] Between 1851 and 1857 he returned to Swinton to work as an independent decorator and was buried there on 11 November 1879.

A number of signed pieces by him have been recorded, including plaques depicting *The Mother's Grave*; *Madonna and Child* and *Derwent Water*.[37] A cabinet plate finely decorated with *The Enchanted Stream* is illustrated in Plate 99, and a large tray in private possession has an enamelled copy of Van Dyck's *Earl Strafford occupied in dictating his defence to his secretary*.

Speight was one of the artists employed on the royal dessert service, as the *Yorkshire Gazette* for 14 April 1832 confirms: 'the Royal Arms by Mr Speight, jun.' (see page 134). In fact much of his finest work was done when he was only just out of his apprenticeship. He was one of a number of young china-painters of particular talent who were employed at the Rockingham Works.

THOMAS STEEL (1772–1850)
The career of Thomas Steel, the famous fruit-painter, has been well documented. Haslem records that he originated in the Staffordshire Potteries and worked at the Derby factory before coming to Swinton.[38] His name does

36. G. A. Godden, *The Illustrated Guide to Ridgway Porcelains*, London, 1972, pp. 64–5.
37. Dr. G. Rice, *Rockingham Ornamental Porcelain*, London, 1965, Colour Plate 12. Also D. G. Rice, op. cit. (footnote 8 above), Plate 149 and Colour Plate VII.
38. J. Haslem, op. cit., p. 119.

147. PLAQUE, 1829. Porcelain, enamelled with a bunch of black grapes by James Ross. Red griffin, mark 52, and painted inscription 'J. Ross 1829'. Diameter of plaque 14 cm (5.5 in). *See page 209*

148. TEA CUP AND SAUCER, *c.*1830–42. Porcelain, of *basket-weave* moulding. Dark-blue ground with yellow flowers surrounding paintings of exotic birds in bright colours. Pattern number 888, ascribed in a Rockingham Pattern Book to Russell. Puce griffin, mark 55. Diameter of saucer 13.8 cm (5.4 in). *See pages 144, 209 and 210*

not occur in any of the local sources, but signed paintings by him on Rockingham porcelain are known, all belonging to the red-griffin period. It is possible that he arrived in Swinton about 1827 with his son Edwin, and left sometime before March 1832, when his name appears in a Minton wages list.[39] Signed pieces by him include a very fine tray with a study of fruit in his characteristic style (in the Rotherham Museum), and the delicately painted small plaque illustrated in Plate 149. In view of the tendency to attribute any fruit painting which includes grapes to Thomas Steel, a comparison of his style with the work of the relatively unknown contemporary James Ross (see page 209 and Plate 147) is of interest.

EDWIN STEELE (1806–71)

Edwin, son of Thomas Steel, tended to spell his surname with the extra 'e'. His name appears in the Swinton militia lists for 1827 and 1828 only, supporting the view that his stay in Swinton was brief. Haslem attributes to Edwin the painting of flowers on the rhinoceros vase in the Victoria and Albert Museum,[40] but no pieces of Rockingham signed by him are currently known. In the Rockingham Pattern Book which the writers have studied, a number of patterns are assigned to the Steels, but although the spelling of the name varies, they are perhaps more likely to be the work of Edwin since they are mainly flower paintings. For example, in teawares:

674 Stone ground, flowers by Ed. Steele
914 1 small flower by Steel

the former being a design of strawberry plants and flowers. In dessert wares:

512 Stone ground flowers by Steel
585 Steel's flowers on a buff ground

HENRY (?) TILBURY

Recorded by Jewitt as a painter of landscapes and figures, but otherwise unknown.[41]

EDWARD WOOD (b. *c.* 1816)

A china-painter at the Rockingham Works listed in the 1841 Census.

BENJAMIN WOOLF (b. 1776)

Described as a potter or painter in the Swinton militia lists and land tax returns between 1803 and 1828. He is listed as a china-painter in White's *Directory of Sheffield* for 1833.

39. G. A. Godden, *Minton Pottery and Porcelain of the First Period 1793–1850*, London, 1968, p. 124.
40. J. Haslem, op. cit., pp. 120–1.
41. L. Jewitt, op. cit., Vol. 1, p. 515.

149. PLAQUE, *c.*1830. Porcelain, with a fine fruit painting in the characteristic style of Thomas Steel. Red griffin, mark 52, and painted inscription 'Steel Pinx. No 5'. A companion piece is inscribed 'No 6'. Length 11.9 cm (4.7 in). *Courtesy of Bryan Bowden.* *See page 212*

A further three china-painters might be added to those already named. In the Swinton Parish Documents each is listed under the more general occupation of 'potter', but since the same names occur in the Pattern Books, it seems likely that they were in fact artists.

THOMAS CHILD (b. 1806)
One Pattern Book[42] refers to 'Mr Child's gold line dinner pattern', and this may have been the Thomas Child included in the militia lists between 1827 and 1831.

THOMAS HOYLAND (b. 1802)
In the Pattern Book seen by the writers, dessert pattern 671 shows an elaborate flower group annotated 'Plants by Mr Hoyland', probably the Thomas Hoyland whose name appears regularly in the militia lists from 1822 to 1831.

JOHN WILSON (b. 1801)
In a Pattern Book seen by Eaglestone and Lockett,[43] pattern 680 is described as 'Mr Wilson's Pattern'. This may well be the John Wilson, potter, included in the Swinton militia lists and parish registers between 1826 and 1831.

42. A. A. Eaglestone and T. A. Lockett, *The Rockingham Pottery*, Rotherham, 1964, p. 55.
43. Ibid., p. 55.

Modellers

It has long been recognized that a similarity exists between certain Rockingham and Derby figures, but the precise reason for this and the link between the two concerns has given much cause for speculation, as previously noted. Recent research, however, has revealed the presence in Swinton of two Derby figure modellers.

Thomas Griffin (b. 1797)

Griffin's name occurs in the Swinton militia list for 1827, where he is described as a potter. He was a figure modeller at Derby before coming to Swinton, as Haslem notes:[44]

> Farnsworth died at a good age in 1821, and Edward Keys succeeded him as foreman of the figure department. Edward Keys left Derby in 1826, and Thomas Griffin, another of the modellers, was then appointed foreman, but only held that position for a short time.

It seems that Griffin left Derby to come to Swinton in 1826 or 1827 and it must have been an achievement for the Bramelds to entice the foreman of the figure department at Derby to their own Works. Archaeological evidence from Swinton has recently confirmed beyond doubt that it was Thomas Griffin who modelled the Rockingham series of Continental peasant figures. The solid base of the master model for figure number 138 was discovered inscribed *Laitiere des environs d'Harlem* and incised on the underside 'by T. Griffin/July 15th 1830'.

Whilst at Swinton, Griffin was also responsible for the curiously original comports for William IV's dessert service. The *Yorkshire Gazette* for 14 April 1832 lists the artists employed on this work (see page 134) including 'modeller Mr Griffin'. It is not known how long Griffin remained at Swinton.

George Cocker (1794–1868)

Another connection between Rockingham and Derby may be traced in the presence at both concerns of George Cocker. Jewitt[45] states that Cocker was apprenticed in about 1808 as a figure modeller at Derby, and from Haslem[46] we learn that after leaving in about 1817 to work briefly at Coalport and Worcester, he returned to Derby where, by 1826, he had his own small establishment. He specialized in making figures and in raised flower decoration. For a time in 1831, however, he was in Swinton, recorded in the militia list as a potter and employed at the Rockingham Works. He may have been there as early as 1829, since the solid base of a master-model of a figure, excavated on the Pottery site, bears the incised inscription 'March 12th 1829/Fox Hunt to Day/Geo Cocker/Last/29th figure', implying that he

44. J. Haslem, op. cit., p. 163.
45. L. Jewitt, op. cit., Vol. 2, p. 108.
46. J. Haslem, op. cit., pp. 159–60.

produced an extensive series of models for the Bramelds. However, no such Rockingham figure matching this description has been recorded. It is now known that figure production continued through to the closure of the Works, and certain Rockingham examples do show a strong resemblance to signed Cocker models (see page 192). Whilst at Swinton he may also have advised on his other speciality, raised flower decoration, since it was at this time that the Bramelds began to produce 'Dresden' flower-encrusted pieces.

In the Rockingham Pattern Book seen by the writers, teaware pattern 684 is annotated 'Gold hoops to match French cups sent by Cocker from Derby', which further points to contact between him and the Bramelds. Similarly, Cocker's advertisement in the *Derby Mercury* for 29 October 1828 states 'George Cocker, Modeller, China Figure Maker, Dealer in Glass, Rockingham Ware &c.'[47] Whilst the term 'Rockingham Ware' is slightly ambiguous, this may be further evidence of a business relationship between Cocker and the Bramelds.

William Eley (b. 1796)

Traditionally, William Eley was the modeller of the bust of Earl Fitzwilliam (see page 194). However, two workmen at Swinton, father and son born in 1768 and 1796 respectively, shared this name and both are described in the militia lists as potters. The elder Eley died in 1830 and since the bust of the earl in the Yorkshire Museum is dated 1833, it seems likely that the son was the modeller responsible for this work, unless the bust was a reissue.

Aston (first name not known)

All that is known of Aston is Jewitt's statement that he was 'clever as a modeller of flowers' at Swinton in the post-1830 period.[48]

Earthenware Painters

Several artists are described in the Swinton Parish Documents specifically as painters of earthenware, but in certain cases it is not possible to distinguish between those employed at the Rockingham Works and those at the Don Pottery, which was established in Swinton in 1801, and possibly some spent periods of time at both concerns. It is characteristic of the documents that the exact occupation is not always given, and included here are the names of workmen described as painters, who may have been engaged in decorating porcelain or earthenware.

Arthur Bennet

Included in the Swinton parish registers, where the baptism of a daughter is recorded in September 1838, his occupation given as painter.

47. We are indebted to Mr Ronald Brown for kindly bringing this extract to our attention.
48. L. Jewitt, op. cit., Vol. 1, p. 515.

JAMES BULLOUGH

A painter mentioned by Thomas Brameld in a letter of 1809 where he states that Bullough 'learnt at Leeds'.[49]

GEORGE COLLINSON (b. 1787)

Collinson is the only earthenware painter for whom there is much specific information. Jewitt describes him as 'the best flower-painter employed at the Swinton Works'.[50] There are yearly references to him in the Swinton militia lists from 1820 to 1829. The *Sheffield Iris* for 29 August 1826 gives an account of his rescuing a boy from the canal at Wath, describing him as 'Mr George Collison [*sic*], landscape painter, at the China Works, Swinton'. His painting is discussed on page 78.

GEORGE ELLIS

This artist was employed at the Swinton Pottery for at least part of his career, as he is recorded in the militia list for 1799—before the opening of the Don Pottery in 1801. He is mentioned again in 1804 as a painter and after a break his name reappears in 1818, but since in the following year he was a tenant of the proprietors of the Don Pottery, he presumably worked there too.

GEORGE GLASBY

This artist is recorded in the Swinton militia lists between 1796 and 1815, where he is described as a painter. In the early years, therefore, he must have been employed at the Swinton Pottery.

JOHN GUILDER or GELDER (b. 1802)

This artist's name appears in the Swinton militia lists and parish registers from 1825 until at least 1842, described as a potter or painter. Since this period corresponds almost exactly with the years of porcelain production, he may have been a china-painter.

JOHN HEWITT

Hewitt's name is included in the Swinton militia list for 1800, described as a painter. His letters to John Brameld indicate that he was lame and could only do work at home.[51]

ABRAHAM NICHOLSON

An earthenware painter mentioned without further comment in one of Thomas Brameld's letters of 1809.[52]

49. Wentworth Woodhouse Muniments, MD 182, dated 23 April 1809.
50. L. Jewitt, op. cit., Vol. 1, p. 509.
51. A. and A. Cox, *The Rockingham Works*, Sheffield, 1974, pp. 64–5.
52. Wentworth Woodhouse Muniments, MD 182.

BENJAMIN PRINCE (1790–1849)
The presence of this artist in Swinton is well documented, there being almost yearly records in the militia lists between 1820 and 1831, where he is described as an earthenware painter, painter or potter. He was buried in Swinton on 18 December 1849.

HENRY SCALES (b. 1787)
Scales is recorded in the Swinton parish registers in 1814 and 1815, his profession given as pot-painter.

JOSEPH SHAW
Mentioned in Thomas Brameld's letter of 1809 as 'Shaw the Painter',[53] this was probably Joseph Shaw, potter, whose name occurs in the militia list for 1796 and in the Swinton parish register for 1801, where the baptism of a son, Joseph, is recorded. Joseph Shaw junior's name appears in a militia list of about 1821, described as a painter.

JOHN SPEIGHT (b. 1795)
The first reference to this artist is in the militia list for 1814, where Speight is described as an apprentice. It is most probable that he was the son of William Speight snr. and brother of William and George Speight. There is a regular record of his presence in Swinton in the militia lists from 1814 to 1829, his occupation given as a potter in every year except 1814, when he is described as a painter. Jewitt quotes a document of 1829 which states that John Speight had charge of 'the painting, &c., &c., in earthenware biscuit work'.[54]

WILLIAM SPEIGHT snr. (1770–1843)
The elder William Speight is first mentioned in the 1796 militia list, his occupation given as a painter. By 1800 he was looking for work as an independent decorator in Knottingley, South Yorkshire, but failed.[55] He was back in Swinton the following year, his presence recorded in the Census, and until his death in April 1843 there are frequent references to him as a painter of earthenware in the Swinton Parish Documents.

Additionally, there are passing references to paintresses. Thomas Brameld's letter of 1809 mentions Elizabeth Barraclough, and Ann and Dinah Hodgson,[56] but for the most part they are anonymous—'flowers by girls' is the usual reference in the Pattern Books.

53. Ibid., MD 182.
54. L. Jewitt, op. cit., Vol. 1, p. 503.
55. Swinton Parish Documents, Poor Law.
56. Wentworth Woodhouse Muniments, MD 182.

Other Workpeople

A number of occupations connected with the Pottery during the Brameld period are given in the Swinton parish registers. They include Joseph Goodwin, flint miller; William Day, china fireman; Samuel Parkin, engineer; and William Stanway, engraver, possibly of copper plates for transfer printing.

Additionally, Jewitt,[57] quoting a document of about 1829, states that Richard Shillito 'was to have charge of the earthenware department as general overlooker, with . . . Hulme to assist him'; William Horncastle 'had charge of the Warehouse, &c.'; George Liversedge 'was overlooker and manager of the printing department'; and William Speight 'had charge of the mill, and also "the care of and management of all gold, colours, and glazes, &c., he giving them out as they may be properly wanted to use"'. This identifies him with William Speight jnr., whose name occurs in the Swinton parish registers between 1837 and 1841, described as 'colour maker'.

A number of the Bramelds' most proficient workmen served their apprenticeship at the Pottery. One such was the George Liversedge, mentioned above, whose indenture dated 9 August 1816 fortunately survives.[58] In this Thomas Brameld agrees to teach him 'the Trade, Mystery or Business of a Potter called a Printer on Earthenware'. Since by 1829 he had risen to be 'overlooker and manager' of the printing department, he clearly had been diligent in learning his trade. As an apprentice he was paid two shillings and six pence per week for the first year, rising to six shillings per week during the seventh.

57. L. Jewitt, op. cit., Vol. 1, p. 503.
58. We are indebted to Mrs R. Scholey for permission to quote from this document.

11
Marks

On Pottery

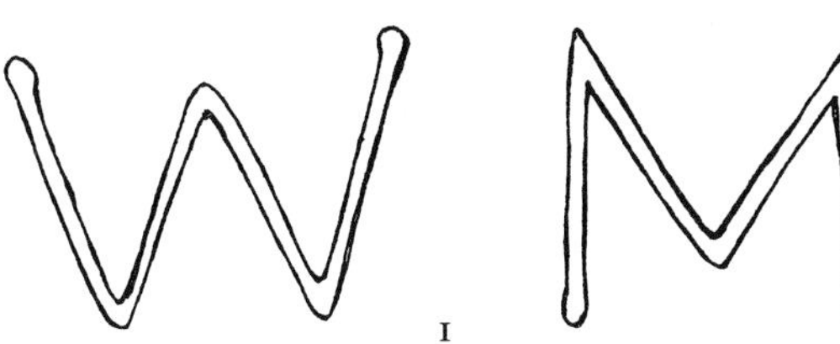

1

1. The embossed initials of William Malpass occur on excavated sherds of slipware dishes *c.*1765–8. Height 2.22 cm (0.88 in). The impressed mark BINGLEY is recorded by Thomas Boynton,[1] but no modern authority has seen it. Possibly of the period 1778–85, or conceivably 1785–1806.

2 3

4

2 to 4 Impressed workmen's marks, *c.*1785–1806. Marks 2 and 3, used also at Leeds,[2] are found on flatware. The fretted triangle, about 0.5 cm (0.2 in) in height, occurs on globular teapots of the type shown in Plate 13.

During the Brameld period, 1806–42, factory marks were regularly applied, although sparingly before about 1820.

1. A. Hurst, *A Catalogue of the Boynton Collection of Yorkshire Pottery*, York, 1922, p. 28.
2. D. Towner, *Creamware*, London, 1978, p. 221 marks nos. 12 and 28.

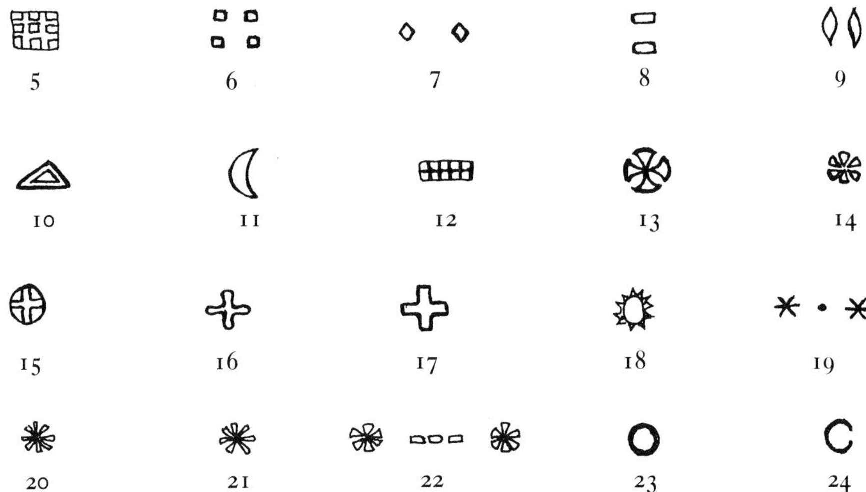

5 to 24. Impressed workmen's marks *c.* 1806–42 on earthenwares; the list is not exhaustive. Potters elsewhere used similar marks, especially star-like devices, hence attribution of wares can rarely be based on these marks alone.

BRAMELD
25

BRAMELD+
26

BRAMELD+.
27

BRAMELD+1
28

BRAMELD
8
29

BRAMELD
30

The impressed marks 25 to 30 were widely used. Flatwares from services are often marked, the principal items less commonly so. Teawares are marked inconsistently.

25. Several stamps were used for this mark, the length of which varies between about 1.6 to 2.2 cm (0.63 to 0.88 in), in large or small capitals.

26 and 27. As mark 25 but with a plus sign, or a plus sign and a dot.

28. As mark 25 but with a plus sign followed by a number, BRAMELD+1 being the most common. Numbers as high as 16 have been reported, but they are often badly impressed, or filled with glaze, and are thus easily misread. Marks are recorded where a triangle or a Maltese cross replaces the number, but unambiguous examples have not come to our notice. The significance of the numbers is not understood; certainly no chronology is implied.

29. Impressed. Numbers up to 13 have been noted.

30. Impressed, usually on flatware.

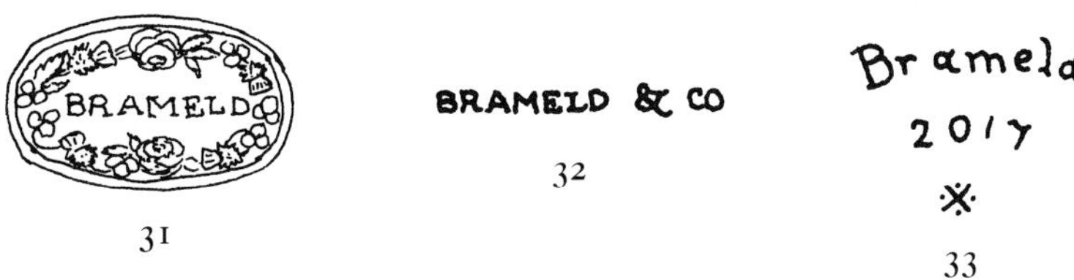

31 32 33

31. Embossed on an applied cartouche. Occurs on cane-coloured stoneware, normally hollow ware, the cartouche being the same colour as any sprigged decoration. A similar mark was used very rarely on porcelain.[3]

32. A very rare impressed mark. A green-glazed Cadogan pot in the Victoria and Albert Museum is so marked.

33. A rare painted mark, normally in red. Usually accompanied by a number in the region of 2000.

34

BRAMELD & Co
SWINTON POTTERY

35

ROCKINGHAM ROCKINGHAM ROCKINGHAM

36 37 38

34. Impressed on excavated sherds of buff-coloured kitchen wares.

35. A very rare printed mark.[4]

36. Impressed, 2.24 cm (0.88 in) in length, on brown-glazed pieces (see page 110). Frequently accompanied by a Cl mark.

37. Impressed, about 2.50 cm (0.98 in) in length, on brown-glazed wares. Of doubtful authenticity (see pages 110 and 112).

38. Impressed, about 1.80 cm (0.71 in) in length. Of doubtful authenticity (see pages 110, 112 and 113).

3. A Rockingham hexagonal vase in the Victoria and Albert Museum (Schreiber Collection no. 794) bears this mark.

4. D. G. Rice, *The Illustrated Guide to Rockingham Pottery and Porcelain*, London, 1971, Plate 38.

39. Impressed, about 2.80 cm (1.10 in) in length, on brown-glazed wares. This is a Wedgwood mark of *c.*1840 and possibly later (see pages 112–13).

40. Impressed, about 3.60 cm (1.42 in) in length, on brown-glazed wares. This is a Spode mark (see page 112).

41. Impressed on pale, brown-glazed pieces, notably jugs. Length across shield 3.0 cm (1.18 in). Of doubtful authenticity (see page 112).

42. Impressed (two stamps) on an oblong, red stoneware teapot, apparently *c.*1820, decorated with moulded chinoiseries. Authenticity uncertain.[5]

43 and 44. Impressed on brown-glazed wares manufactured at Swinton for the London retailer John Mortlock of Oxford Street.

45. Impressed, occurs in conjunction with mark 52.

46. Printed in puce on items manufactured under William Dale's patent, *c.*1838–42.

Other impressed marks have been reported, but have not come to our notice. They are the word BRAMELD followed by two Maltese crosses, and the word MORTLOCK, both given by Jewitt.[6] Similarly, the words NORFOLK and CADOGAN were recorded by Mr Llewellyn.[7]

5. We are indebted to Mr Bryan Bowden for kindly drawing our attention to this mark.
6. L. Jewitt, *Ceramic Art in Great Britain*, London, 1878, Vol. 1, p. 515.
7. G. R. P. Llewellyn, 'Rockingham Ware and Porcelain: Its Marks', *The Connoisseur Year Book, 1962*, p. 140, Plate 2.

On Porcelain

Brameld
2030
✕

47

Brameld

48

Rocking ham
China Works
Sw ton
1826

49

Brameld & Co's
Rockingham Works
near Rotherham
Yorkshire

50

47. Painted in red on porcelain apparently of an experimental nature *c.*1820–5. The vase shown in Plate 65 is so marked; the number varies and its significance is uncertain. An identical mark occurs on earthenwares (see mark 33 and page 84).

48. A rare mark of *c.*1825 or early 1826 painted in puce on a hexagonal vase (Colour Plate H).

49. Painted in red on a coffee cup in the Rotherham Museum.

50. An incised mark *c.*1826 on the bust illustrated in Plate 144.

51. The earliest printed red-griffin mark. It was probably used for a limited period since it is an heraldically incorrect version of the Wentworth crest. The rhinoceros vase in the Rotherham Museum bears this mark and the date 1826. Occasionally occurs in underglaze blue on blue-printed wares.

52. The usual printed red-griffin mark *c.* 1826–30. Used on all types of wares. Occurs rarely printed in puce on post-1830 pieces. Occasionally printed in underglaze blue or grey on porcelain with printed decoration in these colours.

53. Impressed on biscuit figures, some glazed figures and busts. On small items, the griffin and other parts of this mark may be omitted. Almost certainly used throughout the entire period *c.* 1826–42.

54. A rare impressed mark *c.* 1830–42. Noted on a biscuit figure model number 119.

55. The usual printed puce-griffin mark *c.* 1830–42. Occurs on all types of wares, except figures. See also Plate 150.

56. An elaborate puce-griffin mark *c.* 1830–42. Occurs on the royal dessert service and rarely on other pieces.

57 and 58. Variants of mark 55. Probably used *c.*1830 only.[8] See also Plate 150.

8. B. Bowden, 'Royal Rockingham—in Regency and Neo-Rococo Style', *Collectors Guide*, March 1977, p. 74.

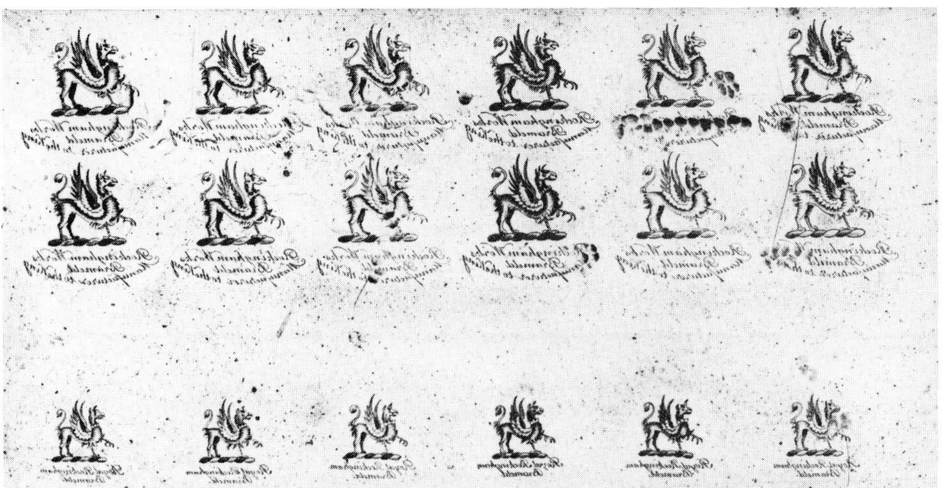

150. GRIFFIN FACTORY MARKS, *c.*1830–42. Direct pull from a copper plate engraved with puce griffins, marks 55 and 57. Note that the griffins are reversed. Length 19.3 cm (7.6 in). *See page 224*

Other marks noted by previous authors which have not come to our attention are: ROCKINGHAM WORKS BRAMELD & CO impressed;[9] *Rockingham* in gilt script;[10] a griffin and either ROYAL ROCKINGHAM/ BRAMELD, or ROYAL ROCKINGHAM WORKS/ BRAMELD, in capitals, sometimes in gilt.[11]

9. A. H. Church, *English Porcelain*, London, 1904, p. 103.
10. G. R. P. Llewellyn, op. cit., p. 146. Dr D. G. Rice records this mark on Coalport porcelain in *Rockingham Ornamental Porcelain*, London, 1965, p. 89, fn.
11. L. Jewitt, op. cit., Vol. 1, p. 516.

Printed Backstamps

A number of backstamps occur on Brameld earthenwares with transfer-printed decoration. All date to the period *c.*1820–42 and were used inconsistently. In the absence of a factory mark they uniquely identify pieces of Swinton manufacture. Examples of the prints associated with these backstamps are shown in the Plates listed below.

59 60 61 62 63 64

59.	*Floral Sketches:* Plate 41.	62.	*Don Quixote:* Plate 53.
60.	*India:* Plate 47.	63.	*Parroquet:* Plate 48.
61.	*Flower Groups:* Plate 40.	64.	*Paris Stripe:* Plate 64.

65 67 66 68 69

65. *Indian Flowers:* Plate 40.
66. *Castle of Rochefort:* Plate 52.
67. Accompanies prints such as *Pea Flower:* Plate 37.
68. *Burns Cotter:* Plate 45.
69. *Rose Jar:* Plate 27.

Marks on Wares Decorated by the Baguleys

After the closure of the Rockingham Works in 1842, Isaac Baguley and his son Alfred continued to decorate porcelain and earthenwares on the factory site until 1865. The pieces are normally not of Swinton manufacture.

70 71 72

70. Printed in red on porcelain. A modification of mark 57, the word *Brameld* having been removed and replaced by *Works/ Baguley*.

71. Printed in red, used by Isaac and Alfred Baguley. Variants occur: i. the griffin alone; ii. the griffin and *Baguley*; iii. the griffin and *Baguley/Rockingham works*.

72. Printed in red on porcelain and earthenwares after 1865 when Alfred Baguley transferred his decorating establishment to nearby Mexborough where he died in 1891.

John Thomas Brameld's London Marks

After the closure of the Rockingham Works in 1842, Thomas Brameld's son J. T. Brameld (1819–92) continued in business in London as a china-dealer until 1851. Several marks were used on wares of non-Rockingham origin:

73 74

The Cl Mark and Pattern Marks

Although not strictly a factory mark, the letters Cl or C followed by a number in the range 1 to about 17, written in gilt or a colour, are unique to Rockingham. This Cl mark occurs on decorative porcelain and brown-glazed earthenwares, in addition to a factory mark which may be present. Its precise meaning has so far defied explanation. It does, however, appear only on gilded items[14] and is commonly regarded as a gilder's cypher, but its true significance lies deeper.

The factory invoices sent to Wentworth House provide some insight as the following extracts show:

1828 1 Rockingham Tea Pot[15] Class 3
1 China Cabinet Cup & Stand Class 7
3 China Vases No. 8 Class 9
1 China Basket F Class 4
1832 24 China Studs Cl 4 Pencilled Foxes
Heads In front & In back
1840 6 Rockingham Tea Pots[15] 2 @ 7/6, 2 @ 6/-,
2 @ 5/- with Gold Class 2

One concludes, therefore, that Cl is an abbreviation of the word Class, but the basis of the classification is not clear. It would seem that this mark was not merely related to the internal management of the Pottery, but was of some interest to the customer too. Nor is the mark linked to the amount of decoration on a piece, since both simply and elaborately decorated items commonly bear the same Cl mark. An extended form of this mark is occasionally seen, for example A No. 8. Cl. 12 appears on a fine trumpet-shaped vase in the Fitzwilliam Museum, Cambridge, in addition to a printed red griffin.

The other numbers or letters which occur in the entries, such as Basket F

14. One exception only has come to our attention.
15. These are brown-glazed earthenwares.

Facing page

73. Printed in puce on porcelain. Variants occur: i. a griffin passant above the garter; ii. with the address 232, PICCADILLY LONDON.[12]

74. Printed in puce on ironstone wares.
In addition, the mark BRAMELD & BECKITT, PICCADILLY LONDON appears on an earthenware plate[13] and refers to the partnership between J. T. Brameld and J. D. Beckitt *c.* 1842–9.

12. T. A. Lockett, 'The Bramelds in London', *Connoisseur*, Vol. 165, No. 664, 1967, p. 103.
13. Illustrated in A. A. Eaglestone and T. A. Lockett, *The Rockingham Pottery* (new revised edn. 1973), Plate XIId and p. 141.

and Vase No. 8, may be references to size or shape. Similarly, certain plate borders are identified by letters and possibly refer to designs in Pattern Books, for example:

1828 6 China Dessert Plates Gadroon A
1829 1 China Table Service C Nr. 488B

In the final extract, 488 is a pattern number, but the significance of the B is not known. The suffix S to a pattern number occurs on tablewares with no gilding and may denote a cheaper product. It is, however, occasionally found on gilded, decorative porcelain following the Cl mark. A small taperstick in the collection of Mr and Mrs J. D. Griffin bears the mark Cl.2:S˙.˙, but again the meaning is uncertain.

Pattern Numbers on Porcelain

At the closure of the Rockingham Works, at least four Pattern Books showing designs in earthenware and porcelain passed into the hands of Isaac Baguley, one of the factory artists who became an independent decorator and continued to operate on the site of the Works. They have remained in the possession of his descendants and are of importance in several ways, for not only do they show in beautifully executed watercolours the patterns which appeared on the factory's porcelain tea and dessert services (Plate 95), but they record the associated pattern numbers, and in several cases the names of artists who were originally responsible for certain patterns (see Chapter 10). Two different series of numbers were used for tea and dessert wares. While such numbers provide a guide to the attribution of pieces in the absence of a factory mark, it should be remembered that shapes too play an equally decisive role in this respect.

The known teaware patterns extend from 404 to 1566, there being a break between 1000 and 1100. A fractional series ranges from 2/1 to 2/99; one instance of 2/143 is known, but this may be an error in marking. It is highly probable that not all patterns recorded in the factory's Pattern Books were actually used.[16] On dessert wares the lowest known pattern number is 409 (Plate 69), while the highest which has come to our notice is 822, although almost certainly this does not represent the upper limit.

Two points are worth stressing. First, a pattern number relates to the decoration only. Second, an early pattern can occur on a late service, and since most shapes introduced during the red-griffin period, 1826–30, continued to be produced in later years, a high pattern number can appear on an early shape.

Pattern numbers do not occur on Rockingham ornamental porcelain, nor on pieces from the factory's earthenware services—but see pages 84 and 86.

16. M. Eaglestone and M. Evans, 'Recorded Pattern Numbers on Rockingham Teawares', *The Northern Ceramic Society Newsletter*, No. 34, 1979, pp. 27–8; No. 38, 1980, p. 30; No. 42, 1981, pp. 41–2.

Fakes and Forgeries

Samson of Paris manufactured 'Rockingham' wares bearing an unconvincing imitation of mark 55 printed in muddy brown. Such pieces are *invariably* made of hard-paste porcelain, quite unlike the relatively soft bone-china body of Rockingham.

An incorrect version of mark 55 occurs on bone china of uncertain origin in which the griffin's raised paw is presented sideways to the observer, and not held downwards.

Refired pieces bearing a false griffin mark are known and are normally easy to detect since on refiring bone china tends to darken. The shapes of such items, typically plates, differ from the true Rockingham products.

Not originally intended to deceive are wares purchased by the Bramelds from other factories when their own stock of porcelain was low and urgent orders had to be completed. These pieces may have a genuine griffin mark as, for example, the Daniel service mentioned on page 148.

Again, not strictly fakes or forgeries are items supplied by other factories as replacements for pieces from Rockingham services. Their shape seldom matches the original, but the decoration normally does so, and rarely being marked they are often the explanation for a 'new' shape in Rockingham tableware.

Finally, attention is drawn to certain brown-glazed earthenwares some of which bear false or misleading Rockingham marks (see pages 110–13).

Appendix I
Sherds from the Malpass & Fenney Period, 1768–78

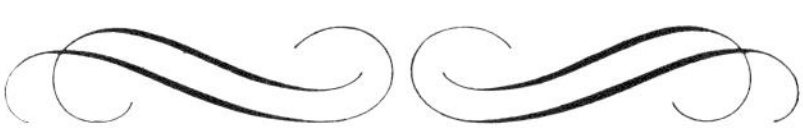

Drawings of mouldings on white salt-glazed stonewares and creamwares. All occur on sherds excavated from the site of the Swinton Pottery. It is probable that the mouldings on creamware continued in use throughout the Bingley, Wood & Co. period, 1778–1785. Comparisons with Greens, Bingley & Co. sherds shown in Appendix II reveal obvious differences.

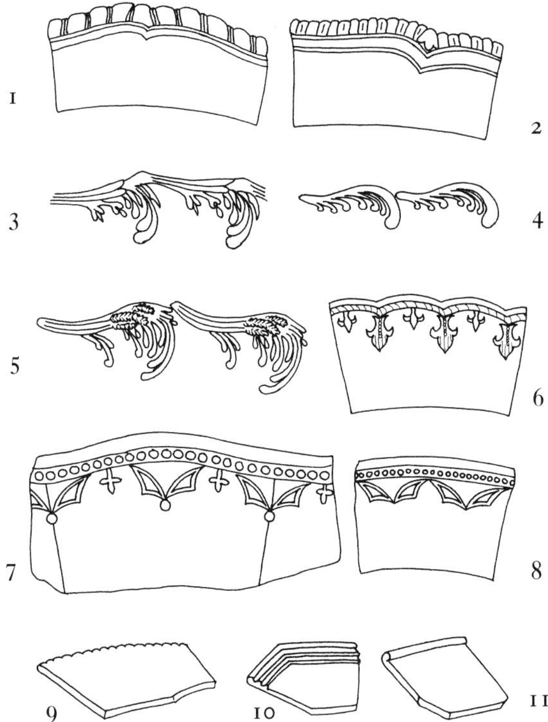

1 and 2.	*Gadroon* plate borders in two versions, on both saltglaze and creamware.
3.	*Cockstail* plate border found on saltglaze only.
4.	*Feather* edge common to saltglaze and creamware plates.
5.	*Cockstail* plate border found only on creamware.
6.	*Fleur-de-lis* border on creamware plates only.
7 and 8.	*Batswing* plate border, found in two distinct versions on creamwares.
9.	*Beaded* edge on creamware.
10.	*Reeded* border on both saltglaze and creamware, on octagonal and round plates.
11.	*Single rib* plate edge found in both saltglaze and creamware.

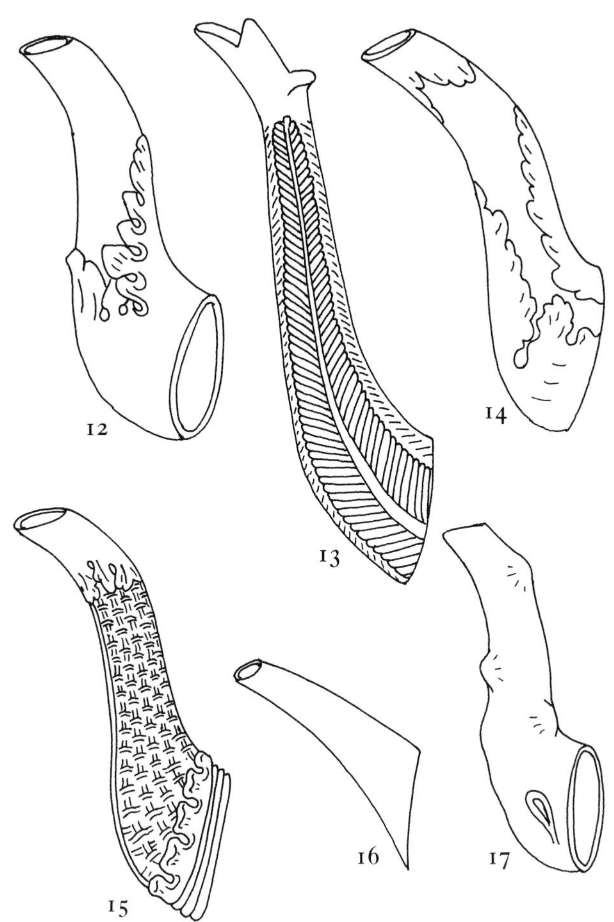

12. Creamware teapot spout with distinctive acanthus moulding.
13. Creamware coffee pot spout with moulded herringbone design. See Plate 10.
14. Creamware teapot spout with acanthus leaves, commonly faintly moulded. See Plate 9.
15. Saltglaze spout with moulded basket-weave and acanthus decoration.
16. Plain, curved spout from a small salt-glazed teapot.
17. Crabstock teapot spout in both saltglaze and creamware.

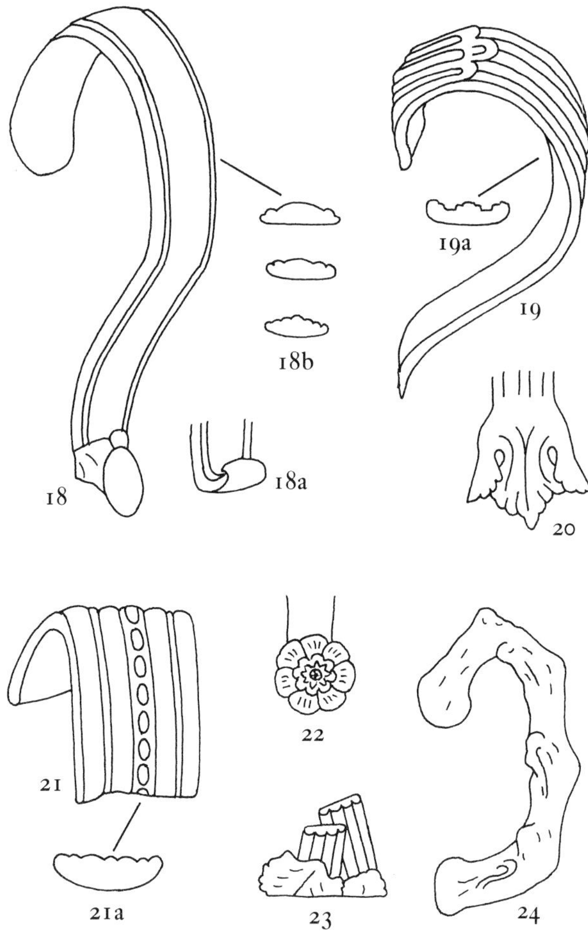

18 and 18a. Saltglaze handle found on jugs and mugs, with pinched or curled end.

18b. Sections of saltglaze handles.

19 and 19a. Creamware handle with unusual ribbed moulding. It occurs with the thumbpiece shown on teawares, but without it on jugs. See Colour Plate A and Plate 11.

20. Creamware leaf terminal associated with handle No. 19. Found on both teawares and jugs.

21 and 21a. Creamware ribbed and beaded handle from a large jug.

22. Saltglaze handle terminal in the form of a flower head. The same flower also occurs on creamware (see No. 42).

23. Saltglaze sherd with broken remains of reeded, crossed handles and leaf terminals. These also occur in creamware.

24. Crabstock handle found in identical form on saltglaze and creamware teapots.

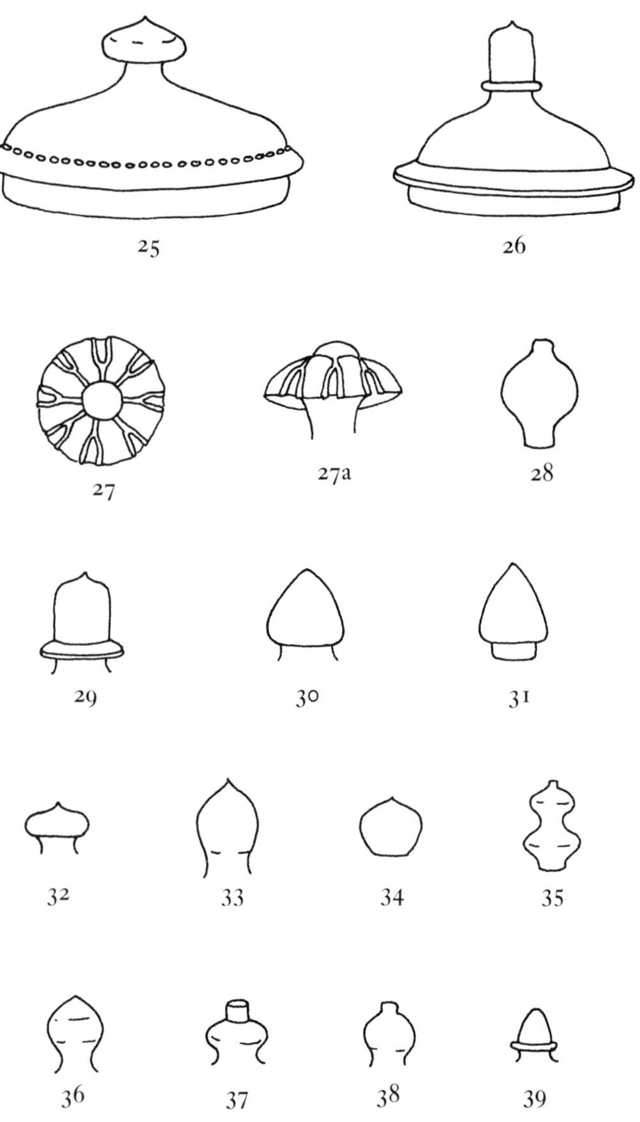

25 and 26. Typical covers and finials from saltglaze and creamware tea and coffee pots.
27 and 27a. Creamware teapot finial which sometimes occurs with terminal No. 41. See No. 44 and Plate 9.
28 to 39. Examples of the wide range of finials from the Malpass & Fenney period, all of which are known in saltglaze and creamware.

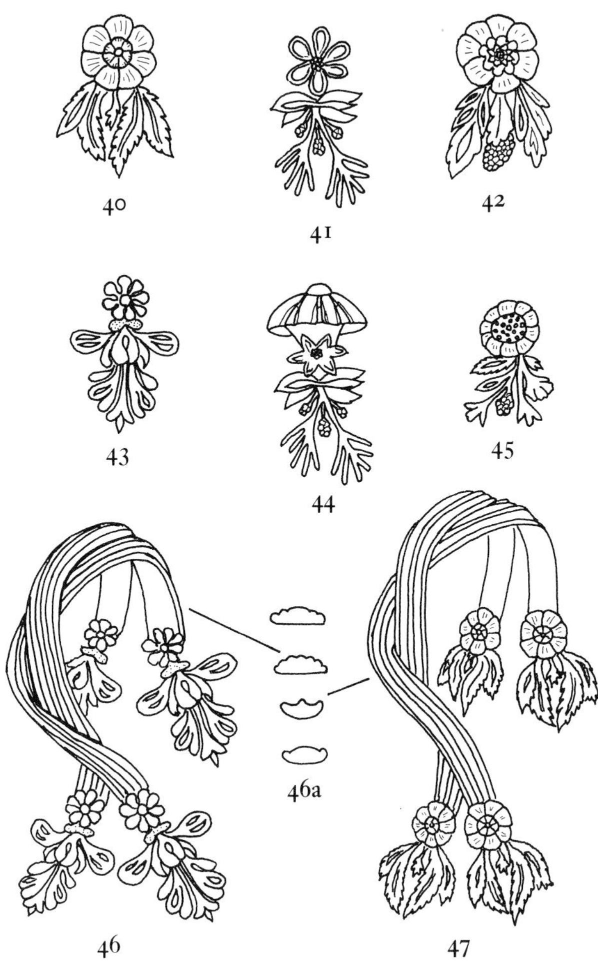

40. Creamware flower-and-leaf terminal, generally occurring with crossed, ribbed handles. See No. 47 and Plate 10.

41. Creamware flower terminal characterized by long 'spiky' leaves. See also No. 44 and Plate 9.

42. Creamware flower-and-leaf terminal with pendant flower bud or fruit. The flower head alone occurs on saltglaze (see No. 22).

43. Creamware flower-and-leaf terminal, perhaps the most commonly found type. See also No. 46.

44. Creamware finial, a combination of the flower head No. 27 and terminal No. 41. See Plate 9.

45. Creamware flower, leaf and bud terminal. See Plate 8.

46. Creamware crossed, reeded handles shown with terminal No. 43.

46a. Sections of creamware handles.

47. Creamware crossed, ribbed handles shown with terminal No. 40. See Plate 10.

Appendix II
Sherds from the Greens, Bingley & Co. Period, 1785–1806

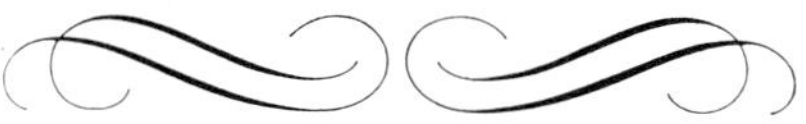

Drawings of mouldings on creamwares excavated from the site of the Swinton Pottery. Comparisons with sherds from the Malpass & Fenney period shown in Appendix I reveal obvious differences.

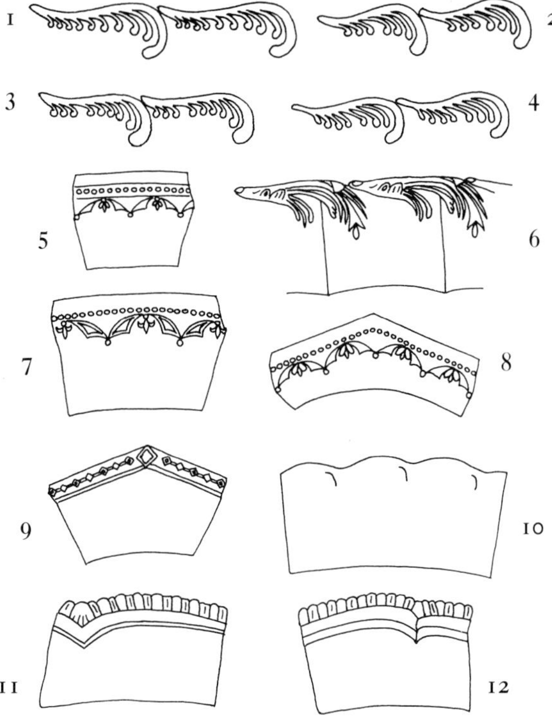

1.	*Feather* edge, ten-barb version.
2.	*Feather* edge, seven-barb version.
3.	*Feather* edge, nine-barb version; identical to that used at the Leeds Pottery.
4.	*Feather* edge, eight-barb version. On large plates this occurs with a different spacing of the barbs, 3:5 instead of 4:4.
5, 7 and 8.	*Batswing* plate borders showing three different versions.
6.	*Cockstail* plate edge with distinctive radial lines around the border. See Plates 14 and 19.
9.	*Diamond-beaded* border with a large diamond at each angle. Found on octagonal plates and dinner ware.
10.	*Lobed* plate edge.
11 and 12.	*Gadroon* borders in two versions.

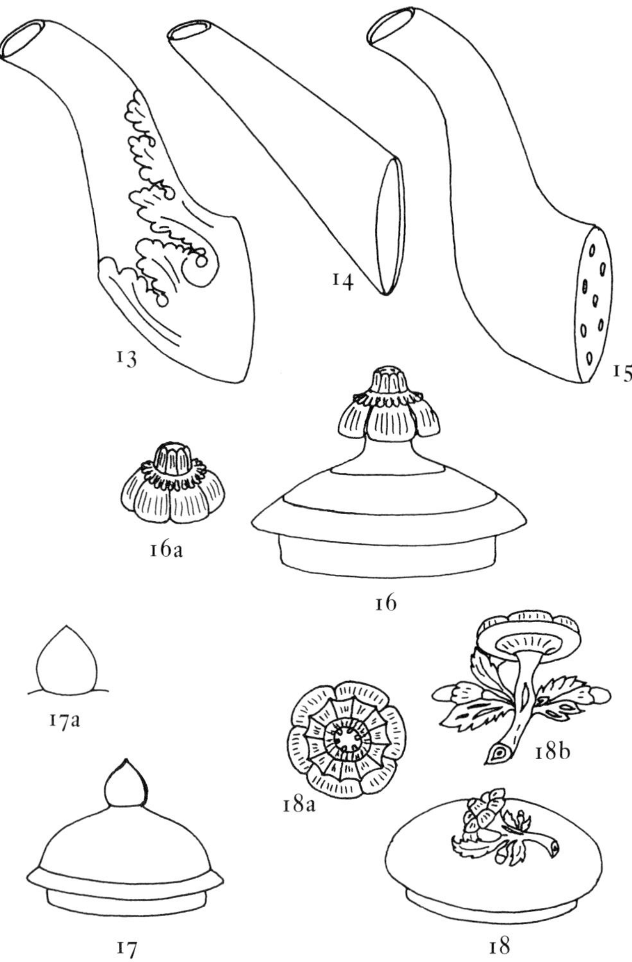

13. Teapot spout with characteristic Greens, Bingley & Co. moulding. See Plate 13.

14. Plain, straight teapot spout.

15. Plain, curved teapot spout.

16 and 16a. Cover and finial from a dip-decorated teapot. The daisy knop is known in virtually identical form from the Leeds Pottery.

17. Round, pointed finial, commonly occurring on tea and coffee pot covers.

18, 18a and 18b. Rose, leaf and bud finial, known in apparently identical form on Leeds wares. See Plate 13.

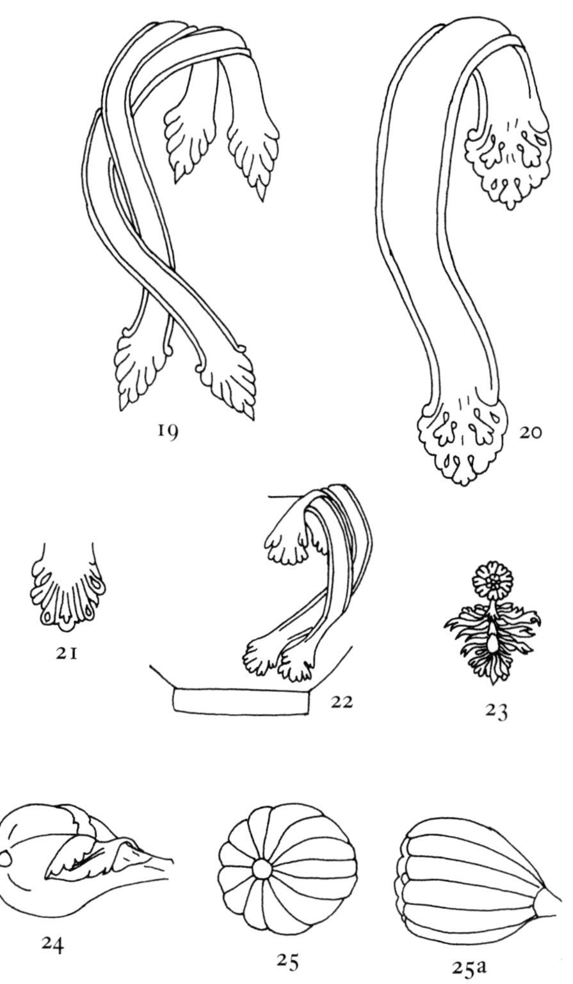

19. Crossed, strap handles with long, pointed terminals, frequently found on teapots.

20. Strap handle with acanthus terminals, commonly found on jugs and mugs. Used also at the Leeds Pottery.

21. Cut-stalk terminal, known on teawares.

22. Crossed, strap handles with simple leaf terminals. These also occur on teawares from the Leeds Pottery. See Plate 13.

23. 'Classic' terminal of apparently identical appearance to those in use at Leeds.

24. Fruit finial from a tureen. Known also from the Leeds Pottery.

25 and 25a. Fruit finial from a tureen.

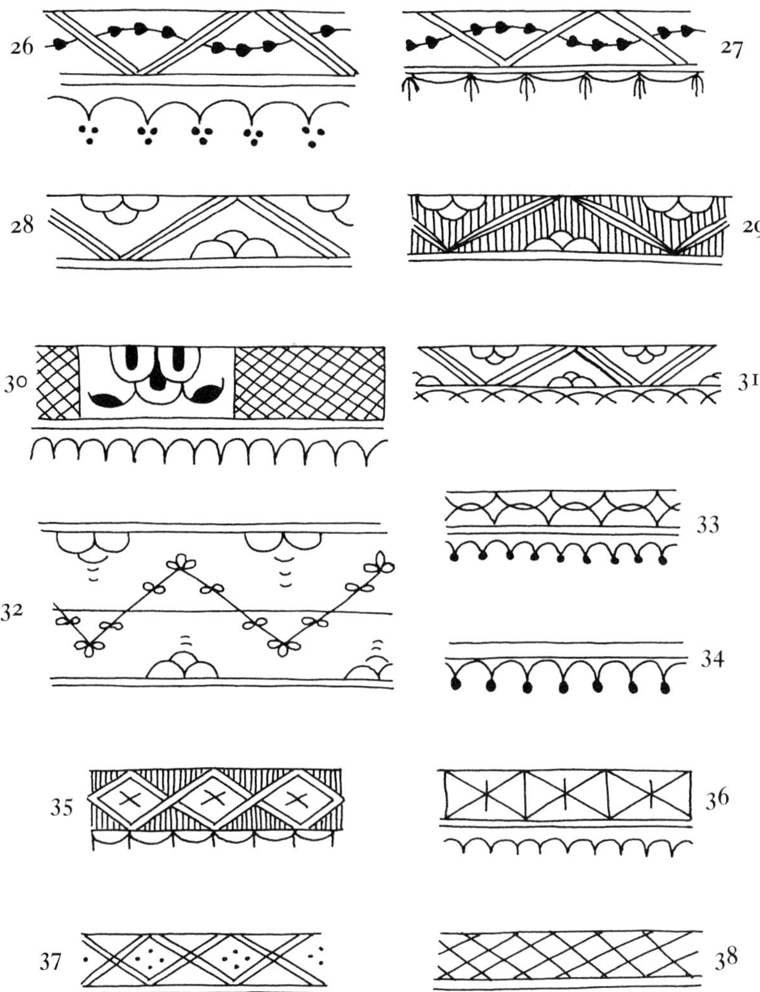

26 to 38. Underglaze-blue painted border patterns from teawares. These simple, but effective, designs were widely used at Swinton. Some of these, for example Nos. 26 and 30, occur in identical form in the Leeds New Tea Pot Drawing Book. They were also used elsewhere.

Appendix III
Selected Financial Statements from the Wentworth Estate Annual Accounts

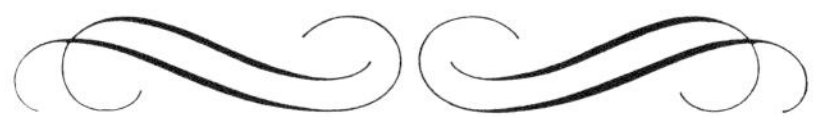

Date		£	s	d
23 Dec. 1806	Paid Messrs. Brameld on their Bond dated this day	2,000		
31 Dec. 1807	Paid Messrs. Brameld further on Account of Money to be Advanced on their Note	1,000		
1 May 1808	Paid Messrs. Brameld to make up the sum of 5,000£ secured on Mortgage of their Property & Effects at the Pottery	2,000		
2 Dec. 1811	Paid Messrs. Brameld on account of erecting a Flint Mill	500		
20 Feb. 1812	Paid Messrs. Brameld & Co further on account	500		
24 June 1812	Do Do Do	1,000		
11 Nov. 1812	Paid Messrs. Bramelds further on Account of erecting a Flint Mill at the Pottery	1,000		
12 May 1813	Paid Messrs. Brameld further on Account of erecting a Flint Mill at the Pottery	1,000		
25 Aug. 1813	Paid Messrs. Brameld further on Account of erecting a Flint Mill at the Pottery	1,000		
25 Nov. 1813	Do Do Do	500		
1 June 1815	Paid Messrs. Brameld further on account of erecting a Flint Mill at Swinton Pottery	1,600		
30 June 1816	Paid Messrs. Brameld in full of Money expended by them in erecting a Flint Mill and other Improvements at Swinton Pottery	400		
30 June 1820	Advanced Messrs. Brameld, for which along with 1000£ remitted to them by Your Lordship they have given their Bond and warrant of Attorney for 3000£	2,000		
1 Jan. 1827	Paid Messrs. Bramelds Assignees on Account of the Purchase of Stock, Fixtures &c at the Swinton Pottery	7,500		
1 May 1827	Received of Messieurs Brameld's Assignees a Dividend of 3/4 in the Pound upon the sum of 10,544£ due on Bond proved under their Bankruptcy	1,757.	6.	8
14 May 1827	Received of Messrs. Bramelds and their Assignees the pur: Money for the House and 24^{a}—3^{r}—6^{p} of Land in Swinton, formerly the			

		£ s d
	Estate of Mr Jn°. Brameld deced but as the property was in Mortgage to Your Lordship for more than the full Value Credit is given for the full sum as received in part discharge of the Mortgage	3,000
	By the following Arrears which are taken Credit for vizt.	
30 June 1827	Swinton Messrs. Brameld the Amount of the Arrears of Rent after deducting the Dividend of 3/4 in the £ which is now discharged in consequence of their having become Bankrupts but upon which a further Dividend is expected	3,901.10. 0
1 July 1827	Received of Messrs. Bramelds Assignees in part of the Principal and Interest due from them on Mortgage being the whole amount of the purchase Money for the Estate	3,000
7 June 1830	Paid Messrs. Bramelds Assignees further on Account of the purchase of the Stock in Trade &c at Swinton Pottery	2,500
15 Aug. 1832	Paid Sir Wm. Cooke & Co.[1] the sum advanced by them to Messrs. Brameld & Co	5,000
30 June 1833	Paid Messrs. Brameld by weekly Payments from the 29th. September to the 31st. December 1832 by Your Lordships Order, in order to enable them to pay their Workmens Wages	1,950
25 Nov. 1833	Paid Messrs. Walker and Stanley[2] the sum advanced by them on Your Lordship's Account to Messrs. Brameld	1,950
14 May 1834	Paid Messrs. Walker & Co for Interest of the sum of 1950£ advanced by them on Your Lordship's Account to Messrs. Brameld	107. 2. 5
30 June 1834	Paid Messrs. Brameld for China furnished by them to Lord Milton and which sum is placed to their Rent Account	47. 1. 9
2 Jan. 1837	Paid Messrs. Bramelds Assignees in full for the Purchase of Stock Fixtures &c at the Swinton Pottery—7500£ having been paid on the 1st. January 1827	500
2 Jan. 1837	Received of Messrs. Bramelds Assignees the final Dividend under their Bankruptcy	135.14. 1
10 March 1838	Received of Messrs. Brameld in part of the sum of 1950£ advanced to them in the year 1832, to enable them to pay their Workmen's Wages leaving 1220£ still due	730

1. Sir W. B. Cooke & Co., Bankers, High Street, Doncaster.
2. Messrs Walkers, Eyre & Stanley, Bankers, High Street, Rotherham.

		£ s d
10 June 1840	Paid Messrs. Cooke & Co the Loan advanced by them to Messrs. Brameld and for Interest thereon	1,138.14. 0
30 June 1842	Swinton—Brameld Messrs. their Arrears being irrecoverable	13,180. 0.10
	Wath D^{o} D^{o}	289. 4. 0
30 June 1843	Mr Brameld sundry Bills paid for Repairs at the House now occupied by him near the Pottery	95. 5. 0
30 June 1843	Paid Messrs. Brameld in part of a Loan of 800£ to enable them to carry on the Flint Mill	215
1 July 1843	Paid Messrs. Brameld in full of the Sum of 800£ agreed to be advanced to them on Bond dated 30th June 1843	585

Appendix IV
Advertisement from the *Leeds Mercury* for 11 March 1826 offering the Swinton Pottery to Let

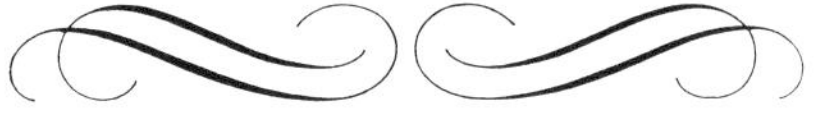

SWINTON POTTERY.—To be SOLD by PRIVATE CONTRACT, all the STOCK-IN-TRADE both of finished and unfinished GOODS, late the Property of Messrs. BRAMELD & CO. consisting of a very extensive and well-assorted Stock of China and Earthenware, together with a large and valuable Assortment of Moulds and Copperplates of every kind, used both for the Foreign and Home Trade.

Also, to be LET, upon a Lease for a Term of Years, or from Year to Year, all that extensive and convenient POTTERY, situate in the Township of Swinton, in the Parish of Wath-upon-Dearne, in the County of York, about Four Miles North of Rotherham, known by the Name of SWINTON POTTERY, (as the same was late in the Occupation of Messrs. Brameld and Co. against whom a Commission of Bankrupt hath lately been awarded and issued,) consisting of Two large Biscuit Ovens, Five Glazing Ovens, with a full Stock of excellent Saggars, Hardening Kilns for Six Printers, Three Enamelling Kilns, 7 Throwing Wheels, with Lathes, Stoves, Benches, &c. &c. large Green Rooms, with extensive Arrangements of Flags, &c. for flat Ware, Slip-house Room for from Forty to Fifty Tons of Clay per Week, with every other Convenience for the carrying on the Manufacture of China and Earthenware, on a very extensive Scale, having a FLINT MILL, with a Steam Engine of Twenty Horse Power, and with an excellent Supply of Water attached thereto, containing One Pan of Thirteen Feet, One of Seven Feet, Two of Six Feet each, Three of Five Feet each, Twelve Colour Pans, Plaster Stoves and Flint Rollers.

The Warehouses are good and extensive, and capable of containing an Assortable Stock of from 1000 to 1200 Crates, with large Rooms for Biscuit Ware, &c. &c. Sheds for Straw and Crates, Cooper's Shops, Carpenter's Shops, a well-contrived Brick Kiln with excellent Floors, a Horse Mill, and a Weighing Machine. The Counting-houses are very commodious, and replete with Fixtures, Iron Safes, &c. &c.

The Taker of the above Premises may also be accommodated with a FARM, containing upwards of 130 Acres of good LAND, immediately adjoining, in a high State of Cultivation, containing some very thriving Willow-Garths and Plantations of Crate-Wood. Also a FARM-HOUSE, with Barns, Stables, and all other suitable Outbuildings in excellent Repair.

The Assignees have continued the Works since Messrs. Brameld became Bankrupt, and they are therefore offered as a going Concern, with all the Advantages of a well-formed Home and Foreign Connection, with a suitable Supply of experienced Workmen, selected at a considerable Expense, and competent to carry on the Concern in all its varied Branches to any extent.

To treat for the above Premises, or for any further Particulars relating thereto, Applications must be made to Messrs. W. and E. NEWMAN, Solicitors, in Barnsley, in the County of York.

Appendix V

Annual Salaries paid to Selected Personnel at the Rockingham Works *c.* 1840[1]

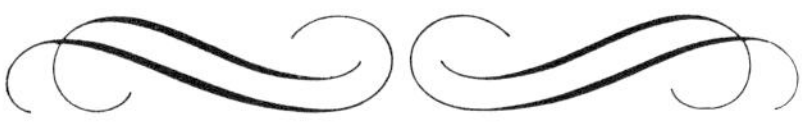

	£
T. B. [Thomas Brameld] General Manager & H. E. B. [Henry Edward Brameld[2]] assistant do	750
G. G.[3] Cashier and Chief Clerk w an assistant Clerk	650
G. F. B. [George Frederick Brameld] Corresponding Clerk and Secretary	100
J. T. B. [John Thomas Brameld[4]] Traveller & Chief of Warehouse department	300
Chief overlooker or Manager of ornamenting & Warehouse	150
Bailiff to assist in the Painting & Gilding depart	100
Bailiff for Claymen	100
Do for Kilnmen	100
Porter at entrance gates	50
Person to Show the Works to Visitors	50

Hours of attendance
8 am to 6 pm.
Dinner 1 to 2

1. Wentworth Woodhouse Muniments MD/182, undated.
2. Thomas Brameld's third son, 1821–1907.
3. From 1818 until at least 1839, George Robinson's signature appears on the factory invoices; it is possible that G. G. is a mistake for G. R. In 1810, William Brameld refers to George Robinson as 'Mr. Robinson our Clerk' (see Wentworth Woodhouse Muniments F 106/11).
4. Thomas Brameld's second son, 1819–92.

Appendix VI
The Brameld Notebooks

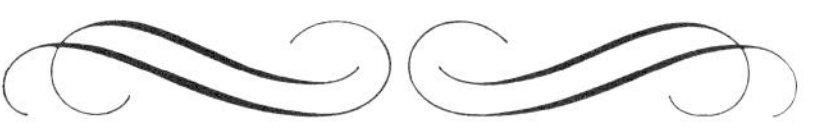

An interesting manuscript notebook, which survives from the Brameld proprietorship of the Pottery, contains details of ceramic bodies, glazes and processes.[1] It includes several references such as 'Bodies used by T B—May 1808' and 'Glaze for Blue Printed & Painted, Brown Printed & col<u>d</u> painted &c by T B—Spring 1811', suggesting that it was kept by Thomas Brameld from the early years of the nineteenth century. He gathered together much information from various sources relating to the manufacture of earthenware and porcelain, with notes concerning the success or failure of a number of the recipes. Some certainly were in use at the Pottery, others such as 'Delph Glaze' were probably only recorded for interest, although there are details for the preparation of tin ashes by calcining the metal, possibly based upon firsthand observations.

The bodies listed include stone body, cream-coloured, pearl, blue and white jasper, chalk body, caneware, numerous recipes for Egyptian black, brown and mulberry body. Glazes are given for creamware, coarsewares and china, and there are details of coloured glazes, dips and enamel colours. Methods of preparing mercury amalgam for gilding and oils for transfer printing are listed, and the production of lustre decoration and how to run down zaffre are described. It is significant that from as early as 1808, Thomas Brameld was collecting recipes for porcelain bodies, including bone china and fritted porcelain.

Very often the source of information is given, and the names recorded are of Swinton workmen and of manufacturers from elsewhere. Among those listed are Yates of Shelton, Keeling, Proctor, Harvey, J. Meyer and William Speight, the Bramelds' own colour maker. In certain cases Thomas Brameld evidently considered it tactful not to name fully the supplier of the information as, for example:

> C. C. Glaze used at Leeds Pottery by S Daniel—before it was Shut up—fm: John N—n. Sept. 1811.
>
> 112 lb or rather more of Wh. Lead
> 34 lb Litharge
> 18 lb Corn. Stone
> 18 lb Dry flint

Additionally, a series of some eighty numbered receipts are listed, many annotated J G—probably referring to John Green, manager of the Swinton Pottery under Greens, Bingley & Co. With these, as with many of the recipes in the book, there are notes as to their usefulness or otherwise, such as 'this is too hard', 'Bad', 'useless', 'good', 'Blisters'. Against one glaze for blue-painted ware is written: 'This Glaze is made of old Leeds Composition & therefore useless'.

1. Victoria and Albert Museum Library, MS Brameld & Co., Pressmark RC–E–31. A photocopy is in the Rotherham Library.

The quantities of ingredients are usually given in the form of relative proportions, for example, Pearl body requires:

4 Cornish Stone
3 Blue Clay
1 Cornish Clay
1½ Flint Glass

More precise measurements are occasionally specified, sometimes in terms of known cup sizes, such as a 'Holland' or an 'Irish' cup.

Some of the recipes include additional notes and are of more general interest. For example, No. 1 of the numbered list of recipes is for Egyptian black body, attributed to J G, and requires:

70 Ochre calcined
10 Mangnese ,,
8 Iron Scales ,,

These ingredients were to be 'well ground together and before it is taken off the Mill add 60 Poole Ball Clay taking care it be dried ground & sifted well before you use it'.

The notebook is obviously that of a working potter, and in a section headed 'Observations & Mem. Various', Thomas Brameld gathered together items of information which he found noteworthy. For example:

> A board of Joe Turners Saucers came out of Biscuit in the same crooked form as they were first put on the board by the taker-off—altho' perfectly straight from the Laithe.

Similarly, he considered it of interest to note:

> 1 doz of 7 In round Bakers placed in Biscuit without rings in one Bung and all out good.

A memorandum in the section describing dips reads:

> Being short of a little good Vinegar James Barrow one Day tried a small quantity of Spirits of Turpentine along with his old Colour & it answered very well
> May 1808—T B.

Other practical hints were also noted:

> In Firing Porcelain Bodies try (as a means of sustaining them in the heat & also of keeping off the Flash or Scorching effect of the Fire)—some fine dry Flint sifted over them so as completely to cover them.

Three porcelain bodies given in some detail are noted 'Proctor', the first consisting of the following:

20 lb best wh: Sand or Flint calcined & gro^{d}
5 lb very wh: Pearl Ashes
2 lb Bones Calcined to perfect Whiteness

Temper it with Gum Water—formed by dissolving the Gum Arabic or Senegal in Water.
NB. This requires a great & long heat—but very good.

However, with its high silica and low bone-ash content, this was not the body in general use at the Rockingham Works. The recipe actually used for the commercial production of porcelain is given on page 118.[2] Thomas Brameld also recorded the types of bones to be used in the manufacture of porcelain bodies:

> Fishes Bones are best; next Sheep's Bones; and next Horse's Bones.

A second notebook survives relating to the Bramelds.[3] Described as an apothecary's notebook, it is full of intriguing miscellaneous jottings from 1748 onwards, but contains nothing of ceramic interest. Its only relevance is that it includes several dates and biographical notes concerning members of the Brameld family. This information is given more fully on pages 57–8.

2. For details and comments upon the Brameld recipes for porcelain see A. Cox, 'The Analysis of Rockingham Porcelain in the Light of Thomas Brameld's Notebook and a Comparison with Some Other Examples of Nineteenth Century Bone China', *Northern Ceramic Society Journal*, Vol. 3, 1978–9, pp. 25–39.
3. Science Museum Library, MS 1762: Special Collection. We are indebted to Mr Ralph Boreham for most kindly drawing our attention to this notebook.

Appendix VII
The Chemical Analysis of Rockingham Porcelain

A knowledge of the chemical composition of ceramics has long been recognized to be of importance, partly from the viewpoint of establishing the provenance of specimens, especially in the absence of factory marks, and also in the study of the evolution of ceramic bodies.

The analysis of ceramics has undergone significant improvements in recent years. No longer is it necessary to remove and destroy a small sample from some object of interest in order to determine its composition. Since the publication in 1922 of Eccles' and Rackham's series of analyses of English porcelains,[1] new, non-destructive techniques have been developed of which X-ray fluorescence spectroscopy is one of the most important. This is based upon the principle that if an object is irradiated with X-rays, it can be stimulated to emit its own X-rays which are uniquely characteristic of the species and number of atoms within that object. Thus if a glaze-free area of porcelain is irradiated, a detailed examination of the spectrum of X-radiation emitted by the specimen permits the chemical composition of the body to be calculated.

The necessary equipment is, unfortunately, expensive and is therefore not in general laboratory use. At the University of York the technique has been refined, primarily for the analysis of ancient glass, but this method of physical examination is equally applicable to ceramics.

A number of specimens of Rockingham bone china from the red and puce griffin periods have been studied in this way[2] and their composition determined, as shown below, where details of six representative samples are recorded.

Analyses of six specimens of Rockingham porcelain expressed in weight percent of the constituent oxides

	1	2	3	4	5	6
Na_2O	0.6	1.4	0.9	1.4	0.6	0.8
MgO	0.7	0.7	0.6	0.7	0.7	0.6
Al_2O_3	14.0	16.5	16.3	15.2	15.8	17.0
SiO_2	36.0	34.7	35.9	36.3	34.0	35.0
P_2O_5	19.8	19.0	18.6	18.8	20.0	18.4
K_2O	2.3	1.6	1.8	1.5	1.8	1.7
CaO	26.2	25.4	25.1	25.5	26.6	25.2
Fe_2O_3	0.18	0.26	0.50	0.34	0.24	0.83
PbO	0.16	0.12	0.22	0.15	0.19	0.15
Total	99.94	99.68	99.92	99.89	99.93	99.68

1. H. Eccles and B. Rackham, *Analysed Specimens of English Porcelain*, London, 1922.
2. A. Cox, 'The Analysis of Rockingham Porcelain in the Light of Thomas Brameld's Notebook and a Comparison with some other Examples of Nineteenth Century Bone China', *Northern Ceramic Society Journal*, Vol. 3, 1978–9, pp. 25–39.

Details of specimens:

1. Comport *c.*1826, anthemion and gadroon border. No mark.
2. Trumpet vase *c.*1826–30, apricot ground. Mark cl 4.
3. Dessert plate *c.*1826–30, shell and gadroon border. Pattern 519 and mark 52.
4. Biscuit figure *c.*1830–42, model No. 119. Mark 54.
5. Saucer *c.*1830–42, from a three-spur tea service. Pattern 1309 and mark 55.
6. Saucer *c.*1838–42, from a single-spur service. Pattern 1450 and mark 55.

Sample 1 is typical of a group of early porcelains which commonly bear mark 51 and 'ring' when struck—they are relatively uncommon. The paste appears to be harder than that normally associated with this factory, but, as is evident, the composition is close to that of the later wares. As may also be seen from specimens 2 and 4, the same paste was used for decorative pieces.

The analysis of sample 6 is especially interesting since it has been suggested that single-spur teawares were possibly manufactured elsewhere and merely decorated at Swinton. The analytical evidence clearly points to a Swinton origin for this type of teaware.

As a general statement, the composition of Rockingham bone china varies surprisingly little, indicating that once a good, workable paste had initially been developed, the basic recipe was changed very little, if at all, over the period of porcelain production. If one calculates the theoretical composition of the porcelain which would result from the recipe entitled 'Another Porcelain Body' recorded by Thomas Brameld in his notebook (see Appendix VI and page 118) there is a remarkable degree of agreement between this and the mean composition of the factory's actual bone china, strongly suggesting that this was the recipe used for the commercial production of porcelain at the Rockingham Works.[3]

In the case of thickly-applied glazes, for example that on brown-glazed earthenwares, it is possible to determine by X-ray fluorescence spectroscopy the relative concentrations of its constituents, such as manganese, iron, lead and silicon, which in many instances are quite characteristic of the glaze used at a specific factory. Thus on the basis of such analyses, it is frequently possible to distinguish the products of one potter from those of his competitors, as explained on pages 110–13.

3. A. Cox, op. cit., pp. 32–4.

Appendix VIII
A Partial Genealogy of the Brameld Family

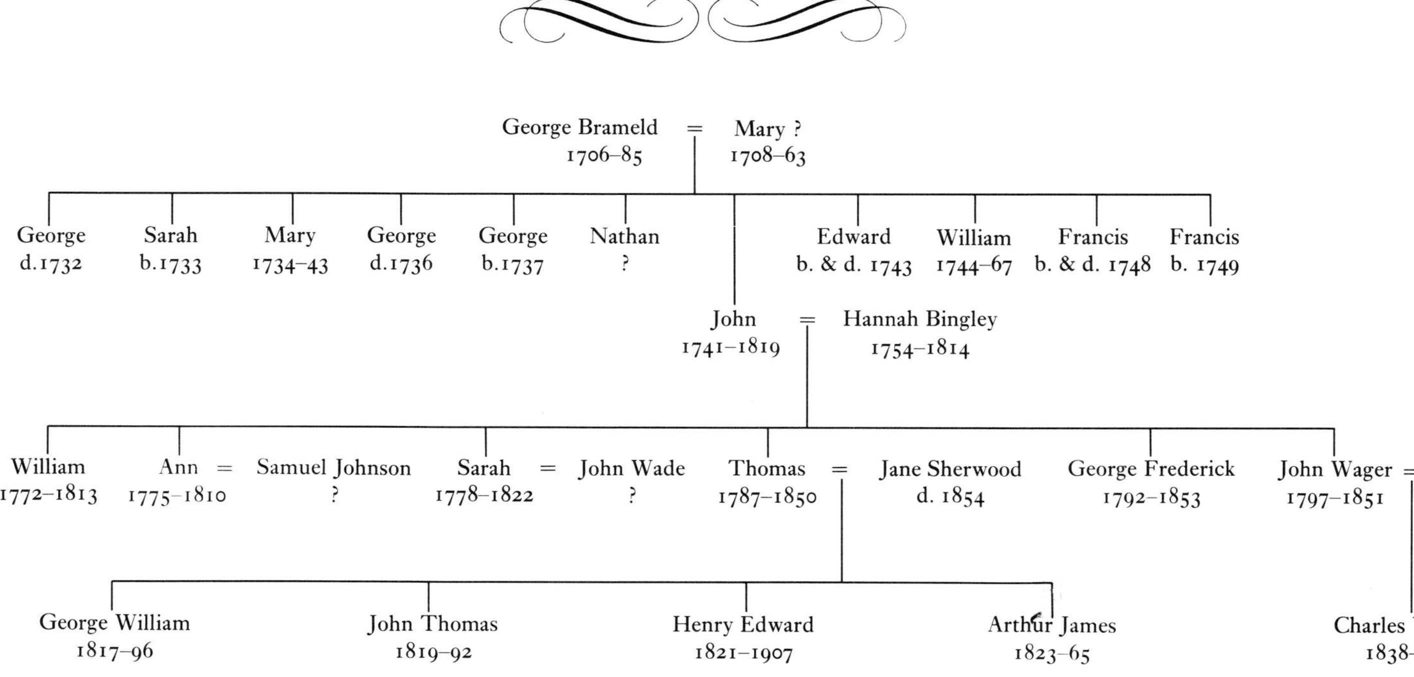

For details of the later Bramelds see H. G. Brameld, *Rockingham China and its Makers*, London, 1910, unnumbered page.

Appendix IX
A Letter from Brameld & Co. to Josiah Wedgwood

Earl Fitzwilliam advanced money to the Bramelds between 1811 and 1816 for the construction of a flint mill (Plate 3) and other improvements at the Swinton Pottery (see Appendix III). A letter in the Wedgwood papers[1] throws interesting light on one particular aspect of this work and indicates clearly that the Bramelds had purchased a costly piece of machinery which they were quite unable to operate.

Swinton Pottery, Nr. Rotherham
8th Oct. 1814

Sir,

Will you excuse the liberty we take in addressing you under the following circumstances—we have incurred a very heavy expense in putting a large clay Wedger[2] to our Engine[3] & now find (after every alteration we can make in it) that the plan is so erroneous that we cannot possibly use it without material improvement—our present request is therefore to beg the favor of you to allow our men to examine yours, & inform themselves fully as to the best plan we can adopt to make our huge piece of metal useful.

We are aware that this is taking a great liberty—but we trust to that liberality which we have, with so much pleasure, before observed in your treatment of your brother manufacturers, to allow us this favor, and therefore sincerely offering our best services to you in any way in which we can at all serve you,

We are Sir with the greatest respect,
Your obed. hum. Servts.
Brameld & Co.

To Josh. Wedgwood Esqre.,
Etruria.

1. Deposited in the University of Keele: Wedgwood reference 22885–30. We are indebted to Mr and Mrs R. Hampson for drawing our attention to this letter and to Josiah Wedgwood & Sons Ltd., and Keele University Library, for permission to publish it.
2. A large, inverted, metal cone inside which revolved blades to cut and mix clay which was then forcibly expelled from the bottom of the cone ready for use in the Pottery.
3. A steam-driven beam engine of 20 horse power which drove the flint mill and possibly other equipment used in the preparation of raw materials.

Bibliography

References to many important papers and articles are cited in the footnotes and are not listed here separately.

Books

Brameld, H. G., *Rockingham China and its Makers*, London, 1910.

Cox, A. and A., *The Rockingham Works*, Sheffield, 1974.

Eaglestone, A. A. and Lockett, T. A., *The Rockingham Pottery* (1st edn. Rotherham, 1964), new revised edn. Newton Abbot, 1973.

Godden, G. A., *Minton Pottery and Porcelain of the First Period 1793–1850*, London, 1968.

Godden, G. A., *Coalport and Coalbrookdale Porcelains*, London, 1970.

Godden, G. A., *The Illustrated Guide to Ridgway Porcelains*, London, 1972.

Grabham, O., 'Yorkshire Potteries, Pots and Potters', *Annual Report of the Yorkshire Philosophical Society for 1915*, York, 1916.

Hadfield, C., *The Canals of Yorkshire and North East England*, Newton Abbot, 1972–3.

Haslem, J., *The Old Derby China Factory* (1st edn. London, 1876), republished, Wakefield, 1973.

Hurst, A., *Catalogue of the Boynton Collection of Yorkshire Pottery*, York, 1922.

Jewitt, L., *Ceramic Art in Great Britain*, London, 1878.

Kidson, F. and J., *Historical Notices of the Leeds Old Pottery* (1st edn. Leeds, 1892), republished, Wakefield and London, 1970.

Mountford, A. R., *The Illustrated Guide to Staffordshire Salt-Glazed Stoneware*, London, 1971.

Rhodes, E., *Excursions in Yorkshire*, London, 1826.

Rice, D. G., *Rockingham Ornamental Porcelain*, London, 1965.

Rice, D. G., *The Illustrated Guide to Rockingham Pottery and Porcelain*, London, 1971.

Towner, D.,*The Leeds Pottery*, London, 1963.

Towner, D., *Creamware*, London, 1978.

Twitchett, J., *Derby Porcelain*, London, 1980.

Walton, P., *Creamware and other English Pottery at Temple Newsam House Leeds*, Bradford and London, 1976.

White, W., *History, Gazetteer and Directory of the West-Riding of Yorkshire*, Sheffield, 1837.

Young, A., *A Six Months Tour through the North of England* (1st edn. Salisbury, Edinburgh and London, 1770), reprinted New York, 1967.

Leeds Pottery *Pattern Book*, Leeds, *c.* 1814 edition. Although commonly referred to as a *Pattern Book*, this is actually a *Design Book*.

Documents

The Wentworth Woodhouse Muniments, Sheffield City Libraries, Department of Local History and Archives.

The Swinton Parish Documents, Doncaster Archives Department. (The authors examined this material when it was housed in Swinton Parish Church, since which time it has been fully catalogued.)

The Freemantle Collection, Rotherham Library, Department of Local History.

Probate Records, The Borthwick Institute of Historical Research, University of York.

Brameld Notebook on Bodies and Glazes, Victoria and Albert Museum Library, London (Ref. Brameld & Co. 1806–13, Pressmark RC–E–31).

Brameld Apothecary's Notebook, Science Museum Library, London (Ref. Special Collection MS 1762).

Rockingham Pottery Pattern Books, in private possession.

Leeds Pottery Drawing Books, Victoria and Albert Museum, Department of Prints and Drawings; Leeds City Library, The Print Room.

Parish registers: Swinton, Rawmarsh and Wath-upon-Dearne.

Newspapers: *York Courant*, *Yorkshire Gazette*, *Leeds Mercury*, *Sheffield Iris*, *Sheffield Mercury*, *Doncaster*, *Nottingham and Lincoln Gazette*, *The Times*.

Index

References to plates are in italics
References to footnotes are denoted by the letter n